IF OUR HEARTS COLLIDE

FORBIDDEN CONTRACT
BOOK 1

VICTORIA DAWSON

PAPER HEART PUBLISHING LLC

If Our Hearts Collide

Publisher: Paper Heart Publishing LLC

Cover Designer: K. B. Barrett Designs

Editing: Happily Editing Anns

ISBN (Paperback): 978-1-959364-11-5

ISBN (e-book): 978-1-959364-10-8

AUTHOR NOTE

If Our Hearts Collide is the first book in the *Forbidden Contract Series* that follows the same two main characters throughout both books. It is advised to read the two books in order.

If you enjoy longer storylines where you get to know the characters on an intimate and detailed level, please consider starting with both the *Entice Trilogy* (*Spark of Obsession*, *Rush of Jealousy*, and *Taste of Addiction*) and the *Toxic Desire Series* (*Inflame* and *Implode*), as story elements are present in those five books that assist in character development and world building.

It is NOT required to read all the prior books before jumping—hopefully heart-first—into the *Forbidden Contract Series*!

The *Forbidden Contract Series* is intended for mature audiences. Sensitive topics discussed could be triggering and not meant for anyone under the age of eighteen.

To anyone hoping to become the passenger princess to a hot and rugged bodyguard…

This one is for you.

1

PENNY

"Hands must be on the table at all times, behind the glass. All phone conversations are monitored by the central operator. You have ten minutes to talk with the inmate before the line will automatically get disconnected. So use your time wisely."

I follow the guard into the cold, sterile room, where a row of glass is partitioned with metal stools and individual wall phones on both sides. I tug my cardigan tighter around me, as I'm led into the booth that is designated just for me. For it being summer, you'd never know it by the temperature-controlled atmosphere in this place.

"Thank you," I mumble, taking a seat.

I can't help but wonder if this meeting will benefit me or if I'm conning myself into participating in a form of self-torture. Now I'm questioning if I'm essentially making a huge mistake by even requesting the visit.

It surely sounded better when my therapist told me to "face my fears" in one of the group sessions months ago.

And this is definitely a fear. I just might have taken the suggestion too literally and out of context.

For the past year, I've been living in a state of limbo, not knowing how to knit my old life to the hope I have for my new life. In a way, I feel like a new person. The Penny before the incident is nothing like the Penny seated here now.

I'm different.

And it's not just because I chose to dye my hair and update my wardrobe color scheme from black and blah.

My parents treat me like I'm different.

My brothers treat me like I'm different.

And I have this sinking feeling in the pit of my stomach that I'll always be seen that way to them—as someone fragile who constantly needs rescuing.

So much has changed that the image of the girl being reflected back to me in the dingy, smudged glass is *not* the same naive person who sees people at face value anymore. I just hope that life hasn't jaded me so much that I'm unable to find my own slice of happiness.

I scoot my stool closer to the table, setting my hands on top as I wait.

Guilt rushes over me as I think of how I used an excuse to go shopping alone as a way to get away from my current residence in Hillsboro. The walls have been closing in on me since my release a few weeks ago.

My parents mean well, but I think they are walking on eggshells and in a constant state of worry that I'll have a mental breakdown again. I mean, the thought has crossed my mind, so it's not out of the realm of possibility. Even I get scared of the unknown.

I learned just how complex the brain is when my thoughts became a taunting ghost to the incident that shattered my life.

No one plans on a break, and when one occurs, it's hard to see your way out of it. I can't go back to that. I can't be a burden anymore.

I'm challenging myself today by even stepping foot inside this prison. But I owe this to myself.

Despite extensive therapy, I still am lacking the closure my heart desires. Sometimes facing your demons is a way to conquer your fears, and that is something no one—not even my brothers—understands.

Sure, my family is beyond amazing, but none of them would approve of today's visit. Everyone sees me as a delicate flower that is waiting to lose its petals at the first sign of rain.

But life has storms.

Some are bigger than others. Some cause the power to go out. But with the rain, regrowth can happen, and sometimes even rainbows can form out of the unexpected.

If I am going to move forward, I need to face the one roadblock that seems to hover in the back of my mind, haunting me with the illusion that I'll never be whole again.

A vision of orange hits my periphery, causing me to look up, as Mark Tanner is escorted in chains to the stool on the opposite side of the glass.

My eyes look at him and then away, almost as if his evilness is blinding. Swollen eyes, a cut lip, and stitches on his forehead all appear to be fresh. His once muscular frame looks smaller, weaker. Prison hasn't done him well, and the petty side to me is rejoicing that he finally got what was coming to him—albeit not because I had anything to do with it.

Mark's expression comes to life and a cocky smirk plays on his lips, as he takes in my face and what he can see of my body, one slow inch at a time. His sinister smile lets me know that he approves of my new appearance.

I feel dirty as his eyes coast over me, like I'm the most interesting person in the world to him right now. He's probably trying to figure out why I'm here. I mean, I'm starting to wonder as well.

When I first decided to come here on an impulse, it seemed logical at the time. Now, after seeing Mark's amusement, I doubt I'll leave feeling anything other than empty.

Mark kicks the stool backward with his foot, steps in front, and lowers himself onto it. His chained hands hit the table so hard that it vibrates the glass. Biting his bottom lip, his eyebrows rise to produce a flirtatious look.

Why am I doing this?

Why am I facing the devil who caused my once seemingly perfect life to shatter at the foundation? Why am I trying to communicate with the madman who almost killed both of my brothers and my now sister-in-law?

Maybe I'm a masochist. Or maybe I'm exactly what I've tried to tell myself I wasn't for all these months…

Crazy.

My nose flares as I bite my inner cheeks to keep from crying. I can't shed a tear in front of this man. He would eat them up like liquid candy, and probably get off to the image of my mascara-stained face later when he's alone in his cell.

Pulling my shoulders back and straightening my

posture, I remove the black phone from the receiver, signaling to Mark to do the same.

It's his labored breathing I hear first.

"Well, if it isn't little Penny Hoffman." He trails his eyes over my lips, my neck, and down to my chest—settling there for way too long. "To what do I owe this pleasure?"

It's Mark's evilness that takes root, growing wildly with unabandoned need and wrapping its hold over every aspect of my life.

I'm tainted—damaged—by his clutch on me. And today is the day I let go of the choke hold he has on my life.

"I'm here to show you that I'm all better. That you didn't break me."

"Well, isn't that cute."

My eyes twitch, as I take in a deep, steady breath. "I'm stronger than you think." And I am. I have gotten through so much.

I watch as Mark places the phone down onto the table and then claps his hands together.

Once.

Twice.

Three times.

His chest rumbles with a boisterous laugh that is so dark that I can hear the echoing hum through the phone. He picks it back up and winks at me, making me cringe from his ability to affect me like he does.

"How can I believe your words when you don't even believe them yourself?"

I bite my bottom lip that can't stop quivering. But I am strong. I've managed to complete intensive therapy. And I came here. "You can't hurt me anymore," I blurt out.

"But I can. And I will. I live in your heart, Penny. And I'll come out to play anytime your insecurities seep through. Just know I'll be waiting on the sidelines. *Stupid girl.*"

"Shut up." I rock in my seat, silently wishing it had a back support.

My fingers grip the phone so tightly, I fear I might snap the plastic in half. I didn't come here to get harassed by him. I came here to show Mark that I'm standing on my own two feet, while he'll be rotting away in prison until he eventually dies. He can no longer hurt me.

"You know what bad girls like you love?" Before I get a chance to even respond to his ridiculous question, he answers for me. "Sin."

"Shut up."

His laugh is manic, like he somehow believes he has the upper hand, despite being in a maximum security prison with no chance of ever receiving parole if he is found guilty. At least that's what everyone—my therapists, my parents, my brothers, our lawyers—tell me.

That's what they *tell* me.

Tell me…

Yet, here I sit, trembling in fear of what this man represents.

He is evil.

He is poison.

He is hatred.

He is permanent…a constant source of anxiety in a life full of variables. Yet he still finds a way to persevere through all of my happier moments, tainting all the goodness that I strive to achieve.

Mark doesn't need bars to keep himself from me—he

already has me. He finds me in my nightmares. He finds me in my reflection in the mirror. And he finds me when I'm trying to start up a relationship that goes beyond the boundaries of friendship.

He finds me.

Every look at me is a power play.

I shouldn't have come here. I should have realized that nothing productive could come from facing the demon who has wreaked havoc in my head.

Mark may not have raped my body, but he raped my mind. He took more from me that day I was drugged than just my freedom and my memory.

He stole my trust in men.

And he stole my trust in myself.

"I may be in here while I await trial, Penny," Mark chants in a singsong voice, "but there are other boogeymen out there in the big, bad world. And they make me look civilized and tame in my sexual preferences. So sleep with one eye open or"—he makes his hands go *poof*—"you may get taken in the darkness as a favor owed to me. And I always collect my debts."

"I hate you."

"No, you don't. You hate yourself."

"You can't hurt me anymore," I snarl.

Mark shrugs. "I'm legally innocent until proven guilty. Wouldn't it be absolutely mind-blowing if I was found *not* guilty?"

"You're going to rot in here."

"I can't wait to see you break down in court. How fun to be reunited again. My lawyers are going to rip you to shreds, and I can't wait for my heyday."

"You're delusional."

Mark's bottom lip gets sucked into his mouth and pops out. "You think I don't have puppets on the outside—just waiting for my silent command? Because, Penny, there's not a Hoffman on this planet that can keep me from gaining back everything I've lost. So be fucking careful. This is just intermission. The main event hasn't even started yet."

Without another word, I slam the phone down and stand up. My legs struggle to hold my weight, but I keep my head up as I walk out of the room. Every step seems unsteady, like I'm going to crumble into a million tiny pieces if I stay still.

So I keep walking.

One foot in front of the other…

And I never look back.

A worker checks me out on the computer, retrieves my personal belongings that I brought, and then I'm released.

When the fresh air hits my face, I'm made aware that I am crying. And like a dam breaking, I let the flood cleanse me of my bad choice in coming here.

Mark is messing with me. He's trying to get under my skin, and I am letting him have that level of control.

I made it easy for him by coming here.

But I am not that broken girl anymore.

And I can prove it.

When I rein in my senses, I forfeit my will to the two men in my life who are always there for me when I am about to crash and burn.

I call my brothers.

"I'm sorry," I cry, as Nic and Graham envelop me in their arms. They got here in record time—probably breaking speed limit laws at every bend. "I know I'm stupid. I know I shouldn't have come. I know, please, I know. I just thought…"

What did I think?

Apparently I thought that the man who almost destroyed my entire family would somehow see me and then magically find remorse?

I obviously came here looking for something…

But what?

A man as vile as Mark Tanner doesn't have an apologetic bone in his entire body—probably because he doesn't think he did anything wrong. To him, everything revolved around a hierarchy of power and money. I was simply a way to help him make more. Except his plan never went to fruition, but I still suffered a mental breakdown as a result.

The day that I met Mark Tanner, when I thought he could help me further my modeling aspirations, was the day that the fuse was lit. It was only a matter of time before he hurt me. He just never counted on my overprotective brothers retaliating and getting him locked up for life.

"Don't cry. Everything will be alright," Graham soothes.

Nic squeezes me tighter. "Yeah, don't cry, Pen."

"I hate him."

Graham rubs circles on my back. "We know. We hate him too."

My sniffles get less and less frequent, and then I'm no longer a sobbing mess.

When my brothers release me from their embrace, a silent message is passed between them with just a look.

But that's what my older brothers do—they fix things. And based on the way they are looking at me now, I know they are trying to think of how to make my life easier.

I'm not looking for easier, though. I just want to find my purpose.

"Mark is going to get out and get me," I whimper. My eyes dart back to the entrance to the prison. "I can feel his invisible pull from here."

"No. No, he's not, Penny," Nic promises. He takes my hand and starts to pull me toward the parking lot, but my feet feel like they are trudging through wet cement.

"He said he has puppets out here in the wild who won't hesitate to follow his orders."

Graham glances at Nic and then back at me. "We won't let him hurt our family again, Penny."

My head shakes back and forth, as I think about every worst-case scenario. "I don't want to go to trial. I don't want to face Mark in court. I won't survive all the questions and the interrogation and the drive from his legal team to discredit me. It'll be humiliating and revictimizing to me all over again. Probably Angie too. She'll probably have to testify. You know? She was hurt by him—by all of them. Not to mention that the whole time, Mark will be staring at us and silently taunting us from his side of the courtroom."

Graham places an arm back around me, pulling me into his unyielding body. "You and Angie won't be testifying."

His words are final, and if he really could control everything in this world, I would believe him. But not everything is in his control.

I look up at my big brother. "Why are you so confident

we won't need to? How will the prosecution get a solid conviction without our testimonies?"

"Trust us, Penny." Pivoting, he looks me directly in the eyes. "That monster is staying exactly where he belongs and won't step foot on free land again. Let Nic and I take care of this, and don't worry yourself sick over it."

"But he might still have influence over people out here" —my hand sweeps out—"roaming around. What if—"

"Trust us, Penny," Nic echoes Graham's previously spoken words. "We won't let anything happen to you."

With a slight nod, I continue walking. Their vagueness is making me cranky. They are always trying to shield me from any pain, and today I gave them all the reason to continue on that pattern.

"How did you get here so fast?" My question comes out as a whisper, but I really don't need an answer. My brothers have their ways of keeping tabs on everyone they care about. So nothing should shock me. "You were on your way already before I called, weren't you?"

Nic opens the back door to the SUV, as I settle into my seat. When my brothers get into the front, I relax my shoulders as Graham pulls out of the parking spot and onto the main road.

Nic sighs, obviously not wanting to confirm what I've already figured out on my own. "Let's get you back to Mom and Dad's."

"Please don't tell them."

"They are worried about you, Penny," Graham says.

"So you aren't mad?"

"We are upset that you came here alone," my older

brother says, speaking for himself and Nic. "You didn't need to come here to prove anything to anybody, Pen."

"I should have never visited Mark," I admit. "The only thing it served me is a fresh, vivid reminder of what evil looks like in human form. Worst part is, Mark doesn't feel bad about a damn thing."

Nic lets out a huff. "That's not surprising." He exchanges a look with Graham, and I know some message was exchanged nonverbally. I swear they can partake in an entire conversation and never actually say a thing.

Glancing at me in the rearview mirror, Graham gives me a stern look. "Don't pollute your mind with scum. You've come a long way with your progress. You don't need to be having setbacks."

I know this already.

I just thought coming to the prison was a move in the right direction for my personal growth.

I was wrong.

"Where did you find Penny?" Dad asks my brothers, when I am supposed to be upstairs showering instead of eavesdropping.

Graham's growl can be heard a room away. "She was at the prison."

I lean forward, trying to catch a glimpse of Dad's reaction. There are two things I hate doing to my parents—being a disappointment and being a burden. I have managed to do both within an hour's time frame.

Dad clears his throat. Even from this distance, I can

sense his unease, where he is usually so calm and collected. "I know she's having a hard time. There's still a lot of healing left to do."

"And she will," Nic chimes in. "But she needs to stay out of trouble and give her body and mind time to assimilate back into how things used to be."

While not normally the optimist, he sure seems to have a confidence when it comes to me. He believes in me when I don't always believe in myself.

"I'll keep encouraging her to touch base with her local therapist," Graham says.

"Yeah," Dad agrees. "That was the compromise for her getting out of the facility. Those sessions need to start sooner rather than later."

Graham coughs. "I'm sorry to say I don't think things will ever be the same."

"Maybe the point in certain times of your life is to not stay the same," Dad says thoughtfully. "Penny now has some life experience she hasn't had before. If she can focus on the positives, then I think she'll be okay."

I lean my back against the wall, allowing my eyes to close. I feel claustrophobic in this house, like I can't breathe right. Too many memories were made here with the Penny before the incident, and it is hard to reconcile with the girl I once was when I'm so vastly different inside now.

"Yeah…" Graham says softly.

"I just hope she learns to ask us for help if she feels like she is sinking," Dad remarks.

Nic clears his throat. "There was no good reason to torture herself like she did today. She can be brave. She just doesn't need to be brave in the presence of that predator."

"Well, thank you for bringing her back," Dad says with a choke, the telltale sign that he is about to cry. "I know you both have a lot on your plates with being freshly married"—he's referring to Graham and Angie—"and a baby on the way"—and now Nic and Claire.

Guilt stabs at my heart. Dad is right. They do have more important things to worry about than my pathetic impulsive urges that seem to get me into trouble. I could have easily called a taxi and didn't need a rescue.

How am I ever going to stand on my own two feet when my brothers are about to slay every dragon that comes my way?

2

COLLINS

"I have a new assignment for you," Graham Hoffman says, passing me the document with the salary highlighted in bold print on the top line of the contract.

It is significantly larger than my previous payouts over the course of the last few years, and even then I felt like I was a bit overpaid. If anything, I'm the one who owes the Hoffmans—for giving me back my life.

"Is there a mistake?" I ask, pointing to the sum. "Perhaps a couple too many zeroes?"

"Call it a bonus. For the loyalty, honor, and respect you have shown our family."

I lean back in my chair, sneaking a glance over at his brother, Nic, who is hanging out near the floor-to-ceiling windows. His fiancée, Claire, is pregnant, and the man is determined to shadow her every movement just in case she stubs her toe or needs assistance with anything that she is fully capable of doing herself.

Graham isn't much different. Angie, his recently

appointed wife, has shaken up his entire world and softened his hardness in a way I never thought could be achieved. How these Hoffman brothers found the two most independent women in the city of Portland is almost comical for their overprotective tendencies.

The women are best friends, working at Plus None, just a few floors below us in this building. While the two of them—and the danger that inevitably finds them—keep my job secure, I can't help but wonder why I am being summoned here today. I'm cocky enough to know that my work is stellar. In a way, I'm the invisible enforcer who keeps the empire intact. With a broken moral compass that got fractured after being discharged from the military, I'm a valuable asset when protecting the loves of these Hoffman men's lives.

What I don't let others know is that this sense of purpose helps me get through my days. I like having a set goal in mind and a plan to execute the mission. Graham Hoffman basically rescued me from my previous life and has given me more than I could ever ask. He helped me heal when he didn't even realize I was broken from the foundation up. Thus, when he is raising my salary this much, it makes me feel a bit of unease.

It's because I need the Hoffmans just as much as they seem to need me.

"You know I'll do anything that you ask," I inform the men.

Without a family of my own, my priorities have shifted into protecting these men and their women that have welcomed me into their lives. Graham and Nic are like brothers to me, and while there is a contract and money exchange involved, the roots of allegiance run thick.

Graham looks toward the window, deep in thought, before returning his gaze to me. “You always have, and thus”—he gestures toward the contract—“your monetary compensation should more than cover any inconveniences this next assignment should bring. And there may be many based on recent history.”

I nod, allowing his ominous words to register. I hope both Hoffman brothers know I would do the work for much less than they are offering. Loyalty can’t be bought, and the bond I have with them is something that I need to maintain. So, of course, whatever they want from me, I will do—willingly and without question.

And if it crosses into illegal territory, so be it.

I’m not afraid to serve time in prison, especially if the outcome is worth the temporary loss of freedom.

But something is off about this meeting. It appears that my next assignment won’t be so straightforward or predictable.

“I’m not used to seeing you nervous,” Nic says in a joking tone.

I tip my head in understanding. “Please forgive me for being a bit taken aback by this meeting. What has changed with the current arrangement?”

Nic clears his throat and joins us. “It’s nothing you have done wrong. So don’t think that.” He lets out a sigh, allowing his frustration to show. “Claire is very stubborn, as you know.” *Oh, I know*.

“It is glaringly obvious that her need for independence is part of her personality, and not just pregnancy hormones—

which I recommend never suggesting to her." Nic shudders, mouthing *ouch*. "She has insisted that anyone I hire to watch over her or assist her with her doctor's appointments needs to have a vag, um, needs to be female."

"Got it…"

He expels his breath, running a hand over the back of his neck. "While I hate pulling you from your assignment, Graham and I have another pressing matter, which is what you were called in today to discuss."

I am a fixer. An enforcer. I'm the problem solver and solutions expert. I do not cave under pressure, nor do I flinch at the first sign of trouble. I've been trained to shoot a gun, and I know exactly when to pull the trigger. My body wears the scars from my past experience of working as a dedicated bodyguard, but the extensive former military discipline is what keeps me grounded and a threat to those who want to double-cross me.

Nothing fazes me.

Nothing challenges me.

Nothing scares me.

"It's Penny," Graham states simply.

Fuck.

Except her—dammit.

I sit up in my chair. "What's wrong? Was there an incident?"

There's something indescribably enchanting about Penelope Josephine Hoffman. There's an aura about her that is sweet and kind, yet there's a fierceness behind her seemingly shy demeanor.

While our interactions have been limited, I've had the luxury of watching Penny on brief occasion from the sidelines. Witnessing her come out of the darkness that once consumed her entire life was a sight to see. She is inspiring—and even that word doesn't encompass just how truly amazing she is. Sure, our paths crossed a few other times when she would visit her brothers on leave from the facility. However, everything was clinical.

This assignment seems personal.

I don't do personal.

Having attached feelings nearly cost me my entire life, and I refuse to give up what I've spent years rebuilding.

With all of my former assignments, I could clearly separate my own emotions from the actual work. But with Penny, there's something about her that tugs on my heart. And I honestly don't know what it is, because it is such a foreign feeling—one I don't think I've experienced enough times to identify and define.

Graham sighs and runs a hand through his hair, stress lines forming on his forehead and around his eyes.

Last year, I worked with the Hoffmans to try to find out who drugged and potentially raped Penny. While it was discovered that she was not physically violated to that extent, Penny suffered a mental break and was in a facility in Seattle for several months—some of which was in a catatonic, nonverbal state.

The grief the family has endured has been intense. While Penny is now home in Hillsboro with her parents, there is still a certain amount of transitioning that has to happen for her life to go back to a new normal.

What that normal will look like is the big mystery.

Based on how her brothers look right now, I'm not so sure they are going to welcome it.

I understand all too well how hard that transition can be. When I was forced to exit the military, I slipped into a dark place. Stubborn to my core, I didn't reach out for help, and I definitely didn't want to talk about my feelings surrounding the discharge.

Witnessing Penny firsthand as she battled her demons was difficult to endure. It reminded me of my own past and all of the internal obstacles I had to overcome to get me to the place I am today.

I owe my life to Graham Hoffman. Just a couple of years after I hung up my time in service to this country, I met the lucrative mogul who was making huge waves in the business world in Portland. Graham hired me to work security initially, but when the drug ring became an issue, my duties shifted to provide that extra protection. It helped that I had nothing to lose and could commit to the task.

I'm not even sure Penny realizes just how many visits I made to Seattle in the past year to check up on the care she was receiving. I was given small requests to scope out workers at the facility, handle therapy arrangements when needed, and was even tasked to scare off a few losers who were sniffing around her.

However, I've never had to officially…*handle* the unpredictable Hoffman princess, so it surprises me that I'm being called upon to do it now.

By the exorbitant compensation staring at me on the contract, something tells me this job will have some twists. I just hope I can handle them all. Retirement is looking better and better. The past year has not been the easiest by any terms. Good thing for me, I thrive on challenges.

Plus, I'm too young to retire by a couple of decades. I'd

grow bored and antsy, just like anyone else dedicated to perfecting their skill set.

"Penny wants to spread her wings and fly," Nic huffs. "Her words, almost exactly. She claims she doesn't want her brothers impacting her relationships or interfering with her affairs." He tosses his hands into the air. "Like we would ever be that intrusive."

I resist snickering. Nic is the worst offender when it comes to overstepping boundaries with his overprotective tendencies, which is an odd judgment for me to have—considering my line of work. Being head of security for Hoffman Headquarters, I'm not surprised that Nic's brain automatically goes to the worst-case scenario—especially after almost losing Claire a couple of months ago. My brain does the same thing. You don't get to be this good at your job if you see the world through rose-colored glasses.

Evil can exist anywhere. It just takes someone who can pull it out of hiding.

"So you want me to do the exact opposite of what Penny is asking for?" I ask for clarification. I'm not shy when it comes to protecting strong-willed women, and I'm almost positive that there isn't a woman who can be more difficult than Angie or Claire. Those two women have caused me more than one migraine. They are always getting into some kind of trouble, claiming they had no idea that something bad would happen, despite all signs pointing to disaster.

But as a result, my loyalty to this family would lead to me cleaning up their messes.

I mean, it's not that I don't like breaking noses in bars and delivering threats to drunk assholes that touch any of the Hoffman brothers' women.

But it also isn't my idea of fun—especially when these women have horrible self-preservation skills.

There is no way Penny could be as difficult.

This may be the easiest assignment I've been given thus far—at least on paper. That's assuming I don't let her manipulate me with her sweet innocence.

Penelope Hoffman is the epitome of the baby in the family. She is as delicate as a freshly transformed butterfly and as rare as a double rainbow.

"Just keep an eye on her," Graham says smoothly. "She knows that there is no possibility of us not keeping loose tabs on her, especially after we got a call to pick her up from visiting Mark Tanner."

"Fuck," I say under my breath. This is news to me.

"Oh, I guess I forgot to mention that."

Things are starting to make more sense now.

And if Penny were mine, I'd be tightening up security on her as well and forbidding her from ever stepping foot in that prison.

What the hell was she thinking going to a place full of criminals—alone for that matter? She was probably a feast for every bastard's eyes who was fortunate enough to catch a look. If I have any say about it, I'll never allow that girl to get that close to her abuser again.

"Fuck is right," Nic echoes. "Why Penny found the need to go see Tanner for the closure he'll never give her is beyond my understanding." He runs his hands over his head, settling them against the back of his neck. "Do you see why we are stressed out? The stunt she pulled was her last burst at freedom, as far as I'm concerned. She better be happy I don't lock her away until the world is a less damaging place. Because if my Claire ever did something like that…"

I nod. I get it. Men in our positions protect those we love, and there's no denying the love the Hoffman family has for their youngest.

Graham clears his throat. "Penny is naive and too trusting. Plus, I think she is going to try to move out of our parents' house—"

"Which neither of us approve of," Nic interrupts.

"Already?" It seems like she just got there. Why the rush?

Graham nods for emphasis. "She wants to be 'independent.'" He adds air quotes around *independent.*

"She wants to be off on her own, doing who knows what. I honestly half expect her to do a repeat visit on Tanner."

"Damn…" I'll never allow it. I feel the tic in my jaw starting, as my heart rate elevates. "Did he threaten her?"

"I can't see how he didn't," Nic says. "I doubt he could resist."

Graham clears his throat. "Given the state of mind Penny was in while waiting for us to come get her, I'd say she was threatened more than she's letting on. She was so shaken up and vocalized to us that Tanner was coming for her. She also fears having to testify."

"Did any of our insiders catch the conversation?" I inquire further.

"Doubtful," Graham concludes.

"His entire empire was dismantled," I confirm. And I had a large part in that destruction. "There's not a credit card trail or even a whisper suggesting he has anyone willing to risk life in prison or death just to lay their loyalty at the altar of Mark fucking Tanner. He has no one."

"Penny doesn't trust us to handle this," Graham says, his tone that of defeat. "She's terrified, and I hate seeing her like this."

Nic paces. "That fucker doesn't need to be in her head anymore. We handled it. He's not going to get out in this lifetime—with or without going to court."

"She's our baby sister, and we just want her to be safe but not smothered," Graham expresses. "If that makes sense. Protect her, but don't let on to the extent of which you are providing the protection."

I nod, absorbing all the information they are sharing with me. I am still reeling inside over the fact she went to the prison unaccompanied. What is wrong with her? What did she really expect to accomplish from something so impulsive?

Penny barely got out of Soulful Mind, just to go and do something reckless in return. If this is how she's choosing to spend her free time, then she damn well better get a hobby. I'm not going to put up with her desire to run straight into danger with open arms.

"So you don't want twenty-four-hour surveillance?"

"No," Graham confirms with a chuckle. "That seems a bit excessive, especially when your other assignment will be some waste management duties."

He's referring to my ability to set up "accidents" for anyone that double-crosses them. "Understood."

"Besides, Penny isn't as adventurous as my Angie."

"And she can't be worse than my Claire," Nic interjects.

My lips form a line, as I think about the potential

requirements. If I'm going to do my job well, I better understand the full scope of services needed. "Credit card statements retrieved?"

"Nah," Graham says, pushing hair off his forehead, "at least not at this moment. But if she starts dating…"

"I know exactly where to hide the body," I deadpan.

Graham and Nic stare at me, studying my facial expression. But when the one corner of my lips lifts slightly, we all burst out into laughter.

"Precisely," Graham jokes.

"Penny knows if she ever needs money, she can come to us," Nic comments. "Just do as you see fit. We trust you to make the right decisions. No need to run everything past us. You know how we operate. Plus, we trust you—fully."

I nod, trying to mentally develop a plan of action in my head. Penny's brothers must have some suspicion that her reckless streak isn't over with the prison visit, if they are officially hiring me.

"Use your discretion. Just make sure she's safe. Run background checks if necessary on anyone she becomes friends with. Fend off the assholes that want to just mess with her for a one-night thrill. Use your best instincts on how to manage her without her knowing she is being managed." A smirk plays on Graham's lips as he crosses his arms over his chest. "I don't see her causing nearly as much stress to you as Angie and Claire have."

I turn to Nic. "What about the trackers?"

He shrugs. "I'm never against them. After the nightmare we endured a couple of months ago at the hands of that madman, I'm done taking any chances with my loved ones."

"Understood, sir."

Between Angie almost losing her life from the kingpins of a drug ring and Claire getting trapped inside this building by an ex-security worker seeking revenge, I completely understand the precautions they are taking with Penny, albeit on the milder scale.

I think they want her safe but not smothered. I can do that.

"We trust you, Collins," Graham says, echoing the similar sentiment his younger brother offered as well. Standing up from his leather chair, he walks over to me. I stand to meet him, accepting his outstretched hand in a gesture of respect that basically turns into a half hug.

"I appreciate your confidence in me."

"You've proven yourself every step of the way thus far."

"And I'll continue to maintain that level of professionalism and respect," I vow.

There's a code I live by, and veering from it is just not something I do. I value discipline and predictability.

I grab the pen off the desk and sign my name on the line, making everything official. It is a technicality, really. I don't need some paper promises of money to continue working for the Hoffmans. Both men have given me back my purpose in life. They are each doing me a favor by continuing to provide me with assignments, even if this one feels a bit watered down.

"Off topic," Nic interjects with a lopsided smile. "But our mom insists on you coming to Hillsboro to celebrate Penny's birthday. I worry what she'll do to us"—he laughs along with Graham—"if you don't show up."

"You know that woman basically thinks we overwork

you without fair compensation and competitive benefits," Graham adds.

"Yeah," Nic says with a chuckle. "She basically has hinted that you should form a one-man union and revolt against us. Sheesh, Mom can be fiery."

I smile. Donna surely is one of a kind. "What day is the celebration?" I know when the official birthday is, but figure I should get clarification in case the party is on a different day.

"Tomorrow."

I can't remember the last time I attended a birthday party. Not knowing what to expect is my biggest struggle socially. I hate unknowns. Recreational parties have never been my scene. "I, uh—"

"Consider it a prelude," Graham says with a chuckle.

"A prelude?"

Nic laughs. "You keep Donna happy, because we all know how pushy our mom can get. And getting to see the *new* Penny will be a field experience bonus."

I shift my weight on my heels. "New?"

"Oh, she decided to do a few changes on her appearance. You'll know when you see her in person," Nic says with a smirk. "The party starts at four tomorrow. Dinner, cake, you know the drill. Everything is casual and small."

"Donna-style," Graham chimes in.

So not small at all. "Sounds good. I'll see you guys tomorrow."

"Come hungry," Nic insists, "or bring a moving van for all the leftovers our mom will pack up for you. She's also convinced we don't give you a lunch break—ever."

I can't hide my smile. That woman can't help mothering each one of us from a distance. It's engrained into her.

And there's no part of me that doesn't welcome her affection.

When I exit Graham's office, I take the elevator down to the Plus None floor. Old habits never die. Nearly every time I'm here, whether I'm on or off duty, I check in on the girls —even if they are unaware of me doing so. Claire and Angie are family to me. I would lay down my life to protect either one of them.

Seeing that nothing is out of the norm, I opt for the stairs the rest of the way down to the lobby.

Since Nic's been appointed head of security here, the building has undertaken a revamp on all of the cameras, access points, and daily operation protocols. Graham spared no expense with turning his building—which encompasses the management of his jewelry company—into a fortress.

Stepping out onto the sidewalk, I breathe in the warm mid-July air. Living in Portland, I find the summer weather enjoyable. I pull out my shades from my suit pocket, placing them over my eyes. It sure feels good to be back on an assignment after taking a couple of weeks off to relax my brain. Granted, Graham forced those days on me.

He was right, though. I feel energized and ready to go.

I unlock my Tesla, slipping into the driver's seat. I would be lying if I said it wasn't a guilty-pleasure purchase. I can't take all my money to the grave with me, so I might as well splurge once in a while.

My lifestyle has adjusted to the perks of working for Graham Hoffman. Sure, both brothers assign me work, but it is Graham who usually takes the lead on most matters. He values hard work and loyalty. My bank account is proof that staying on his good side has profound financial benefits.

I only have to go a few blocks to get home. I park in the garage, directly in my assigned spot. Exiting the car, I lock the doors with the key fob and enter into the waiting elevator. I hit the button for the eleventh floor.

With a short walk down the hallway, I am at my unit. I tap in the code to unlock the door and enter my foyer. Sitting on the storage bench, I untie my dress shoes and place them perfectly on the shelf underneath.

Everything has its place, and when everything is in its place, I feel calm.

During my vacation, I hired a designer and several contractors to gut my condo unit and update all of the features. My place was livable before, but now it has all of the modern luxuries it was lacking during the original build.

Now I have a built-in sound system, new tiled floors, and a complete switch to all stainless steel appliances. I upgraded the master bedroom and even had some fun features added—like special lighting and a four-poster bed. Not that I ever bring women back to my sanctuary. I much prefer hotel rooms for anything casual but intimate. There's fewer strings to cut later if things get emotionally messy.

I don't do drama, and I definitely don't like messy.

Regardless, at least when I do come home, it's a place I want to be.

Without having a full schedule for my assignment of watching over Penny, I may be able to carve out time to catch up on some of my hobbies. Focusing on myself these days has been a rarity. But maybe hitting up a social scene or two will bring me some sexual satisfaction that I've been missing. There's really no other way than to chisel out time for that desired release.

I make my way into the master bedroom, undoing my belt and fly as I walk into the newly renovated closet. Deciding that I needed more space for all of my suits—which are perfectly organized based on color—I opted for the walk-in version.

I remove all of my clothes, fold them, and place them neatly into the hamper meant for dry cleaning. Once a week, Hilda swings by to tidy up the place, bring me groceries, prep meals, and handle all of my laundry needs. It took me a while to trust someone inside my residence while I'm not here. The hidden security cameras scattered about the place help build my confidence though.

Part of me wishes I had more of a conscience. But in my line of work, being soft gets you taken advantage of—or killed. You either eat or be eaten. While I don't have many personal items to protect, I still value the luxury of knowing that what I do have is not going to be stolen away from me.

I'm sure to others, I appear to be quiet and rigid—a man set in his ways. But you don't become one of the top sought after bodyguards for one of the richest men on the West Coast by being sloppy.

I am all about those details.

Slipping on a pair of workout pants, I forgo my shirt and head to my home gym. The good thing about being introverted is that I waste less time by avoiding all of the pitfalls of social media or going out to bars. It's just not my scene. I'm methodical with my choices of where and how I decide to spend my free time.

I start on the pull-up bar and keep my reps around

fifteen for three sets. Today is arms day. With the metal music playing through the sound system, it's easy to lose myself in this room.

Thirty minutes is all it takes to be drenched in sweat and ready to hit up the shower. As the water pelts down around me, I think about my new assignment—one I didn't see coming.

I am also shocked about being invited to Penny's birthday. I can't even remember the last time I bought anyone a gift—let alone for someone of the opposite sex.

What would someone sweet like Penny like? If I'm going to try not to stand out, I better figure it out—and fast.

3

PENNY

"Penny?"

I turn to the sound of the knock on the door and my momma's concerned voice. "Everything's fine."

"I heard you crying. Do you want to talk?"

I flop back on the bed, covering my hands over my eyes. Even being surrounded by the fluffy cotton candy cloud of my pink comforter isn't very comforting. I am tired of talking. I am tired of feeling like I'm surviving as only half a person. For the past year, I've been forced to talk—forced to *feel*.

And now I'm done.

I just want to move forward with my life, the best way I know how.

Visiting Mark Tanner in prison was not one of my brightest ideas—even I can admit that. However, seeing him did actually help me unload some of the feelings blistering my heart from the inside out. Despite feeling emotionally drained by the time Graham and Nic arrived to pick me up, it was therapeutic to see the person who trashed my life behind bars. Unfortunately, though, I think it only served to make my brothers more on edge.

And when they are nervous like that, freedoms get taken away.

Poor Angie and Claire…

How do they even cope with my controlling and possessive brothers?

"Pen?" Momma asks, reminding me I never responded.

I sit up in bed, dragging my fingers through my hair. "No, Momma. I promise I'm fine." I want to believe that. I do. Maybe if I keep saying it, I eventually will be.

I quickly dry my tears, throw on a shirt dress, and open the door. My smile is forced, but I know that there is major cause to be concerned considering I just spent the better part of the last year in a mental facility. Now everyone in this house is walking on eggshells around me, worrying that if they take the wrong step, I will break and go back to my unresponsive self.

It's a lot of pressure to put on myself to act like my emotions are in check and to go through life wondering how many people are filtering their words for my fragile ears, when all I am yearning for is normalcy—which for me means drama.

Controversy.

I crave it.

I just want to feel like myself again and not this washed-out, broken version of me. My eyes don't even recognize my own reflection anymore, and maybe that's for the best. Maybe I can reinvent myself beyond changing my hair.

Maybe I can start over again. Perhaps, I can reacquaint myself with what I want out of life.

"You would tell me if something's wrong?" Momma asks, reaching for my hand to hold.

"Yes, Momma, of course." I glance at the watch that was a gift from Graham for Christmas last year, seeing that I've slept way too long today. It is now afternoon. Maybe if I had something I'm passionate about, I'd be better able to channel my energy and focus my mind. I need a hobby or, better yet, a job.

"It's nice out."

"Yeah?"

"Sure is. I can pack you up food and you can eat out in the garden or by the pool if you want."

My smile is genuine this time. If it wasn't for my momma who sent me weekly letters while I was in Seattle at Soulful Mind, I may not have recovered as quickly as I did. Her love is pure and without measure.

I'm just in a slump. Or maybe it's a mood. Regardless, it's probably because I'm turning another year older tomorrow, and I'm still struggling to find my purpose.

I get it—I am young.

At least that is what everyone around me tells me. They say I have so much time to figure it all out, yada yada. However, I am ready *now*. If I wait until tomorrow, I will miss out on all that I can accomplish today.

I need to make a road map. Some plan of action to get me out of this mental rut and on to bigger and brighter things.

I follow Momma into the kitchen and help her wrap up some fruit, pasta salad, and a sandwich.

"Is Dad still working?" I ask, noticing that the house is quiet.

It's always quiet here.

Too quiet.

At Soulful Mind, I got used to the nightly check-ins and the sound of footsteps outside my door. At one point I think they had me on suicide watch. I would never have taken my own life—even at my lowest. That's just how the staff viewed me when I first arrived. I was just a shell. And it took them months to even crack through enough to get me to talk during sessions.

My mind was constantly moving, though. I was just not brave enough to provide the verbal commentary until I felt safe.

I know it was scary for my family. I was scared too. I thought I would never be able to break through my own mental block to get free.

"So much for retiring, right?" Momma says with a huff.

I laugh. "Yeah, but he promised he would once Claire has the baby. I think he is using being a grandfather as a way of letting go of his dedication."

"Pssh," Momma says, making a face. "That man will never lose his passion. He'll just redirect it. He has already created blueprints for the baby's nursery furniture. Ya know, just a little weekend project to keep him from getting bored."

"You don't have room to talk, Momma. I wonder who designed it?"

"It's not my fault those big box stores lack the elegance and finesse that the baby's room needs. I'm just glad that Claire is finally accepting help."

"Did she have a choice?"

Momma props her hands on her hips, giving me a fake glare. "Always. But some people just need some gentle persuading."

"That's one way of looking at it, I guess."

"So..."

"So...?" I brace myself for one of Momma's abrupt changes of topic, because they are usually way off course.

"Ivan has been asking about you."

Who? Ivan... He must not have made that big of an impact on me if I can't even remember him. "Your friend's son?" I finally inquire.

"Oh,"—she claps her hands together in unnecessary glee—"you remember him."

Barely.

We met a few times when his mom would visit in between trips to Colombia, and apparently we used to be friends as toddlers while attending the same indoor play space in town. I'm pretty sure the only coffee we'll ever drink in this house is the good kind from their country. But in reality, I really don't think we'd be a good match—and this is what this line of conversation is about. I can tell from the hopeful eyes of my momma looking back at me.

Please, just stop.

I don't do well with the whole matchmaking thing. It's as if everyone else thinks they know what's best for me.

"You guys go way back, you know?"

I shrug. "I honestly can't remember too much about him." I *think* he has dark features and is really good at sports. My bank of knowledge is basically supplied by an overstepping mother who loves to "help," which translates to meddle.

But I could also be wrong, and he's a serial killer who collects fingernails in a jar in his basement.

Momma smiles a knowing smile. "Well, he can't make it to your birthday, but he did get you a gift."

What? Why? We don't even know each other. I mean, not really. Maybe we did before as babies. But definitely not now.

That's weird.

I take the box that Momma hands me and pull off the lid.

"Oh, that's nice."

And I didn't even have to fake my enthusiasm—because it *is* a very nice gift.

As predicted, guilt strikes me right in the heart.

Ivan was being thoughtful.

"Well, what is it?" Momma bounces on her feet, trying to get a better look.

I pull out the hoodie shirt that has the Colombian flag printed along the front. It is lightweight enough for cooler summer nights. "I love it."

"Ivan has been working under Dad at the office."

"Oh, yeah?" I feign interest. I have to balance between being nice and trying not to give my momma some type of illusion. I honestly have no clue what she actually tells her friend and what could potentially get back to Ivan.

"So, maybe him mentoring someone young and fresh will help him step away from the business."

"Yeah, maybe."

"I still am holding out hope that the baby arriving will make him want to slow down."

"That's a good point." And probably a step in the right direction. Dad deserves to rejuvenate with much-needed time off and enjoy his next season in life.

I pack up the food and then grab a can of sparkling orange juice from the fridge. I turn back to Momma, who is sorting out a stack of mail that is resting on the counter.

"I still can't believe Nic is on board with Claire's desire to wait until delivery to find out the gender. Or maybe he paid off the ultrasound tech just to know ahead of time. It's not like he or Graham have any patience when it comes to things they cannot control."

Waving some junk mail into the air, Momma lets out a laugh. "Well, both boys have met their match with their ladies. Serves them right for all of the stress they caused me over the years. Getting pregnant with you was the universe's way of giving me some balance."

I smile. My brothers deserve happiness, and they sure found it with the women who have consumed their hearts. "I'm just glad neither had to be bailed out of prison."

"Ha, I wouldn't place a bet on that. You know how hotheaded they can get when it comes to those they love."

"Yup." I nod in agreement. "They have quite the reputation at the facility."

Momma smiles. "Oh, without a doubt. You know every gray hair that I try to hide on my head was caused by them. I blame them for everything. It's how I cope."

I giggle and move over to the back door. At least I can find some small amount of humor in my life. "I can only imagine the impressions they've made when I wasn't around to witness their behavior."

Momma looks to be deep in thought. "It's probably for the best we never find out."

I slip on my pink Converse shoes and grab the tote bag I have hanging on a hook. I double-check that my journal and pen are inside. Part of my ongoing therapy sessions involve self-reflecting and understanding my triggers that make me shut down. I'd like to think that all of the self-talk I do has been helping, but honestly, some days I doubt I'll ever go back to being the carefree Penny who used to trust everyone —especially men—without reservation.

Maybe I should stop trying to go back to being my old self and just learn to get to know the new me. So much has changed that I'm not even sure I can knit the two versions together.

"Oh, here, Penny. This just came in the mail. Dad had some sent to the house to check the quality before distributing them to the masses. Maybe you'd be interested?"

Turning around, I take the flyer from Momma's extended hand and look down at it. "Oh, the annual charity auction for Dad's work. I missed last year's…"

"But you can attend this one if you want," Momma quickly interjects, her voice hopeful and jolly.

"Yeah," I say, almost as an afterthought. I tuck the oversized postcard into my journal, so I can look at it later.

I wave to Momma and slip out the door, with my packed bag and a rolled-up blanket tucked under my arm. The smell of jasmine and freesia overwhelms my senses, as the rush of sweetness fills up my nostrils.

When I make it down to the patio, I can't help but feel a

sense of peace wash over me. That's what this place does to me. It provides the perfect dose of nostalgia, paired with the safety net of having two parents who love me dearly.

The pool's surface glistens in the sun. Bending down, I glide my hand through the water, testing its temperature. It's just right. Maybe later I'll take a dip.

When I was getting treatment, I often spent my days outside in the sunshine. Soulful Mind is one of the top places in the country for mental trauma and rehabilitative services. While I didn't particularly enjoy being there, it was a way of overcoming some of the hurdles keeping me from living a full life again.

But it still feels like I'm lacking the passion and drive to do more than just mope around and sleep. I guess it could be depression? Although, I really don't feel sad. Maybe I'm just lonely—or bored.

I place my bag down onto the grass and then spread out the pink-and-white checkered blanket. I thought changing my hair and buying a few new clothes would shake me out of this rut. However, I think I need to set some reachable goals and come up with a viable action plan to home in on what I really want to get out of this next chapter of my life.

If there was one thing I learned this past year, it's that the time is now. Tomorrow is not guaranteed.

Mark Tanner might still think he's the demon lurking around in my life, but the real predator is time and our inability to stop it from progressing forward.

Second by second…

No matter how I look at it, I lost opportunities while at Soulful Mind, and that's time I'll never get back.

But I did gain a better understanding of my own self.

And that intrinsic knowledge is priceless.

While I might lack the foresight to achieve my goals, I at least have self-awareness of what I really want out of life.

Simply put—I want to live. Live for today. Live for tomorrow. And live for the hope of a better future.

I pull out my journal and pen before finding refuge in the center of the blanket. Birds tweet melodically in the neighboring trees, while my newly dyed blonde hair blows in the breeze.

I push the top of the pen against the notebook to extend the point. I flip through the filled pages, noticing that my entire journal is full. I don't even have a page left. How did I not notice until now? I flip open the back cover and decide that the empty margins will work for now. I can always transfer my list to a fresh book later.

I start writing, allowing my brain to just dump ideas out onto the small section of blank space.

Goals for the Summer:

1. Make at least one female friend
2. Find a job
3. Learn to shoot a gun
4. Move out of my parents' house
5. Step out of my comfort zone
6. Buy something frivolous
7. Get my driver's license
8. Kiss a ~~boy~~ man

I take a deep breath as I think about the last couple of goals that I need to work on in order to overcome some of the mental stress my brain endures when faced with a few triggering challenges involving men.

9. *Allow someone to tie me up*
10. *Give a man permission to blindfold me*
11. *Kiss a random stranger*

I reach into my bag and pull out my sandwich. Peeling back the wrapper, I take a bite. I reread my scattered list, trying to think of anything else to add to it. At least I have a road map to what needs to be done to gain a bit more independence and be a little less fearful of everything that crosses my path.

Mark Tanner may not have raped me when I was incapacitated. However, my brain still hasn't been able to separate the feeling of being violated from what actually happened. If I ever have hopes of getting a boyfriend, I need to be able to fully function when things get intimate and not freak out at the first intentionally suggestive touch.

Ha. Who am I kidding? I'm pretty sure Graham and Nic will scare off any guy that even tries to get near me—long before clothes start shedding.

They proved as much when any guy at the facility would go from talking to me to completely ignoring me, in a matter of days. If I'm going to work on my goals, I need to do it without my two overbearing shadows.

Who needs an overprotective father, when you have two controlling brothers who basically have zero qualms about background checking anyone who comes within a six-foot radius? How Angie and Claire can function with their hovering men is a mystery to me.

But I love them with my whole heart.

Stubbornness runs in our family, so we are all bound to clash at times.

I twirl my pen into my hair, wrapping a strand around it. And just for fun, I add a few more goals. If you can't challenge yourself, then your life will forever be boring.

12. Have wild, passionate sex (and actually enjoy it)
13. Go to a sex toy store (and buy something fun and unexpected)

Feeling satisfied with my to-do list, I roll to my side and reach for my beverage. I pop open the tab, hearing the satisfying sound of the fizz. Despite the therapy facility having stellar food, I often would hit up the vending machine during our walkabout hour each evening and make a junk food buffet, using the exorbitant amount of money my brothers would add to my account card. I guess it was my way of preserving some normalcy in my life, when everything else seemed so out of place.

As much as it's nostalgic living back here at my parents' house, I need to do things on my own. Tomorrow, I'll be another year older, and the last thing I need is to get comfortable being stagnant.

Grabbing my phone, I open up the search engine and type in "roommate needed in Portland," and then click to search. Several app and service ads fill up the screen, allowing me to scroll through to see which one looks the most professional. Settling on Roommate Finder, I open up the App Store and download it. I eat some fruit while I wait for it to install.

Knowing that I want to live in the city helps me narrow down the location. I want to stay west of the rivers to avoid some of the college students seeking out a roommate. I have no intention of going back after being gone for so long. Even when I did attend, I wasn't sure it was the right choice for me anyway. A formal education may have worked for Graham and Nic, but I've always been the one to go against the grain.

I guess I could look for a modeling job. I am less naive than I was before. Trauma will do that to a person. I could also waitress or apply to a clothing store. My skill set is limited, but at least my willingness to put forth the effort is abundant.

I fill out the personal information form for the app and allow the tool to find me the perfect rental and roommate based on what I need and what I can comfortably afford. Maybe I'll even meet someone friendly and we can become friends.

Dropping out of college early definitely took away several opportunities to meet and connect with people my age. Sure, I had friends in high school, but our lifestyle choices didn't align, and connections faded over time. Then, being in Seattle and having people there just temporarily didn't allow me to develop strong friendships.

I'm nearly positive I'd have made a horrible friend during that chapter of my life anyway.

Friends listen. Friends share emotions. Friends want to hang out.

I was incapable of doing any of those things. If you don't nurture relationships, they don't tend to grow.

When the app stops searching, I have eighteen possibilities to sift through. I choose my top three favorites and do a virtual tour of the building and rental units. A thrill of excitement rushes through me at the chance of starting fresh again. I can be anyone I want to be, and it's my choice on what to share or not share with others about my hiatus this past year.

Feeling daring—something I haven't felt in so long—I click "accept" for the apartment that appeals to me after the tour. I have a month to test out the lease. If I am not happy there, I can always move again. The bonus is that on this particular unit, there already is a match for a roommate that meets the requirements for the filters I set for the search. Win-win if you ask me.

Gathering up my items, I pack them into my bag and make my way back toward the house. Things are already feeling brighter. Maybe I can assimilate myself back into the real world more smoothly than I was originally planning.

I just hope that Graham and Nic aren't going to be hurdles to jump over. I need to do some things on my own. Surely they can understand that? I lost too much time to be idle and complacent now. I just need to play my cards right and give my brothers the illusion that they are in control. The last thing I need is for them to jack up all of my plans.

4

COLLINS

"I'm so happy you're here, Collins," Donna greets.

She takes my gift and sets it on a small table near the door, and then gives me a hug—a real one.

I take a polite step back after we detach, lowering my gaze toward the floor. "I'm very thankful to be asked."

It feels good to be wanted—especially by the matriarch of the Hoffman family. She has always given me the warmest welcome. I'd be lying if I claimed not to compare her active presence in her children's lives with what I grew up missing.

I wouldn't call it jealousy. It's just an observation—paired with admiration.

"I know my Graham works you to the bone. I wouldn't be surprised if you all of a sudden quit."

I chuckle over her coddling. She may appear sweet, but she packs a punch with her spitfire personality.

Something tells me that Penny will share that in common with her mom.

I've gotten good at standing back and observing. I can learn a lot about a person just by watching them—their mannerisms, reactions to adversity, and nervous tendencies. All these clues let me in on the core of a person. It's like my brain creates a virtual catalog of the information, tucking it away for safekeeping, as a just-in-case resource.

Nic joins us in the foyer, smacking hands with me in greeting. He knows I'm here for business and as a family friend—a relationship that has evolved over the course of employment. While celebrating the birthday girl, I still plan to assess the situation and see just how much effort I'll need to make to keep Penny content and safe.

She must be getting antsy, and her brothers just want what they think is best for her. Who could fault them for wanting to keep her safe from the cruel and mindless negativity of the world? I would be doing the same if I had any siblings—especially a baby sister.

The sound of the door opening causes us all to turn to see Graham and Angie arrive hand in hand—looking more in love than ever.

"Good to see you, Collins," Angie says, separating from Graham to give me a hug. She pulls back from me to look with awe over my appearance. I think she likes to try to get me to smile. She probably even makes a game out of it. "Hmm, never thought I'd see the day where you would choose to wear jeans and a T-shirt. Very casual. I like it."

Graham wraps his arms around her from behind, nuzzling the side of her neck. "You better not be flirting with my staff, sweetheart. We know that never ends well for *you*." His voice trails off to the point where I can no longer hear, but Angie's cheeks turn pink, and I glance away to avoid seeing her in her state of vulnerability.

At one time, Graham may have been serious about the accusation. However, there should be zero doubt in his mind that his wife would ever turn an eye to anyone other than him. She is so utterly in love that her entire demeanor outwardly expresses just whom she belongs to, and I can't see that ever changing.

"Stop," she scolds, smacking him on the arm. "Ignore him, Collins. As you know, my husband's jealousy streak has not lessened since our nuptials. If anything, it has—"

"Gotten more extreme," Donna chimes in, making us all laugh. "If you all will excuse me, I need to check on a few things for the party. Make yourselves at home and relax."

I shake hands with Graham when he detaches himself from his wife, who hits him on his side to keep him from smothering her.

"Where's Claire?" I ask Nic directly.

"She's upstairs helping Penny get ready. I sure wish she would just stay off her feet and quit it already with this need to do all the things. She thinks the baby is going to change her life so drastically that she is in marathon mode trying to be everything for everybody."

I give a nod. Claire definitely is a ball full of energy. It's hard to imagine that giving birth will cause her to calm down entirely.

"I'm doing my part," Angie says softly. "But I can only force her to take so many breaks in the office before she starts shooting me with her daggers of sarcasm."

Nic sighs, running his hand over the back of his neck. "I'm on the verge of hiring a nanny for her while the baby is in the womb. I'm going crazy worrying about her every second she is away from me. She's probably upstairs doing Pilates or human pretzel twisting exercises just to prove to herself that she still can."

"Just wait until the baby is born," Germain says, joining us. "Your attention will be split between the baby and your wife. You'll be too exhausted to worry."

Nic growls at his dad. "I'm going to go nuts."

Germain excuses himself into the kitchen and returns with four bottles of beer under his arms. I am about to decline when one is offered to me—since I never drink on the job—but Graham shoots me a look across the room to signal that I can relax my standards if I so choose.

I guess one drink will be fine. It's a birthday party after all.

"If I need to pull out the hard stuff, I won't object," Germain says, patting Nic on the back. "It doesn't feel like that long ago when your mother was pregnant with you, and I was worried sick over her drive to manage everything. Women are superheroes in my eyes. They can basically do it all, but why should they?"

"Exactly," Nic says, clinking bottles with his dad.

At the sound of footsteps on the stairs, we all look over, expecting to see Penny. Instead, Claire is walking down. Even though she's not even at the halfway mark, I can see the hint of a bump growing round on her petite frame.

I suck in a breath and brace myself for the middle Hoffman's wrath. I can almost predict his exact words before they are spoken.

"Hold on to the damn rail, woman," Nic scoffs, joining

her mid-descent to assist with a hand. "They aren't there for decoration."

"I'm pregnant, Nic, not some invalid."

"You've been getting dizzy and—"

"I'm sure you'll be assigning some watchdogs to me. Or better yet, a water person. You know, someone who follows me around with one of those liter bottles with the huge straw."

Claire's eyes glance to me, making me take in another deep breath. Angie and Claire are best friends. However, they have very different personalities. Where Angie is subtle, Claire leaves nothing up to the imagination in what she is thinking.

And I know she's a bit salty over me being assigned to her prior to my vacation time off.

"Be careful what you suggest," Nic says smoothly, but it is obvious by his tone that he is on edge. "You are only supplying me more ideas."

"And they better be bitches and not your intrusive militia man squad who hover more than bees on flowers."

Claire's finger points at me, and I instinctively hold my own hands up in defense. "I was on leave." And I was. It's a legit defense. But yeah, I heard all the drama that happened —and am apparently still reliving it.

With Nic as the focus for her rant, she continues, "I've never been more embarrassed than when trying to go to the obstetrician's the last time."

Sighing, he squeezes his eyes shut, as if to fight the effects of a migraine. "I have it handled. Just don't blame Collins. He needed a vacation."

Angie makes her way over to her best friend, pulling her

into a hug when she gets off the last step. She has a way of defusing a situation. I'm thankful, because these women can gang up and combine forces. And now with Penny back in the area, I can only imagine what dynamic the three of them together will be.

"If my son messes this up," Donna states from across the room, "do not hold grudges against me, Claire. I've told both boys multiple times not to jack up the best thing that's happened to them."

We all laugh. Donna is not one to mince words either—which actually comes across as endearing. You know she likes you when her filter seems a bit broken.

I relax into my stance and take a long sip of my beer. I glance at the label—seeing that it is local—and savor the bitter flavor.

It's almost impossible not to think about love when you are around the Hoffman brothers and their women. It's also the perfect reminder that I'm a loner. In a way, I always have been.

From an early age, I've been conditioned through a series of bad events to trust my instincts—not people.

Men like me don't settle. We just survive.

And with that closed-off attitude comes a lot of no-strings arrangements. I can't call them relationships, because that would be an insult to the ones I am witnessing right here in my presence now. Plus, I'm not consistent enough with my needs to label it any other way.

Seeing movement out of the corner of my eye, I turn toward it to find Penny waiting at the top step, looking down at the crowd gathered below. We are here to celebrate her and yet her eyes tell me she is uncertain if she even wants to come down.

The darker hair she used to have is a thing of the past, being replaced by a honey-blonde shade that surprisingly suits her perfectly. Half is pulled back in what I assume to be a clip. Feathery strands highlight the roundness of her cheeks, which are painted with the palest pink shade. Her smile is sweet, causing her to look even more…

Innocent.

No, that's not the right word. Because if she was in fact innocent, then my mind would be able to separate right from wrong—unlike what is happening now.

Maybe "untouchable" is a better word.

Off-limits.

This is my first time seeing Penny since she has been discharged, and her brothers are right in the physical transformation she has done with herself.

Her delicate hand reaches for the rail, as she takes the first step down. Dressed in a pale pink dress made entirely of lace, she looks stunningly feminine—elegant but still casual.

If she looks this stunning in clothes, I have zero doubt that she'd be a vision out of them.

Every exposed inch of skin is the color of fresh cream. The harsh sun hasn't damaged her or caused her to be flawed in any noticeable way. Every freckle seems to be perfectly placed, as if they each belong in the exact location in which they reside.

She is a masterpiece.

My eyes focus on Penny's bare feet, with nails painted the shade of bubblegum. Each step she descends causes her ankle bracelet made of linked hearts to shift. Her fingers play with the hem of her dress, curling and uncurling around the delicate fabric. Her hand moves up to fix a piece of hair behind her ear, drawing attention to her exquisite neck and jawline.

In this moment, it's like meeting Penny for the first time.

The swell of her breasts rises and falls as I watch her breathing increase—probably from a bit of nerves or excitement. I am completely entranced by the way her toes bend and flex as she makes her way downstairs. It's like the world has stopped spinning on its axis, and the only thing that matters in this fragment of time is Penny.

Penny.

She's the girl I'm supposed to guard and protect. She's the baby sister of the two men I can never repay for the life they have given me.

Yet, here I stand, just a few yards away from the girl, and I can't seem to stop wondering—what if?

What if we met under different circumstances? What if I never decided to start working for Graham Hoffman? What if we weren't on two vastly different playing fields and at two vastly different times in our lives?

Her eyes catch mine, and a rush of guilt coats my insides as I feel like I have violated part of an unwritten code that I live by—with my wayward gaze alone. I plaster on my professional filter and offer up a half smile, careful not to give away any of my thoughts or allow any more blood to rush to my freaking cock.

Well, damn.

I am rarely caught off guard, and in just the moment of

seeing Penny, it feels like everything I thought I knew is now a jumbled-up mess. Perhaps it's the higher alcohol percentage from the beer or the fact that I haven't eaten dinner yet. Regardless, I need to keep my head on straight and remember my role in this family.

And my role is definitely not one of betrayal.

Penny's attention is on me, and it feels like I'm back in the danger zone. The longer I look, the higher the risk of getting swept up in a sea I have no business wading in. But, no matter how hard I try, I cannot look away.

She captivates me, and yet, causes such unrest within my soul.

This girl may have changed appearances, but something inside me has changed as well.

Penny's hands twist together in front of her, as if she's trying to decide what to do with them. Her enchanting blue eyes hold so much mystery and emotion. She's the type of girl that men would move mountains for—she is that sweet.

She fixes a stray piece of hair behind her ear, revealing a pair of heart earrings that are similar in style to her anklet, and most likely a product of Jealousy—her oldest brother's jewelry company. She bites her bottom lip, and then—

Fuck.

Her tongue sweeps across her lip, licking the sheer pink gloss. It's the most erotic thing I've ever seen, and I'm going to go to hell for enjoying it so much.

If I make it out of this assignment without landing in a body bag with Graham and Nic fighting to zip it up first, then I'll consider myself the victor. Perhaps even a saint.

Oh fuck, she's moving closer.

Taking one bare foot in front of the other, Penny closes

the distance between us. My heart catches, causing me to feel a bit lightheaded.

What is happening to me?

I've been around Penny for over a year, and I never thought of her as anything other than the baby sister of my bosses. But now as she meanders toward me—looking like a delicious strawberry cupcake—there is nothing sweet about my thoughts.

Dammit.

I can actually feel my cock stir with the influx of blood rushing to the damn thing. So much for priding myself on discipline when it comes to the opposite sex. Right now, the only thing I have is a semi hard-on that needs to simmer the fuck down.

"Happy birthday, Penny." My words come out gruff. Did I just hit puberty?

"Thanks, Collins."

I want to say more. I always want to say more—yet never do. So instead, I make it awkward by defaulting to silence.

"Glad you could come. I, umm"—she rocks on her feet while glancing around the room—"don't know many people other than family."

"You'll make friends. It just takes time." It's a stupid thing to say—something I don't even have experience to justify saying. I just hate seeing her disappointed.

Penny gives me a nod and then moves to give her brothers each a hug in greeting. The whiff of strawberries and cream permeates my senses, coating me with the sweet smell that radiates off her. The fragrance is delicious, like the freshest berry patch. She is a freaking treat now for my eyes and my nose.

"Well, everyone," Donna says, signaling for us to turn our attention to her. "I have a barbecue buffet set up outside around the pool. Feel free to help yourself to the food and bar. The pool is the perfect temperature, so get in at your leisure. Let's just enjoy everyone's company and wish Penny a happy birthday."

"Happy birthday, Penny," we all say, making our way outside.

The attention makes her shy, but I can tell by the smile plastered to her face that she is excited to be putting some of her past trauma hopefully behind her.

The pool is curved in shape and is surrounded by lounge chairs and tables. Donna is a designer, with an eye for pretty things. She can really make even the most ordinary things sparkle.

I stand back on the sidelines and just take in the scene, not feeling any big drive to put myself in the middle of conversations. Aside from the few social events connected to Graham and Angie's wedding, I haven't really attended too many nonwork-related parties—especially ones that are this personal. So, I'm not even sure if I should insert myself and try to look less stiff or hang back like I am.

Nic makes Claire a plate of food she initially scoffs at, but then gobbles up every morsel with minor coaxing. Angie relaxes on Graham's lap, while he feeds her grapes. Donna buzzes about, straightening anything that appears to be crooked or out of place, all while Germain hugs Penny to his side.

From the little bits of information I gathered from

working with Graham, Germain took it extremely hard when Penny was victimized. He must be ecstatic that she is on the mend—albeit a bit nervous that it will be short-lived.

No one wants to see Penny fail and go back to Seattle.

Growing up with my grandparents raising me, I never had the luxury of an intact family unit. I was the only child. When my grandparents passed away when I was still very young, I had no one to take up that role.

So I entered into the broken foster care system.

And that is where I really grew up—and fast.

I got really used to temporary.

In a way, I'm very much a recluse to this day. However, it is moments like these, where I am surrounded by the outpouring of love, that I wonder what life would have been like if I had the comforts of a forever family.

After years of speech, I've managed to outgrow my stuttering problem that shadowed me throughout grade school. Kids can be cruel, but I learned early on that no one bullies the kid in class that can beat the shit out of everyone else. I was smart, methodical. I knew how to defend myself without getting caught or in trouble. Plus, no one would have suspected the quiet kid to pommel anyone. It just took sticking up for myself physically one time in the cafeteria before word got out that no one should mess with me.

After that day, no one did. I carried that reputation until the day I graduated from high school. And even decades later, I still think about those fuckers who did me wrong. They were the driving force pushing me into service for this country. It was my attention to detail and my quick thinking skills that moved me up in rank.

I don't have a temper by any means. I pride myself on

being disciplined enough to know when to strike versus when to keep my cool. Not every battle needs to be fought with force, and none need to involve any type of emotions.

Emotions can get you killed.

I scan the patio area and make my way over to the serving table. Everything looks amazing, and the smell of real food makes my mouth water. I grab a plate and scoop out some pulled pork from the tray, dressing it with a sweet and spicy barbecue sauce. Grilled pineapple on skewers catch my attention, and I add one to my plate.

"Come join us, Collins," Angie says, motioning for me to come over to the furniture area.

"You too, Penny," Claire calls over.

I find a free spot on a two-seat couch, making sure there is ample room for Penny, as she takes her place beside me.

My legs alone make her look even more petite—delicate. She is a graceful butterfly who just needs her wings to heal.

"How does it feel to be another year older?" Graham asks his sister.

"It makes me a bit anxious, actually." She fixes a piece of hair behind her ear, and I realize it is her tell. Anytime she is stressed, she curls her toes or touches her hair. "I feel like I lost an entire year of my life, so this next one has to count."

Graham gives Penny a look of concern. "That's a lot of pressure to put on yourself."

She shrugs. "I made a list of a bunch of things I want to accomplish."

This catches my attention.

"Oh yeah?" Angie asks. "That sounds fun."

"What are some of your goals?" Graham asks, attempting to sound casual, but I know he is simply asking to seek out information and save himself a step of asking me to retrieve all of it for him.

I'm thankful he asked. This list definitely has me curious and a bit impatient. Her answers will help me to understand the scope of my duties, because right now, I'm not sure just how much my services are really needed.

Penny shifts in her seat. "Well, for starters, I want to learn how to drive."

"Now that seems fun!" Angie says with a giggle. I think she hears her husband growl beside her—or maybe I'm just imagining his reaction because it mirrors my own.

"Maybe I can sign Claire up with you for classes?" Nic volunteers softly.

"Hey!" She smacks him on the arm, almost making his beer spill. "I may only have a half working brain right now, but my ears aren't affected. Plus, I have my license, you loon."

"A refresher course would never hurt," he counters.

Angie can't contain her laughter, earning a glare from her best friend. I've witnessed Claire's driving, and it is scary. I don't blame Nic in the slightest for outlawing her from going behind the wheel—especially now that she is carrying their child.

Nic sighs. "Then settle for a self-driving car."

Claire shakes her head. "No. We've had this discussion already. It would just stifle my creativity."

"That's the point, Claire." He lets out a harsh laugh. "Driving isn't meant to be wild and carefree."

I resist reacting as I see Nic's face turn visibly stressed.

He sure has his work cut out for him as he navigates this new territory of keeping his pregnant fiancée happy while also keeping her safe.

Maybe watching Penny won't be bad at all. I very well could have dodged a bullet—shaped like Claire Nettles.

I've been broken in and initiated by watching the Hoffman men's women in the past.

Can Penny really be worse?

Nah.

"What else do you have as a goal?" Graham asks his sister, keeping us on topic.

She finishes chewing and then crosses her feet at her ankles. "Moving out, getting a job, making a friend, and learning to shoot a g—"

"No," Nic says flatly.

Claire pats his arm, in the place she once smacked him. "Baby, you can't keep your sister in a box forever."

"I can try." His words come out as a growl. He is on edge. I wish there was a way to defuse the situation and help him relax.

"You know you can't control the women in your life," Angie interjects.

"Yeah, you basically have the authority of a crossing guard," Claire teases her man, earning her a hard look, which translates as playful rather than angry.

"Why do you want to shoot a gun, Penny?" Graham asks.

I'd like to know as well. And I'll find out. I always find out. And if it has anything to do with the fucker who violated her, I will handle the situation myself before she ever confronts him again. The last thing this family needs is to be hiring a fancy lawyer to get Penny released of charges when she tries to show up at a prison with a gun.

Penny looks thoughtfully at the ripples in the pool from the gentle breeze blowing through. "I just want to learn a skill. Do something invigorating. Partake in something I wouldn't otherwise want."

Graham and Nic both glance at me. I know what they are thinking. If they want me to be discreet, then they have to allow Penny to have some sort of freedom. I don't like the idea of her shooting any kind of weapon. However, I understand her desire. She wants to feel in control again. Who could blame her?

I store all of this information inside my head. I might need to keep tabs on her credit card spending and make sure she doesn't step near a shooting range without my knowledge or try to purchase a gun on her own.

I'm also hoping that I can convince her somehow to reconsider. Maybe if I offer to teach her some self-defense moves, it will keep her content.

"I think your goals sound wonderful," Angie says, reaching over to pat her on her hand. "As for the job, I'll be in contact with you. Maybe you can come by Plus None."

"I'm not sure…"

"Don't eliminate us as a possibility," Claire chimes in. "We would be honored for you to join our team."

Penny bites her bottom lip, and my eyes are instantly drawn to the simple act. "Fair enough."

Germain whistles from across the pool, causing us all to look at him and Donna, as they make their way toward us. Lit candles flicker in the sunshine as Donna carries a three-tiered, strawberry-topped frosted cake. It is big enough to feed an army.

We all sing happy birthday.

"Make a wish," Donna urges, setting the beautiful cake down onto the coffee table in front of her.

I turn to look at the blushing girl beside me, who no longer represents the fragile person I would see at the psychiatric facility. No, this girl is strong. Resilient. Empowered. She just doesn't realize how much she has overcome.

Discreetly, I snap a picture of Penny with my cell and then tuck it back into the pocket of my jeans.

Penny's eyes move about the space, locking with each individual present, until she circles back to her cake.

Twenty-two candles.

Twenty-two years she has been alive, and almost half my age of thirty-eight. It's hard for me to remember what I was like when I was twenty-two years old. I'm not even sure much has changed in me on an intrinsic level. I have the same mindset as I did over a decade ago. It's just that now I have the resources to fulfill any plans I have for the future.

But what are my plans? Do I even have a vision?

I never really cared before now. I have been too content working for Graham Hoffman to care about much else at this stage of my life. I do my job, I go home, and I wash-and-repeat.

Sure, I work out and partake in some sexually freeing fun. But other than that, I don't have much of an identity.

I definitely don't have a legacy built on a family name like the Hoffmans do.

So why have I been satisfied up until now when I see how intently Penny is staring at her lit candles? She is preparing her wish, and I'm not even sure what I would wish for if I was given the chance to make one.

Penny blows out her candles, and secretly I hope that whatever she wished for comes true. A girl like her deserves what her heart desires.

I lose track of the scene around me, and it isn't until Donna passes me a slice with a strawberry on top that I realize the cake has been cut and served.

I eat in silence, having a hard time swallowing each bite, as I think about my own life.

What am I striving to be?

What goals do I have?

Closing my eyes, I make a wish of my own…

And it's to take more risks.

5

COLLINS

"Everyone knows it's not a party at the Hoffmans without—"

"Alcohol!" Nic chimes in, making his mom stop all movement.

I can't help but smirk. I also can't help but be drawn to Penny and her expressions of joy.

"No. Well…yes, but that's not what I was thinking."

"Oh, I know!" Graham yells, raising his hand animatedly. "Mom sharing embarrassing stories of my childhood."

"No, but speaking of which… Did I ever tell you all the story where Graham watered the house plants by peeing on them? They all died within a month."

"No, you didn't," Angie says, turning to look at him.

He shrugs and tries to appear innocent. "It was all natural irrigation."

"Gross!" Nic yells.

"Oh, but did I tell you about Nic's childhood obsession with"—Donna pauses to let out her own laugh—"stickers?

Well, I came home from the grocery store one day, and he was so proud to show me his fancy sticker project. You know, the one where he took menstrual pads and stuck them all over his bedroom wall."

"You didn't," Claire says, shaking her head.

"It was my most creative project to date."

"And then there's P—"

"Storytime is over," Penny says in a hurry, probably trying to move on before her mom shares something about her. "And I think I know the answer to Momma's question. It's family games."

Donna smiles with pride. "Finally, someone gets me."

We all watch as Germain carries out a big box to the patio. "This arrived just in time," he says, using a retractable blade to slice through the packing tape.

Donna pulls back the flaps and peers inside the box, scrunching up her nose in disgust. "I've been a victim of a hate crime."

Graham shakes his head. "Mom, falling for an MLM pyramid scheme is not a hate crime."

We all laugh.

"It is when they were supposed to send me light-up medallions," she snaps, holding up the most obnoxious handmade beaded necklaces made of fraying yarn.

"I could only imagine what you'd do if a man pulls up with a van and offers to show you his puppies in the back," Nic mutters.

Donna shakes the plastic disk on a string in front of him. "These don't even light up. Scammers."

"Anyway," Germain says cheerfully, probably trying to distract his wife, "let's start the games. Partner up."

And everyone does, with Penny and me having no logical choice but to choose each other.

"I play to win," she says with a giggle.

I raise my eyebrows in challenge. "I do as well."

"We are on the same team."

"So make sure you bring it."

"Oh, I plan to."

Donna flitters about, handing us each a paper airplane and a strip of paper. "The goal is for one person to fly the airplane and the other person to move the runway in order to safely land that airplane."

"Sounds simple enough," Claire says, nodding to Nic.

"I'll fly it."

She props her hands on both hips. "We'll take turns."

"Then I'll brace myself for the crash and burn."

She smacks him on the arm, making us all laugh.

"You must be at least three yards away from the takeoff position and the start of the landing strip. The winning team is the first team to safely land the plane. Get ready. Get set. Go."

Penny flies the paper plane while I move the strip as it is midair to see if we can land it safely.

Fail.

"Try again. You're doing good," I encourage.

The plane takes off and falls short of the strip.

After another two tries and adjustments, we land the plane.

"Victory!" she chants, jumping up and down.

Donna keeps track of the win on the scoreboard, and then starts pulling out supplies for the next challenge.

I help her carry over a stack of mini folding tables and

set them up in partners across from one another. Each table on the left has a bowl of tennis balls set up as the centerpiece. The accompanying tables each have three empty tennis ball containers arranged in rows.

"So this next game is called Pucker Up and involves transporting the tennis balls using only your mouth to the containers, with your partner of course. We have two minutes to see who has the most balls collected."

"Seems easy enough," Penny says, rocking on her heels.

"Assuming we can work as a team."

"Just don't drop the ball and we'll be fine."

I let out a chuckle at her playful pun.

"Get ready, go," Germain yells, not giving us much warning.

Penny and I rush into position. "On the count of three, we lower ourselves to the top ball," I instruct.

"And then we hum to the count of three and rise."

"Sounds good."

"One, two"—we both line up our lips on opposite sides of the top tennis ball—"three."

"Hmm, hmm, hmm…"

I join in on the laughter and silliness as we waddle over to the empty containers to drop off our first ball.

And it's the first time in ages that I fully enjoy doing the simplest of things such as playing a game.

"Bloody hell," I whisper under my breath, as Penny comes out of the pool house wearing a pink ruffled bikini. It is strapless and looks so pretty, yet seductive, on her perfect body. Creamy skin, from head to toe, makes her look like a porcelain doll. She's a flawless temptress and a feast for my eyes.

Does she even know the alluring appeal she has?

My unhinged jaw should be validation alone.

I know Penny has a fighter spirit to assimilate back into her old life, but she is clearly making another type of statement. I doubt the version of Penny prior to the incident resembles this version of Penny.

I have to respect the effort though.

Feeling underdressed in my black swim trunks and a pair of shades, I at least have the luxury of staying shielded from all of the glances I keep taking of the blonde bombshell.

I can't even remember the last time I've been to a pool party. Maybe never. I definitely can't remember the last time someone from the opposite sex has affected me this badly.

I stand frozen in place as Penny leans over the pool's edge, lifting her arms above her head. Her breasts plump to almost spill out of the scrap of fabric. Then, she dives into the water—fully dry—barely making a splash. When she resurfaces, her blonde hair looks golden in the sunlight. She shakes her head, spraying water droplets, giggling at what I can only imagine is an invigorating feeling. She looks relaxed and carefree.

Utterly beautiful.

Graham and Nic join me, as I try to look like I wasn't just ogling their sister. The sunglasses help to keep my stare from being obvious.

Nothing good can possibly come from my developing

infatuation with Penny Hoffman. I'm not a stupid man, and yet, every thought fluttering through my brain right now is one hundred percent insane.

"Can you understand now why we're compensating you with an abundance of money?" Graham jokes, nudging his chin toward Penny.

Nic smirks. "We might need to consider a raise."

"On my unofficial first day?" I say with a chuckle.

"Yup," Graham says with a grin.

"I'm bracing myself for when all the fuckers in the city start panting over her." Nic tilts his beer at me. "Feel free to freshen up your carving skills."

"The money is an afterthought. I'd do that for free."

"We appreciate it, man," Graham says, his eyes laser focused on the pool.

I swallow hard and redirect my attention as Claire and Angie enter the water. The hum of excitement has taken the edge off my inappropriate desires, sobering me for the responsibility I have with protecting Penny.

There most definitely will be fuckers after her.

Just look at her.

She is hypnotizing.

I've seen Penny struggle with exorcising her demons. I never want to see her that broken again. And I sure as hell don't want some man taking advantage of her good nature. Just the thought makes my blood heat inside my veins.

If her brothers are right about her wanting to spread her wings and take some risks, I'll need to make sure no idiots bother her. Because they will. I know how asshole-ish my gender can be when someone like Penny crosses their path.

If she wants to find someone, she will have no problem at all. But they will have to get my approval first.

Any guy worthy enough to have her better the fuck know how lucky he is. Women like Penny don't come along often. So, she better be cherished.

And respected…

Yup. I am a hypocrite.

Glancing at the pool, I watch as Penny laughs with the girls. Her head bends back, exposing the muscles of her toned neck as she wets her hair. If she's not careful, her top is going to slip.

Damn…

While I'd like to think I'll always have Penny's best interests in mind, a small part of me doubts that my attraction to her will ever go away. I just need to make sure my thoughts don't become actions. There's no way to guard someone adequately if there are too many personal strings attached. This is precisely why I refer to my clients as ma'am and keep the formalities. There's an invisible line that mustn't be crossed. Yet, I already feel like I've failed with my inability to keep my eyes off of the pool.

Why does Penny have to practice backflips right now? Why does every innocent stroke or movement cause my cock to jerk in my trunks?

What the hell is wrong with me?

Penny keeps unknowingly testing my self-control, and if she continues, I'm going to fail.

"Yeah," Nic mutters, mainly to himself, "it's definitely not enough compensation." His eyes stay focused on the pool. "I'm jaded enough to know that those girls can only bring trouble."

Nic's not off the mark. Each one of them has had her fair share of problems. I can only hold out hope that Penny can be receptive to reason. I have to gain her trust and pray that she will let me guide her. But if she is anything like Angie and Claire, she won't accept having me hovering on the sidelines as a positive. Thus, the less she knows, the better.

"I'll make sure nothing happens to your little sister—with or without any compensation. You both have been very generous already."

With the right type of investing, I'm set for life.

It's the work I need—not the money.

I value the work.

But it's the promise I'm making to them that I'm also making to myself. If I keep reminding myself that Penny is the innocent sister, then maybe my thoughts about her will stay platonic in nature and not be laced with the lustful energy that wants to keep charging through my veins.

Nic clears his throat, while rubbing at the back of his neck. "Good. Because I just got notification today that Penny has already found an apartment."

My eyes snap to his. "That was fast."

"She is determined and perhaps desperate."

"Add stubborn," Graham adds.

"Reckless," Nic continues.

Graham glares at his sister from afar. "She is sneaky."

"Oh, I got another," Nic chimes in. "How about purposely defiant?"

"That's a good one," his older brother agrees.

I nod in agreement. Penny is most definitely all of those things.

Taking a glance at the pool, I watch as Penny climbs onto a huge rainbow unicorn float and then reclines into a relaxing position in the fleeting rays of the setting sun.

Her alabaster skin is now a golden tone. I really hope she remembered to put on sunscreen even though it is evening. Her complexion is prone to burning easily.

"I'll run background checks on the landlord, as well as try to get a list of all of the current tenants for the building whenever she decides to officially take the leap." I imagine it'll take a month or so for the unit to be move-in ready. "Is it clear if she'll have roommates or not?"

"I know she'll have at least one," Nic says flatly. "Spending all that time alone in her room at Soulful Mind is probably making her crave social interaction. I can only hope she finds someone who meshes well with her. Girls can be so petty."

If her roommate turns out to be the spawn of Satan, protecting her will be much more difficult. I can keep her safe physically. However, the emotional toll that females can cause to each other can be even more damaging, with lifelong effects. I can only hope Penny gets matched with someone who is good for her and good to her.

"Oh, I know just how much too," Graham says with a sigh, probably thinking about his past with his ex. "Just be prepared for anything."

"I always am."

"I appreciate it, man," the eldest Hoffman brother says, patting me on my back. "I know Penny is in good hands."

"Agree," Nic says. "My hands are full with Claire and the arrival of our baby. It helps to know that I don't have to worry about Penny, on top of all this added stress."

I swallow down the lump in my throat. If I'm going to do my job, I need to get over this infatuation. The best way to do that is to fulfill my desires through other methods. I need to overindulge and get my deprivation sorted out. Maybe if I can get my rocks off with some unattached sex, I'll be able to maintain the professionalism that my day job requires. Getting too close to the subject I'm trying to protect will only lead to trouble.

In this very moment, I could use a bit of a release of the adrenaline running through my nervous system.

The sound of clinking glass echoes from across the pool, making everyone turn their attention to Donna, as she wheels in the decorated cart of gifts that were collected upon entry into the house. "It's present time."

I see mine resting along the side, and I feel the uncertainty flutter into my stomach, wondering if I missed the mark.

It is such a foreign feeling. I'm usually confident in most decision-making. Maybe I'm just wanting Penny to feel special today. She has a lot to celebrate. I think we all feel the pressure to make her day memorable.

The girls exit the pool and dry off, wrapping themselves just in towels and taking seats around a gas fire pit table. Graham claims his woman, circling his arms around her. Nic hugs Claire to his chest. I take the solo chair opposite the love seats and anxiously wait for my gift to be opened.

"This is from your mother and me," Germain says, passing Penny her first gift. It is a huge silver gift bag, overflowing with tissue paper.

Penny digs inside and pulls out a designer handbag that

is a pastel shade of pink. She turns it over in her hands, a huge smile brightening her entire face.

"Thank you so much. It's beautiful. I love it."

"Of course," Donna says with pride.

"And my favorite color."

"Like we could forget," Germain says with a laugh.

There was a time when Penny opted to wear only darker colors—never pastel. I think as she healed, her trauma response was to wear colors to outwardly express her mood.

I have to say though, these softer colors look gorgeous on her. She's as sweet as cotton candy, and it makes me happy to see her this content.

"Open ours next." Claire bounces with anticipation. "It's actually from Angie and me."

"Oh fun," Penny says, lifting off the huge lid of the gift box. "Wow." She peers inside the box. "This is too expensive."

"Our men are made of money." Angie laughs, making us all join in. Graham tickles her, nearly causing her to bounce off his lap.

"Well, show us," Donna demands, bubbling over with anticipation.

Penny holds up a pair of ice skates, jazzed out with pink glitter. "How did you know I wanted to…" Her eyes turn from excited to confused to livid, as she looks between both of her brothers with her finger pointing.

Both Graham and Nic hold up their hands in defense. "We had nothing to do with this," her oldest brother says. "Complete coincidence. I swear."

"You both lie through your teeth," she snaps. "You

know how I feel about my privacy being violated. These skates were on my own personal wish list."

Angie gets up to sit next to Penny, hugging her to her side. "While the idea of spying and overstepping boundaries is not out of the realm of possibility, the guys didn't have anything to do with this."

Penny gives her brothers a sheepish look and then looks up at Angie. "Then how?"

"You basically were glued to the television last Christmas when you were watching the figure skating holiday special. Claire and I just figured you would appreciate your own pair of skates."

"I love them. I've become very interested in skating. But I don't even know how to skate," she says sadly.

I'll teach you, Penny.

I haven't in years—maybe even a decade—but those skills are never forgotten. The body has an amazing way of retaining muscle memory.

"Then, maybe it's time to learn a new skill," Claire says with a smile. "The new place just opened outside of town, and we got you a season pass to go and enjoy the facility at your leisure."

"Get Iced?"

"Yeah, that's the one," Angie confirms.

"Thank you. I appreciate the thoughtful gift. Ironically, I was just looking up training videos on how to skate this past week." She looks at her brothers. "Sorry for accusing you of spying on me."

They manage to look innocent, although I know that them keeping virtual tabs on Penny is the norm. As much as they try to stay disengaged from their sister's private life, I know that when it comes to her track record of trusting the wrong people, they are very much concerned. This is probably the main reason my services are being shifted. The last thing they need to know is personal details about their sister and how she spends her free time. That's a line they are not willing to cross—on their own. Hiring me to do the job... Well, that's their decision. They don't need to be privy to every detail of Penny's personal life.

"This is from Graham and me," Nic says, reaching over and passing Penny a small box with a huge silver bow.

Penny shakes it up to her ear. "I wonder if it's jewelry," she teases.

"You would be wondering wrong," Graham laughs.

She pulls off the bow and rips off the lid, gasping as she sees the contents before any of us are aware of what she received.

"What is it?" Donna asks hurriedly.

Dangled on one manicured finger, Penny reveals a set of keys. "Holy shit," she mumbles. "Is this what I think it is?" Her eyes light up with hope.

"You will have to learn how to drive first," Nic says, chuckling as she throws herself into his arms, making him stumble back from the shock as he catches her midair.

Graham opens his arms to embrace Penny when it's his turn. "You are now the owner of an Audi A1 and—"

"I can't believe it!"

"Just promise me you'll be careful," Germain says quietly from where he is seated nearby.

Penny detaches herself from her brother and does a little jump from excitement. I think all of the Hoffmans are surprised by her energy—I know I am. I didn't know Penny before she got wrapped up in a bad escort agency and was drugged. However, I would like to think that some of the old Penny is morphing into the woman she is now. I'd hate to think that the one turning point in her life kept her from revisiting her old self entirely.

"Please make sure you stay on top of these driver's lessons," Nic whispers to me, as he watches Penny twirl around from the buzz that must be coursing through her.

"Understood."

"I know we can count on you," Graham chimes in, for only my ears to hear.

I excuse myself from the conversation, as I find my present to give to the birthday girl. I hope she likes it, because it was very difficult shopping for someone I barely know.

"Here's my gift to you, Penny."

Her eyes light up with joy. "Thanks, Collins. I wasn't expecting you to get me anything. I just thought…" She shakes her head. "Anyway, I appreciate the gesture. That's really sweet of you."

Just how she says the word "sweet" makes me feel a rush of warmth coat my insides. I am nearly positive "sweet" is never used to describe me, when ruthless, methodical, and unyielding seem to do a more accurate job. Thus, the sound of it coming from her lips feels so foreign.

While I'm not an asshole to women by any means, I'm not exactly what someone would consider boyfriend material either.

Our hands brush against each other's as I hand over the gift box that contains what I think Penny would appreciate. But what do I know? I haven't picked out a personal gift for someone in quite some time. I definitely haven't been around to watch anyone open something that was hand selected either.

I rock on my heels as Penny rips off the paper and tosses the box lid behind her. Her bottom lip slips between the cage of her top teeth, and I can't stop wondering if her skin there is as soft as it appears.

"You got me a year's pass to the Japanese Garden?"

I shrug, not really knowing how to feel. "Yeah." My shoulders tense as I watch Penny pull off the tissue paper.

"I love it there," she says thoughtfully. "I haven't been there since…"

Seattle. Shit. I want her to be happy, not sad. The last thing she needs are reminders of all she has missed.

"And a journal?"

I nod.

She eyes me with curiosity. "How did you know I just discovered my current one is completely filled?"

"I didn't know." The only thing I knew was that her therapists encouraged her to write in one. "There's one more thing." When she looks confused, I point toward the journal that is engraved with her name across the top. "Inside the cover."

Within seconds, Penny is squealing and hopping up to—

"Whoa," I mutter, catching her midair as she pounces on me.

I stumble backward a step, taken completely off guard by her sudden outburst of unfiltered joy. Her still damp body feels good against mine.

My hands don't know where to touch that isn't bare skin. Every part of her that is covered by a swimsuit feels inappropriate to touch. So I have no other choice but to press my hands against her warmth.

Penny is magnetic, in personality and in the physical sense. If I'm not careful, I'm going to jeopardize the best job I've ever had and sever more relationships than I can afford to lose.

I may not have had a forever family, but I do have a found family.

And I can't afford to mess up the one place where I feel like I belong.

Dammit.

Our hearts are beating so rapidly, it is hard to tell whose is whose. And in this moment, I gained more than just a hug; I gained a memory. An embedded concoction of emotions, wrapped up into a singular event in time…

"What got you so excited, Penny?" Donna asks, laughing over her reaction.

Penny's eyes lock on to mine, as I slowly release her and set her back on her feet. "You got me Grace and Jace tickets for their fall concert?" she asks, obviously surprised by my gift.

I clear my throat. "I did."

She examines the tickets. "They are playing at the garden. Oh, ha, that's why I have passes there too. And they just announced their tour dates. I didn't even know tickets were being sold. Yeah, this is basically awesome."

Her words come out as one stream of consciousness, and if I said it wasn't adorable, I'd be lying.

But in the span of just a few days, I've gotten really good at lying to myself.

To think that I can do this job and maintain the loyalty a man with honor upholds…might be the biggest lie of all.

"Collins?"

"Yes?"

"Thank you."

I am enchanted by her free-spirited excitement. It's contagious.

The concert tickets were an on-a-whim purchase. "Glad you like your gift."

Grace and Jace often play at the Hoffman Hotel. However, their outdoor fall tour seems to be popular among their fans. And Penny most definitely just confirmed she's a fan.

Penny's cheeks heat to a bright shade of pink, and a shyness coats over her entire demeanor. I want to comfort her and tell her that it's okay, as to how she reacted. I really am relieved she loves her gift. She doesn't need to be weird around me. I can keep her emotions safe and never make her feel awkward with her outward expression of them.

"Like is too mild of a word," she jokes, trying to catch her breath. "I'm in love"—she turns the tickets over and over again in her hands—"with my gifts. Plural. Because you got me so many things. Kind of unexpected too. Thank you."

Penny is unexpected.

"You are very welcome. Happy birthday, Penny."

Seeing her smile does something to make me soften. I hope there never comes a day where I'm responsible for a frown on her sweet face. Penny deserves happiness. She deserves a chance to move forward with her life. I just hope

I can find a balance between keeping her safe and letting her live the life she is desperate to live.

Donna brings out bite-sized snacks and desserts while we all float around in the pool. Despite Nic having a fit over Claire overexerting herself, we form a guys versus girls water volleyball game, which we end up winning.

I can't even remember the last time I smiled so much. Being around these people does this to me.

They make me realize what is important in my life. And right now, doing the job I was hired to do is what really matters. My head may be cloudy from every soft curve of Penny bouncing out of the water, but when it comes down to business, keeping her out of trouble will be my top priority.

I owe it to her brothers. I owe them my loyalty.

I just hope that I can—

Fuck.

What is Penny doing? Why is she swimming closer to me? And why the hell is she pouting out that bottom lip of hers, as if she's already predicting the answer to be no?

When she is so close I can count her freckles, her distraught face morphs into game on. Her hair is matted along the side of her face, as her hands slick it back off her forehead. Her skin looks kissed by the sun. Water droplets settle along her nose, and the way her lips curl up into an earth-stopping smirk…

"Can you hoist me up on your shoulders, Collins?"

Why? "Umm…"

"Angie and I are going to battle it out."

My eyes dart to Graham, who looks equally confused but has no choice but to submit to Angie climbing up his back like a bear cub to get onto his shoulders. She leans over him to grab a pool noodle and puts on a fake angry face. She then bursts out laughing over Graham telling her she's going to get hurt.

"Women are not made of paper, you know," she teases.

Penny tugs on my arm expectantly. "Please, Collins." Her bottom lip pouts out again.

If it wasn't the sexiest thing I've ever seen, I may have said no. I may have come up with some excuse or even suggest someone else to fulfill her request.

I am technically working. She may not realize that, but I know her brothers who are now staring at me understand the need for me to separate business from—

Pleasure?

Ugh. Why does every other thought I have seem to be laced with a sliver of indecency?

I am better than this. I know better. I can do better.

Penny bobs up and down in the water, whining as she bats her eyelashes. "Pretty please."

I shake my head over the thoughts running through it. Guilt creeps into the voids, making me feel even worse because of what Penny has been through in the past, her age being just twenty-two years old, and the fact that her brothers are now my friends—not just my source of income, pride, and stability.

They trust me. Problem is, I am starting not to trust myself with each second spent in her presence.

"Turn around." My voice comes out raspier than expected.

Penny's face beams with a huge smile, as she complies with my simple command. I reach for her slender waist, picking her up with ease. My vision fogs with the soft curves of her ass, while I lift her above my head. Her thighs spread around my neck.

Penny is very light, and yet I feel like the weight of the world is resting upon my shoulders. I feel her shift above me, and I grip her calves to steady her from falling, as she reaches into the water to pick up a pink pool noodle without warning.

"Game on," she says to Angie, and then gives a fake growl.

My eyes lock with Graham's, and he actually looks relaxed. That's what Angie does to him though. She has a way of getting him to lose some of his rigidness.

I wonder what the right woman would do for me?

There's no point fantasizing. My lifestyle doesn't leave room for anyone to get close to me. I am all about work. I am a loner and a bit of a hermit. I like things done a certain way and have no qualms about avoiding anyone who disrupts my rhythm.

The only type of women I attract are those who thrive on temporary arrangements, with no long-term commitment or hope for the future.

"Three," Angie starts.

"Two," Penny counts down.

"One," Claire chimes in from the pool's edge.

"Fight," the girls scream in unison, reminding me of what this is all about.

Then the two go at it, as the giggling gets more vocal. Claire waves her hands, chanting some made-up cheer that has some filthy connotations to it—but I can't pay attention enough to be sure.

I steady Penny, shifting my weight in the water to dodge some of Angie's moves. I've played football with both ladies before, so I know how competitive they can be, and how rules are merely suggestions to them. However, based on how Angie isn't going full throttle, I know this is simply meant to be fun.

Everything about today has been fun.

"I don't even know who to root for," Claire calls out while attempting to jump during her sporadic cheer moves.

I have to laugh over Nic's hovering. It's as if he's spotting a guy bench pressing in the gym. The dude needs to chill a bit, or Claire's going to go into labor early from just the stress alone.

Penny gets a couple of good jabs in with the noodle, missing one time and hitting Graham in the face.

"Oops," she mutters.

He laughs. "I'm starting to question if that was an accident."

Doubling up her pool noodle, Angie catches Penny off guard, as she swings and hits her on the side. Penny giggles and loses her balance, causing us both to fall into the water. Her hands grab at my arms, as I pull her up to the surface.

"You okay?" I ask, laughing at her tangled mess of hair in her eyes. I sweep the wayward locks back, tucking some behind her ears. "There, is that better?"

Her doe-like eyes look up at me as she nods. "I appreciate it."

"The pleasure is all mine," I whisper, instantly regretting how impassioned it sounds.

Get your head on straight.

I pull my hands back, keeping them down at my sides. I

know my way around the female body, and yet everything about Penny is foreign territory. Every touch seems different. Every emotion running through me is new.

"That was fun," she admits.

Penny breaks eye contact and then swims to the opposite end of the pool. She exits via the stairs and then meanders over to the dessert area to fill her plate with pink French macarons and some fresh berries with whipped cream. The girls join her, and the giggle fest continues, as I catch bits and pieces of their conversation.

The night concludes with a toast to Penny, more wishes of happy birthdays, and then some sparklers in the backyard. Penny says goodbye to her brothers and their women, and then turns to me with a warm smile.

"Thanks for being here, Collins. It means a lot."

My lips curl into a smile. "I wouldn't have missed it, Pen. Happy birthday."

Penny's face lets me know that tonight brought her joy. She's running on a high, perhaps from having her family surrounding her or simply from just being home.

She looks happy.

Content.

Fulfilled.

And in this moment, that is all that matters.

6

PENNY

It's when I'm calm and my heart is quiet and at a peaceful rest that the demon finds me, putting his evil hold on everything he can touch. Images of terror still flutter through my head, like a ghostly incubus trying to bring me down to its nefarious world.

I thought time would heal the wounds that were caused when I was drugged and almost raped. But the more time that passes only makes me doubt my inner strength and, in return, lose hope that I can one day be released from all this subconscious baggage.

The pain from that horrible experience is so deeply rooted in the decisions I make now that I'm starting to wonder if it is now part of my identity.

While staying at Soulful Mind, I toyed with the idea of starting up a relationship. However, my mind could not cope with the uncertainty of whether or not I would get hurt by a man again.

Sure, I flirted with a few of the outside workers who

would frequent the center. But I knew deep down that the chance of having an actual connection was unrealistic.

Who will want to be with me, when I flinch at the first signs of intimacy? I'm a freak, and it's not the good type of freak that men want in bed.

I am jumpy and timid.

While I only had one real sexual encounter before the whole incident with Mark, I'm still very much the awkward girl fumbling around with her hands and her messed-up feelings. I don't even know what to search for, when I'm too inexperienced to notice when I actually find it.

One thing is for certain; I am desperate to connect in a meaningful way with something—or someone.

Anything.

My heart yearns for a feeling of fullness.

Sure, I have a loving family that continues to grow, but I want more. I need more.

So perhaps if I flood my system with relationship opportunities, I will detox my brain from all of my triggers and be able to function again as a normal, healthy woman in her twenties.

I grab my old journal off my nightstand and double-check the list I created for myself.

I'm tired of being stagnant. I am tired of limiting myself by my past.

Today is a new day—a starting point.

I know I have some baggage to carry, but if I don't try to move forward, I will forever have the burden of my past on my shoulders.

The problem with not being able to drive is that I'm at the mercy of someone to be available in my life to take me places. I hate relying this heavily on others. If I'm going to be independent, then I need to learn how to drive.

I still can't believe Graham and Nic bought me a car. It is a big step for them to relinquish this level of control over to me. They must realize how determined I am to start living my own life again.

I go back to the search box and type in "driving lessons," waiting for Google to present me with some viable options. I click on a few of the top-rated links, jotting down the information for some classes. I already had my permit from passing the written knowledge test a year ago. However, I haven't really had practice out on the road.

Perhaps I was a late bloomer.

While everyone in high school and college craved the feeling of being behind the wheel, I was too spoiled with my brothers basically hiring a personal driver to tote my ass around town.

It never really bothered me that I wasn't driving—until now. If I want to keep off my brothers' radars in every little thing I do, then I need to prove to them that I can handle my own life.

Rolling off my bed, I make my way into the bathroom and start the shower to heat up. I have plans to meet Angie and Claire at the Plus None offices for brunch. It was a last-minute idea that was coordinated the night of my birthday party. Knowing how amazing these women are to me, I couldn't say no, even though I'm pretty sure I know the nature of this meeting.

I slide out of my pajamas and step under the hot water. Steam billows out around me, making my skin tingle.

I know the girls would love for me to come work with

them, but I just am not sure I would be the right fit. I haven't modeled in a long time, and when I did, I'm not even sure I was good at it. Maybe everyone was just telling me what I wanted to hear in order to manipulate me.

That's what Mark did.

Or perhaps Angie and Claire feel obligated to include me in the business for the mere fact that I am family.

I don't need a pity invite. I want to genuinely be considered—and to actually feel like I'm good at it—before accepting any offers.

I crave the rush that comes from being passionate about something and actually miss the invigorating feeling of belonging and having a purpose.

I squeeze strawberry shampoo into my palm, rubbing my hands together vigorously to work up a lather. I massage my hair with the soapy foam, working my scalp.

I can't believe I'm twenty-two years old. It seems like just yesterday I was so pumped to turn eighteen. Then the thrill of turning twenty-one was lost in the commotion. Now I am a year past that and more excited than ever to face challenges head-on, to take risks, and to prove to myself that I can live again.

I scrub my face with a sugar and honey mixture that I made using a recipe I found online. I'm not that big into organics like Claire is, but there is something special about putting together homemade ingredients. The scrub smells incredible, coupled with the backdrop of strawberries lingering in the air.

After I rinse completely off, I towel myself dry and throw on a skirt and a floral tank. I add some curl gel to my fingers and work it through my hair. I accessorize my outfit with strappy heels, some jewelry, and a pair of sunglasses. By the time I get to Hoffman Headquarters, my hair will be dry and hopefully not a frizzy mess. I wrap a hairband around my wrist just in case.

I exit my room, making my way downstairs to find Momma.

"Good morning, Penny," she greets with a warm smile. "Well, don't you look lovely. Going somewhere fun?"

"Hey, Momma. Yeah, I have a brunch date with Angie and Claire at Hoffman Headquarters."

She gives me a nod, glancing at her phone. "Did you call for a ride yet?"

"No. I was about to."

"No need," she says.

"Why…?"

"Because you don't really need to."

I curl and uncurl my toes. "But why, Momma?"

She looks down at her phone again. "Because Collins is almost here. Graham just texted me."

I let out a sigh. Seriously? "Welcome to the start of the micromanaging," I grumble. "Courtesy of my brothers."

"You know those two would move heaven and earth for you."

Guilt stabs at me, forcing my shoulders to slump. "I know that. I just"—I push my wavy hair back over my shoulders—"want to do things my way. Without…"

"Interference?"

"Exactly."

"It's been a very rough time when you were gone, Penny. We are all still adjusting. Some of us just have a different way of dealing with the pain of wondering what if.

So, please give your brothers some prevenient grace. They know you are unable to drive right now, and in the meantime, they have Collins available to give you a lift."

"I guess I should thank Graham for the ride." I try to leave the sarcasm out of my tone, but it seeps in anyway.

Momma smiles. "Seems fair."

"While we are on the topic of my independence, I found a place."

"Seems rushed, yeah?"

I shrug. "The opportunity presented itself to me." It's a bit of a lie, because I specifically hunted down this particular opportunity. Regardless, I think this will be an amazing move.

Momma shifts her weight to her other foot and leans her hip against the counter. "Penny, I hope you know that you can live here forever."

That's exactly why I need to move out.

It's the safety net that sometimes feels stifling. "I know. I appreciate that too. But I need to be in the city. I've been gone from Portland too long and I miss it."

"Your father and I have saved up money so you—"

"Momma..."

She holds her hands up in defense. "Okay, fine. But just know that if you need help," she says, giving me a pitiful smile, "you can ask us. Always. And if this place is a hot mess, you don't have to keep living there. You always have a home here."

I take a step closer and wrap my arms around her back. "You are the best momma on the planet. You know that, right?"

I feel the vibrations from her trembling and know that

she is trying to hide her tears. "I just want you"—she sniffles—"to have a good life."

"And I will. It feels like I got a second chance at life, and I'm not blowing it on being afraid to fly."

So maybe paying Graham and Nic a visit today while I'm at the office will help set them straight on their priorities. It may take multiple reminders, but surely they can understand my desires.

I pull back from Momma, and she turns her head to hide her tears. I think she's afraid she will break me, and that alone should be reason enough to need to move out. I can't be under the same roof as her and walk around trying not to make her cry. I won't be able to live like that. She needs the separation as well, even though she'll never admit it.

"Momma, I appreciate you. Please don't cry. I love you with all my heart. I'm going to be okay. I promise. And if I slip back into a bad state, I know the signs and what to do about it. Please trust me."

She offers me a weak smile, and I mirror one back. "As long as you know that you can always come home, then I will let you leave."

Donna Hoffman is basically my favorite human. I can only hope to grow into the woman she has become.

I gather up my belongings and slip out the front door, only to find Collins leaning against the black SUV. I'm still getting used to seeing him so casual, but I'd be lying if I said he didn't look good doing it.

Like the leaning, for example…

The man isn't a leaner. He is a poker straight spine type of man.

Yet just looking at his strong body resting against the vehicle is doing things to me.

It's simple.

It's also unexpected.

Collins takes his shades off his eyes, propping them onto the crown of his head. My eyes scan up his jean-covered legs, all the way up to his black buttoned shirt, where his sleeves are cuffed up and situated comfortably at his elbows. He is either off duty or my brothers have released him of the strict dress code. Either way, I approve.

Dayum. I *really* approve.

We are in the thick of the summer, and he doesn't look like he is breaking a sweat.

I'd like to think I made my ogle-fest less obvious than what it probably was. At least Collins doesn't make it known. He's probably used to women giving him the once-over.

Men as attractive as he is can't get to his stage in life and be oblivious to it.

"Miss Hoffman," he greets with a downward nod.

"Mr. Stone," I counter back sassily, with a fake curtsy.

He gives me a smile. Also rare. What is going on?

Collins straightens his posture, rounds his shoulders, and opens the back door for me to enter. I sidestep him and open the door to the front passenger seat, sliding in. I snap on my belt, snickering to myself, as Collins shuts the back door and circles the front of the vehicle. I can see a smirk playing on his lips, and it does something to my insides to see him so confident and in his element.

Sure, at the pool party he was in casual attire. However,

there is something about seeing him today that is intentionally different.

And dare I say, devastatingly handsome?

Not in the conventional sense, though. No, Collins is rugged, yet sophisticated. I just can't figure him out at the core, and part of me wishes that I could pull back the layers one by one to see the real him.

Collins takes his place behind the wheel. "How are you today, Miss Hoffman?" he asks politely.

I can tell he wants to say more, but the man never uses more words than what are deemed necessary. He literally just saw me at my birthday party where we were laughing and having chicken fights in the pool. He also got me the most amazingly thoughtful gift—that I'm still in shock over. Now, he is calling me Miss Hoffman like we aren't even becoming friends? Why all of a sudden is he trying to act over-the-top professional?

Holy shit.

And then it dawns on me.

Unbelievable.

Collins is here more than just to tote my butt around the town. I suspected as much when I saw my brothers talking with him at the party. I just never really thought they would stick their right-hand man on me when they each have their own women to protect.

I haven't even done anything bad yet, so why provide this assignment for your most valuable employee?

Are they still angry over me going to the prison?

Maybe I should have called someone else to give me a lift from there.

I glance back toward the house and then to Collins, who

is looking at me expectantly while we sit in silence, not moving.

"Everything alright, Miss Hoffman?"

"No."

His eyes soften, as his eyes scan over my body. "What's wrong? Are you ill? Can I get you anything, Miss Hoffman?"

Every time he says my name the way he does, anger simmers inside me. Is he trying to make me boil over and snap? If so, it's going to happen.

"Nope. I'll be better though if you cut the formalities and simply call me Penny. You know, the name you called me at my birthday…"

I cross my arms at my chest as I study him. At the party, he even called me the shortened version of my name—Pen.

But today he's in ultraprofessional mode.

And I don't like it, not one bit.

"Understood."

"Unless, of course, you want to admit that my brothers hired you to watch out for me. Which, by the way, is not far-fetched considering how many times you were assigned to both Angie and Claire. Oh, and also by the way, I am doing things on my own this go-round, so it best be remembered that giving tabs back to my brothers is just"—I shudder as I make a disgusted face—"gross."

"Breathe, Penny."

I shoot him a glare that translates to *shut it*, but I do take a deep breath.

The last thing my brothers need to know about is my dating life—or my sex life. I've been officially off the market long enough. Maybe taking a dip in the dating pool is what I need to challenge both myself and my brothers. If they can succeed at allowing me some liberties, I'll be more accepting of the other little gestures they so frequently make.

But apparently they already made a gesture—a big one—by downright hiring Collins to do their bidding.

Collins starts the engine, readjusts his shades that rest on his forehead, and then shifts in his seat to give me a thorough look. Every inch of territory he covers with the attention of his gaze causes me to wilt slightly. He, too, seems to be studying me. I don't like it. It makes me feel vulnerable and under a microscope, and I spent the better part of a year feeling those same exact emotions.

I sigh. "Listen. You can't intimidate me."

"I'm not trying to."

"I'm super resourceful and capable of slipping away from anyone trying to snuff out my first taste of freedom."

"I'm aware," he says simply.

"I know you are hired to follow me around. I get it. Graham and Nic need some type of assurance that I'm safe. But what you all don't understand is the utter devastation I face every time I wake up and realize it is a new day. Another day in my life that is wasted. I'm done wasting time, Collins. Call it a life crisis if you will, but I am done going through the motions of a day, just to sleep and wake up, and then do it all again." My shoulders slump forward. "I want to feel alive. I am going to take some risks to find myself again—wherever she may be hiding."

Understanding hits Collins's eyes, and the tension I've been holding in my shoulders releases, causing me to melt into my seat. I close my eyes to collect myself, waiting for the taciturn man to say something—*anything*—to confirm what I think I'm witnessing in his demeanor.

Nothing.

He says nothing.

Not a word. Not a hum. Not a sound.

When I cannot take any more silence, I turn to face Collins—who has yet to pull out of the driveway—and break down.

It surprises even me.

"Oh, Penny," he says, reaching for my hand to squeeze.

I bite my lip between my top teeth as pangs of guilt hit me all at once. He is just trying to help—to do his job. And here I sit on some invisible self-appointed throne acting entitled, spewing my rant like some privileged rich teen. I'm not a kid anymore, yet I sure have been acting like one.

I did it with my momma and now I'm doing it with Collins.

"Don't cry. Please."

His touch feels so different.

It's like we aren't supposed to cross some emotional boundary, and yet he did so without thought.

"I'm being a brat. I know I am. I just don't know what has come over me. I'm acting cra—" I shudder at the thought of the implication of the word I was about to say. I'm acting like I am. I just can't bring myself to complete the second syllable and make it feel real.

Crazy.

It's a one-word accurate representation of my latest mood swings.

"You've been nothing but good to me and my family,

and here I am just ranting and raging and I regret it. I'm sorry."

"No need to apologize."

"It's just that you came to my birthday party and gave me the most thoughtful gifts, and while I would love to think that you did that all on your own, I'm nearly positive my brothers are micromanaging every move you make and have basically hired you to shadow me. It makes me feel claustrophobic, and I hate feeling caged in. They probably even wrapped up the package and forced your hand to give it to me, if just to appear friendly. *Normal.* Yet nothing about the life of being the youngest Hoffman is normal."

"It was my idea," Collins says with sincerity.

"Huh?"

"The gifts. They were all from me." His eyes soften to a shade that is the color of melted caramel. "I completely understand why you would think otherwise, so no harm done."

My level of paranoia must be strong because I even accused Angie and Claire of using my brothers' spy tactics to know I was interested in ice skating. "What about the rest?" I press further. The idea of not knowing what my brothers are up to will just make me more probable of doing something risky to avoid their watchful eyes.

"Yes, I'm assigned to watch out for you."

"I knew it," I snarl, tossing my hands up into the air. The car feels suddenly smaller with the tension simmering between us. I want to be mad at Collins, but who I really am mad at are my brothers. The least they could have done was consult with me.

Collins holds his hands up in defense. "I'm not going to

interfere with your life nor share details back that are not appropriate. Trust that I can keep an eye on you but still let you accomplish your goals."

Well, he hasn't seen them—and won't see them. Some are a bit spicy…

"Did they assign you to me because I visited Mark?"

"You won't be doing that again whether I'm your guard or not. Do you understand?"

I shrink back in my seat at his stern authority. "Got it."

Collins lets out a sigh. "We can even work together."

"Together?"

"Form an alliance." He shrugs, eyeing me carefully. "A partnership, if you will."

"That seems counterproductive, don't you think?" I furrow my brow. "I'm sure that will probably break some major code in the professional bodyguard conduct book that my overbearing brothers probably made you sign. Why are you smirking? I'm being serious. This is my life."

"I'm not going to break any rules, Penny."

"I'm no expert, but I'm pretty sure my brothers wanted this whole assignment to be secret from me."

"You are smart, Penny. I never expected you not to figure it out. Albeit, I thought I had more time to get you on board before you try to derail me." He glances at the time. "I made it a solid seven minutes before you called me out."

I don't even know what to think. Although I knew my brothers would have some type of watch, I never expected them to be this blatant about it. Collins can't possibly understand my needs right now, especially since I'm still struggling myself with where to channel all of my energy.

This is not how I expected my morning to go. Not at all.

I can feel my breathing pick up, and I say a silent prayer that I won't have a panic attack—at least not here.

When I'm alone in the confines of my bedroom is one thing, but to have an audience always makes things awkward.

"I'm simply asking you to comply with the normal safety protocols that your brothers will want in place."

I think about Collins's words, mulling the idea around in my head. I don't know what to say. I can tell he is struggling with how to handle me, and maybe he deserves some of my grace. But I don't even know how to cope with this confession on his part. I just need some time and space to manage my emotions.

After several long minutes, Collins grips the steering wheel so tightly that his knuckles turn white. Maybe he's mad I'm not talking. I mean, what is there to say?

All of the humor I once saw on his features has now vanished, making me wonder if I imagined it there in the first place. "Maybe your brothers went about this the wrong way by not consulting with you first."

"You think?"

Collins purses his lips as he pulls out of the driveway. "I need to keep you safe, Penny. That's not up for negotiation."

"Safe from what?" When he doesn't answer, I connect the dots. "Oh, myself." I allow that thought to sit with me. "Is it because everyone is worried I'll make bad choices?" Again more silence. "You do realize that every nonanswer is an answer, right?"

Collins sighs. "Let's come to some understanding so neither of our lives are made difficult."

"Can you at least provide me with some examples of the

safety protocols you want to put in place so I can yay or nay? Because right now, Collins, my mind is thinking of tracking devices, prison style ankle bracelets, and other archaic methods."

"Huh."

"What?"

"I wasn't thinking of ankle bracelets before, but that is a really good idea."

My eyes jerk to his, which are looking at the road. "You cannot be serious."

A laugh escapes his lips, and it is so unexpected I burst into giggles as well.

"Background checks," he supplies, his voice unwavering.

"Can you be more specific?"

"I'll need to run them on anyone you decide to share close contact with." His words come out gruff, and the raspiness does something to me that I cannot put into words.

"Anything else?"

"There will be a security system install or upgrade."

I glance out the window as we leave Hillsboro, heading toward the city. "Fair enough. Anything else?"

"My"—he clears his throat—"duties evolve depending on the threats."

I turn to look at him, despite his eyes staying forward on the road. "Maybe there will be no threats. Did that ever cross your mind?"

"This isn't about me."

"Except it is."

Collins lets out an exaggerated breath. "I'm just following through on a job I was assigned."

I growl. Mark Tanner threatened me, but that psycho just wanted to get under my skin. All of the bad guys are locked up and going to spend the rest of their miserable lives behind bars. "Maybe my life will be completely boring and your position will be"—I sweep out my hand, catching his attention—"discontinued."

"If it helps you to think like that, go for it."

I should be happy that Collins isn't filling the silence with more silence. That's what he does, though. He avoids talking. So, since he has shared with me more than I ever expected, I *should* be thankful. Relieved, even. But I'm not. I'm anxious and on edge.

Knowledge isn't power at all. It is fuel for my anxiety.

Collins sharing the behind-the-scenes arrangement wasn't for my benefit. No, it was for his. Maybe he thinks that if I know the basic plan, then I'll submit and let everything run smoothly with his position.

Too bad. I'm done following the rules. I'm done having people tell me when to eat, what to eat, or how much to eat. I'm done with curfews and bedtimes. I'm done with safety checks and drills throughout the day. I'm done with having a gatekeeper.

Everyone can think I am the youngest Hoffman princess. However, no one is going to come between me and my goal list—not even the broody bodyguard that is stewing beside me, probably working himself into a tizzy. I can already tell he is conjuring up some epic plan to derail me.

Problem is, my liberation plan is better.

7

COLLINS

Whatever initial thoughts I had about this being the easiest assignment to date, I obviously take it back. Nothing about Penny Hoffman is going to be simple.

I thought I would go off the path and introduce the idea to Penny of me keeping an eye on her. I figured this would gain her trust and buy her acceptance by being upfront with her. However, seeing her fidget in the passenger seat beside me, twisting her golden blonde locks around her manicured finger, and sucking on her bottom lip to the point where I'm about to yell at her to give it life…

Yeah.

I misread this whole situation.

I pride myself on picking up on social cues and analyzing what is best based on the scenario. Yet, here I sit, at yet another red light, trying to figure out how to get us both back on track, without any clear path to success in sight.

"Why are you so resistant to working together?" I ask

nonchalantly. I need to get her to talk. When Penny starts ranting, I gain way more information than I normally would about what she is thinking.

I see the rise of her chest in my periphery. I hate seeing her stressed out, and yet, that is exactly what I'm doing to her. This is not how I envisioned our morning going. When I arrived at the Hoffmans' house to pick her up, I expected a car ride of small talk and pleasantries. I got the opposite.

I slow down as another light changes to red, wondering if this ride will ever end. I just want to get Penny safely into her brother's building, so I can take a moment to decompress.

"Can you please stop at the coffee shop on the corner?"

So this is what it's like to be on the receiving end when someone wants to avoid questions. I know I've driven quite a few people mad with my lack of words. Now I know how frustrating it feels.

"Aren't you going to be eating brunch with the girls? I imagine that—"

"I need to bring something to contribute. I also need a coffee but don't want to blatantly show up with caffeine in front of Claire. So, I'll need to loiter a bit until I finish it."

Oh yeah, Claire. Nic wouldn't be too happy if anyone made her hostile.

Helping with hiring the perfect female entourage to keep Claire safe was no easy task. And to think she was my most difficult client…

I nod as I pull in front of the shop, and then lean my arm over Penny's seat to look behind me as I park.

"You are good at that," she mumbles.

"At what? Hiding my true feelings?"

She pauses and then bursts out laughing, making me join in. I can't even remember the last time I laughed this much around anyone. It feels so foreign, and yet the past couple of times we've been together, I can't keep it contained.

"I was referring to your driving. Although your self-awareness is on par."

I hum, just because I'm not sure what to say.

"I'm nearly positive I would have hit the curb and then that convertible that basically came out of nowhere."

I kill the engine and turn to study her. Is she joking or being serious? "The parked one?"

"Oh." She sucks her bottom lip back into her mouth, and then looks back at the immobile car. "Huh. I thought I saw it move. Anyway, do you want anything?"

"I'll escort you in."

"No, sir. You stay here and practice restraint. I can escort myself. So what'll it be?"

"Latte with extra shot of espresso." I reach into my pants pocket to pull out my wallet, hoping I even have cash on me. If I'm going to be hanging around Penny more, I'll need to figure out her routine and be prepared. This rare feeling of not knowing what to expect has me off-kilter, and I hate all parts of it.

"It's on me."

"No, here." I hold out the fifty-dollar bill, coaxing her to take it.

"You're my unwanted bodyguard, not my much-needed pimp."

Before I can argue or dissect what she just muttered, she's out of the car. I didn't even get a chance to open her door or help her out. My eyes bulge out as I see way more of her thighs than she probably intended.

Fuck.

Can her skirt be any shorter? How did I not notice that before now?

Just the other day I was graced with her perfectly curved body in a bikini, but there is something utterly sexy about a girl in a skirt. Perhaps it's the accessibility or the idea that it's intentionally casual. Regardless, she can wear cardboard and look enchanting.

Penny is one of those girls who has natural beauty.

Now, what is she doing? I stretch upward as I watch Penny double over. Shit. Is she hurt?

I grab my door handle and leap out of the driver's seat, walking briskly toward the sidewalk.

"Penny? Are you sick? What's wrong?"

She straightens her posture, turning to me with her palm opened to the sky. "It's good luck."

I stare into her hand and see the shiny copper penny glimmering in the sunshine. "Oh." I sure hope it's good luck. I also hope that I'm on the receiving end of some of it. I watch with awe as her lips curl into the biggest smile.

"You keep this one," she says sweetly, which is in direct contradiction to how she was feeling just moments ago in the SUV. "I love finding them in the wild, just waiting to be claimed. Each one I find is my little reminder to make a wish."

I accept the penny from her hand and offer up my own smile. I welcome this shift in her mood and realize that her emotions directly affect mine.

Rotating the penny between my fingers, I marvel at how something so simple can bring someone so much joy.

I have a feeling I'm going to learn a lot from this blonde, blue-eyed girl.

With a pivot, Penny makes her way inside the Ground Floor coffee shop, in way better spirits than I've seen her with all morning. She is an anomaly to me. She's a princess, yet has an edge about her that has me wondering what makes her tick at her core. I want to know what excites her and what makes her melt to become more pliable.

Because right now, Penny's stern and rigid, determined and stubborn.

I want to exorcise her demons and get to know the real girl, hidden inside the layers of protection. She's afraid to trust again, yet is brave enough to put herself out there anyway. That combination is exactly why she needs me. Her vulnerability will make her prey for any asshole looking for an easy target to manipulate.

I make my way back inside the SUV. Checking my phone for messages, I send a text to the lead security guard at HH, alerting him that I'll be arriving soon with Penny in tow.

I look into the shop, seeing Penny next in line to order. She is making conversation with the young guy in front of her, who is smiling way too much not to be annoying. In a way, I'm glad I'm witnessing this normal—and seemingly innocent—interchange.

It's realistic.

Penny is going to fall in love and hopefully find the right man. The more I keep reminding myself of that, the better it'll be.

He'll just have to get through me and my extensive background checks first.

Penny is the type of girl who men will flock to, but few will actually be worthy.

When I see her nearing the exit, I hop out of the SUV, circle the front, and open her door. Except she isn't alone.

I want to ask what the other guy is doing here. I want to ignore the fact that he is helping Penny carry a package of mini pastries that could only be going to the brunch at Plus None. Nothing is out of place. Yet, I can't calm down the gnawing feeling inside my head that everything is wrong. The whole imagery is wrong.

I accept the drinks from her hands, placing them on the hood of the car.

"Thanks, Rex," she says, giving him a hug and then taking the box from his hands.

Rex? Who names their kid Rex? He already sounds like a dog. And not the cute and cuddly type. No. This mutt is the eager kind that begs for attention and needs a treat every time he wags his tail.

"Hope to see you at the event."

Penny flutters her hand into the air, waving goodbye. Rex walks away, glancing back to us midstride to catch another look. Did I just witness him figuratively peeing on a tree?

Yup. Yup I did.

I feel my muscles clench and my jaw twitch. "What event?" I bark out, harsher than I initially intend.

"Oh, just a thing."

I eye her with the expectation for her to continue. "Penny…"

"Hmm?"

"What thing?" I try again.

"Apparently the shop is closing down for one evening and doing a speed dating event."

Sounds fucking horrible. "Sounds fun."

She looks at me with an expression of amusement. "Oh, you're cute."

Huh? "What?"

She motions with her finger, up and down my body. "It's cute when you lie."

I straighten my back. "How do you know I'm lying?"

"Me going to the event is like your worst nightmare for background checks and all things security. All these men, vying for my attention…" She stifles a laugh into her elbow, and then shrugs. "Who am I fooling? Anyone that knows anything about me will just run for the hills. Pretty sure as soon as someone figures out my last name, they'll either see dollar signs or caution tape. Excuse me."

I can see the tears form in her eyes as she flutters around me to get to the backseat, where she gently places the box of baked goods onto the bench. She maneuvers her body so I'm unable to see her face, which just pisses me off, because I want to see how badly she is hurting.

"Pen?"

"Hmm?"

When she doesn't turn around, I gently place my hand on her elbow, spinning her so she can look at me. I have every urge to say something profound. Anything to cheer her up. But, I can only just stare.

"I don't want your pity, Collins."

My mouth dries over her assumption. "Then it's a good thing I'm not giving it. I just—"

"It's okay." She pulls away, slides into the front passenger seat, and snaps her belt into place. "I don't need fake sympathy either."

I hand her the paper cup labeled "Princess Penelope," shutting the door gently. I can't help but smirk over the name she gave for herself. She despises whenever anyone uses her legal first name, so it is a bit surprising to see it spelled out in front of me in bold caps.

I then grab my cup and laugh over all of the writing on the side. First I see "Control Freak" written with black sharpie marker and then crossed out. Under that name, I see "Stubborn and Silent" jotted down and then scribbled out. When my eyes connect with the name Penny finally settled on, I don't know whether to laugh or applaud her for her determination and originality.

"Not My Bodyguard."

It's clever. I have to give her that.

Except I *am* her bodyguard. And no amount of resistance on her part is going to change that fact.

I take a slow sip, savoring the taste. I round the front of the SUV, and then settle behind the wheel. I glance over to Penny, who refuses to look at me. She just stares at the people entering and exiting the Ground Floor coffee shop, sipping her own steaming beverage.

Penny's moods flip so fast between lighthearted fun to serious doldrums that it is causing me a bit of emotional whiplash.

"Penny?"

"Drive or I'll just get out and walk."

I bite the inside of my mouth, snap my belt into place, and pull out of the parking spot with ease.

It kills me not to ask her what's wrong or try to comfort her on whatever turmoil is going on inside her head. I get that Penny is still recovering and going through maintenance therapy sessions locally in the city. However, I doubt a therapist is going to help her in triggering moments like these—especially if she doesn't quite understand herself what set her off.

I round the block and park us in the designated spot in front of her brother's building, Hoffman Headquarters. Giving me no time to exit and help her with her door, Penny is already on the sidewalk, pulling out the pastry box from the backseat.

I reach into the car, grab our coffees, and then manage to catch up to her at the main entrance. We walk quietly side by side, through the lobby, where I'm greeted with nods from the security staff.

Since Nic has become head of security here, the day-to-day flow has been vastly better when it comes to entering and exiting the building efficiently.

He has pioneered cutting-edge technology to tighten the security here, and despite having the massive incident with the madman who kidnapped Claire a couple of months ago, things have been smooth overall.

There was a time where I was stationed here most of my day, helping out with the behind-the-scenes checks of the staff, while still guarding either Angie or Claire.

Now my days are going to be filled with trying to manage this sassy princess.

When we arrive at the elevators, I hit the up button,

signaling the doors to open on cue. Penny cuts in front of me on the way in, and instead of selecting the floor for Angie and Claire's company, Plus None, she hits the button for Graham's office.

"Detour?" I ask quietly.

"You know it."

My shoulders round as I take in her stance. She's trying to be strong, but I can tell she's about to cry. Sweat builds on my neck beneath the collar of my shirt. It feels weird to be in this building dressed so casually in jeans, but I understand why the release in formalities. Penny's case is different. Since she's family, her brothers didn't want to be intrusive.

Her soft sniffles gnaw at my heart. I want to pull her to me, cup her head against my chest, and—

And what, fucker?

Go behind the backs of the two men who have given me my own brighter future?

Pretend this will work out with a happily ever after?

Nope. I don't do the whole playing house thing. And I sure as fuck can't be to Penny what she needs from a man.

I resist a growl over my impulsive thoughts. If I wasn't so egotistical in my service to the Hoffmans, I would resign and ask for a different assignment. However, I don't trust anyone to look out for Penny beside myself.

"Here, drink some coffee." I take the box from her hands, passing her the coffee she ordered from Ground Floor. I watch her steadily, as I finish the rest of my beverage off.

"Stop staring at me."

Am I staring? I barely glanced her way. "Why?"

"It makes me nervous."

I stifle a laugh. "I just wish I knew what was going on inside your head."

Her shoulders lift into a shrug, as she reaches over and hits a new number on the panel. "I want to negotiate the terms of our deal."

My mouth opens and shuts as I am caught off guard—yet again. "Some things aren't up for negotiation," I say simply.

It's the truth. I won't budge on certain safety measures—no matter what she wants to bargain.

"Fine. But you'll hear me out anyway."

I watch as the car stops at the floor for Plus None, and Penny exits. I follow her with the box of pastries into the office space that is devoted to the subscription box service company designed to empower women. Claire and Angie built it from the ground up, and the success of their platform is getting national attention for the speed at which they've been able to execute their business model.

It will only be a matter of time before the women delve into the international market.

I toss my empty cup into a trash can, while Penny's cup joins mine. "When would you like this meeting to occur?" I'm not used to taking a passenger seat to being in control, yet here I stand on the abyss of uncertainty, waiting for Penny to call all the shots.

She glances down at her nails, while biting at her bottom lip. "The sooner the better. I've got so many goals to accomplish, and the last thing I need is someone"—her eyes rake up and down my body—"standing in my way."

My eyes narrow at her perusal. I'm also not used to the

blatantness of her distrust. If she only realized how many times I have already looked out for her and had her best interests at heart.

She has no reason not to trust me, but yet I feel like I'll have to put forth major effort to get her to relinquish some control.

"I'll pick you up from this office in"—I glance at my watch—"two hours."

"And?"

"And we'll go somewhere private to *negotiate* my terms."

"*Our* terms," she counters.

"Deal."

"See, you can be reasonable after all," Penny says in a teasing tone.

"How about you draw your conclusion after our discussion."

"Fair enough."

"See you soon, Princess Penelope."

"I'll be counting down the seconds, Not My Bodyguard."

8

PENNY

As soon as Claire and Angie catch sight of me entering Plus None, they greet me with a group hug. At one point I would cringe over this level of affection, but considering the turmoil my emotions have been in all week, I am welcoming the comfort that their embrace provides.

These women love me. Not just because they are forced to as we are family—but because we all share a common bond.

Each one of us has been the carrier of pain, and with suffering comes understanding.

Angie and Claire *get* me.

"Good seeing you ladies again so soon." My words come out muffled, as my mouth is pressed into fabric. I try not to squeeze too hard, since Claire has mentioned how sore her breasts have become.

She has to be the cutest pregnant person ever. Despite my brother being overbearing on a good day, I understand why he is so. He just wants to keep her as happy and comfortable as possible.

From the looks of her swollen feet, I'm wondering how much relaxing she can possibly do here at HH. I mean, she has a freaking treadmill under her stand-up desk.

How she managed to get Nic not to veto that arrangement is pure magic.

"Plan to see more of us," Angie chimes in. "We have a lot of discussing to do."

"Oh boy," I mutter, knowing full well what their intentions are in inviting me here today. I catch Collins dropping off the pastry box out of the corner of my eye. "You are welcome to help yourself before you go about your"—I wave my hand in the air while thinking about my next word —"mission."

I honestly don't know what he's going to do for the next couple of hours. He'll probably be bored out of his mind just hanging around loitering. I know I would. It takes everything in me not to snap at him to go home and learn some hobby—maybe even a musical instrument or second language—but I know he won't. He is just too loyal and too disciplined to veer from his target—*me*.

"I appreciate it, but I'm good," he calls back.

I wave goodbye at him as he slips from the room, quietly exiting our ladies' brunch without a word.

Maybe that's what his presence will be in my life, just a soft reminder that he is here to look out for me, but will not interfere in how I want to spend each of my days.

Surely, we can come to some type of understanding, because if I know anything about my brothers, they aren't going to back down—even if I protest. That will just spur them on further and probably stick me with two guards instead of one.

I know they are worried about me. The thing is…

I'm also worried about me.

As much as I want to thrive, I'm concerned that everything outside of Soulful Mind will get sabotaged by my own inability to see the world for what it is.

I'm jaded. And jaded people have a hard time finding happiness.

The last thing I need is to feel like a failure before ever really trying.

"Please tell me there's sugar in that box," Claire groans with delight, eyeing what I brought. She always has a way of making those around her relax. "I'm at the stage in my pregnancy where eating an entire key lime pie is normal. And I'm starving. Feels like I haven't eaten in a week."

"Or an hour ago," Angie teases, grabbing the box of pastries and moving it into another room that is an offshoot from the main office space.

"Hey, I'm making another human in here"—Claire points to her belly—"and the thing basically never sleeps and treats me like its Snack Bitch."

Angie giggles, coming back out of the room. "Sure, blame the baby."

"Oh, I do. For basically making its daddy want to trap me in some gilded cage for safekeeping."

"I'm sure he'll spare no expense on the cage though," I tease, making Claire laugh. "Just sayin'."

Angie places a hand around my back. "Come, check out the brunch setup. We have a lot of talking to do."

I feel the rush of nerves flitter through my system. I

probably should have had a high-protein snack when I drank my first cup of coffee less than an hour ago.

I allow Angie to lead me into the room where a huge buffet is set up with every food offering imaginable—but in bite-sized portions.

"Wow," I mumble, taking in the atmosphere of the room.

It's filled with live plants, instrumental music playing in the background, and the sweet smell of vanilla filling the air. I really could get used to being here. The girls really nailed the aesthetics.

I circle the room, taking in all of its features, marveling at how calm and collected I feel in this space. No wonder they seem so happy here.

Once I make my round, the girls and I fill up plates, and then Claire and I gather back around a table that is set up with different juices and a pitcher of water. Everything looks fresh and magazine worthy. I love how bright and airy the room feels. It's weird because it is a closed-in space, but yet the least claustrophobic area of the entire office.

"So, Penny," Claire says, obviously about to change the subject. "How about you come work for us?"

"Wow, you're extra blunt today," Angie calls out over her shoulder, as she grabs a muffin from the buffet.

"It's hormones. They dissolve my already sheer filter."

"I, um…" I stutter.

Claire props her hands on her widening hips, underneath the surface of the table. "Okay, fine, I'll just use guilt."

My eyes bulge as I think of the direction she is going with her thoughts.

"I'm pregnant," she states simply.

"That much is obvious." I laugh.

"Hey now, I realize that I'm looking extra blimp-like but go easy on me. Anyhoo, we are a women empowering women company. Thus, dicks are welcome, but not part of our brand recognition. Unless we use Nic as inspiration and create a Man-Child Box."

I hiss. "Ouch."

"I don't mean that," Claire says in a rush. "I love your brother, and it is scary just how much. I think me being pregnant has unleashed more of his overprotective tendencies, and I'm still learning to cope with all that entails."

"Aww, but you are doing a really good job."

Part of me wonders if Nic's need for control over me is stemming from his inability to control aspects of the pregnancy with Claire.

"Anyway, I digress. Back to why you should work for us. You have a gorgeous personality and face, and you have an appeal about you that many people will be able to relate to. Plus, you have modeling experience."

"Not much," I interject. "My past experience is a dumpster fire at best."

Claire waves off my comment, as if I'm just being modest. "I already included you on my latest vision board, as wishful thinking, so you gotta now."

I let out an awkward laugh.

"Oh, and you are family and we trust you and yada yada. *Please*." She is jumping out of her skin. Begging.

It's not that I have jobs lined up or really a clear path to getting one. Working at Plus None is a great opportunity to be part of something that has the potential to grow. Angie and Claire have already accomplished so much with their start-up in a short amount of time. They would make great role models.

While part of me thinks they are hiring me simply because I'm the youngest sister of their partners, I know that when I'm determined, I also put my heart and soul into a project.

Perhaps there is a real place for me here at the company. Maybe I can even make a difference to other women around the world.

"Penny, come and get more food," Angie coaxes me back toward the buffet. "You barely took anything. And Claire, quit harassing my favorite sister-in-law. Give her time to think."

"Hey…" She pouts out her bottom lip. "I thought I was the favorite."

I appreciate Claire's ability to keep things lighthearted. It does help to not be so serious all the time.

"Maybe if you ever tie the damn knot around your man" —she animatedly expresses with some waves of her hands —"you can slide into the spot of being a contender."

"Wow, your spirited language is a bit offensive," Claire goads, obviously teasing.

"Oh, shut it," Angie pretend snarls. "You know that man of yours is ready to take that leap. He might as well cuff you to him until you settle on a date."

"Well, he does like a bit of kinky goodness in the—"

"He is my brother!" I blurt out, covering my ears in fake dramatics but unable to contain my laughter.

The more I hang around these ladies, the more I yearn for a friend of my own. I just don't know how to even go about meeting people these days—especially those who just want companionship. I lack the commitment to socialize regularly and enjoy doing things on my own terms.

Plus, I'm not even sure what I have to offer. I almost forget what it feels like to try to make an effort and hope to be liked. It feels very middle school vibes, and yet that is what my heart really wants. Fake drama. Normalcy.

I want someone to treat me like I'm not seconds away from breaking.

Over the next thirty minutes, I munch on finger foods, laugh with the girls, and try to picture working here. It isn't hard to imagine. At least I would know the work environment isn't toxic. Having Angie and Claire as my bosses would be a bit weird—especially if I fail to produce their visions—but I know that their gentle guidance is what I need right now.

I have a habit of trusting the wrong people, so this would be one stressor in my life that I wouldn't have to second-guess. I know they will never take advantage of me.

"So, hypothetically," Angie says with an attempt to be casual, "if you were to come work with us, we would offer you some equity, a comparable and competitive salary, the ability to get promoted, and a full benefits package."

"Can I just ask one thing?"

Angie shifts on her feet, placing her empty plate onto the table behind her. "Yes, of course."

"Did my brothers put you two up to this?"

Claire spits her water into her cup, as she laughs. "Ha, even if they did"—she pauses to glance up at me—"which they didn't—it would just make us do the opposite."

"She speaks the truth," Angie chimes in, giggling.

"Have you not realized that while those two bossy

brothers of yours like to call the shots, neither Angie nor I give a damn? We basically make it our life's mission to drive them nuts. They make defying them too easy."

All of the tension in my shoulders releases as I let out a laugh. "You have a great point."

"Penny," Angie says softly. "Yes, you are family, but you need to build up some confidence in yourself. I used to hide in the shadow of my twin brother, James, always thinking he was the outgoing one or the one that everyone loved. Well, it sucks to feel inferior, but those feelings are put onto us by ourselves. So, stop."

"Okay…" Angie is right. I am hard on myself.

"You are enough, just as you are. We have a certain image we are looking for, and you would be a great asset to our subscription boxes. The way to build a brand is to have that likability factor. And trust me, girl, you have it."

I try my best not to cry. I want to cry. I want to contradict her kind words and brush them off, but I resist. Sometimes I just need to take that leap of faith. "I'll do it."

"What?" Claire and Angie yell in unison, while looking at each other like they won a lottery, and then back at me.

"I'll accept the job."

"But you haven't heard the salary or benefits package yet," Angie says in shock.

"I trust you," I state simply, and I do. Plus, I'm not doing this for the money. "Ooff…" I stumble backward as I get clobbered by a surprise group hug. It is unexpected, catching me off-balance. I stay upright, careful not to let Claire fall. "Were you really doubting my decision?"

"Um, yeah," Claire says with astonishment. "And Nic basically told me that there was no way you would be—"

She quickly shuts her mouth, covering her hand over her lips to resist from blurting out her next word.

My eyes narrow. "*Sensible*?"

Angie bites her bottom lip, confirming that the talk between my brothers has been full of speculation. Ugh, they can be so annoying…

"What a *punk*," I mutter, recalling the nickname, Punk, I'd given to my brother growing up.

"Anyhoo, you can't decline now. It's written in my tears of joy."

I shake my head over their enthusiasm. It's not even noon, and I already have managed to accomplish an important item on my goal list. Not too bad for just starting out.

"When do I start?"

"Soon. Probably next week or the following one. Your hours will vary, and some of your shifts are dependent on the weather," Angie explains, "as the photographers might need certain lighting to capture certain shots. Don't worry though. You have the flexibility to take time off as needed. We are confident that you will love it here."

"I believe I will."

I help clean up the brunch items, throwing away trash and wiping down surfaces with cleaning spray I find in the break room. After I say my goodbyes, I head out into the hallway.

My eyes scan the area, looking for Collins, but I don't find him.

A chill runs up my spine, as I take a few steps toward a group of chairs outside the bathroom.

Then I feel it… A hand on me.

My eyes snap to the source, finding the calloused grip of a man on my arm.

And no matter how hard I try, I can't protect my mind from plummeting into the pit I spent most of my days trying to resurrect it from at the therapy facility.

Don't touch me.

My arms wrap protectively around my midsection, squeezing my abdomen until pain radiates through my core.

And with a growl that confuses even my own ears, I twist and turn, trying to dislodge the hand holding me prisoner in my own mind's maze.

Get off of me!

9

PENNY

Flashes of memories flitter through my brain at high speed of Mark Tanner on the night that changed my life forever. Claws scratch at the delicate walls of my mind, digging into the fragile darkness, and restoring freedom for the evil, vile man to resurrect.

His scarred face…

His sinister smile…

And the way his eyes track me…promising me that he is coming for me. He'll be relentless.

Prison walls won't keep us apart, not when he is taking up camp right here—in my own mind's playground.

"Tsk-tsk, Penny…" His words are a hollowed-out echo, bulldozing through all the work I've done on myself, shattering me from the inside out.

"Don't touch me," I yell, not even sure my voice is making a sound that is outside my own head. My shoulders round inward, and I tighten my band of arms.

Please, don't touch me.

I squeeze my eyes shut as I feel my body rocking back and forth, swaying to the rhythm of my frantic heart.

"Stay buried, stay buried, stay buried," I chant in my mind.

The calloused hand touches me again, and as I resurface for air from the depths of the darkness, I reclaim my willpower.

"You dropped this," the masculine voice says softly, now squeezing my shoulders, giving me a little shake. "Hey, are you okay?"

"I'm not falling for your charm." My fist swings around —desperate to connect with anything. Anything to make this pain stop. But I miss and flop my body into the hardness of someone else. Someone safe.

"Here, I'll take it," the new voice cuts through the static sound crinkling in my ears.

Collins. He has me.

I let out a whimper but don't dare open my eyes. My mind has played evil tricks on me before…tempting me to come out of this tight, little cocoon of protection…

Just to be deceived again.

"Penny?" His voice is in my ear, hesitation evident in his concerned tone, as he rubs soft circles along my back. "No one will hurt you."

I clear my throat as I choke on a sob. "He was here."

"Who?"

"Mark."

I feel the tension radiate through his body, as he takes a step back, cups my chin, and coaxes me to look into his eyes. "Penny…"

"He was. I saw him."

"No. He's locked up. He'll never hurt you again."

Except he is…

My eyes scan the room, searching for the vile man, but he's nowhere to be seen.

Of course he isn't.

Mark Tanner may be rotting away behind the bars in prison until he has his trial, but he lives rent-free in my damaged mind every day I exist.

"I'm sorry," I say, as tears fill my eyes—for what, I'm not too sure.

My stare grows wide. I know if I blink, I'll be a crying mess.

"He can't hurt you, unless you keep allowing him to."

"He finds me." I bite back a sob. "Every time I am vulnerable. He finds me. Every time a stranger brushes against me. He finds me. And those instances make me want to lose myself into the darkness and never come out. I want to hide."

And that's what I did that night—I hid—and never resurfaced until months later.

Collins pushes back a strand of hair that I'm sure is sticking to the side of my sweaty cheek. His eyes study my face, looking for what—I don't know. "How can I help you?"

"I just need a moment."

"Let's find you a place to sit. There's a chair in the hallway."

It takes all my energy to nod. I feel like a freak. If physical touch can trigger me this much, how will I ever be able to have a healthy relationship—let alone an actual sex life?

"Here, take my hand."

Reluctantly, I reach mine out and Collins envelops it. His touch feels different—safe.

"I'm sorry." My words come out soft, almost as a whisper that I'm not even sure is loud enough to be heard. "I scared that person." I know I did. There's no amount of convincing me otherwise that will be believable. Not when I know the truth.

"Everything's going to be alright. Just take a couple of deep breaths."

His steady pace guides me blindly to a comfy chair several yards away from where I exited Plus None. I feel foolish. Being triggered this easily is not proving to anyone that I'm healed from the trauma that got me sent away in the first place. Maybe Graham and Nic's fear that I was released too soon is valid.

Right now in this moment, I would have to agree.

I slowly open my eyes to find Collins kneeling at my side, my hand still in his. Tears drip out, and I move my head to get my shirt to capture some of the excess off my cheeks. I take a few deep breaths, allowing the stress to detach from my brain and melt away.

Mark Tanner can't hurt me anymore.

And while his influence on my life hasn't fully gone away—and maybe never will—I no longer need to keep living in the shadow of his evilness. I can choose to push forward.

"Penny, you can talk to me."

"No, I can't."

Collins's eyes twitch. "*Yes*, you can." He sounds offended.

I mean, what does he expect?

"Everything that has happened thus far will get passed along to my brothers. I have no one to confide in where they won't find out. And while I do trust Angie and Claire, I don't need to put them in a position to withhold the truth. So, no. I don't have anyone to talk to. No one."

Collins's eyes confirm my fears. This is why I need a friend. Someone neutral and not obligated to walk on eggshells around me.

After several long minutes, he clears his throat. Then he places the ponytail band I must have dropped in the hall that started this whole emotional shitstorm into the palm of my hand. "I won't say anything."

"And why should I believe you?"

"Because I've been looking out for your best interests all along. Besides, my position is not to be a middleman."

"Well then, what is your position?"

Collins stands, pacing in front of me. "We really need to have a conversation. But not here. We need to go someplace private."

"That seems silly." I watch as he stops moving to look at me. "You hate talking."

I see a smirk play on his lips, and it does something to me in the pit of my stomach. At one time I thought Collins was incapable of showing any facial expressions, as if he was pumped up with Botox or just physically unable. Now, I see that he is just selective with his emotional expressions. So when he offers me one, I am tempted to savor it and commit it to memory.

My breathing settles as I recall our earlier discussion. It's not that I forgot, but I guess I wasn't expecting Collins to be waiting around for me while I toured Plus None. Doesn't he ever get bored?

I start to stand and move past him.

"Where are you going?"

"I'm going to use the restroom." Now that I'm no longer in an equilibrium state, I feel a bit raw and vulnerable in front of him.

He nods, sucking in a breath. "I'll be here waiting."

"No doubt," I mumble.

I turn and rush into the ladies' room, feeling the sweat beading on my face. What is wrong with me?

I'm being silly.

This is how I react when any guy gives me a little attention—albeit completely platonic. I act silly. Awkward.

I finish up and wash my hands in the sink. I dab a clean paper towel on my cheeks, trying to tone down some of the blotchiness from my skin. I look like I just went for a jog.

Dammit.

Giving up hope, I toss the crumbled-up paper towel into the trash and exit back into the hallway, where I find Collins at his post like a perfect soldier.

"Ready to go?" he asks, eyeing me with suspicion.

Stop looking at me. I'm fine. "Yes, sir." As soon as the words register to his ears, his eyes twitch and the rare smirk is playing on his lips once again. Shit. This isn't helping. "Where are we going?" I quickly ask, trying to change the subject.

"You'll see."

"So you aren't going to tell me?"

"I'm not planning on it."

"So this is how it's going to be?"

"Most likely."

"Grrr…"

I pick up my pace to keep up with him as he hits the button for the elevator. Our descent to the lobby is less ceremonious compared to our frantic arrival earlier, where my indecisiveness got the best of me.

When we cross through the open space, several employees tilt their head toward us, as a sign of respect—at least I would assume. I think the attention is primarily directed at Collins, who spends exponentially more time here than I do, but I smile in response anyway. I can't even assume people know who I am. It's not like I've been back in the area long. But who knows when it comes to my brothers. There may have been a special briefing among staff where a printout of my face was used for reference.

The warm Portland air hits me as soon as the glass doors open to allow us out. Any day here without a canopy of rain clouds in the sky is a good day. Everything can look so doom and gloom when the sun is hidden.

Collins opens my passenger door and helps me inside with a gentle hand to my elbow and one to the small of my back. I don't need that assist, but the gesture feels nice.

I'm still trying to figure out why some people can touch me and nothing scary happens inside my head, while others can cause such unrest and madness.

I dig into my bag and pull out the new journal he got me. Earlier, I transferred my goal list to the beginning pages, letting this gift be my main keeper of my thoughts.

If there is one thing I've learned through the numerous daily therapy sessions I endured, it is to write things down. There is something magical that can happen when I release my brain from holding on to the lingering information that could potentially be dragging me down.

Collins opens the driver's side door and slides into his place behind the wheel. His eyes catch the journal he got me, and I can see a slow smile brighten his otherwise emotionless expression.

My lips pull into a smirk. "What are you smiling at?"

"Oh, nothing," he says, clicking his tongue.

"Liar."

"Perhaps."

Every encounter with this man brings me more information that I'm trying to piece together. Why is he the way he is? Does he always use his calmness to subdue those around him, or does he really not have that much to say?

"I love the journal, Collins. Thank you."

"I'm glad, Penelope." Upon my groan, he chuckles and then corrects himself. "Penny."

I look out the window as we pass through the city, heading northwest. Based on the direction we are taking, I think I know where we are going. However, I don't bother asking. I know Collins won't tell. He is the type to dole out information if he chooses—not answer questions like an interrogation.

But I can't resist filling the silence. So I do what I do best. I make things awkward. "Do you have any family?"

I glance over to see Collins looking extra uncomfortable. His eyes darken, and I can see the twitch starting in his jaw.

"Doesn't everyone?" His words are cold. Calculated.

"Not an active one, no."

"Then, no."

"I'm sorry."

"I don't need pity."

"Good thing I'm not giving it. What happened to them?"

"They died."

What? "How?"

"I was raised by my grandparents. They passed and then I entered into the foster care system. Every few months, I got a new family."

"Do you have any relationship with any of those families now?"

"No."

"Why not?"

He clears his throat. "Because there was no one who made a positive impact on my life other than to give me a reason to build a fortress around myself."

My eyes fill with tears as I think about Collins as a young boy, being tossed about from house to house. "This is breaking my heart."

His sigh cuts through my sniffling, as he shifts in his seat. "Not every card in the deck is meant to be in your hand. Some people start out having better luck with life. Others have to make their own. What I have going for me that is going well, is my own doing. I'm not sorry about that. I have no one to thank, but also no one to blame."

My lips press into a hard line. I can't imagine what my life would be right now without the love and support of my parents and brothers. No matter how overbearing I sometimes think they are, I know deep down that they are coming from a place of goodness.

"Okay…"

"Okay."

I want to know more about Collins. He has a deeper backstory. We all do. But something tells me that few know about it.

Collins and I drive in silence the rest of the way, until he pulls up to the entrance of the Portland Japanese Garden.

"I didn't bring my season pass you got me."

"I have my own," he states simply.

"You come here often?" I can't keep the surprise from my tone. Why is a man like Collins coming here so intriguing?

"If I need to think, I do." He parks, cuts the engine, and then turns to look at me sternly. "Wait here, Penny."

I watch as he rounds the front of the vehicle and makes his way to my side. Why is he being so formal all of a sudden? I surely can open my own door without putting a crease in his impeccable manners. I'm a twenty-first-century woman after all. The kind that can open her damn door.

I give the handle a try, pulling it toward me. Nothing. Seriously?

Then Collins grabs it from the outside, tugs it open, and offers a hand to me. I'm a bit intimidated not to take it, just by how determined he looks in this display of outdated chivalry.

I walk in step with him toward the entrance in silence. He seems too serious. It's making me anxious.

"Are you mad at me?" I whisper.

Nothing. Seriously—what just happened? I can feel the cosmic shift in his entire mood.

We get to the perky female worker who is scanning passes, probably silently begging for someone to engage her with some meaningless chitchat. She just appears to have the personality of someone who needs that social interaction.

Collins shows her his phone where there is a barcode loaded. She's oblivious to our silent standoff because she asks if we've been here before and mentions about a new hybrid plant that the facility has adopted to grow.

I answer all of the questions, while Mr. Grump Grump sulks.

Sheesh.

This man is going to ruin all of my Zen that I should be experiencing by coming here. Instead, he is harboring a lot of emotions and, quite frankly, giving me anxiety.

If Collins wants to talk, then he will talk. He is a grown-ass man who can make his own decisions.

The thing is, I'm a grown-ass woman who is trying desperately to hold on to my own decision-making capabilities. The fact that he's struggling to see this is what irks me the most.

We walk through the main entrance, and I allow Collins to take the lead. Surely that will cheer him up. I've been here several times before, so when we end up in the Strolling Pond Garden, I'm thrilled to be at one of my favorite places here.

Our pace slows as Collins slides his hand along the rail bordering the path. While he's not verbally expressing his thoughts, I can see that he's visibly distressed—as am I. The garden might represent peace and tranquility, but I feel everything but those things.

"I take my job very seriously, Penelope," he states

directly, reminding me yet again of the formal name I despise hearing.

We continue our annoyingly gentle stroll, pass over the Moon Bridge, and then through the irises. He keeps his gaze forward.

I stop the walk, turning to look Collins straight in the eyes.

"I imagine you do," I comment, "but I'm not going to budge on moving forward with my goals. So, no matter what you or my brothers say, I'm not going to back down. I've wasted too much time already."

His lips flatten into a pensive line. "Taking care of yourself is not a waste of time."

I bite my bottom lip that seems to want to quiver. "Fair enough. But that doesn't change my determination to move on to a new chapter in my life."

He gives a single nod, glancing off into the forest of trees. "Fine."

"I just hope it isn't a chapter that ends in tragedy."

"It won't if you just trust me."

I soak in my surroundings. It really is magical here. The special thing about the Japanese Garden is that everything here is intentional and beautiful. It is majestic, yet not overdone. It's easy to get lost here and still remain on the path, while thoughts drift into the serenity.

"It's not that I don't trust you, Collins."

"Then let's set some ground rules."

I lean my butt against a handrail, crossing my feet at my ankles as my mind races with all of the possibilities. Collins has obviously given this some thought already for him to suggest it in the first place. And by the rigidness of his jaw and the way his back is in perfect alignment, I'm guessing this meeting will be less of a negotiation and more of a ruse to get me to comply.

So, out of pure curiosity, I entertain his train of thought. "And what might those be?"

His posture relaxes. "I become your official driver."

"No."

"No?" His nose twitches, as I veto the first of his demands.

"That's weird."

"Weird?"

Did he really think I would make this whole thing easy?

"Yeah," I answer.

"Please explain," he grinds out between clenched teeth.

When I'm reluctant to provide a valid explanation, he raises an irritated eyebrow at me—relaunching my self-preservation skills. He isn't going to let me off the hook with this one, that much is clear. Anxiety forms in the pit of my stomach, multiplying and spreading outward. My teeth gnaw at the inner liner of my mouth, as I teeter on my heels.

Crossing my arms at my chest, I let out a sigh. "Fine. For starters, I'm going to be living in the city. So, I will either walk, get a taxi, pass my driver's test, or hitchhike with some stranger."

"Penny, I don't—"

"Oh my goodness…" I toss my hands into the air. "The last part is a joke. Chill."

He looks so confused. "A joke?"

"Yes, silly—a joke." I shake my head at him. I know he knows how to laugh. I've seen him do it at my birthday party which seems like a lifetime ago, because this discovery has literally been bogging me down the last few hours.

"Why can't you just call me when you need a ride?"

"And I will do that—"

"Good."

I glare at his unnecessary interruption. "About seventeen percent of the time."

"That sounds oddly specific," he grumbles. His hand rubs at the back of his neck, and my eyes instantly narrow in on the tone of his arms through the fabric of his shirt.

Stay focused, Penny.

Do not get blinded by the biceps.

"My point is, I need some space. I hate feeling claustrophobic, and if you are going to be hovering on every sideline of my life, I'm going to"—my hands wave frantically in front of me as I think of my next words—"fill in the blank."

I'm not even sure what I'm capable of doing, but I know I can only be pushed so far before I break.

"Why does my hovering upset you so much? We know each other. I've been working for your brothers for some time now. You can obviously trust me with your life and be confident that I have your best interests in mind. Why is this such a big deal?"

"Because I'm planning on having sex," I blurt out. "Lots of it! Ooey-gooey sex." I'm on a roll now, so why stop? "The type that you don't want to know about. The kind that my brothers don't need updates on or even acknowledgment of."

"Penny…"

"I'm a grown-ass woman, Collins. I'm going to make mistakes that a background check and a fancy security system won't be able to remediate. Let me. Just let me live my own life in peace and harmony, humping whomever I want and how often I want." My voice is raised, as the words flutter out like caged birds seeking freedom, unable to be contained any longer. I don't even know if I can actually complete a sexual act after the trauma I endured, but I sure am going to try to desensitize myself to all the things that would typically make me panic. I just don't need Collins lurking around the corner, cockblocking me with his unrevealed-to-me orders from my brothers. "There, I said it. Happy now?"

I feel absurd, yet relieved, to get that off my chest. That's the root issue. I really need to keep my private life private. Graham and Nic wouldn't understand because the women they are protecting are actually in relationships with them. Who knows, they may even like their overbearing ways. But I don't.

I glance over at Collins, who has the backdrop of peaceful trees swaying with the wind behind him, yet nothing about his demeanor hints that he's at ease. "Well?" I probe.

"Well what?" he snaps

I know he's not this dense. "Are you happy?"

"Happy?" he asks, tension building in his shoulders, extending up to his now hard jawline. "You think any of your verbal confession makes me happy, Penelope? You are barely out of the facility. What about the hallway incident today outside of Plus None? Do you think you are even ready for that next step? But here you are threatening to go throw yourself at anyone with a semi-hard cock. And for what? To say you can? To prove your defiance?"

My mouth dries at how he says the word *cock*. A chill runs through me over his spitting rage. "Why are you upset? If anything, I'm the one who should be mad for you forcing me to overshare. You make me snap."

Collins runs both hands through his short brown hair, grasping on to whatever he can and tugging. After a few minutes of silence and what I perceive to be the expectation that we are going to continue our discussion until we can come to a mutual understanding, Collins instead pivots and starts walking along the path toward the Sand and Stone Garden.

Why is he retreating?

Are we done?

I rush to keep up, nearly tripping to maintain the pace. "Is that it?" But my words fall on deaf ears. He is too far ahead of me to actually hear. I break into a slow jog, reaching for his arm to try to stop him from completely deserting me in the middle of the park. "What's with you?"

Collins pauses his stride. And we just stare at each other. No understanding passes between us. It is emptiness. Like his mind has already been made up, and maybe if I'm lucky, he'll let me in.

My throat burns from the harsh intake of air as my breathing levels.

"We are done here."

"*You* are done here," I correct, propping my hands on my hips.

And just like that, he is back to power walking. "I'm taking you back home."

I run to catch up again, tugging on his arm. "So that's it?

No more talking? You decide we are going, so we're going?"

His eyes lack the anger from earlier and are void of any real identifiable emotion. It is eerie. It's like he turned into a stone-cold statue, shielding himself from whatever stress guarding me is causing him.

"There's nothing left to discuss."

10

COLLINS

I thought I could do it. I really did. But I can't.

Well, at least not in this heightened state that I'm in currently.

We need to have time apart today to really comprehend what was said and the implications of it all.

This is not how I envisioned today going, but it is what it is…

I've experienced difficult women before, but with them it was usually an act. Some like the thrill of being a brat.

With Penny, there's no acting. She is being true to herself, even if her honesty is driving me into the red zone —a place I rarely go.

After hearing Penny rattle off all of the things she plans to do, I don't think I can just stand back and watch her implode.

Her brothers gave me the impression that my role was to be a low-intensity bodyguard.

However, in the span of thirty minutes, my job requirements just got more rigorous.

Keeping Penny out of trouble will be difficult if I don't tighten up my reins of control.

This girl is already testing every ounce of self-control I have. How will I even survive the duration of this contract?

Penny best be glad I don't carry her over my shoulder and toss her into a cage and conveniently lose the key. Until she can learn how to show some respect to me—and herself—I'm taking no chances with her.

This girl has a way of getting under my skin, like no one has ever in the past.

She needs boundaries.

She needs discipline.

She needs someone who won't back down.

But for now, I need to get us into the vehicle and drop her off back at her parents' place.

We need some distance between us to clear the air.

My abdomen hits the turnstile bar that keeps count of people leaving the park, and the annoying-as-fuck worker tries to get me to interact—again.

"Here's a list of our sister parks that you can get a discount with on your season pass! There's a coupon for ten percent off on the back, sir! And if you fill out the customer survey, you can be eligible to receive a fifty-dollar gift card on your season pass renewal!"

With a wave of my hand, I dismiss her. I'm not in the mood and would willingly pay her just to shut up.

I swear I hear Penny mutter something about me being rude, and it is then I realize she has been trying to keep up with me this whole time.

Fuck.

I slow down as I near the parked SUV, as pangs of guilt for walking so fast consume me.

I turn as I hear Penny gasp while tripping, but she catches herself before hitting the pavement. Her shoe falls off, and with a groan, she bends over to retrieve it—declining to put it back on.

Dammit.

Why did I not even pay attention to the type of footwear she chose for today?

I should have walked slower and considered how uncomfortable she must be with the pace I was forcing upon her.

My success as a bodyguard is spent being observant, and yet I missed this important detail when I decided to stride off in full dick-mode.

I want to apologize, but the words get stuck in my throat. Saying sorry now just seems so…

Pointless.

She's upset. I'm upset.

I tried.

I *really* tried to make this work.

I thought that I could get her to bargain and be on my side. Nope. Her words about all of the sexual encounters she plans to do is what did me in. I feel murderous thinking of how I'll have to stand on the sidelines and endure whatever recreational activities she wants to subject herself to.

Men are going to want to bury themselves into Penny, and I'll have to bury them into the ground because I won't be able to handle it.

Penny is my responsibility, but something gnawing at

me from the inside is telling me that she is more than just that.

At least with Angie and Claire, they were committed to their men. Penny, however, is single. From the way she described her plan, she has high hopes of bouncing between multiple men, all at the expense of her own safety.

She might feel like she has to make up for lost time, sowing her oats and being reckless.

If her brothers find out, I think they may lose their minds. How do I even explain to them why I can no longer guard their sister? They deserve an explanation. They will demand one actually. How do I even paraphrase the things Penny said?

I open the passenger side door and step back to allow Penny access. I don't dare touch the soft skin of her elbow or the perfect curvature of her lower back. In such a short amount of time, I've already gotten close to her.

I've gotten so close that I've committed her fresh-picked strawberry scent to memory. I've gotten so close that I know when she is stressed by how she touches her hair or when she is excited by how she bites at her inner cheek to contain her smile.

But she isn't smiling now.

Nope. She is not happy at all.

It's her off shoe that makes it into the vehicle first by the toss of her hand, followed by the other one that she kicks off onto the floor.

Then I see them—angry red blisters. Just the sight causes my breath to catch in my throat. "Fuck," I say breathily. "Pen, I'm sorry."

"Just shut the door, Collins. We are done here."

Her words, echoing the same ones I spoke just minutes ago, sting. I'm an idiot for not considering her well-being. "I'm so sorry."

"Just go. I promise not to get blood on your pristine mats."

I wince over her attempt at indifference. "Let me make this better."

"Don't bother. Just take me back home."

She reaches for the door to close on her own, but I stop her. Bending my body into the car, I lean over her to open the glovebox. I can hear her breath catch as she exhales.

"Let me help you."

"I'm *fine*."

"No, you're not." I rustle through the insurance information and emergency supplies, until I find the first aid kit tucked in the corner. "I caused you to get these sores, so at least let me tend to them."

"Coll—"

"Please."

"I'm fine."

My fingers tighten around the kit, causing my knuckles to turn white. "Dammit, Penny, you're hurt. So just accept that I'm going to help you, and quit being so utterly stubborn." Is this normal for her, or is this the result of spending the morning with the girls at Plus None?

Before Penny has a chance to protest further, I squat down onto the gravelly parking lot, take one of her feet into my hands, and turn her foot slowly to assess the damage. At a closer examination, it is worse than I first thought. Some layers have peeled back, causing the redness of her skin to shine through the cracks. She must be in pain because the sight alone is causing me distress.

Fuck.

I caused this. For someone who prides himself on being observant, I completely missed the clues as to Penny's discomfort. I didn't even look back to check on her, when I knew she was following after me—trying to keep pace.

Opening the first aid kit with one hand, I pull out a tube of antibiotic cream. I rip open several bandages, squeeze the ointment into the cloth pad of each strip, and then place one onto each blister. I go slow and take my time to make sure I don't cause her any additional pain.

I've done enough. This is the least I can do.

"Thanks," she mumbles, as I place the kit back into the glovebox and then straighten my posture.

I want to linger. I want to evaluate her wellness further. However, both of us are teetering dangerously on our breaking point, so why tip the scales? Just by the way Penny is gripping the hem of her skirt, white-knuckling the shit out of it, is indication enough that I'm already driving her to the edge.

I shut the door, round the front, and then situate myself behind the wheel.

Taking a deep breath, I rub the temple of my head.

This whole afternoon was a disaster, and the only thing it revealed was that my work just got a whole hell of a lot harder.

I'm usually good at predicting outcomes to situations, but I was not prepared for Penny's big confession.

Does she really think I'm going to sit back while she brings a harem of asshole boys back to her place, just to prove a point to herself? The thought of someone touching her claws at my insides and makes me irrational—something I rarely ever am.

No, I'm not like that at all.

I pride myself on being calm and collected, especially when in volatile situations. And just hearing Penny talk about how she is going to have casual sex, whenever and wherever she wants, makes me want to lock her up in a room and protect her from all of the dangers of the world—including herself.

I don't even trust my reaction to her future plans if faced head-on with a situation.

She makes me ready to commit murder on anyone who touches a hair on her sweet head or even dares to think they have a chance with her.

What the hell is wrong with me? Not once in my life have I cared this much about anyone, which is precisely why I need to distance myself from her today and rethink this whole arrangement.

I turn to look at Penny, as she blatantly refuses to look my way.

"I'm sorry," I say softly. Why is she not acknowledging me? Why is everything so difficult?

I don't expect her to answer, and yet it hurts when I'm met with indifference. It's a silence so loud that it says everything as to how she is feeling in the moment.

She hates me.

So I allow her the silence to sit with her feelings and don't muddy the air with another word.

It takes longer than usual to get to Hillsboro, and when we do, Donna is arranging flowers outside on her porch in huge wicker planters. When she stumbles backward trying to carry one over to the other side of the house, I quickly park and jump out of the SUV to run over and relieve her of the weight.

"Here, I got this, Mrs. Hoffman. Just tell me where you want it."

"First off, never call me that. It's insulting. Second"—she gestures with the wave of her hand—"you can put it over there next to the cobblestone path."

I laugh over her directness. It's not surprising her daughter has the same aversion to formalities. "Sure thing."

In my periphery, I see Penny slowly get out of the vehicle. Her feet must be hurting, as she walks barefoot, carrying her shoes in her hands like broken trophies.

My pulse quickens with yet another visual reminder that I'm responsible for her suffering. Maybe a warm bath and going shoeless the rest of the day will help her heal faster. It's not like I can provide any input now with how tense her shoulders look and the way she is deliberately avoiding eye contact.

"Oh, and third," Donna says loudly, "I made my famous Mississippi pot roast today, and it will be a travesty if you don't join us, Collins."

"Umm…"

"With secret ingredient mashed potatoes."

"I…"

"And a salad with the little candied walnuts and crumbled-up goat cheese…"

I need to make a clean break right now from Penny, and yet here is her mom unintentionally blurring the lines further and taunting me with homemade food.

Donna always makes too much, enough to easily sustain the entire town. I'd be doing her fridge space a favor by staying just this one time.

But I can't.

"I, um, don't—"

"A trav-es-ty," she reiterates, exaggerating the syllables.

"I'm not sure…"

"Oh dear," she says, a frown marring her otherwise kind appearance, "you are a newly declared vegetarian?"

"Ha," I say with a laugh, "no."

"He probably has plans, Momma," Penny says, not even bothering to turn around, as the door shuts a bit too loudly.

I spare a glance at Donna, giving her a shrug. "I don't want to intrude." I never do. It's actually part of my life's mission to never get too personal with people. Sitting down and sharing a meal together seems personal. Sure, I've done it here on a holiday, and most recently, Penny's birthday, but staying now is surely just going to make things worse.

I can't do worse.

"Nonsense. Don't be silly. Stay. Eat. Hell, go for a swim if you want. It's so hot out here, I think my face melted half off. If you see it"—her eyes move around on the ground—"please pick it up for me. New ones cost way too much these days."

I smile over Donna's sense of humor. She has this ability to make everyone feel welcome and at home, despite me never really having a solid home after my grandparents passed just months apart.

They tried their best, in the limited time they had with me. So I can't fault them there. At least they stepped up to the plate when my biological parents didn't.

So to have this level of welcoming and a sense of motherly compassion is rare for me. I'd be lying if I said it wasn't refreshing—to be wanted and appreciated. It sure is a contrast to how Penny sees me at the moment.

I think about how I'm going to get out of having to stay. Saying I have other plans seems like a lie that Donna will see through in an instant. She's not the bullshitting type. I imagine raising boys like Graham and Nic did that to her. While I'm several years older than they are, Donna still treats me like I'm her son. That's just how she operates.

I rock on my heels, placing my hands into my pockets. I want to decline. I want to just go back to my place and work out until all my simmering animosity is settled. But it's her eyes and the persuasive kindness that gets me every single time.

Do I even have a choice?

I give a nod, as her lips curl into a satisfied smile.

"I know my boys have you watching out for our Penny."

"I, um…"

Donna raises her hand up for me to stop. "Well, they actually keep me in the dark on basically everything, but I know. I'm very"—she furrows her brow—"*observant*. Anyway, Germain and I appreciate it. The least I can do is make sure you are properly fed. It would hurt my heart to think you were going to get takeout from one of those horrible-for-the-environment Styrofoam boxes or worse yet, warm up a meat and cheese pocket thing." She shudders, placing a hand on my back. "Gross. Come. I insist. You like pot roast, yeah?"

"I love it."

"Perfect."

The lump in my throat plummets and expands into the pit of my stomach. I already feel guilt stepping foot onto her soil, knowing that I'm doing a shitty job of taking care of her daughter, and the job barely started. The hopefulness in her eyes is nearly my undoing. The entire Hoffman family has some deeply rooted trust in my capabilities, yet I'm dropping the damn ball every time it's thrown my way.

I haven't visited this house often prior to this week where I've been here twice, but nearly every time I have, there have been memories made with Penny. I think back to the time we played football together for Thanksgiving, our paths crossing a few times over Christmas, the rehearsal dinner here for Angie and Graham's wedding, and the memory of her walking down the stairs on her birthday just two days ago. Those experiences are vastly different from just minutes ago with how Penny slammed the door—shutting me out of her life in a figurative gesture that may lead to permanent consequences.

I don't belong here. I don't really belong anywhere.

And maybe that's what bothers me the most. That the more time I spend with the Hoffmans, the more I'm reminded of all that I lack in my life. But no matter how different our backgrounds are, the Hoffmans are basically family to me.

"Don't be shy," Donna coaxes, opening the door and holding it for me to pass through.

And I do. I walk into the very house where all three of her children were raised, and which I imagine holds so many wonderful memories.

The Hoffmans are the type of family I would read about in books. I would fantasize what it would be like to love and to be loved. And there's no shortage of love that Donna has for her three children.

And here she is extending that compassion to me.

The smell of dinner cooking makes my stomach growl. I often skip meals during the day and fuel up in the evening via a food delivery service. However, Donna is right that most likely I would be warming up something mediocre if I decided to go back to my place now instead of staying here for dinner.

Germain greets us from the couch in the living room as I follow Donna deeper inside her house. It feels different being here this go-round. Maybe it's more intimate because there are fewer people. Or maybe it's because I am harboring some unprofessional feelings for their only daughter.

"Thank you for having me," I say softly, my voice barely a whisper.

"You are always welcome," Donna reassures. "You're family, Collins. Go sit, enjoy a break for once. I'm not sure where Penny went…"

"She's up in her room," Germain answers, looking toward the stairs. "She said she had a phone call to make. Sounded important."

Curiosity strikes me as I think about what could be so pressing that she had to retreat to her room upon entry into the house. It's not like I can ask her and expect a truthful answer. We aren't on speaking terms at the moment. Part of me wonders if things will ever go back to how they were. So much has changed in just the span of twelve hours.

Now I can't help but wonder if this girl actually does hate me.

11

PENNY

When I get to my room, I allow the tears that I've been holding back most of the day to cascade down my cheeks. I needed to make some excuse about having to make a phone call so my dad wouldn't stop me on the way to my pity party.

I don't need an audience for this.

So I recline in bed and just cry.

And after several minutes, I feel so much better.

Today was a lot. Between meeting up with the girls at Plus None to arguing with Collins publicly at a garden meant to provide serenity, I just need one evening of calm.

Rolling over, I reach for my phone to check my messages and am shocked to find one from Collins. We just spoke not even half an hour ago.

Collins: You left your wallet in my car. I'm going to give it to your mom.

Penny: Thanks

I hate the tension between us, and yet every time I think of his sole purpose in my life, my blood starts to boil. How could he not expect the two of us to clash? We both have entirely different goals.

When I come down the stairs for dinner, wearing an oversized shirt with a giant teddy bear on the front and a pair of mismatched pajama bottoms, I'm surprised to see Collins being fawned over by my parents at the dining room table.

So much for a calm evening at home.

Like, seriously…why is he still here?

I'm mad at him.

While my anger might be displaced, I can't help but feel trapped and confused about the whole situation. I just want to keep moving toward achieving independence. Yet, everything about Collins screams dependency.

I can't drive.

I technically still live at home.

And the job I just accepted is located at a building that my brother owns.

How would anyone expect to actually do anything profound with these limited conditions?

My movement causes Collins to turn his head and take note that I have arrived at the table.

He better shut his mouth over my choice of attire too. I am comfortable.

But he keeps staring at me.

At least I kept my bra on, although I wouldn't turn around and get one if I hadn't.

"Stop it," I whisper under my breath.

"Stop what?"

"Looking at me."

How am I even going to be able to eat with him here? I take my seat, place my napkin on my lap, and then down my entire glass of iced water in a few gulps. My mouth is parched, and I think it has to do with how deeply I'm breathing.

"Penny, isn't it nice that Collins can join us?" Momma asks, obviously smitten with the man. It's a bit obnoxious.

Thanks, Momma, you traitor.

"Oh, it's just lovely," I say as sweetly as I can muster up, while plastering on the fakest smile I can produce.

Collins gives me the side-eye, making me want to laugh at my own jolly-good sarcasm. I shouldn't be laughing right now. If I laugh, I'll forget that I'm angry, and that is a feeling I want to embrace wholeheartedly.

I should be mad. I'm entitled to be mad and for as long as I want.

Dad gives me a look, and I know he senses my unease but is too polite to ever call me out on it in front of a group.

And then it dawns on me. This is yet another reason I need a place of my own. Everyone is so damn polite around me, always afraid to mess up or say the wrong thing or freak poor Penny out.

I just need my space so I can learn to assimilate myself back into society, or I might go insane. It's not that far-fetched of a possibility either. I did spend months at a mental institute. No wonder everyone seems to walk around on eggshells around me.

Momma walks to Collins's side of the table first—since he's the guest—and shovels piles upon piles of pot roast onto his plate despite his soft protests that she can stop.

"Whatever you can't eat, I'll just wrap you up a plate. It's no biggie. That's what they made Tupperware for."

Why not just let him spend the night, Momma?

At this rate, he'll never want to leave.

Maybe he can move in, while I move out. I stifle a giggle over the absurdity of my idea.

"Something funny?" he whispers to me, while my parents are distracted.

"Kudos to you for winning my parents over."

His smile is bright. "I do love to win."

My eyes glare at his. "Oh, I bet you do—except when I'm your partner for family games."

"Oh, you're still bitter over that?"

"You legit caused us to lose."

"I carried our team."

"Psst," I hiss, sticking out my tongue.

Then he reciprocates, and I nearly fall out of my chair.

Why is he so lighthearted all of a sudden? What has changed? He's usually so stern and rigid, hiding behind his hard exterior shell.

When it's my turn to get served, I take a small scoop of the meat and an even smaller scoop of the mashed potatoes. I'm just not feeling very hungry at the moment, with everything that's going on. Plus, my feet hurt horribly from the blisters I got trying to rush through the gardens at a speed I could barely maintain. I should have just parked my ass on a bench and refused to walk.

Most people think I'm stubborn anyway. I might as well rock that label while I can and embrace the shit out of it.

"Nice shirt," Collins says softly.

I look down at the teddy bear printed on the front and then back up at my annoying bodyguard. "Are you mocking me?"

"Never. Wouldn't dream of it."

"Your mood swings are giving me whiplash," I sneer, as Momma turns her back to put the serving bowls on the buffet table.

He places some meat into his mouth, chewing it up. "Likewise."

I spin my fork into my potatoes, swirling them around on the plate. Stabbing some meat, I take my first bite and close my eyes over the taste. Momma is the best cook. She can make a thirty-cent pack of ramen turn out amazing. However, when she really tries—like she did today—she can make magic happen.

"This is really delicious," Collins says to the table. "Thank you for inviting me in."

Suck-up.

I spare a glance his way, and right as I do, he looks over at me at the same time. Quickly, I grab my phone and check through my text messages, settling in on the unknown number. Scanning through the detailed message, I see that the apartment I chose to rent can be accessed now. I just need to get the key from the lockbox near the mailboxes. Seems easy enough.

I already wired over my deposit and rent payment. Digital signing of documents makes life so much easier than having to physically go during business hours to fill out forms. I am basically all set.

Anxious to meet my roommate and get started on figuring out how to move my stuff from here to there, I decide that going there tonight to check out the location and logistics would be best. I can take pictures, measure out some of the dimensions, and brainstorm on how I want my space to look.

Being in Hillsboro, there is no taxi service that is local. If I need to hitch a ride, I have to give a lift company in Portland ample notice so the driver has a chance to get here to pick me up. So, I Google a company and fill out the form to reserve a ride in about an hour. By then, dinner will be over and I will have had a chance to throw on some normal clothes that don't make me look like I am eight.

"So, Collins, do you have any summer plans?" Dad asks, leaning back in his chair and taking a sip of his wine.

Collins clears his throat, places his napkin down onto the table, and then gives a half smile. "Just work."

"Now, that doesn't sound like fun at all," Momma says with a pout. "No time off to travel and relax?"

"Actually, Mrs. Hoffman, I—"

"I thought I warned you before to never call me such a formal title."

"Oh, ha."

"That is basic rule number one in this household," Momma says, keeping her voice stern, but conveying through her eyes that she is really joking.

He dips his head. "My apologies." He spares a glance at me, and I can't seem to take my eyes off of his. "I recently had a break in my schedule. The time off was good, but I really like to keep busy."

"Maybe you should find a hobby," I interject. "You know, like take up painting or learning a musical instrument… Or leaf collecting."

Collins's eyes lock on mine. He knows I'm being sarcastic.

"Just don't let Graham overwork you," Momma says, ignoring my snarky comments.

My humor is wasted on these people.

"I won't," Collins says with a smile.

"Penny, do you want more salad?" Momma asks.

"No, thanks."

It's driving me nuts how she is allowing me to text at the table and get away with other rude behavior. *Just treat me normal.*

Momma gives more to Collins.

"I really hope Graham appreciates all you do."

"Your son—actually *sons*—treat me very well. I've been very lucky to be under their employment."

"At my expense," I say with a grumble, but only for his ears to hear. Bored, I shoot him a text.

Penny: Suck-up.

"Well, at least relax while you are here. Think of our house in Hillsboro as a retreat. You can escape those boys of mine anytime. Heavens knows they don't visit here often enough, so this would be the last place they would expect to find you hiding."

Collins's laughter causes the knot in the pit of my

stomach to release. Maybe after all of this awkwardness blows over, we can eventually be in the same room as each other and it not be this intense.

I'm playing with my food when my phone lights up with an incoming text.

Collins: Your mom is hard not to like.

I type back a quick response but don't actually send it.

What's left to say? Momma has the gift of hospitality.

It's not Collins's fault he fell victim to her persistent invitation to come in for dinner.

The meal wraps up with a coconut pudding dessert that Momma made from scratch. I carry mine up to my room, forgoing the chitchatting that seems to be endless downstairs. Maybe by the time my ride arrives, Collins will have already left.

In between bites, I toss on a yellow sundress. My feet hurt so bad that the only logical thing I can wear until they heal are flip-flops. I brush out my hair and braid it down the side.

I'm not sure who will be at the apartment right now, but I want to be prepared to make a good first impression just in case.

I finish up my dish of pudding and carry it down the stairs into the kitchen, finding both my parents embracing in a hug. Even after all of these years, they still find a way to love each other.

"Hey," I mutter, walking into the room. "Collins leave?"

"Just a minute ago," Dad answers. He takes in my attire. "Going somewhere?"

"Remember how I told you guys that I wanted to get a place of my own? Well, I'm able to go take a look at the one place tonight. I'm too excited to wait until tomorrow."

"Do you want us to come with you?" Momma asks. "I've been getting some notifications that the rain may be heavy at times. A big storm is moving into the area from the coast. I'd feel safer if one of us accompanied you. Yeah?"

"I'll be fine." I hate seeing her this anxious—this hopeful.

She looks up at my dad to see his reaction. "We can give you a ride."

"My taxi should be here soon. I appreciate it, though."

Momma nods, wrapping one arm around Dad's back. I know she doesn't want me to move out but respects me enough to understand my need to do so anyway.

"You'll be extra safe?" Dad asks, trying to keep any emotion out of his tone.

"Of course. And I'll be back tonight to sleep here, just a bit later than usual."

"Oh, okay." His relief pulls at my heartstrings. "You have your key?"

"Yup. Also, once I move out, you can use my room to store baby stuff until Claire gives birth. The extra space will probably be welcomed."

"You will always have a room here, Pen," Momma insists. "Always."

I step closer, joining them in a group hug. "You both are amazing parents."

After a long minute, I break the hold and use the bathroom before heading outside.

I'd be lying if I said I wouldn't miss living here.

Because I will. My parents are basically the best—albeit a bit intrusive at times. I will miss the smell of fresh flowers that my momma has been nurturing and the ease of having someone to talk to at a moment's notice. I'll miss the comfort that home brings, but this is the right step for me. And I think deep down, they know it as well.

Fishing my phone out of my bag, I find the taxi service app. Based on the tracker, my ride should be here in about five minutes. I meander along the front porch, observing Momma's new plant additions. Maybe when I get settled into my apartment, I can spruce it up with some greenery.

I am lost in thought when I see movement from the corner of my eye, causing my head to jerk toward it.

"Collins?" I ask, placing a hand over my heart. "I thought you left. Where's your SUV?"

He gestures with his chin toward the end of the driveway where his vehicle is idling. From the confusion on my face, he elaborates with, "You left your hair tie in the cupholder."

As his hand extends, and his fingers open up, I see the pink stretchy ring in his palm. I don't even remember removing it from my wrist. My fingers brush his, as I accept the offering. His touch tickles, causing goose bumps to trail up my legs, all the way to my arms. Our eyes lock, and there's more exchanged in the simple look than just a hair tie.

"Thank you," I say softly. It's as if the tie serves as some peace offering I'm not sure I should even accept.

In the distance, heat lightning flickers over the mountains. The wind is warm, and the smell of my momma's flowers fills the air. It would be tranquil here if I wasn't so on edge around Collins. He makes me twitchy.

"You mad at me?"

I shrug. "A little."

Collins nods in understanding. "I'm not trying to ruin your life, Penny."

"So you say."

"Things will work out. You'll see."

I rock on the heels of my feet as a car flies past the driveway, screeches to a stop, and then backs up down the road.

Then the headlights come flickering up the lane. Based on the rev of the engine, I'm not quite sure it will even make the short trip.

Collins turns to look at the source of the light coming toward us, his eyebrows drawing in. "Who's that?" His voice is stern, cold.

"I don't know," I lie. I don't even recognize my own squeaky voice.

"Yes, you do. Tell me," he presses, somehow knowing that the junk of a vehicle coming our way has something to do with me. Maybe he does have some sort of sixth sense.

I bite my bottom lip and brace myself. "My ride."

His eyes bore into mine. "Your ride?"

I plaster on a smile. It's not often I get to shock someone like Collins, and based on how his back is poker straight, I'd say I managed to do just that. I pull back my shoulders and clear my throat. "Yes, my ride."

Collins takes in my attire, seeing that I've exchanged my ratty pajamas for something more sophisticated. "To where?"

Oh, and now he's a bit snappy. "To wherever my heart desires."

"I'll give you a ride wherever you want to go, Penny. Can you just ask? Is it so difficult that you are unable to relinquish this desire you have inside to make everything so complicated?"

My hands prop on my hips, as I stare at him. The driver of the other vehicle passes by Collins's idling SUV and stops in front of us.

"Who is he? Do you even know him?" When I don't answer, he rubs along his jawline while closing his eyes. When he opens them again, I know I'm in trouble. "Please clarify if I'm wrong. You called some random person to give you a ride, and they just pulled up in a rusted tin box?"

"Maybe."

My toes curl, making me wince when my blisters rub against the flip-flop straps. Shit. I bite at my bottom lip to suffer through the sudden pain.

"Have you lost your mind?"

His words sting, and I don't think he has a freaking clue just how much. "No. But you have," I bite back.

"It's moments like these that solidify the fact that you need someone to watch out for you. Your brothers were one hundred percent correct in taking that initiative."

I take a step toward him, placing my hand on his muscular chest from pure annoyance, as I push with all my might. "Back off."

"You're the one coming at me, little girl, not the other way around."

"I'm not little."

Oh, do I hate being referred to that way.

All my life I've been the baby of the family. My nose flares as I push harder. And harder. And—

Nothing. I don't even move this boulder of a man. Not even an inch. If anything, I'm just entertaining him.

I hear the car door open and smell the pungent scent of something more than just nicotine.

"Ya need my help, miss? Dis guy bothering you?"

In unison, Collins and I turn toward what can only be described as a walking stereotype—fresh out of a classic nineties movie. Between the sideways hat, the cigarette resting behind the ear, the stained white T-shirt, and the nasty scent of a skunk, I think there is no way in hell that Collins will ever let me get within a yard's radius of this once-a-pizza-delivery vehicle and this teenaged hoodlum.

And I know the junk-mobile used to be for pizzas because I can see the outline of an entire pie molded into the rusty side.

The boy clears his throat again and moves his fists to be in front of his face, in a self-defense pose.

"Is this some kind of joke?" Collins asks, taking in the scene and then looking at me for a reaction. But I don't give him one. Because what is there to do? I feel like I'm also being pranked.

"I've been practicing my moves," the kid says, slicing his fists through the air. "I made it to level seven in *Mortal Kombat*. That totally has to count for something."

It only takes one glance at the impromptu karate demonstration for my shoulders to quake. Then I double over, laughing so hard that I fall toward the pavement.

"Penny," Collins calls, squatting down to brace my landing. "What the hell is going on?"

I look up into his concerned eyes. "This explains why the ride was so cheap. I mean, from Hillsboro back to the city was only like twenty bucks."

"If you think I'm going to let you get inside the car with that crackhead, you've completely—"

"Don't touch her," the kid yells. "I also forgot to mention that I took the junior ninja training obstacle course at the local YMCA. Don't mess with me." He bends his knee upward, flicking his foot forward like a broken pendulum. Losing his balance, he stumbles backward, breaking his hold and crashing into the side of his beat-up vehicle.

I just can't stop laughing. Tears drip down my cheeks as I remain curled up in a ball on the driveway. "He's a ninja," I echo.

"I'm basically a badass to the first degree."

Not fazed in the slightest, Collins helps me up. He hands me my bag that managed to spill out a bit onto the driveway. I shove items inside in a hurry, careful not to miss any of the action. And then with calculated coolness, he turns to me, leveling himself with my face. "This is not up for debate. We are going to walk down to my SUV, and you're going to get inside without any type of argument. Understood?"

But before I have a chance to answer, Collins is already escorting me. I cringe as the kid starts to yell at him.

"I got ripped off. If you think I won't lawyer up, then you obviously have underestimated my ability to blow through my parents' money. I drove all this way and for what? To get cockblocked by the dude with the bigger vehicle. Classic. Just classic."

"Please don't get into a fight at my parents' house. Please," I beg, as I see Collins's shoulders tense. I already know who would win, and it's not the guy probably wearing cartoon boxers still.

"I can carry his body down the road first before my fist connects with his face. Would that make you feel any better?"

I look up at him, trying to evaluate whether or not he is joking. I can't tell. I know Collins is capable of joining and winning a fight. My brothers would never hire someone who wasn't prepared to get hit. Being wrestlers themselves, I'm sure they had a list of physical qualifications before choosing a bodyguard.

He opens the door for me, but I hesitate.

"Get inside."

"Quit being so bossy."

"Get in the fucking car, *Princess*."

Princess.

Any other time… By any other person…

I would have cringed.

But from Collins, I like it. And secretly, I'm wishing he would say it again.

And again…

I did refer to myself with the label Princess Penelope this morning at the coffee shop.

If the tiara fits…

"I need to pay the dude, even if I don't accept his service."

"I got it. Just get inside and do not get out." He eyes me sternly. "No matter how much blood you see."

"Collins," I snap, reaching for the door.

He shakes his head at me. "Just teasing, Pen. Now get in this damn car."

I climb inside, strap my belt on, and toss my bag onto the floor near my feet. The door shuts, and I turn to watch Collins walk back up the driveway, joining in a conversation with the taxi driver. I hit the button for my window to roll down when things look to be sketchy.

"No fighting on my parents' property," I chant, causing the men to back up from each other.

Collins hands over several bills from his wallet, never taking his sight off the kid.

It isn't until the beat-up car is barreling down the driveway that Collins makes his way to his own vehicle. I roll up the window as he gets into the driver's side.

"Well, that was fun," I mumble, trying to defuse the tension.

"You can't be pulling stunts like this again."

I whip around in my seat to glare daggers at him. "How was I supposed to know that the taxi service was a dud? Huh? Like this is somehow my fault?"

"It's most definitely your fault."

"No, it's not."

"Yes, it is."

"What are we—five?"

"You are doing everything in your power to not accept my help. So, yes, forgive me for being a tad bit heated and mad right now."

"Mad at me?" Is he for real?

"You've proven to me that you one hundred percent need a keeper. And if I need to improvise and change the protocol to deal with this…" He pauses as he struggles for the right word.

"This?"

"*Situation*."

My jaw unhinges, losing control as my mouth gapes open. "I am not a *situation*."

Collins looks thoughtfully out his window, and then, turning his focus back to me, lets out an awkward laugh. "You are right. You are the problem."

12

COLLINS

I can't even look at Penny. If I do, I'll say something I'll regret. I am that mad.

No, actually. That word doesn't even encompass the ferocious nature of my blood circulating through my body—pulsating and urging me to prove a point or make Penny see reason.

She doesn't know what I'm capable of if pushed hard enough. She doesn't even realize how much I reined myself in back there—for her sake. Sure, I can be calm and decisive. But challenge me like she did and…

I turn into a monster, an unrelenting beast of a man.

And I'm one people shouldn't cross.

There's a reason why the Hoffmans want me on their payroll.

And there's a reason why society says, "It's the calm and quiet ones you need to worry about."

My fingers grip the steering wheel so tightly that I may damage my knuckles in the process. I guess it's better that this object is taking the brunt of the abuse from my anger and not that poor spud's face.

What the hell was Penny thinking hiring some no-name taxi service? Is she that hell-bent on putting herself in danger just to prove her independence? She could have called her brothers if she didn't want my help. Her dad would have given her a ride, I am sure. But no. Instead, she basically defaults to the worst-case scenario with every decision she makes.

I'm so confused by her choices that I can't figure out if her naivety is a blessing or a curse.

If Penny were mine, I wouldn't let her get off this easily with a simple punishment. No. She'd definitely know her boundaries and where to not push me.

Fuck.

Mine?

When has anyone ever been mine?

I must be losing it. There's no other explanation for these impulsive, carnal thoughts flittering through my overactive imagination. That's what Penny does to me. She makes me react.

I pull onto the highway, leveling my breathing, as I come down from the high. I inwardly scold myself for getting this worked up.

"You seem deep in thought," I comment.

Turning in her seat, she glares daggers at me. "If I'm such a *problem*, then why even bother?"

Out of all the things said, that is what has her so hostile? "I—"

"I mean, seriously. I thought you could handle anything

and anyone. You're supposed to be this demolition man for my brothers and—"

"Demolition man?" I can't help but snicker, which only adds to her frustration.

"Don't interrupt me! Yet you get assigned this cakewalk task of watching little ole me. Maybe my brothers are punishing you with this obvious demotion. They are kinda passive-aggressive like that."

I chuckle over her word vomit. And just like that I'm no longer angry with her. She doesn't even have a clue what effect she has over me. If she did, I'd be in a lot more trouble.

Gathering her hair, Penny wraps the pink hair tie around it, twisting it into place. I can't evict the smell of strawberries that radiates off her body from my nostrils and also don't want to. It's a welcome scent in comparison to the ashtray-smelling boy she hired to give her a ride—probably into a ditch somewhere as he had a tire approaching flat.

The sun is nearly set, while the dark clouds roll in. We hit little pockets of rain as we get closer and closer to the city. It is weird having this state of peace right now on this drive, and I can't help but wonder if it is just the calm before the storm—figuratively and literally.

I glance over at Penny, take in her dress, the way her ankles keep crossing and uncrossing, and how her fingers can't keep still on her lap. With every glimpse I get of her feet, anger simmers through me over just how bad her blisters are.

Dammit.

I know better.

"Where should I take you, Penelope?"

"To the circuit court so I can change my name. Why must you insist on the formalities?"

I smile to myself over her outburst but ignore her question. Her mouth is going to get her into trouble.

Sassy little thing.

After several minutes, Penny shifts in her seat, reaching down to retrieve her phone from her bag. "Um, the address is 625 Monroe. Building is called—"

"Sky View Apartments?" I snap.

"Ah, yeah, how did you know?"

"Why the fuck do you need to go to an apartment building at"—I glance at the dashboard for the time—"seven o'clock at night?"

I rub a hand down my chin as it is starting to make sense. Her dress… The way she called a ride instead of asking me for one. Her secretive demeanor…

"You are going there to have sex with someone?"

Her body turns in her seat as her mouth drops. "What?"

She studies my face for any humor, surely never going to find any. This isn't a fucking joke. I'm definitely not laughing. If she thinks I'm just going to drop her off at some asshole's place so she can check whatever goal off her freaking goal sheet, I'm going to most definitely have a say about it.

So, don't look so surprised, shortcake.

"Sure," she says with confidence. "We'll go with that explanation."

I seethe in my seat, slamming my fist to the steering wheel. "I'm not dropping you off at some random person's residence so you can be taken advantage of."

"Then let me out. I'll drop myself off."

"Here?"

She crosses her arms over her chest. I try not to notice how her breasts get pushed out. I try not to notice how her bottom lip gets caged between her top teeth and how her pouty eyes are the most adorable thing I've ever seen. I try not to notice how my damn cock stirs, straining against the fabric of my pants.

Dammit. What the hell is happening, and how am I going to get this whole situation back on course?

"I'll just walk."

My eyes look to hers and then back at the road. "We still have eight miles to go. And it's going to pour."

"I can hitch a ride," she says smoothly. "Can't get worse than the guy I tried to hire that—"

"Are you trying to give me a heart attack? Because if you are, it's working."

"You are so annoying."

"So are you," I yell back with equal passion.

I continue driving Penny toward the apartment complex, not because I want to drop her off at some dude's place, but because I know she'll get there one way or another. At least if I break his hands or nose, then a trip to the ER will slow down this roller coaster's trip into the bedroom that Penny is so determined to ride on.

We drive in silence the remaining fifteen minutes, when I pull up to the Sky View parking garage entrance.

"You don't need to park, Collins. I can just hop out."

"I'm not just dropping you off, Penny. I know that but so do you."

She pulls out a tube of pepper spray from her bag. "I have protection."

How often has she been hanging around Angie? They both have delusions when it comes to protection. I let out all the air from my lungs. "In real danger, that wouldn't do anything but just aggravate the perpetrator. That's assuming you can get the safety cap off in time and not drop it on the floor for him to grab and use against you."

"Wow. You have little confidence in me."

If Penny knows what's good for her, she will put her pouting lip back in its original location. I don't have time for my fantasies to run wild right now—fantasies I'm going to go to hell for inevitably.

"Just sharing another perspective, that's all."

I think back to some of the poker nights where Graham shared how he discovered Angie carrying pepper spray early on in their relationship. I think he found it cute at the time.

I don't find this cute at all.

Penny is being irresponsible.

"Well, this is just backup until I can learn how to shoot a gun."

I can't contain my exaggerated sigh. "Learning how to shoot and actually carrying a weapon are two different things. I can teach you how to shoot. However, you will need a license and a permit to carry within the city limits."

And quite frankly, I'm pretty sure her stay at Soulful Mind disqualifies her in the state of Oregon. I'm hoping I don't have to research any of that and Penny just changes her mind.

"I would really like one to be in a lockbox in my bedroom. Like in a nightstand drawer or something."

I nod. I'm relieved she didn't say under her pillow.

It makes sense. Although, I worry over someone else finding the weapon. Being able to use a gun during a crisis requires quick thinking. Penny's trauma at the hands of Mark is probably spurring her need to feel safe.

And I want to foster that sense of safety in her.

"How about we start with some basic self-defense moves?"

"Taught by who?"

"Me."

"And you trust me not to use them against you when I get angry?"

"I trust you to try."

"But you don't think I'll actually do any damage?"

I clear my throat. "Self-defense is less about damage and more about escaping the threat. So if you go into any lesson hoping to learn street fighting skills, then maybe self-defense isn't for you."

"Fine." She exaggerates the one-syllable into three. "I'll try it."

My lips curl up over her agreeableness, which is rare for her.

But a win is a win.

I park the SUV, hop out, and open Penny's door. My breathing picks up as I anticipate what is going to happen once we get inside the building. Through the parking garage, we take the elevator up to the lobby, where an attendant is waiting for us to grant access. This is the main reason I love this building. The security is top-notch.

"Mr. Stone," the attendant greets with a smile.

I dip my head in a nod, glancing down at Penny as confusion makes little lines on her forehead.

You'll know soon enough.

We pass through the lobby to the opposite side where there is another line of elevators.

"Okay, you can go now," she says expectantly. "Please."

"No."

There's no way in hell I'm leaving now.

She turns to take in my strong stance. "No?"

"That's correct."

"Why are you making this so difficult?" she asks, visibly shaken over my unyielding nature.

After a long pause, she turns, marches over to the mailboxes and then to the side where there are lockboxes. She pulls out her phone and glances at the screen, scrolling through messages until she apparently finds the information she's looking for. Finding the lockbox she needs, she undoes the lock and pulls out a key.

I follow her as she goes back to the elevators and then hits the button for the eighth floor once we get inside. I guess I should be relieved that wherever she is going is not going to be some nasty place. This building is nice and well-kept. However, that does not negate the fact that she has only been back in the state of Oregon for a couple of weeks. That would have left zero time to make any real connection with anyone of the opposite sex. Whoever this guy is that she is meeting better be worth it, have his driver's license ready, and not look like a complete loser. Even then, I might just drag Penny out of the fuck-buddy situation kicking and screaming.

And I will. No problem at all.

Or maybe I can just embarrass the shit out of her and make this whole night turn sour.

I'm on a roll already of getting under her skin, so I doubt I have to provide much effort to continue on the trend.

"You are making this feel weird," she mutters, right as the doors open to let us out.

"Good."

Her nose scrunches up as she makes a face at me. I make one back. She laughs, and in return I laugh.

"You drive me nuts."

"The feeling's mutual," I say with a smirk.

I allow Penny to lead us down the well-lit hallway, stopping in front of 815. She places the key into the lock, turns, and then pushes open the door. I'm not exactly sure what I was expecting, but it definitely isn't what I find in the room.

Emptiness.

There is nothing inside. Just a bare apartment, with all of the normal amenities and appliances, polished and waiting to be smudged.

Even the walls smell of fresh paint.

"You aren't meeting anyone here, are you?" I ask.

"I'm not a slut, Collins," she snaps, looking over her shoulder to take in my posture and stance.

"I, ah—"

"You thought it. So don't even try to deny it."

"I'm sorry I implied otherwise, but you said in no uncertain terms at the Japanese Garden that your goal was to have unbridled sex." My eyebrows rise in challenge. "My intention was not to shame you but to just make sure you weren't doing something—"

"Stupid."

"Reckless."

"Which translates to 'stupid' in bodyguard talk."

"Penny…"

"Believe it or not," she says, "I have learned from my mistakes of trusting the wrong men and making rash decisions. The taxi driver was just an error of judgment based on an online ad. It was my fault but not something I plan to make a repeat mistake on."

I finally connect the dots. "So, this is your new place?"

Penny walks deeper into the room, spinning around to take in the entire space. "Sure is. Ain't she a beaut?"

"She sure is." But I can't take my eyes off the dazzling girl who is capturing my full attention with her rhythmic dance moves in the center of her apartment. She glides about like a ballerina.

Prancing over to the window, she looks out. "Breathtaking."

Sidling up beside her, I take a deep breath. "The view of the river is amazing. I never tire of looking at it."

I marvel at how the water ripples with each gust of wind. From up here, I can see rain starting to fall farther out, creating a misty fog along the horizon.

I follow Penny from room to room as she tells me about what she wants in each one. It is relaxing hearing her get excited over going furniture shopping and making this place her own.

My phone buzzes in my pocket. I pull it out to see Nic Hoffman's name across the screen. Sliding the bar, I accept the call. "It's Collins."

"Hey, man, my mom keeps calling me wondering why Penny isn't answering her phone. Is everything okay?"

I motion to Penny that I'm going to take this call out in the hallway, and then proceed to exit the unit. "Yeah, I have

Penny with me now. She actually just found an apartment and we are here checking it out."

"Oh, yeah? Where's it at?"

"Sky View."

Nic laughs. "Well, your life just got easier."

I would never equate those two things—especially right now. Nothing thus far has been easy. "From a security standpoint, I know this place is sound."

"And from a convenience standpoint," Nic interjects with a chuckle, "monitoring her just got vastly easier."

"Yeah, really."

I'd never tell him that everything about his sister is difficult. Granted, deep down, I think he already knows. Otherwise he would have hired someone with a less rigid demeanor.

"Okay, I'll let Mom know she's with you. She's pretty hard set on giving Penny space, so there's no need to let Penny know she's being checked up on."

"Noted."

"I know you have this covered, and I trust you to take care of my baby sister."

My tongue sticks to the roof of my mouth, as I think of all the times in the last couple of days where I've thought of Nic's baby sister in a less than professional manner. I'm the worst kind of human.

When I go back inside, I find Penny on the hardwood floor in the living room, lying on her back and moving her arms and legs around like a malfunctioning windmill. My feet cement themselves, as I can't take my eyes off her.

"Oh, hi," she greets.

Her hair is in disarray, getting tangled with every movement of her head. Her perfectly toned legs get more and more exposed—and I can't stop from wondering how they would feel in my hands as I press her against the hardwood.

Or the wall…

Or the table…

Or the mattress…

Or the shower.

I know Penny is fearful of men, but I'd show her great pleasure at the work of my hands. But being with me means pushing limits, as I'm a demanding partner. And I know she would never be ready for all that I'd have to give.

Rolling to her side, she takes in my stance, trailing her gaze up my body until it settles on my eyes. She looks like an angel, and her innocence is even more reason to keep our relationship fucking professional.

Penny is my client.

I am her bodyguard.

Her giggle pulls me back to the present.

I clear my throat. "What are you doing?"

"It's good luck to make floor angels in a new place. It's a ritual."

"I've never heard of it before."

"Oh, I just made it up. But doesn't it sound fun? Come join me," she invites.

How do I say *no* to that? We've been fighting for most of the day, and now that things are finally back to an equilibrium state, why would I want to rock the boat again and risk drowning in drama?

So I comply by lowering myself to the floor, lying opposite of Penny. I wave my arms and legs around, until she's laughing so hard a snort comes out.

"What?" I ask. "Am I that entertaining?"

"No, I mean yes. But you're doing it wrong."

"How so?"

"More enthusiasm. Get passionate. Think drunk quadropus."

"What's a quadropus?"

"An octopus but with four tentacles—obviously."

Her words make my eyes twitch. Penny's so stinking cute that I'm certain she is unaware of the effect she has on men. But I do what she requests. I lay my head back, and I go all in.

Snap.

Snap.

I lift my head and see Penny's eyes twinkling with mirth. She clutches her phone to her body, as the realization that she's taking pictures of me acting a fool come to light.

"Pennnnny…" Her name on my lips takes up more syllables with how I drag it out. She is playing with fire now.

"Hi."

Hi? Don't hi me. I sit up and edge toward her. "Delete them."

Moving to her knees, she scoots backward a few inches. "No."

"No?"

"I may need these for blackmail purposes," she answers seriously.

"Is that so?"

Her eyes widen and then without warning, she flips to all fours and starts crawling away from me—like she actually thinks I won't catch her. She turns to look back at me, only a few feet between us. When she sees what I can only assume is a sparkle in my eyes, she hops up to run—giggling and squealing—as I dart toward her.

I chase her into the kitchen, cornering her around the island.

"I promise I won't show anyone."

"Lies."

We move in a circle, both on guard—until Penny tries to make a dash for it. But I'm faster.

"Let me go," she says, out of breath from all the laughing.

Her body feels so soft in my arms, as her back is pressed against my front. Beneath my fingers, her heart beats rapidly. Wisps of her hair tickle my neck, as she tries to break free.

She is light—too light. It's as if I'm holding a delicate strawberry, afraid to press her too much and cause her to bruise.

I should let her go, but I don't want to. I want her to stay here just a little bit longer, so I can savor the feel of perfection.

"Please." I can tell she is pouting just from the simple word.

"Not until I get the blackmail material."

But then she goes limp, catching me off guard and wiggling free. She darts back across the room, giggling as I close the distance yet again.

She holds the phone in front of her, splitting her attention between me and her screen. "You better hope I don't post these on social media or upload them to some random dating app. Actually, that sounds so fun." She gives me a dazzling smile. "It could be a good way to get laid—if you needed help in that department."

I stalk toward her, ignoring her soft mewling protests as she pins herself to the wall of windows, never taking my eyes off her. "Do you really think it's wise to threaten me, when I obviously have the upper hand?"

"Who says you have the upper hand? I'm the one holding the—"

My hand thrusts forward, snatching the device so fast that Penny has no time to react. "And you were saying?" I ask smugly.

"Hey! Give it to me."

I turn my back, walking away. I'm privy to the passcode, but the last thing I need is to make that information obvious. Nic Hoffman is a cybersecurity genius, and anything digital that I need, he can usually retrieve. Sure, I'm overstepping a bit here with the only-use-when-necessary code of conduct, but having—

"Gotcha," Penny growls, jumping onto my back and trying to grab at the phone in my hand.

She can only weigh about one hundred ten pounds, but I let her think she has me. She hammers my back with her little fists, groaning after a couple of hits.

"If you are trying to hurt me, you are instead going to hurt yourself."

"Too late."

I give up on the photos, reach back, and pull Penny down to face me. I look at her hands, seeing that she will probably bruise tomorrow—or at the very least be sore. She is that delicate.

"Can you keep yourself from getting any more injuries today?"

"They are all your fault."

"How is hitting me *my* fault?"

"Maybe if you weren't built like a freaking ice sculpture of a Greek god"—she shoots me a glare with her angry eyes—"stop laughing at me. It's true. Anyway, I wouldn't have pain right now. So, yeah. This is your fault. And I'm pretty sure you don't have a soft spot on your entire body."

Oddly enough, I'm developing one for you.

Penny reaches out her hand, wiggling her fingers. "Gimme."

I hand over her phone, taking a step back.

She is unbelievable. Just when I think I have her all figured out, she turns the dial the opposite way and shows me a different layer. I'd be lying if I said I wasn't intrigued. Everything about Penny is interesting.

Her phone dings and she looks down at the screen. "Oh no."

I straighten my spine and check my own phone for notifications, seeing none. "What's wrong?"

"My momma just messaged me to tell me that there are a few road closures leading into Hillsboro. Apparently a storm blew through and knocked down a bunch of trees and power lines."

Both of our phones buzz, with what I'm assuming is a weather warning. "It's heading this way."

"Oh no. How am I going to get home?"

"You can stay with me at my place," I say, not really thinking of the logistics. I just know it's unsafe to be traveling in a storm, and the last thing we need is to be stuck on the road due to a closure.

"Where do you live exactly? Close by?"

"Very close."

"I can just sleep here."

"Penny…"

She gives a shrug. "I'm officially renting it after all. It's not like I'd be squatting."

"It's unfurnished." There's no way in hell I'd let her sleep on some hardwood floor in a vacant unit. Plus, if the storm is in fact coming this way, I want her close by me.

"My brothers live near here. They have guest rooms."

"You're staying with me and that's final."

I can tell she is thinking of more alternatives, but what she has yet to fully understand is that I'm stubborn as fuck.

Her teeth grind into a straight line, while she props her hands on her hips. "Fine."

"Isn't it fun just to be agreeable to my ideas?" I ask, my tone jovial.

"Oh yes," she says with fake enthusiasm. "Fun like a carnival."

I feel my smile getting even bigger, as I can't contain it from spreading. "Yes. See? You get it."

Penny's eyes roll, and if she wasn't so freaking adorable doing it, I'd call her out on her disrespect.

Just one glance her way has every cell in my body wanting to ignite.

What is this girl doing to me?

"Take me to your cave, Mr. Stone."

13

PENNY

"Where are we going?" I ask, watching as Collins hits the button for the eleventh floor. "Are you taking me on a tour of this building? It's going to probably storm, so shouldn't we vacate and not go on a joy walk?"

"Have some trust in me, Penny."

I do.

I don't want to admit it, but I do.

Collins is like the sun, a constant and consistent source of comfort—even though he seems to be driving me to frustration on most days. He's basically the most resourceful Boy Scout you would want to be stuck with in the middle of a disaster.

And deep down, I'm thankful he is here with me, and I'm not alone.

If anything, he's a man of his word.

He says what he means and does what he says. There are no hidden messages.

I find it oddly refreshing.

Collins studies me, and it causes a stirring deep within my abdomen.

It's his attention that unnerves me. No one has ever looked at me more than a glance, and here I stand rocking on my heels, while he seems to be memorizing all the parts of me that I have expertly hidden all these months.

His closeness knocks me off-balance.

He's an enigma.

A contradiction between known chivalry and potential corruption…

And I'd be lying if I said I didn't want to peel back the layers of Collins Stone and see what this man is all about.

When the doors open, I follow him out, then down the hallway. When he pulls his keys out of his pants pocket and places one into the lock, I'm dumbfounded.

"Coming inside?" Collins asks, punching in the code to disarm the security system on the wall.

"You live here?"

It's a stupid question—even I know that. Who the hell else's place would this be?

"I do."

"Just a few floors above my new place?"

Collins shrugs, removing his shoes and placing them perfectly on the rack beneath the bench. I toe mine off and haphazardly kick them toward their final destination, which is nowhere particular and wherever they happen to land. Shaking his head at me, he takes them and neatly arranges them next to his.

It's the simplest thing and yet there's something so spellbinding about seeing the two pairs side by side.

My eyes connect back with Collins's. "Talk about

convenient," I mutter, knowing his job has got to be easier now with me voluntarily this close.

I think about how he'll be able to monitor my coming and going. He'll know exactly who I invite over. And can even poll the neighbors about who knows what.

And then it dawns on me. "Hey!"

"What?"

My finger wags in front of his face. "Did you plan this?"

His lips curl up into a full-on smile, one I didn't even think his facial muscles knew how to form, it's that big.

He's amused. And the realization that I caused him that level of happiness warms me from the inside out.

But I have to play it cool. "Don't you dare smirk at me!" I poke my finger into his chest. Dayum, he has the muscles. "You did plan this!"

I knew it.

Taking several steps backward, he retreats from my accusation and makes his way toward the glass windows on the opposite side of the unit. I join him, feeling the coolness of the tiles under my bare feet.

My eyes focus in on a row of five little pots that are resting on a table.

Collins is a man of many things. Security expert… Neat freak executor… But a connoisseur of succulent plants was not something I could ever have predicted.

I'd be lying if I said I wasn't intrigued.

My fingers trail along the boney leaves. Maybe Collins does have a nurturing bone in his body. His plants are well cared for and, more importantly, alive.

A distant flicker of light has me peering out the window at the angry, dark sky. It looks like the clouds are about ready to explode with an epic temper tantrum. I just hope everyone I love is safe. It's going to be brutal.

"I'm a man of many skills, Penny," Collins says with a chuckle, "but predicting the future is not one of them."

"Then how?"

"It's a coincidence. I knew you wanted to move to Portland, but I didn't know where you would end up. I'm actually a bit surprised you found a unit so fast and signed rental agreements without even seeing the place."

"I looked at many places in the city before I went to college. I knew that at this hefty price point, I wouldn't be disappointed. But are you sure you didn't hack my Internet and make it so that when I searched for apartments, only the ones you pre-approved of popped up in some type of cyberspace magical voodoo? Stop laughing at me. I bet Nic would have those capabilities."

Collins tries to hide his grin by rubbing a hand over his mouth. "Maybe so. But you and I both know that Nic is a bit distracted right now."

"Yeah, I agree, but I still know what you all are capable of. I've seen the eyes on Angie and Claire. You all probably get alerts every time they pee."

He gives me a nod, not denying anything I spew. "Watching out for those we care about is a code we men live by, Penny. It's best you get used to it."

"But why do you care?"

I watch as Collins swallows, looking away but just for a second. "I cared the moment your brother found me and needed my services."

"So it's about the money? Maybe I can outbid my brothers and hire you to *not* watch over me."

He bursts out into laughter. "Are you really trying to bribe me, poach from your brothers, and renegotiate what they have already put into place?"

I peek up at his face between my eyelashes. "Is it working?"

"No," he states flatly.

I hold up two fingers, squeezing them together but leaving an inch. "But you are a little bit tempted?"

"No, Penny, and it's a horrible idea."

But is it?

I cross my arms over my chest. He is making me twitchy with anger. "Why is that so unreasonable?"

"Because I'm not doing this for the damn money, Pen. It's never been about that."

"Then why are you taking an assignment you obviously do not like?"

"Loyalty."

Damn these men and their secret code of conduct. "I just hate that I'm in the middle of all of this."

The loud cracking sound of thunder echoes through the room, causing my body to jerk.

It's amazing how it can still be heard through the insulation and thick glass of the windows—but it can.

Shivers run up my spine, as goose bumps form on my arms.

My attention goes back to the windows, watching the rolling clouds darken and explode with rain.

"Is the power going to go off?" I ask, but more to myself.

"It might. We haven't had a storm of this magnitude in a while, but most power lines are protected around here."

I hate the dark. My mental demons find me there. Hell, they have no problem finding me in the light as well.

A loud buzz simultaneously sounds coming from our devices.

Collins grabs his phone and opens what appears to be the radar, running a hand through his hair.

"What's wrong?" I'm afraid to look at my own phone, knowing it's an issued warning.

I can see all the color wash out of his face. "It's that, um…"

"No. Don't sugarcoat it." Worry fills my body. "Please."

Sighing, Collins looks down at his phone and then back up at me. "There's a possible tornado forming on the upper east side. It's best that we prepare for the chance of one forming here."

"Those are super rare for the Pacific Northwest."

Collins nods in agreement. "They are, but still possible. The coastal states basically get three or four a year."

"Why do you know so many things?"

He shrugs. "I love trivia."

As soon as the words leave his mouth, our phones buzz again with the automatic alert system warning us to take safe shelter.

I quickly open up my messaging app to text Graham and Nic to make sure they are safe at their places. They respond within seconds that they are home. "My brothers already know I'm with you?"

"Yes," he responds. *Of course they do.* "And safe."

"What should we do?"

"The best place to be right now is away from the windows and preferably underground. I'm going to go gather some supplies, and we will make our way to the basement. A building with this type of modern architecture is almost always safe, but it's best that we prepare for the what-ifs since we have the luxury to do so."

I bite at my bottom lip as I try to think of the last time we had a storm this big. I can't even remember. Collins grabs a backpack from the coat closet and starts tossing items inside. Bottled water, a few snacks, hand sanitizer, battery USB chargers, a pack of batteries, flashlights, and a fleece blanket.

I can't tell if this all is just extra precaution or if this is how he prepares to do mundane tasks like go to the grocery store.

"I'll go grab you some clothes," he says, moving toward a hallway, "if you prefer to get into something comfier."

Looking down at my sundress, I nod. I suppose I didn't prepare for a potential crisis when I chose to wear this. I'm sure our building will be fine, but no one wants to get hit by flying glass or sucked out the window if it does touch down.

My feet stay cemented in their spot on the tiled floor until Collins returns with an armful of clothing. Accepting his offering, I hurry into the bathroom to change. Thunder booms through the room, startling me and pressuring me to move faster. The lights flicker, hinting to the realization that we will probably lose power after all.

I pull my dress over my head, folding it onto the vanity. I slide into the gray jogging pants and powder-blue T-shirt —both several sizes too big. I tie a knot into the bottom of my shirt, shrinking it in size, and cuff over the waistband of the pants several times to keep them from falling down.

I quickly use the toilet, wash my hands, and fix my hair

into a messy bun. I join Collins at the door, slip on my flip-flops, and allow him to escort me out of his unit and into the already crowded hallway.

"We can't take the elevator," he says, opening the door to the stairwell and pulling me inside with him. "For one, I imagine other people are thinking the same thing. And also, it's not safe to be stuck there in a true emergency."

Groups of people are making their way down the concrete steps. We merge into the cluster, getting bumped into by the herd of people. He reaches for my hand, and I allow Collins to hold it as we descend to the next floor.

"You okay, Pen?" he asks, taking note of my appearance.

"I'm good." It's a half-truth.

By the sixth floor, I feel my blisters throbbing, and my breath is a staccato rhythm from all of the cardio. At least my mind is focusing more on the pain, rather than the way every random person bumping into me makes my skin crawl.

"Your feet."

"I'll be okay," I say, trying to keep up the pace with the cluster of people.

My phone buzzes in my pocket. It's probably another weather alert, based on the mere mass of people trying to get to the bottom floors. I wish I could look up statistics right now on tornadoes hitting apartment buildings and see if any have gotten destroyed. However, right now, I'm trying to stay calm and focus on getting to where Collins is taking me.

"I'm going to carry you."

"I'm fine," I say, groaning as someone accidentally steps on my feet. "Ouch."

"Put your arm around my neck, Pen," he instructs, slowing down just so I can do as he says.

When I hesitate, Collins takes initiative, scooping me up into his arms when we get to the next landing. I'm not sure how much I weigh, but regardless, Collins doesn't seem affected in the slightest. He is built like a statue, and while I have seen him shirtless at my birthday party, it's an experience having him hold me like this during a potential crisis.

He makes me feel safe. Like no matter what happens, he'll know how to handle it.

"Do you think Graham and Nic will be alright?" I ask, worried over my family.

Collins's smile is warm. "I'm certain of it. Your brothers know how to take care of themselves." He shifts my weight when someone bumps into us and shoots the man a warning look.

"It was an accident." My words come out jumbled. My fear is kicking in, thinking about what would happen if I didn't have Collins watching over me. I guess I would just figure things out like I usually do. It's just nice now not having to be alone, after I've been alone for so long.

The fluorescent lights flicker. I close my eyes and tuck my head into Collins's neck, trying to block out all of the panic. It isn't until I hear a door open and feel the cooler air hit my face that I open my eyes.

"We are going to the parking garage?" I ask, not seeing the logic.

"I have a special card that grants me limited access to

the underground parking lot. It’ll be safer and less crowded there.”

I nod and watch as Collins runs with me to another car parked in the lot—a Tesla—and places me into the front passenger seat. Through the access points to the outside, I just see darkness as the rain pelts the side of the concrete building. Whistling wind blows around trash inside the garage, making garbage cans tip over, spewing soda cans and paper about the area.

Collins slides into the driver’s seat and backs out. He follows the arrows leading us to the underground parking, which is more like car storage for the elite. I imagine residents store their nonseasonal vehicles here. Convertibles in the winter and trucks with snow tires in the summer.

Several other residents have the same idea, and I watch as more people join us in their vehicles. Collins lowers the windows, parking his car in a numbered spot.

“Nothing bad will happen to us, Pen,” Collins reminds me, cutting the engine. “We will just wait this out, and when the storm passes, we can go back up.”

I glance out the window. “Okay…”

“Listen I’m being way overly cautious, but I was hired to protect you, and this is how I am assuring that you are safe.”

“I’m just glad I’m not alone.” My words come out in an emotional rush.

My hand gets squeezed, and it’s such an innocent touch that it makes zero sense for the warmth to seep into all of my limbs like it is.

Collins looks at his phone. “I have zero Wi-Fi signal.

But Graham texted me to let me know that this should all pass in about an hour."

I nod. "Okay, good. Glad he's alright." I undo my seatbelt, stretch out my legs, and turn to look at him. "So, we just wait this thing out?"

"Yeah, basically. But I brought a few things to entertain us."

"Oh, yeah? Like what."

Reaching into the backseat, he unzips his backpack, removing a pack of Uno cards. "Care for a game of Uno?"

"I should warn you, I'm very good at games."

He wiggles his eyebrows. "I've seen you play before. I'm not worried."

"Hey!" I fake scoff.

It feels weird again, laughing with him. It's like the incident from the Japanese Garden never happened. It's as if I fabricated the entire event in my own head. My feelings haven't changed just from this moment of interlude, but it does give me hope that we can eventually coexist and be amicable toward one another.

I watch anxiously as Collins shuffles the deck and deals out our seven-card hands. With eyes full of determination, he examines his cards. I organize my stack, sighing over the fact that I have zero wild cards—the best ones in the deck. I do, however, have a crazy amount of plus twos.

"You first," I insist, looking at the yellow eight that gets turned over from the main pile that is situated on the center console.

Collins places a red eight on top of the face up card, changing the color of the playing stack. I follow it with a red two. He eyes me carefully, as if he can see my cards with some type of X-ray vision. Who knows, maybe he can. He appears to have a sixth sense when it comes to danger, and I play to win. To some men, that may be intimidating, but something tells me that nothing scares Collins. The man is fearless.

"Wild," he says cooly. "Blue."

"Unlucky for you. Get ready to start collecting some cards." I throw down a blue plus two, with a dramatic flare to my wrist, followed by a green plus two, and two yellow plus twos.

"I better mix up the deck more next round, because it seems to me you are a card shark."

I wiggle my eyebrows, as he finishes picking up all of his cards. When I no longer have any yellows or matching cards to add to the pile, I am forced to pick up from the main stack.

"Not so cocky now, are you?" Collins teases, laughing every time I groan when I get nothing of value.

"I feel like I'm being sabotaged."

When I finally get a yellow five to place onto the deck, Collins follows it with a yellow seven. I frown, and then start picking up cards from the main deck all over again.

We lose track of time playing back and forth, turning a short card game into the longest game I've played in a while.

"Uno," Collins says happily, making me jump.

I change the color to green and hope he doesn't have a match. But he does.

"Good game."

His smile is genuine. "Thank you."

Collins rummages through his backpack, pulling out a

bottle of water for each of us and some beef jerky. "Hungry?"

I accept the offering. "Yes, thank you."

We eat in silence, turning on our phones and checking the weather app to see if we have a signal.

Collins sighs. "Any luck?"

"It's weak and things are taking a while to load."

He continues messing with his phone, and then turns the engine on, rolling up the windows as the air conditioning kicks on. "There's a lot of hall movement according to my security system footage, so I think we are in the clear to go back up. Storm should have passed by now."

"I hope the elevators are safe. My feet cannot take any more abuse today."

Collins glances over at the floor, where my shoes have already been slipped off a while ago.

"You should soak them in a bath tonight."

"Can I get back home to Hillsboro, do you think?"

"No, Penny, you are staying with me until at least morning. I have space, and the roads may be flooded or closed along the way."

I nod, glancing at the clock on the dashboard. It's almost eleven at night. I could stay with either of my brothers, but I imagine getting there would be a challenge if there are downed power lines or emergency vehicles trying to get where they need to be.

Collins drives us back up to the main parking area, shuts off the engine, and grabs his backpack. He helps me out of my side, grabbing my hand to pull me toward the elevators. The wind is still whistling through the garage, but everything seems to be in good standing.

Collins hits the up button, which produces a weird buzzing sound. Then he pushes open the stairway door. Without even asking, he scoops me up, making me yelp.

"There's too many floors to be carrying me," I protest.

"You don't think I can do it?" he challenges.

"I, um"—my eyes flash up to the next landing—"no. I mean, I'm sure you can. But why would you want to? Seems excessive."

"I already feel horrible about your blisters, Pen. Just let me take care of you tonight, okay?"

I swallow hard. He's planning on taking care of me for more than just one night. That's the resistance I have, right? I want to do things on my own. I want to have a say in how I spend my free time. I want to do what I want, when I want.

Yet, it feels good to be cared for in this manner. Except it's…

Professional.

It's a job to Collins.

And I'm the job.

14

COLLINS

I can't remember in this lifetime if I ever drew a bath for someone. But here I stand with bubble bath in hand, making sure the water isn't too warm. It's the first time the tub will even be used since the new remodel.

I didn't buy all of this girly-smelling stuff either. All of the products were a housewarming gift from the realtor who helped me find this place years ago. I mean, things like soap don't expire, right?

Ironically, everything smells like the torturous scent of strawberries. It's the fragrance that reminds me of innocence —and Penny Hoffman.

She is going to fight me at every turn. That's what capable women do. They are stubborn as hell and resist help when they need it the most. She would have climbed all of those flights of stairs with her sore feet if I let her, never asking for help. That's just who Penny is. She's fierce, sassy, and determined.

I shut off the water for the bathtub, lay out another set of lounge clothes on the vanity, and place a new toothbrush on top.

Since living here, I haven't had a woman in my place, other than the designer who helped with the upgrades and my cleaning lady who manages more than just the dust. There's no weird comparison memories or flashbacks playing in my head right now. Yet, what I'm doing for Penny seems natural—as if I know exactly what to do to bring comfort to her.

I am a fixer. It's what I do. I anticipate needs and come up with the plan on how to deliver services. Granted, all of my other assignments were straightforward and the requirements were easy to execute. With Penny, I'm constantly thinking outside the box. Hell, I'm pretty sure Penny arrived carrying the box in her hands, basically crushing it so she'd never be tempted to hop back inside it ever again.

I hear the soft footsteps behind me and turn to see Penny resting her weight against the doorframe.

"You have a really nice place, Collins."

A smile forms on my lips. "Thank you. And you will too."

Her eyes look around at all the details. "I don't know. This place is pretty snazzy. I don't think the Furniture Depot is going to give me the same effect."

"I recently had some upgrades done. I can't even take all the credit in the styling, because quite frankly, I don't have style."

My eyes coast along the tiled features, the soft lighting, and the built-in storage units. Well, I had a say in the features but not in the cosmetic aspects as much.

"The floors are so nice."

"They heat on the cooler days, which will make it extra nice in the winter. I'm happy with the results."

Penny takes a step inside, trailing her hand along the polished edge of the vanity. Picking up her toothbrush, she turns it over in her hands. It's pink. I didn't plan for my spare box in the closet to have girly-ish supplies. But maybe my realtor was just being humorous with her gift—and a hell of a lot presumptuous. I never would have expected to need all of the supplies she gifted to me in a big basket. Sure, I could have gone out and hunted for them, but this is almost too convenient.

The more minutes Penny spends in my space, the more she feels like she belongs here.

"Are all of these things for your girlfriends?"

I laugh over her curious doe-like eyes.

If she only knew how far from the truth her statement really is.

I'm not a dating man, and I'm definitely not a Casanova. Sure, I know my way around the female body, but that is a skill set, not a lifestyle.

I can tell Penny's teasing, so I smile just to not make it awkward, yet I feel like I need to say something as well. "These items were gifted by my former real estate agent. There are no girlfriends, Penny."

It's true.

I prefer fewer-strings-attached arrangements. Those are better for all parties involved. Having some easy exit strategies keeps me calm and limits the potential for any drama that may result when things get heated.

If I want to fulfill a sexual need, I just hit up the club scene. Women there will volunteer. This isn't me bragging.

This is just how it is when you give just as much as you take. When you have a reputation for not being an asshole, it's easy to have your pick of women for a drama-free evening.

"Is that a personal choice?"

"As opposed to what?" I ask, trying to understand the motive to her questions.

I don't like being scrutinized. And yes, I get the irony.

Her shoulders lift. "Maybe you aren't allowed to date. My brothers keep you very busy."

"That's what you think?" I cross my arms over my chest, leaning against the vanity.

"I mean, it wouldn't surprise me."

"No, Penny. I'm allowed to have a personal life. I just choose not to have one that involves a girlfriend."

"And *why* is that, Collins?"

I let her question mull around in my head, trying to find some type of explanation that will appease her. Maybe all this time, I just assumed that women want a man who can be emotionally engaged with them and their relationship. I just have no interest in going beyond the physical with any woman. Even though the people I surround myself with are madly in love with their partners, it doesn't mean that I'm capable of that level of commitment.

Not anymore… And definitely not after being burned as badly as I was from a past that I can't seem to forget.

I'm just not the type of man who can love. I am too analytical of a person to allow my heart the chance to break in order to open it up to the possibility of the undefinable emotion.

I am a black-and-white type of person. I don't need

those fuzzy gray in-between feelings that muddle up the water that wants to stay clear.

The way Penny stares at me with expectation makes me wonder if we are cut from the same cloth—holding others to the same standard that we hold ourselves.

"I'll let you have some privacy," I say, ignoring the question. Nothing good can come from this topic of conversation. "There are extra towels in the closet. Help yourself to anything I have here, and if you need something specific, I can get it delivered."

"Thank you."

I can feel the tension building in my muscles, as I restrain myself from saying something stupid, or worse, inappropriate. It's bound to happen the more time we spend near each other, so cutting ties seems to be the only logical solution.

Heading out of the bathroom, I travel down the hallway and into my office. Even if we lose power in the building, I have a backup power supply. Luckily, the storm has passed.

My phone buzzes. Pulling it from my pocket, I see that it is the boss.

Graham: Everything still okay there? No power loss? Penny's fine?

Collins: All is well here. Putting Penny up in the guest room until her place gets furnished and until it's safe to bring her back to your parents'.

Graham: Thanks for taking care of her.

I swallow the lump in my throat. The guilt radiating through me is so extreme, it literally makes me nauseous. How am I going to avoid betraying the Hoffman family by being unprofessional? Can I even be around Penny and not break every boundary my traitorous body wants to cross?

It feels like I'm holding on by a thread of self-control.

Checking my email, I absorb myself in work and read the prison reports that get sent to me from some of my spy contacts. It pays to know a lot of people in this business who can give favors out.

It also helps that so many people fucking hate Mark Tanner and want to see him rot.

If his threats made to Penny during her visit had any validation, the Hoffmans would want to know. And while the brothers think they are just empty scare tactics, I'd rather be thorough and not underestimate the asshole—even from his prison cell.

The day that fucker takes his last breath will be celebrated like a holiday.

And to think of Penny testifying in her still fragile state? Never. I'll never allow it.

So, time is ticking on when Tanner can be snuffed out and it made to look like an accident or self-inflicted, and there's only so many opportunities where no one goes down with the sinking ship for conspiracy and manslaughter.

Graham and Nic are in the clear from testifying, and now that Angie is married, she's granted those same privileges. But Penny hasn't been awarded any luxuries, except for the fact that there's no way the men in her life will ever allow her to testify. We just have to keep fending off the lawyers who want to start the trial prep.

Too bad there's not going to be a damn trial.

My eyes start to grow heavy over the play-by-play of Tanner's day. I get a list of what he eats, how much, and who he has contact with when it comes to the outside world.

Oddly, other than Penny, no one has come to visit him.

It's as if anyone who may have been close to him either has already been handled or he really is just that unpopular.

When the drug ring was dismantled, Graham and Nic made sure I looked under every rock to find anyone connected with the predator. I scoured the earth for months analyzing digital records and a huge list of contacts until I took every single one of them down.

So it's not shocking that Mark has no one on the outside left to throw him a lifeline.

"Collins?"

I turn to see Penny standing in the doorway, her hair high up in a wet, messy bun on top of her head, while she is looking utterly adorable wearing my black sweatpants and old basic training T-shirt I refuse to discard. It's one of those pieces of clothing that I tell myself I should get rid of but never do. Now I want Penny to own it.

Her fingers trail along the bottom hem of the heavily worn fabric. "You were in the military?"

"I was."

"I didn't know that. So you retired?"

I'm not ready for story time. "Not exactly." I was discharged.

"Oh… What happened?"

I lock my screen and get up from my chair. "Did you find everything you need?"

She nods, changing her stance to lean against the doorframe. The outline of her body is even more visible in the dimmed light, as my eyes focus in on the threadbare fabric of my shirt, and my mind instantly floods with images of what she has on underneath the cotton—if she even has anything on at all.

Fuck.

These thoughts aren't helping me maintain the boundary line—that's for sure.

I'll never be able to look at that article of clothing again without fantasizing about Penny's perfect curves touching it.

Seriously though, the way she can transform something so masculine to look delicately feminine is mind-boggling. The girl can wear anything and make it look tantalizing.

"Can you please show me my room?" She shakes her head, as if trying to clear her mind, and in this instance I wish I could read it. "I mean, the guest room?"

It feels bizarre her referring to the room as a guest room, because she'll be the first person to ever sleep in it and will probably be the only one to ever use it.

"Come. I'll show you."

I slide past Penny, my arm brushing against hers. I watch as she shivers, and I inwardly smile that maybe she is as affected by me as I am by her. That if a brush of my arm can make her hair stand on end, then what will happen if…

Dammit.

I need to get my head on straight. I need to stop thinking about Penny sharing a room just yards away from my own. I need to stop guessing if she is wearing panties and a bra or wondering if her pussy has the scent of sweet strawberries just like her hair does.

I casually adjust my waistband of my pants, as every naughty image I have of my boss's little sister plays on repeat in my head, an endless loop of curiosity over what Penny would sound like if she were lost in a moment of release. Would her skin ripen to my touch? How would her body respond as it learns its commander?

I am going to go straight to hell.

And that would be a better place to be than having to endure the wrath of Graham and Nic Hoffman. I've actually exacted revenge on men that have done their loved ones wrong—so I know exactly what they would want done to me.

And it would be fucking painful.

Sure, I may not die, but being blacklisted from every type of job I would want on this entire coast, while knowing that I betrayed the two men who have given me a life, will probably be equivalent.

I push open the door to the guest room, allowing Penny to enter first. When I remodeled my unit, I never expected this room to actually get used, so the furniture and decor are minimal but functional. However, watching Penny's face soften, her eyes exploring the room, lets me see my place with a brand-new lens.

I think she likes it.

"This looks so nice, Collins." Her voice is breathy, as she takes in the space.

The bed is a queen, with a big, fluffy, white comforter and a pile of pillows. All of the furniture is in a modern black style, with clean sharp lines that draw the eye in. Now that Penny stands inside, it's easy to see what has been missing from it.

Sunshine.

That is Penny though. She's a bright ray of light, a contrast to the sterile monochrome theme that I've grown accustomed to accepting. Yet she looks good here, like she belongs in every inch of my once quiet, undisturbed space.

Sometimes you don't realize how lonely you are until you experience the comfort of someone else's presence. For years, I've been a solitary man. I go about my business, never bothering to rely on others. I dine out for one, order takeout for one, and expect nothing from anyone.

I'm not bragging. It sucks to feel this cold in my own place—in my own skin. That's what years of bitterness can do to a person.

Maybe it took Penny walking into my home for me to realize that it isn't a home at all. I have rooms. Sure, they are filled up with materialistic possessions, but there is nothing warm about the actual atmosphere.

I lean against the doorframe as I watch her hand touch the fabric of the comforter, squeezing it between her fingers. I hope she likes it. I never cared before, and yet I'm already contemplating buying her a new one if it would make her happy.

"Feel free to adjust the temperature of the room. There's a thermostat box outside of the closet. If you need anything to make yourself more comfortable, just let me know. I'm just down the hall."

With a nod, she jumps onto the bed, splaying herself out like a deflated hot air balloon.

She looks ridiculous and perfect all at once.

"This bed feels like an endless cloud."

I chuckle as I watch her roll around to her back, stretch

her arms out above her head, and groan out a yawn. My eyes narrow in on the bare span of skin exposed at her stomach, and I adjust my stance. She looks content, and that makes me smile.

How can I not be happy she is happy?

Liking Penny is the easy part.

Controlling my impulses? That's the impossible part.

The only way for me not to jump on the bed with her and tickle her until she begs me to stop is to walk away.

There's no way out of this situation that doesn't involve someone getting hurt.

"I'll see you in the morning, Pen."

"Good night, Collins."

Just the way she says my name is a signal straight to my groin, and I'm certain she has zero clue the influence she has over me. I'm still trying to make sense of it myself.

I head down the hall with my semi-hard dick straining against my pants. The only thing cockblocking me is my own conscience, and thankfully so, because I value my life.

I start to undress as soon as my door shuts, yanking my shirt over my head and throwing it across the room into the hamper.

Penny messes up the order of my perfectly constructed life—which I built for myself out of nothing. Growing up without love helped me to value the progress I've made at not becoming a statistic. I value organization, consistency, and predictability. I like to know what to expect and when to expect it. My mind and body thrive on control.

But Penny scatters everything.

She's the one person making me want things I told myself I couldn't have, wouldn't need, and didn't deserve.

Meandering into the bathroom, I wash my face and brush my teeth. Slipping on a pair of low-rise black pajama pants, I make my way into the bedroom, startled to find Penny in the doorway leading out into the hall.

Her eyes trail up my body like a slow, lingering caress, stopping at different landmarks along the way. Her eyes travel from the V of my waist, to my chest, to the script tattoo I have on the underside of my arm. She eventually stops at my twitching jawline—the one that won't stay still—as her mouth opens and then closes.

I reach up to rub at the back of my neck.

Does she like what she sees?

Penny tilts her head to the side, as if she's trying to figure me out. "I didn't know you had a tattoo."

"Plural. I have more."

"Hmm," she says with a hum, looking to the side of my room where my king bed rests. This is my domain—my safe place.

Her eyes connect with mine again. "How did I not notice when we were swimming at my birthday party? Surely I would have seen it."

I shrug. It's not like I try to hide it, but it isn't like I make it a point to show anyone. I never expected Penny to see it, especially when it is in a discreet place and often concealed if my arm is down near my side.

"Lilost?" she asks, looking for clarification.

I raise my arm to give her a better look since she clearly is curious. "Litost," I correct.

"What does it mean?"

I never thought my tats would be the topic of deep conversation, but it seems like Penny is intrigued. "It's a

Czech word that's actually difficult to translate, but it basically means to be tormented by the eye-opening sight of your own misery."

Penny takes a step closer, shortening the distance between us. My ink artist did a fabulous job with the lettering. Often, the clarity gets muffled over the course of time. I got this one done about five years ago, and it still looks crisp along the edges, and I never had to get it touched up.

"Wow," she says, reaching her hand out and trailing a finger along each letter.

A shiver starts in my toes, slithering up my legs, over my torso, and through my limbs. Penny is a devil in an angel's disguise. Does she know how freaking badly I want to pull her to me, cup the porcelain skin of her face, and make out with her pouty lips? I want her to know how a real man kisses and not these boys she probably will end up dating.

Ugh. That reminds me that she is going to go to that dating mixer event. How the hell am I going to be able to control my urges to tell her they all suck ass? I mean, I haven't met any of them yet, but I can make that prediction with almost ninety-nine percent accuracy. I know how men think.

They are dirty.

I am dirty.

Why the hell am I even worrying about this right now? It's not like I'm staying in this position. It's not like I have some claim over Penny—no one does.

"I want one."

My eyes slide to hers. "Hmm?"

She removes her hand from my skin, making me feel the void at the loss of her touch. "A tattoo. I want one."

I frown. The thought of Penny enduring the pain of the needle makes me cringe. "Why?" My question comes out harsher than I intend.

"I want to have the thrill of knowing that my skin is being branded with an idea all of my own choosing."

My hand twitches, thinking of other ways to brand her, mark her, and make her mine.

This sexual frustration has to be because I haven't fulfilled that need, that avenue, in too long. I could be lusting after anyone right now, and having Penny in close proximity just makes it easier for me to picture her in every corner of my life.

I need to get out of town. I need an outlet to channel all this pent-up aggression, especially before I start making mistakes I won't be able to undo.

"Your skin is too pure to mar with the tainting of ink." Unless I'm there to witness it and help her through the precipice of pain.

And unfortunately, I can't do that. I can't be the support system she needs.

Penny bites at her bottom lip and rocks on her heels. Confusion forms in her eyes. We both have gotten wrapped up in the moment, neither of us appearing to understand how we got to this place in time.

Has the universe lost its mind too or is this part of some cosmic plan—to put us together only to tear us apart?

"Did you need some—"

"Oh yeah," she interrupts and then glances off to the side, looking a bit sheepish. "Sorry. Um, I came here because I wanted to ask if you have a night-light. I know it's stupid, but I have a hard time sleeping when it's so dark in the room. I know I can open the curtains, but it just freaks me out too and…" Her words stop. She looks embarrassed.

It hurts me that she's still affected by the darkness of the past that must seep through the cracks in her waking thoughts. I can only imagine what evilness awaits her once she closes her eyes and drifts off to sleep.

I know therapy has helped with her coping with the drugging incident. However, memories and fragments of memories are ticking time bombs—waiting to come out and cause damage when she probably least expects it.

"No worries, Penny. I think I have one in the kitchen. Let's go check."

"I appreciate it," she says meekly, tears forming in her eyes.

"Hey," I say, pulling her closer to me, "it's going to be okay."

"I just get"—she sniffles—"scared sometimes."

I nod, giving her a squeeze as we walk into the kitchen. I release my hold on her to open the cabinet where I keep batteries, flashlights, and other random things. Everything is neatly labeled in bins for easy access. I find the package of night-lights, handing two to Penny, along with a pocket-sized flashlight.

"Is that enough?"

She nods. I can tell she wants to break down, and it tears at my heart to know she's ashamed near me. She never has to feel that way. I understand demons. If only she realized how alike we really are.

I lead her back to her room and watch from the doorframe as she finds free outlets for the lights.

"Good night, Penny," I whisper, taking a step backward in retreat.

"Good night." Her tone is sad, and I know I won't be able to sleep knowing that she is here feeling uncertain.

"Collins?" Her voice is barely a whisper.

"Yeah?"

Her shaky hands fix her hair, as she shifts her weight from foot to foot. "Do you mind sitting with me until I fall asleep?"

"I don't mind at all."

15

PENNY

“Thanks for the ride,” I say, as Collins pulls up the driveway to my parents’ house.

I take a sip from my disposable coffee cup that Collins picked up for me at a drive-thru on our way here, insisting I have something on my stomach. I’m learning how to pick and choose my battles with that man. I mean, the bacon and egg wrap was really delicious, so I don’t have a lot of room to complain over his bossiness.

Collins’s eyes scan over the house, probably looking for any potential threats. It’s how his brain must think. “No problem, Penny.”

“Thanks for washing my clothes and drying them from yesterday.”

He smiles. “It’s no problem at all.”

“And thanks for letting me spend the night.”

I hate this feeling of being weird around someone who is paid to protect me. I also hate that I asked Collins to stay with me last night until I fell asleep, only to find him camped out on the armchair the next morning.

How can an act be so intimate and we didn't even share the bed?

Do I talk in my sleep?

Maybe I drool or have other equally embarrassing habits.

Who the hell knows…

"Please call or text if you need anything."

"Of course."

"You mean that?"

"No."

"And this is why there are tracking devices…"

I make a face. "Ew, gross. I'm going to pretend you were joking."

"Of course."

"You mean that?"

He makes a face. "No."

Well, I guess I'm also going to need to scour all of my belongings for anything that could potentially be a GPS locator.

Fuck.

I exit the car, shut the door, and jog up to the house. I'm barely inside when Momma greets me with a big bear hug, startling me and making me drop my bag.

"Momma," I gasp.

"I was so worried over that storm. The roads and the power and the trees down. Not to mention the flash flooding. And you weren't here, and I was just scared."

This is what smothering feels like, and there isn't a darn thing I can do because I'm thankful someone cares.

"Collins took care of me," I say simply, trying to breathe from the force of her embrace. "No need to worry."

"Carrying you for nine months in my belly gives me the privilege to worry about you anytime I want."

I pull back and smile. "I'm fine," I promise. "Really."

"You keep growing up so fast that if I blink, I'll suddenly be old. And I know I won't age well, I just know it. I did one of those age zap things on this filter app, and I was appalled. Even my future turkey neck had a turkey neck. Life can be so cruel sometimes."

I laugh over her gift at keeping serious situations still lighthearted. "I'm going to go to my room and start figuring out what to pack. I got to see my new place last night, and it is going to be fun to furnish."

"Can you ask me if—"

"Momma?"

"Yes?" Her eyes are full of a hope I never want to diminish.

"I would love for you to help me shop." I give her another hug. "I have a hard time committing to colors."

Her squeeze tightens. "Oh yes, we can turn it into a girls' day. If you want, we can even invite Angie and Claire to tag along and go get our nails done and just eat comfort food and—"

"I am on board for all of that. However, I haven't met my roommate yet, so I don't want to overstep boundaries and pick out living room items yet that she may not like. Let's just focus on my bedroom."

"Do you know her name yet?"

"Not yet, but I'll definitely have one," I say softly. I'm

pretty excited to hopefully meet a friend who I can bond with and talk about guys with. It is hard to see Angie and Claire together and not long for a bond like that for myself.

Momma bites her bottom lip. "What happens if you both don't mesh well?"

"I can get out of my lease easily. The building doesn't have a problem occupying its units, so having that stipulation isn't going to backfire on them."

"Oh, wow, that's nice—and rare."

"That's why I jumped on the deal fast. I figure if it's a bust, I have little risk—other than all of the time I spent moving in. I'm still holding out hope that this will be a good match."

"You have to take that leap of faith sometimes, right?"

I smile. "Exactly."

"Well, are you free tonight to do dinner out with the girls and then hit up some of the boutique shops in downtown?"

I think over my schedule. The perk right now of not having a social life is that I'm free most of the time. "I think tonight will work."

"Oh, good. I'll text the girls to see if they are free, and if they aren't, we can still go just us."

"Sounds good. Thanks, Momma."

I make my way up to my bedroom, tossing my belongings onto the bed in a haphazard pile. I use the bathroom and then pull out my luggage from the back of my closet, placing it on the bed. I crank up the music on my phone, allowing the sound to play through the wireless speaker I have resting on my nightstand. I dance my way around my space, tossing in items I can't live without. I figure now is a good time to donate a bunch, plus keep a stash here in case I spend the night for holidays and other family gatherings.

Feeling sweaty from shaking my ass to Beyoncé, I take off my clothes and slip on my magenta bikini. I slather on sunscreen, dig in my nightstand drawer for a pair of shades, and then make my way downstairs.

"Oh, good," Momma says, "I may join you in a bit after I do some gardening."

I smile. "Perfect."

I pour some tea over ice in a cup with a lid, adding a straw through the center opening. When I get outside, the air feels smoldering. I pull out a float from the pool house, tossing it into the water. Situating myself on the steps, I carefully climb on top, surprisingly not spilling a drop of my drink. I twist my hair on top of my head and recline into the cushions.

I'm going to miss the quietness that Hillsboro brings. However, I'm also looking forward to living on my own. Well, technically with a roommate. I can't forget about her.

My mind drifts to yesterday and the revelation that Collins and I will be sharing a building together. How is that ever going to work? He doesn't even have to work hard to find me. Selecting that apartment for rent literally made his job a whole hell of a lot easier, but in return made my quest at freedom a whole lot harder.

Leaning up with my eyes closed, I take a sip of my drink and then settle back into the comfort of the cushions.

And I float and float, as the sun warms all parts of me.

I must have dozed off, because when I wake, Momma is getting out of the water.

"What time is it? I must have fallen asleep."

"You did," she says with a laugh. "I think it's almost three? The girls can meet us for dinner around five, if that sounds good to you."

"Sounds great," I say, taking a sip of my tea that is already past the cool stage. I slide from the float into the water, feeling the chill hit my heated body from my head to my toes. "I'm going to go shower so I'm ready for later."

"I will do the same. Glad we all can hang out."

"I am too." The more I get to know Angie and Claire, the more I like them. They are sisters to me, and in just a few days my employers.

Things seem to be falling in place for me. Maybe I'll be all right after all.

"Some storm last night, huh?" Claire asks, plopping down into the chair at the cafe that is situated along the water. "I'm pretty sure I ate all my feelings from the stress alone. I kept imagining I was going to give birth and that there would be no way of getting to the hospital."

"Oh no," I commiserate. I know how stress can eat at someone.

"You know people have given birth in their cars on the side of the highway, right? Like, that's a thing, you know? I can't even find my shoes in the car when I kick them off, let alone be able to find the baby if I were to give birth in one. And you know Nic would just freak. He threatens me daily that wrapping me in bubble wrap is still a viable option if I misbehave. Sheesh."

When she finally takes a breath, we all give her a sympathetic look. Nic warned us via text prior to Claire arriving that she has been having some extreme anxiety lately. She still has a while to go, and worrying about every little thing is not good for her or the baby.

Momma sighs, clutching her heart. "Oh dear, I trust my son would be able to handle any curveball that gets thrown his way. Here"—she stands up to grab the extra chair to pull it closer—"put your feet up. You need to relax." Momma glances down at her phone, buzzing on the surface of the table. She snickers at the message, turning the screen over and laying it again flat.

A growl escapes Claire. "He just texted you, didn't he?"

"Umm…"

"So," Angie says, clapping her hands together, "did Penny tell you she is going to work at Plus None?"

"I was there, remember?" Claire snaps, looking enraged.

"I was talking to Donna," Angie says smoothly.

"She did," Momma says with a smile. "I think that's wonderful."

I look up from the menu, glancing toward Angie and Claire. "I'm really excited."

"You are going to be a great asset to our brand," Angie says with pride.

I'm not sure why she has so much confidence in me. Maybe it's my last name and the assumption that I'll be stubborn and determined to get things done right. It's in the Hoffman blood.

"I think it's exciting you found your own place too," Claire interjects, taking a big bite of the bread from the basket in the center of the table. Maybe she was just hangry upon arrival.

"Well, I'm guaranteed a roommate. I just haven't met her yet."

"Luckily you get along with basically everyone, Pen," Momma says, making me smile. She is always so complimentary.

I lean over and give her a squeeze.

When the waiter returns with waters, another basket of bread, and cold strawberry soups, we place our main food orders—mine being a spinach and goat cheese salad with fresh mandarin oranges.

"So, Penny," Angie says, "your brother was telling me that you were in the city when the storm hit."

"Yeah, I was given access to my apartment and was checking it out. I got all of these warnings on my phone to take cover. Collins was with me because"—I motion with my hand—"well, I can't drive yet. Anyway, there was no damage to the building, and I was glad not to be alone."

I watered down the entire story, but how do I tell them that I have a bit of a crush on my secret bodyguard? How do I tell them that even a brush of his hand can cause me to want things I spent a year thinking I would never want again? Sure, I flirted with a couple of the workers coming in and out of the facility while in Seattle, but I was really just testing the water—desperate to rearrange my emotions to mimic something that looked normal.

That's all I want for myself. I want normal.

Nothing about Collins Stone is normal though. Just the way he stayed with me last night—without expecting anything in return—is not normal. Guys don't do that. Bodyguards don't do that either. I doubt he ever spent time in either of Angie or Claire's bedrooms. Sure, I was at his place, but he could have easily retreated when I finally fell asleep.

But he stayed.

Plus, he is older—a lot older. So no wonder why every time I look at his hands, I imagine him knowing what to do with them when given the chance. He's probably been with dozens of women.

"For those of us who thought being alone was inevitable," Angie continues, "it's a wonderful feeling when you let down your guard to allow someone in."

Her words hit me harder than I think she intended them to—but I'm not letting Collins in. I'm actually trying to push him out. He's the roadblock I'm trying to avoid right now. And based on everything he divulged back at his place, I doubt he'd ever want more with anyone.

Maybe Collins is being tortured by his own misery. I mean, why would he get the type of tattoo he did without it having some sort of symbolic meaning at the very least?

Claire makes a disgusted face at her best friend, drawing my attention back to Angie's sweet declaration. "Barf. Vomit. Ugh."

"Why? Just why?" Angie asks, as we all laugh.

"Love sounds good on paper," Claire explains, glancing at her phone. "But this man of mine"—she turns to Momma—"no offense, Donna, but he is going to send me straight to some island where all they serve is chocolate pudding and is free of any person sporting a dick."

"Being offended is a choice I never choose," Momma says nonchalantly.

Turning to Claire, I ask, "Why? What's going on?"

"Apparently Nic and Graham have taken it upon themselves to buy the ten top-rated video baby monitors on the market." She holds up her phone to show us a picture of the devices arranged on the floor. "From around the world, mind you. And they are now trying to hack into each of them to see which has the most superior firewall."

"Can you say nerds?" Momma asks, making us burst out into laughter.

Claire points to the corner of the photo where there is something lying on the floor. "See the baby doll? That man is obsessed. One night I caught him practice burping the thing."

"That's cute though," I croon, holding my hands over my heart.

"Then the head fell off."

Momma shakes her head, leaning back in her chair. "I thought for sure I raised more well-adjusted men. Those two are going to drive me to that island with you, Claire. But I'll need all the dicks. Big ones. Like an entire bag of them."

"Momma!" I scoff. And she manages to look innocent. I just can't with her.

"Come on, Penny," Claire pouts. "You'll come to the island too?"

"Count me in," I add without hesitation. "I could get used to daily doses of chocolate pudding."

"Good. But I'm serving it with pickles."

"That's nasty, Claire," Angie says, making a face. "And I didn't even think you like pickles."

"They aren't for me." She pats her stomach. "They are for the uterus inhabitant."

It feels good to laugh, to cry from laughing, and to just…

Be myself.

Asking Momma to help out with interior design work is basically like taking a kid to a candy store. She's on a high, walking around the store, feeling up fabric and looking at us girls for an appropriate reaction—which none of us must give her because she scrunches up her nose and then sighs in true Donna-drama fashion.

"Just pick something, Momma," I say with as much calmness as I can fake. "Everything looks amazing in here." And it does. I'm having choice paralysis basically.

"I can't just *pick something*, Pen. This is art."

I turn to Claire and Angie. "Well, I must suck at art."

"Us too," Angie laughs. "I would have settled on Dave's Discount Furniture but was afraid to suggest that."

We are camped out on the display living room set, surrounded by vases of fake flowers, French macarons in glass bowls, and throw pillows fit for a queen.

"How much for the macarons?" Claire asks, her tone serious.

"I think they are just for show," I answer.

"So, I can eat them?"

"If you like plastic," Angie giggles. "They are fake."

Claire picks one up, turns it around in her hand. "Huh. They sure look real."

"I think that's the whole goal," I add, stifling a giggle.

"Seems like the shittiest thing I've ever seen. Talk about a tease."

Momma takes out her phone and snaps some pictures at various angles. "I think I found my vision."

"Oh, good, because I think the store is closing soon," I respond, relieved that this outing is going to come to an end. I knew going into this adventure that my feet would hurt, but I didn't expect just how much. My blisters are going to be raw at this rate.

I'm messing around with my phone when I see a new message pop up onto the screen. It's from Collins and it looks as if he sent me an image.

I open up the message and see a picture of the guest room at his apartment and my hair tie resting on the nightstand and his finger pointing to it. I send back a laughing emoji in return. I honestly have no idea how I can keep leaving my ties all over the place. First in his car, then in his apartment. I must be the reason they sell them in packs of one hundred.

Momma clears her throat, causing us girls to look up. "Everything is all set, Penny. We are good to go."

"Yeah?"

"Yup. Delivery is expected in the next five business days. You'll get a text confirmation with a window of time you should be at your new place to let the delivery people inside."

I nod. "Thank you, Momma. I really appreciate it."

"I would do anything for you girls," she says, bending over to give each of us a hug.

"Where to now?" I ask, getting up from the comfort of the display sofa.

"I'm hungry again," Claire says, her tone serious. "And before any of you make a snide comment on how I'm"—her face distorts and her voice changes pitch—"*letting myself go*, it is the macarons' fault."

"Snacks it is," Momma announces, causing us all to laugh.

16

PENNY

I am jamming out to Grace and Jace's upbeat album they put out two years ago, feeling the pangs of nostalgia to a time when I was living my best life. I mean, anything has to be better than the doom and gloom feeling that flutters into my conscious thought when I find myself alone.

This is why I listen to music so much. It helps me to feel less isolated.

Puttering around my apartment, I struggle with what to clean next.

I'm running out of stuff to do here without officially moving in, and I'm growing bored. It's pointless getting too settled yet without the addition of furniture, so I spent the better half of the day grocery shopping at the store next to the building and stocking the fridge, cupboards, and pantry with the essentials.

That's the perk about living in the city—everything is relatively close. As much as I want to learn how to drive, I don't really need to yet. Nothing is urgent, except for my desire to feel productive and successful.

I twirl around the space, allowing my skirt to flare about around me, when I hear a light knock on the door, followed by the doorbell. I prance over to the door, check the peephole, and then try to contain my excitement when I see a girl waiting patiently outside. Yes. Finally.

Pulling open the door, I give a polite smile. "Hi. I'm Penny."

She looks confused. "Hi." She pushes back her hair, smoothing it behind her ear. "I'm…" She gets distracted by the music blasting through my sound system.

"My roommate," I finish, nearly bouncing on my feet. She looks harmless and friendly—both plusses. "Do you want to come in?"

"Actually…" She looks around me to see our unfurnished place, and I instantly want to tell her that we can fix it up the way we want. And then she clears her throat and says, "I'm just delivering this"—she hands me an envelope —"for you."

"Well, that's super embarrassing."

Of course, now I see her shirt with the Sky View Apartments logo.

"Aw, don't sweat it. Can you sign here? It's certified mail."

Scribbling my signature, I mumble, "Thanks."

I wait for her to leave before tearing open the envelope. Pulling out the card inside, it has one word written on it —One.

Weird.

What was the point of going through the trouble of delivering something so uneventful?

I didn't even think anyone knew I lived here yet.

Looking closer at the envelope, it has my name on it, along with my new address.

Knowing that most people get more junk mail than real mail, I place it into a bin in the kitchen that I'll start designating for the shred pile.

And then I take the card out and decide to use the back of it to make a shopping and to-do list.

As I brainstorm about the things I still have to do, I remember my other responsibility—maintaining my outpatient therapy sessions.

When I left Soulful Mind, I promised my brothers I would take part in a program. Basically it was a stipulation for being released from the facility.

I don't want to do it.

Talking about my feelings is not something I particularly enjoy. My counselor's favorite phrase is—How does that make you feel?

At the time, when I was first brought into the facility, I wasn't sure how to feel. So many months were spent with Mark on the loose—terrorizing my family members. He haunted my nightmares and still does.

But now he's in prison. While that is amazing, as long as he takes a breath, I know that he can still have an influence on me. He knows he still has one over me, too, and said as much when I visited him.

I should have never gone to the prison.

I hate him more than anyone else on this planet.

So, how will therapy fix any of these growing feelings

of anger? Answering the question—how does that make you feel—is lame.

Like, how would anyone feel after being drugged, their memories being foggy and incoherent, and then to have their predator gloat from behind bars?

My brothers claim I won't need to testify at trial. But how will Mark Tanner's body stay behind bars without my testimony? Or Angie's?

Angie might be strong enough to endure the cross-examination, but I know I won't. And with her being married to Graham, who has special connections to the whole take-down operation, she won't need to confess anything.

And Graham won't allow it anyway.

He says he won't allow me on the stand either…

But what if he's wrong? He may think he has control, but I've seen too many criminals get released when all the evidence led straight to them.

Mark Tanner's release will not be the plot twist in this story.

Hell no.

So the lawyer team is right. They need me.

Unfortunately, I could jack this whole thing up. I know I'll cave at the first sign of tension. I'll spiral out of control mentally if I'm forced to try to relive the nightmare.

But I'll only be reliving what the pieces of the puzzle allude to—because I can't remember much from the horrible night.

And maybe that's why my brain is protecting me by not remembering.

Maybe recalling the horror will cause me to slip right

back into the hellhole that got me sent to a therapy facility in the first place.

So in order to keep functioning in the real world while Mark Tanner awaits his trial, I'm going to need to make the effort to hold up my end of the bargain and attend a session. It's already set up. I just need to show up.

But showing up is the hardest part.

Looking at the clock, I worry I'll be late.

Grabbing my purse, I run down the hallway toward the elevator. I hit the button and check the time on my phone. I should still be okay.

When the elevator doors open, I step inside and am shocked to find a man there. My heart stops as I glance to his scarred hands, wincing and squeezing my eyes shut. Shit.

Why does this keep happening?

"Miss?" His voice is gruff. Deep.

"I, um," I stutter. I take a couple of steps back, only opening my eyes wide enough to see the floor, as my neck refuses to gain the strength to pick my head back up. "I'll take the stairs."

I pivot and rush into the stairwell, instantly feeling the pangs of claustrophobia.

And utter embarrassment…

Taking five deep breaths, I try to settle my growing unease.

This is the prime example of why I need forever therapy. It's because I'm a freak, and deep down, I doubt I'll ever be whole again.

It doesn't matter where I am—Mark will find me. He's

haunting me like a ghost, looking for a host to give that nightmarish night back its life.

I don't want to keep being his victim.

I force myself down the stairs. And when I finally get to the lobby, my blisters are crying from the abuse.

"Miss Hoffman," the lobby attendant says. "Can I please help you?"

Adamantly, I shake my head. "I'm just a bit overwhelmed. No cause for alarm."

The person behind the welcome desk joins his coworker, squats down beside me as I slump into the oversized chair. "Miss? Can we get you anything? Water? A snack?"

No. And the fact that these two workers already know my name is alarming enough, and they could very well be on the bodyguard squad's payroll. Just your everyday heroes saving one panicked girl at a time.

Feeling like a loser, I peel myself off the cushions, give the men a reassuring smile, and then walk over to the water dispenser to pour myself a cup of chilled water. I don't even think I drank anything today.

Glancing outside the main doors, I see the scarred hands man enter into an awaiting taxi. He didn't deserve my horror, and the thought that I caused him emotional harm makes my stomach twist.

Not every man I encounter is Mark Tanner.

Not every person with scars is Mark Tanner's minion.

Feeling the need to move, I make my way outside into the fresh summer air.

"Miss Hoffman! Please…"

I turn to see the apartment building worker shadowing

me. This is just obnoxious. "Yeah?" I need some time by myself.

"I'm under strict"—he pauses where the word *orders* should have been said which only adds to my suspicions—"I would love to assist you in any way and to see that you have safe travels. If you could simply afford me the opportunity to adequately do my job, then…"

"I'm going to walk," I say with certainty.

The worker keeps his irritation at my refusal in check, teetering most likely on the edge of dropping his professional facade and going straight to military tactics. Collins and my brothers only hire the most drill-sergeanty people.

Every ounce of his willpower is being challenged, and I'm the one delivering the test. I watch the vein in his neck as it pulses manically, momentarily distracting me from my initial fight.

Without being granted permission, I walk down the street and into a nondescript commercial building, leaving my entourage behind.

The good thing about my therapy sessions in the city is that they are discreet and held in a rented-out office space—not a facility with the huge title blaring across the door. I can slip in and out of my session and not feel like everyone knows what I'm doing.

There shouldn't be a stigma over caring for your mind—yet there is.

Sure, my entire family knows I need to partake in my recovery protocol, but I don't need them involving themselves in my matters anymore or the entire world finding out.

I don't need a caregiver, and I sure as fuck don't need a bodyguard.

Having that level of eyes on me just freaks me out.

I hate feeling like someone is watching me.

When I enter Room 536, Margo is waiting for me. I'm a few minutes late, but I doubt she'll say anything about it. No one wants to rattle me or make me snap. It's annoying.

Margo and I met prior to my discharge to get acquainted while still in Seattle, so I'm already at ease.

"Glad to see you, Penny."

I give a small smile. "I'm just following the rules."

Margo lets out a laugh. She doesn't look like the typical therapist one would encounter, and I've seen enough of them to know she is different.

Maybe that's why I like her best. She doesn't put up with my crap.

"So you came for a sticker on your reward chart. Got it."

I shrug and then full-on giggle. "Only if they are the good kind. I want the ones that are scented."

"Only the best for you," she agrees, and I instantly relax. "Take a seat."

I join her across from a round wooden table that overlooks the city. The building is full of start-up businesses, a coffee shop, and a marketing company. Any empty space, I assume is for things like this—freelance meetings.

Getting comfortable, I cross my feet at my ankles and settle in as much as I can for a medium-tier office chair.

"How have things been going?"

My shoulders lift in response. "Okay."

"Just okay?"

"Yup. Just okay."

"So they suck."

I give Margo a look. "Some days, yes."

"And how does that make you feel?"

"Oh, I love it. Sucky days are my fave."

"Penny…"

"Margo…"

"You need to work with me."

"You need to ask better questions, because if you only knew how badly I don't want to be here, then you might consider making it worth staying."

Margo leans back in her chair. "Why are your days sometimes sucky?"

"Because I feel like an outsider in this world."

"Hmm…so do I."

"Well, that isn't helpful as my therapist."

"Isn't being honest the number one road to success?"

I shrug. "I guess so."

"Then I was just being honest. But are you?"

We go back and forth on our banter—seconds turning into minutes—and then finally the dam breaks and I burst into tears, sharing how every man who resembles Mark makes me freak. I explain that being in a closed-in space with a stranger—specifically a man—freaks me out. I express the fear that I'll never get over him and how stupid I was to visit him at prison. That entire trip there was a disaster waiting to happen, and I did that to myself.

Because I'm a masochist.

I share that I think I left the facility too soon but I'm too in love with not being there to ever go back.

I spill it all… Every fear. Every panic moment. And

every bit of false hope that the future could be somehow different.

We talk.

I break.

We talk some more.

And once my tears have dried up, I don't even realize that seventy minutes have passed—twenty minutes past my session limit.

"I'm proud of you, Penny. You did amazing today."

I want to snap back for her not to patronize me. I want to respond sarcastically. I want to make some silly joke.

But I don't.

Because I'm proud of me too.

"So now what?" I ask. "What should I work on?"

"You work on walking into your future as a warrior who has done battle but has already won."

"Umm, how do I do that?"

"You make a goal list of the things you want, and you start conquering them off that list one by one."

And who would have thought I was the overachiever without even realizing it.

I nod. "I can do that."

Margo levels with me. "Of course you can. Because you are stronger than anything that has happened to you in your past. It's not about forgetting those memories. It's about forgiving yourself for what you think you failed at. You didn't fail, Penny. You persevered."

I persevered.

"And maybe get some guy friends. And rewrite your brain from thinking all men *are* assholes to all men *have* assholes."

"Ha… I'd be happy with a female friend first." It's on my goal list after all.

"Baby steps."

"Got it."

After Margo and I say goodbye, I head out of the building and decide to go for a walk at the river. At least I'm not too late to enjoy the sunset on the water. Picking up food from the food truck that waits in the same place every single day, I enjoy my Mediterranean rice bowl.

I have what I want—independence.

And yet I am consumed with a fierce loneliness.

I miss Collins.

17

PENNY

I nearly dump an entire marshmallow-flavored cappuccino all over myself on the way into Hoffman Headquarters. It probably doesn't help that I'm also juggling my box of desk essentials that I picked up on the way here. And by essentials, I mean anything random that caught my attention. Plus, I included all the normal items like a desk calendar with motivational messages, a bedazzled gemstone stapler, and a little heart-shaped picture frame with a photo of my family inside.

My job wasn't supposed to officially start yet, but after giving it more thought, Claire and Angie wanted to transition me into the office. Having my own desk was unexpected since I expected to mostly be modeling.

I'm honestly thrilled to have something to focus on other than overanalyzing my forward progress with therapy and all the backsteps I have taken. Despite just starting it recently with Margo, I already feel overwhelmed with the case of what-ifs that I doubt even she can control.

What if I'm not fully healed?

What if I get sent back to the center?

What if I'll never get over my past?

What if there doesn't exist a guy who will understand that I'm a product of my trauma?

But I am here. I got out of bed this morning and ate a non-sugary breakfast and made the choice to not be afraid of my own shadow—at least not today.

Today is full of new possibilities. And being here feels good.

It feels *right.*

I even got through security and check-in without an obvious escort paving the path. It feels invigorating to finally have some independence and do something on my own. Maybe Collins took the hint, or better yet, got reassigned.

One can only hope.

That man has the charisma of a hungry lion. And yet, I think I would miss his looming presence. He's different from all my other guards in the past. He's smarter than they are and more thorough, which is probably why I find it so odd that he isn't here now lurking in the shadows.

I glance around the space. Or perhaps he is and is just really good at hiding.

Regardless, I feel empowered and ready to take on new challenges—no matter who is or isn't watching it live.

I don't need a babysitter anyway, and having a watchdog here will only make it feel like I got this job because I'm family or because it would be way easier to keep an eye on me in my brother's building than if I were to work elsewhere.

But I can't get inside my head. I need to walk with purpose and with poise.

Just like a model…

There's no space for self-doubt in my life today, at least not when I'm on a high from the unexpected need for me to be here in the office.

But maybe a little self-guided pep talk could do me some good, like it has in the past.

I can do great things.

I can be an asset to this company.

I can prove to the world that I can triumph even in the face of adversity.

Rolling my shoulders back, I take a deep breath.

Just don't get fired.

I can't imagine how awkward family gatherings will be if I get fired or know I should be fired but am kept on payroll out of guilt. I'd just resign if it were the latter.

I take the elevator up to the correct floor and resist going to Graham or Nic's offices to harass them about hiring me a secret bodyguard who isn't so secret. Honestly, if there hasn't been a conversation about the whole thing yet, then there's no point having one now.

What's done is done.

Graham and Nic must really just think they pulled one over on me.

Oh well, it's better for everyone to think I'm clueless or naive. It makes ditching my watchdog easier when I really need to get away.

When the elevator doors open, I step out of the car, walk down the lounge-like corridor, and then enter through the main doors into Plus None.

"Penny, I'm so glad you could come on such short notice," Angie says, giving me a hug.

That's definitely the pro to not really having anything else going on in my life, which is basically sad if I overthink about it too long.

Several other employees glance over at us. But I shove down any feelings of trepidation over anyone thinking of reasons why I've been hired in the first place. Everyone seems nice, and I don't need to taint that opinion with negative self-talk.

Angie takes the box from my hands, glancing inside at all of my random things.

"It's too much, isn't it?"

"Oh no. Of course not." She studies the box of some of my gadgets. "I love the sand tray and the little desk fountain. Oh, it has mood lighting—nice."

I'm second-guessing all of my purchases and silently vow not to shop again while under the influence of too much free time.

The truth of the matter is, I don't have an official style. For years, I would allow Momma to pick out my clothes and organize even my own bedroom.

In a way, I figured she'd do a better job, so why bother when she was willing to make my space look great and enjoy doing it?

And it did look great.

But after being discharged from Soulful Mind, I realized how short and fragile life really is, and through that self-reflection, I'm starting to see that it's okay to not have everything figured out.

"I wasn't expecting to have a desk."

Angie gives me a half squeeze, while trying not to drop anything. “Of course, you’ll have your own space. And I know you’ll make it your own.”

I look at my box of items as she places it down on the empty desk that already has a Penny Hoffman engraved name holder. At least I stuck to a theme—controlled chaos. I unload a few items, rotating them to see where they’d look best next to a modern desktop computer. “I may have gone overboard.”

“Impossible.”

“You’re just being kind,” I say with a little laugh.

I have fun sorting through my purchases and find the perfect location for my little Zen garden sand tray that has little glass pebbles.

“You know, everyone in this office is either going to steal that one or demand you tell them where you bought it.”

I rake through the sand, creating little ravines. It really does have a relaxing effect. “It clearly is my best purchase ever,” I joke and hand over the rake for Angie to use.

There’s a few people in the office working, but they all have headphones on and appear to be deep in thought. Despite taking a moment to look at me when I first arrived, they all seem to now be in work mode and not paying me any attention.

I like it that way too. I’m not one who enjoys being the center. I’d much rather stand on a sideline.

Angie glances at her watch. “If you don’t mind, I have a few things to discuss with you before Claire arrives.”

I swallow the spit pooling in my mouth. “Okay.”

She smiles. “It’s not that I want to go behind her back,

but I bet she'd feel more comfortable as a result of my efforts in hindsight."

I know Angie is coming from a good place, so I don't feel anything but gratitude that she would want to include me in her discussion at all.

Angie guides me over to the sofa section. How cool is it that a corporate office—one I'll now be working in—has a section for relaxing and brainstorming? Everything about this place lives and breathes warmth and inclusion.

I'm obsessed.

The dress code is relaxed, yet everyone appears to choose to be professional. Living plants rest on stands and in pots near the windows. And there's an amazing lounge that is stocked with healthy snacks.

I really could get used to this.

Angie and I each take up a sofa.

"So, I've been thinking…"

I cross my legs at my ankles. "Okay…"

"I know the original plan was for you to model for Plus None, and that's still definitely something Claire and I both want. But the work is sporadic and is centered just around photoshoots and not as much the office."

I nod, trying to predict what she's going to say next.

"With Claire going on maternity leave later this year—at Nic's request, not hers—I would like to have employees be more versatile."

"Of course. That makes sense."

"Although, I imagine once Claire holds her baby for the first time, she may completely jump ship and enter the stay-at-home mom life. Anyway, I'd like to get you trained on the marketing aspect of the business for the off chance we need a bit more help while she steps away temporarily."

"Or permanently."

"Yup. That's always a possibility. Claire can be unpredictable at times, but I know her well enough to know she'll always have a firm foothold in the company she helped create. Her role might just look a little different than it does now, where she is putting in so many hours."

"She is a determined and driven person."

Angie nods. "She's out right now meeting with potential partners for Plus None who might place products in our subscription boxes."

"How wonderful. I can't wait to see what gets decided."

"So, you'd be willing to learn some of the behind-the-scenes marketing techniques and strategies? And also brainstorm with a team your ideas on what colors to use, fonts, and motivational monthly slogans? This would involve field testing, surveys, and analyzing already successful marketplaces." Angie takes an exaggerated breath. "Sorry, that was a lot. I'm a lot."

I laugh. "I can do all of that, just as long as you understand that I have zero experience but am very eager to learn."

Angie smiles brightly. "Hiring you is our game changer."

"But you barely know me."

"I know enough. And I make decisions based on my intuition which rarely lets me down. Besides, this is a low-pressure type of thing. If you try it out for a while and really don't like the work, we can reassess and come up with a new game plan. But I'd really like to see where this goes right now. We already have a decent-sized following. It's just about staying fresh and keeping our clients always wanting more."

I nod. "This sounds like a lot of fun."

"Did someone say fun?"

We turn to see Claire looking as adorable as ever. I know when she first found out she was pregnant, Plus None decided to host a pregnancy subscription box that has really taken off. There wasn't a ton on the market and definitely not one that was meant to progress with all months of pregnancy.

I can only hope that I can learn a lot and help relieve some stress that might occur to the company if Claire takes an extended leave.

"Good seeing you, Claire," I say, getting up from the sofa to give her a hug.

"Same to you, Penny. Oh, I saw your new desk. I love your choices. Where did you get the sand tray? I feel like I need one of those in my life for when Nic drives me crazy with worry over this"—she points down to her small bump—"sweet potato."

We all laugh.

And it feels so good that I know accepting the offer to work here was one of the best decisions of my life.

18

COLLINS

When I signed up to be Penny's bodyguard, I honestly didn't expect to work this hard at trying to keep her safe.

While Graham and Nic initially hired me for periodically checking in on their little sister, it easily morphed into needing to keep a closer eye on her.

That's because no matter where Penny goes, she seems to attract some type of unwanted attention. Granted, she's oblivious to it most of the time, but that doesn't make it any less annoying.

The girl didn't even realize I followed her to the office the other day, through security, and managed to clear the hall of any men prior to her arriving at Plus None. The last time she was there, someone spooked her, and I didn't want that to be a repeat situation.

Maybe I should be glad that she doesn't see me when I'm running surveillance on her.

Regardless, I would feel more comfortable if Penny was equipped to handle some basic self-defense moves in case

I'm not there to knock some teeth out or crush some fingers for her honor.

It's been days since I've been graced with Penny's snarky and defiant attitude.

And oddly enough, I miss it.

I have several people on my payroll to monitor her entering and exiting our building, and just a few days ago there was an incident where she arrived at the lobby basically in a panic.

While nothing checked out as being out of the norm, I decided right when I was reading the update report that Penny needs to work on her confidence in case a problem were to arise.

Maybe if she had some type of defense if someone were to get handsy with her, she wouldn't spiral every time a nonthreatening encounter occurred.

While this wouldn't replace the benefit of having actual self-preservation skills, maybe it would be a step in the right direction to assimilate back into society.

And that's the hope—that Penny can learn to function outside of Soulful Mind and develop the coping skills needed to live a full life.

"You know I don't take kindly to being summoned," her melodic voice sounds behind me.

I reserved the matted room in the apartment building's gym to conduct my private lesson with Penny.

I turn around and am faced head-on with Penny's eclectic wardrobe choices.

We are going to the gym, not the club.

Sure, she's wearing gym attire, but this isn't what I had in mind.

Her booty shorts and halter top reveal too many square inches of butt cheeks and belly.

Fuck.

"I'm glad to see you respond to my texts."

Why can't I divert my eyes?

It's like I'm staring straight into the sun and am oblivious to the burn.

"I was afraid that if I didn't show up, I'd find myself kidnapped in the back of your SUV."

"The day's still young," I deadpan. Although I'd have to use the discreet exit in the back of the building because there's no way Penny's going to be seen on the streets in this attire.

She takes a step closer. I can smell the strawberries radiating off her. Did she bathe herself in their essence?

"You wouldn't know what to do with me if you had me."

Without warning, I grab hold of Penny's wrist, tightening my grasp to provide the restraint but gentle enough not to hurt her.

"Hey!" she yells, trying to tug her arm away.

"This is your first lesson on how to get out of wrist grabs."

"That's why we're here?" she scoffs. "I thought it was going to be something fun."

"Would you have come willingly if you knew the details?"

"No."

"Precisely. So this is why we're here."

"Why?"

"Because I'm looking forward to the day you have the

confidence to defend yourself and take back all that you think you lost over the last year."

Penny's jaw unhinges. The snarky words that typically teeter on the end of her tongue get swallowed back inside her mouth as it slams shut.

She pulls on her wrists, trying to wiggle free. Her high ponytail of hair flings into her face, and she swings her head the opposite way to get it to cooperate.

"So how do I get out?" she growls.

"Are you in the right mindset to learn?"

Her face softens. "Yes."

"Then ask nicely."

Penny wedges her knee between my legs, bending it to the side. I twist her around, my fingers still able to restrain her wrist, while I secure her other one behind her back.

"Use your good girl words, Penelope. Ask nicely."

Her hair blows out from the side of her face as she lets out an exaggerated exhale. She feels good in my arms—too good.

Our eyes connect in the wall of mirrors along the perimeter of the room.

"Please teach me, Master. I want to learn."

"Hmmm… You still sound pretty defiant. And defiance will get you hurt. Try again."

Her spine softens against my core and her breathing levels. "I would like you to teach me, Collins. Please."

As a test, I release Penny from my hold and wait to see if she attacks.

Good.

"The first step to defending yourself is trusting your instincts."

"How do I do that?" Her tone is of genuine curiosity.

"You use your senses and a lifetime of pattern development to assess situations and listen to the inner voice inside that may be alerting you to danger. Too often people ignore that inner monologue of self-preservation by falling to the trap of the bystander effect."

"What's that?"

"It's where you rely on other people's lack of instincts to dictate your own during a potentially dangerous situation." When she still looks confused, I elaborate. "For example… If you are at a store shopping and someone walks in that makes you question their intentions of being there, don't look around to see if anyone else looks uncertain. Leave immediately. Trust yourself."

"Got it. Okay."

"So let's start with basic wrist grabs and work our way to getting out of certain holds. But Penny?"

"Hmm?"

"None of what I'll teach you today is going to replace common sense and trying to avoid danger in the first place. This is only meant to supplement what you should already be practicing."

"Like not getting into cars with strangers," she supplies.

"Exactly."

I reach out my palm. "Let me have your arm."

Penny complies.

"To get out of a single hand wrist grab, bring your arm up to your face and rotate your hand so that your thumb is facing you." I wait until she mimics my directions. "Then thrust your hand down and out to break the grip."

When we try it a couple of times, I switch roles.

"You try to grab me."

And she does, except her small fingers can barely make it around half my wrist.

"The goal is to get away from being the prey and *not* to in turn switch and become the predator."

An hour passes of practicing various grabs and holds.

"You're a fast learner."

"I still can't get you knocked down."

I chuckle. "That wasn't ever the point."

"Collins?"

"Yes?"

"I'm trying to absorb all that you taught me, but sometimes when I freak out when someone touches me, I also black out."

"How often does this happen?"

I can tell she is thinking. "About once a month."

"I'm sorry that happens to you, Pen. I wish I could make it stop, but I can only help you overcome some of your fears by fueling the inner strength you already have."

I hate seeing her sad. Maybe if she can be less afraid of the dark, then maybe she can learn to function in that shadowy space in her mind.

"I have an idea," I say, walking to the edge of the room where I have a gym bag resting on a bench.

"Okay…"

"I know you said you don't like the dark…" I pull out a band from my bag that I sometimes use to wrap my hands for sparring. "But what would you think to being blindfolded and trying out some of the self-defense moves?"

Penny's eyes latch on to the black band in my hand. "I'd

say your teaching methods are unconventional and I'd question your logic."

I make my way back to the center of the mat and try to hide my grin over Penny's bold nature. I've seen her in enough situations to know she's nowhere near as comfortable with other people as she is with me.

And I like it.

She doesn't trust freely, and I value her ability to let her guard down around me. I won't take that for granted.

"Come sit," I say, lowering myself to the floor. I wrap the band around my fingers, as I think of the right words to say.

"Okay…"

"I know you don't like the darkness, but you find yourself in that dark space when you shut down during a stressful situation."

Penny glances away from me. "It's just that I get scared," she whispers.

"I know. And I want you to work through those fears. Maybe if you practice being in the dark, you can desensitize yourself."

"What if I can't?"

"Just try."

Her hesitant nod causes my heart to increase its rhythm. Taking the band, I gently place it over Penny's forehead, tightening it into a secure knot.

I look directly into her eyes. "I want you to listen to me, because I'm being very serious about this."

"Okay…" I barely hear her.

"If you get too scared, then take your hands and move the blindfold up to your forehead like it is right now. It's that simple. You have control here, and I won't let you fall."

"Promise?"

"You have my word."

I help Penny stand back up and give her the patience and time she needs to cover her eyes with the band on her own free will.

And she does.

"I want you to relax. And I want you to use all of your other senses to evaluate your environment, all while staying in the present."

"Okay. I can do that."

Silence fills the space, and I allow this moment of calm to flourish.

"I don't want you to think of the darkness as a negative. I want you to utilize it as a way to center yourself and regain focus. Remember, this is about trusting your instincts."

"What if mine don't work?"

"The only thing that's not working is your confidence, Penny. Do you remember all of the moves I taught you?"

She shifts her weight to her other foot, curling her toes into the mat. "Yes, I think so."

"We are going to practice the same thing but blindfolded. The best approach to self-defense is to escape dangerous situations and not hang around to potentially get hurt."

Wrinkles form on her brow. "How am I supposed to escape if I can't see?"

"That's the point of this exercise. I think you can function in the dark, but just don't have a lot of practice."

I can tell Penny is finally understanding the task.

With her blindfold still on, I take a few steps back away from her. Careful not to make a sound, I circle her—slowly.

And when I think she has let down her guard, I jump into her space and watch as Penny mimics the motion in reverse.

"Great job."

"You scared me," she whimpers.

I gently pull her into my arms and slide up the blindfold to her forehead. Tears fill her eyes, and when one escapes, I wipe it away with my thumb.

Touching her is my weakness and yet I can't leave her standing here in the middle of the gym floor, looking like she just might break.

"I know you are scared, but that isn't the intention of this lesson. You did phenomenally well. Even without your sense of vision, you were able to dodge my advance."

Her bottom lip quivers but she rounds her shoulders. "Let's do it again."

"Are you sure?"

"Yes."

I wait until Penny pulls the fabric down over her eyes again and take a step back.

Allowing several minutes to pass, I grab hold of Penny's wrist as fast as I can and revel in her reflexes to break free in less than three seconds.

Sobs break out from deep in her throat, and the sound makes shivers run up my spine.

"I'm sorry, Penny."

I pull her to me, rip off the blindfold, and fold her onto my lap as I settle on the floor.

"It's okay." Her words come out as fragments as she

sniffles and buries her face into my chest. "I really needed this."

"I don't know. I'm having major doubts right now. Maybe we did too much too soon."

She shakes her head no, but I can't see her eyes. It's her crystal blues that allow me to see her truth, but she is hiding her face from me.

"I just want you to hold me."

And I do.

I sit here on the mat and hold the beautiful girl who is starting to mend her broken wings and relearn how to fly.

And it's in the quiet that we find each other.

"Your turn," Penny whispers, bringing me back down to earth.

She pulls back, and the rejection reminds me that what I'm doing with her is wrong. We are blurring lines faster than we are using them to construct the boundaries.

Standing up, I offer her a hand. *Just a hand.* "My turn?"

She swings the band around her head like a lasso. "Yes. Your turn."

Smirking, I place the band around my eyes, making sure it is secure.

"Now, spin around in a circle ten times."

"That doesn't seem fair." But I do it anyway.

My senses and adrenaline kick in as I wait for Penny to make her move.

Hearing some rustling coming from my left side, I clasp my arms together, pulling Penny into my chest.

"Got you!" she yells, making me burst into laughter.

"Pretty sure I got you, but who's keeping score?"

"Next round."

We go back into position.

But this time I allow Penny this one victory.

"Got you good," she screams three solid seconds before jumping onto my back.

I heard her a mile away and braced myself for her attack.

I fake fall to the mat with her attached to my back.

"You aren't supposed to warn people before you pounce on them. And self-defense never means attacking first," I reiterate.

Peeling back my blindfold, I pull Penny around and onto the mat.

"You like my mad skill?"

"What am I going to do with you?"

Her eyes focus in on my lips. I'm giving her mixed messages and that's not fair.

It's not fair that my inability to keep things professional is warping with her mind.

"Kiss me?"

My eyes dart to hers. I had to mishear her. There's no way she is requesting this right now.

But here I sit, stuck in a haze of attraction, unable to comprehend the reality that it can be mutual.

Damn fucking hell…

"No, Penny."

Her face reddens, and she pulls away.

"I'm your bodyguard."

"Some boundaries are meant to be crossed."

"I can't."

"But…" She stands up and starts fast-paced walking to the door, clearly embarrassed. Turning back around, with tears staining her cheeks, she looks at me like I just crushed her entire world. She wants to say something. It's as if the words are on the tip of her tongue. "Oh, never mind."

And then she walks out.

I've made a lot of mistakes in my life, but allowing Penny to walk away without me fully explaining my side of things has to be in the top three of mistakes.

Not only have I made things worse by not clarifying my feelings and reasoning as to why I couldn't kiss her, I have created this irreparable distance between us. I can feel it. I don't need any more confirmation that it exists other than the collective ignoring of my texts and attempts at contact that Penny has been giving me for the last three hours.

She is shutting me out, and I don't blame her.

If anyone is at fault, it's me. I have given her mixed messages, and now the look of devastation over my rejection will be a permanent memory in my mind.

And it was all over my weakness toward her.

I failed her.

The only way to make this better is to step aside and allow someone else to take over for me.

Thoughts of teaching Penny how to drive flutter through my brain. Who is going to help make sure she's safe on the road? Who is going to verify that her apartment is up to code? Does she actually plan to attend that dating mixer at the coffee shop?

Whoever I recommend to watch out for Penny must

understand how precious she is to her family. Keeping her safe has to be top priority.

I have a list of contacts I can use that have already been semi-vetted. Surely someone will stand out from the crowd as a potential replacement, and most likely I'll have to fly that person to Portland since I know everyone in the business already that is local, and no one person in particular stands out as a viable option.

Penny needs someone who won't crack under pressure or be bribed with her sweet antics, and I know she'll try.

I'm not a quitter, so the mere idea of giving up seems so foreign. I'll suck it up for a week to gather my references for Graham and Nic, and then officially resign from this assignment.

Ugh.

I don't even want to think about the disappointment that will be evident on their faces. The Hoffman brothers have trust issues. I've earned their respect over the years. This is out of character for me, and yet I really have no other choice.

Penelope Hoffman has fluttered her way into my heart.

And the only way to function is to deny the hold she has on me.

19

PENNY

I'd be lying if I said I wasn't sad to say goodbye to Momma as she helped me bring in my purchases to my new residence. I haven't even officially spent the night here, but there's now no reason not to do it. I have my bed, dresser, and all of my essentials right here in this place. Yet, as much as I wanted to have this level of independence, I am already lonely.

And perpetually embarrassed over the kiss request incident with Collins.

Who the hell asks someone for a kiss?

What am I—ten years old?

Not only has the man probably kissed a hundred women in his lifetime, he managed to look sympathetic toward me when I asked him for one. And that there is the worst.

He pities me.

Hell, at this point, I pity me.

To him, I'm some little naive girl who has a silly crush. I might as well grab a holographic notebook and doodle our names together with pink hearts drawn around them, while the "Collins and Penny sitting in a tree..." song plays on loop from the sound system.

Ew, how mortifying.

How am I going to function with him bodyguarding me when the only person I need protection from is myself and the stupidest things that can be spewed from my mouth?

And that there is the real dilemma.

So here I sulk in my dream apartment with my newly shopped for furnishings that fit my momma's style more than my own, and the only thing I can celebrate is the loss of my dignity.

The only hope of surviving yet another day where I feel awkward and silly is to stay busy and focus on a task. Maybe then my mind will stop thinking about how comfortable my parents' house is and the warmth of my momma who would cuddle me in a heartbeat.

I try not to think about how my momma makes the most delicious breakfasts or how my dad and I chat about pop culture around the island in the kitchen—where most discussions seem to occur.

And I'll try not to think about how before the incident, I was a carefree girl who faced challenges head-on, and not want to curl up under the covers and drown out all the humiliation I brought on my own life.

I just need to center myself and make this new space feel the same way the comfort of home feels like—but with my own flavor. I did it with my Plus None desk, so I just need to follow that same recipe here.

This is my first big-girl apartment, and I should at least find joy in doing things my way for a change.

Right now, boxes are stacked along the walls in the living room, and my luggage is open and arranged on the floor in haphazard piles.

It isn't like Momma didn't offer to help me unpack. She always volunteers. I just need to not use her as a crutch for every big decision I make. If I want to spread my wings, why would I constantly try to do so in the safety of a cushioned cage?

You can do this, Penny.

I take a few deep breaths and then find a playlist on my phone to get me in the mood.

When I was at Soulful Mind, I used music a lot to cope with the stress and anxiety I had festering inside of me. I even did music therapy classes, as well as horseback riding there. I loved being with the animals because they never judged me for not talking or not acting a certain way. Animals can sense moods, and it helped to have that ease of companionship without the pressure to be perfect.

No matter how happy my family is to have me back in the area, they are still expecting me to go back to being my old self, and I hate disappointing them. That version of myself died the night Mark drugged me.

They are never going to get her back.

I grab the highest stacked box from the pile and peel back the strips of packing tape. I never bothered labeling anything because I don't have a lot of possessions. When living at home, it never benefited me to have my own dish or silverware set. All of those kitchen items and gadgets can just be bought new.

When I dig inside the box, I find some of my favorite pairs of shoes. I dance my way down the hall to my bedroom, dumping my armful of shoes onto the floor near my closet. Kneeling down, I arrange them onto the built-in rack.

An amazing feature of this particular unit is how big the bedrooms are. Both rooms have the same square footage and similar layout, so I don't feel guilty for choosing mine first.

Picking myself up from the floor, I meander back into the living room. I have so many more boxes to open. It'll probably take me all week to get everything situated.

But no matter how hard I try to visualize my new space, I'm struggling to see the big picture.

Grabbing my phone, I shoot a group text to Claire and Angie.

Penny: I am at my new place and I am not sure how to go about decorating it. Want to come over and help me brainstorm?

I get a response almost immediately.

Claire: Of course! I live for moments like these! I'll bring the supplies.

Angie: I can pick you up, Claire. I would love to help.

Penny: Supplies?

Claire: Think arts and crafts…

Angie: But on steroids…

Claire: For our vision board! Woot woot!

While I wait for the girls to arrive, I skip down to the little home décor boutique that is literally just a few minutes' walking distance from my new place.

I don't have a clear style, but I definitely enjoy the concept of color to transform a space.

Grabbing turquoise knobs for my bedroom nightstand, I place them on the checkout counter. Then I go back to get some matching ones for the en suite.

"Did you find everything you needed?" the worker asks, her voice kind and helpful.

I glance around the shop. "Umm, do you have any paintings or wall art?"

"I sure do. There's a whole gallery lineup in this room on the side. Here, I will show you."

I follow her into the attached room that I never even noticed before now. "Wow. These are wonderful."

Various photos, paintings, and sculptures fill up the space.

"Did you have something in mind?"

I shrug. "I don't have any style. I am just grabbing things that catch my eye to brighten up my new apartment."

She smiles. "A lot of us have evolving styles. I think it's wonderful to allow your taste in items to be organic. Get what speaks to you in the *now*."

And I do. I find the most amazing aqua and gold butterfly painting that looks majestic and warm.

"This is the one," I say with pride.

"I love it. Amazing choice. And just remember that in a year or whatever, you might want something different for your wall. And that is okay. There are no rules when it comes to making a space your own."

It's funny how complete strangers can set you on the right path without even realizing it.

I like the idea of doing things that feel good now, without any type of commitment or pressure to get everything right the first try.

If only I can put this practice into other aspects of my life…

When Angie and Claire show up to help me create a decorating game plan for my new apartment, I wasn't expecting them to be pulling a wagon full of art supplies.

"Isn't this a little over-the-top?" I hesitantly ask. I'm kind of afraid to set off Claire. This is clearly her idea. Angie is just the accomplice.

Claire starts laughing like I just said the funniest of jokes.

Angie, on the other hand, looks at me and shrugs. "You should have seen what she really wanted to bring. I got her to tame down some."

Claire claps her hands and then flutters about my place like a pregnant butterfly, oohing and aahing over all the possibilities. But she isn't telling me what to do or trying to control everything. She is simply asking me various questions and helping me to articulate what I have already envisioned but was too inside my head to see clearly.

Calling these girls was the best thing I've done all day.

Already, I am rearranging furniture the way I want it, and their confidence in my ability to do it gives me strength.

"Oh, I love that idea, Penny," Angie says, helping me to hold the painting while we mark the location of where we should put the nails into the wall.

"What still needs to be done?" Claire asks me, pulling out a pad of paper and some colored pencils. "We can make a vision board so you have an idea of what is left to do."

"I think I would like an armchair for the bedroom and maybe a duvet?"

"Oh, yeah, that sounds good," she agrees. "Let's work on a color scheme. It will make searching for the items a lot less exhausting."

Claire's phone rings, and we all turn to look at the device.

"Who is it?" Angie asks.

"My ball and chain…"

I laugh. Yup, Nic has turned into quite the overprotective fiancé, that's for sure. "I'm shocked he even allowed you to come here without a five-man escort."

"Oh, they are waiting in the lobby," she says coolly. "But there's six of them. One for each of my personalities."

Angie smirks. "She's not lying."

Claire answers the call. "Hello, stalker. Yes, I'm drinking water." She motions with her hand, and I run into the kitchen to get her a glass. She takes a sip and then gargles it—probably to provide him proof—before swallowing. "Okay, fine. Yes, I will allow them to escort us back."

"Time to go?" I ask, when she ends the call.

"Yeah, apparently I have another ultrasound appointment that slipped my mind."

"Oh, fun."

She looks at me like I have five heads. "Oh, yeah, super fun. The last time, Nic almost fought with the ultrasound tech when they refused to answer any of his questions, stating something about it being protocol. Well, your brother thought they were just being 'unnecessarily difficult' on purpose and told them they were making up rules as they go."

"Well, at least there's never a dull moment," Angie says, making us all laugh.

"That's one way of putting it," Claire grumbles.

I see the girls out and close the door behind them, already feeling the pangs of loneliness from being here all by myself.

20

PENNY

As a way to celebrate being in my new place, I order a bunch of my favorite appetizers for dinner with extra ranch—the runny kind. I don't do thick ranch.

I guess the good thing about being here alone is that I don't have to share my food, and I can double-dip these boneless chicken pieces into my sauce—guilt-free.

Yum.

Grabbing the remote control, I scan through the show options and settle on old game show episodes that were probably popular when my parents were my age.

Maybe that's why my parents are obsessive when it comes to family games. Perhaps they watched too many of these types of shows. They are fun and relaxing to watch.

I play along with the contestants, enjoying the taste of comfort food.

When a commercial cuts in, I skip off to the kitchen to peruse my newly stocked fridge, settling for some lemonade to quench my thirst.

I move back into the living room, happy that I found my coasters earlier during some unpacking of the boxes.

“Well, hello, Sunshine!”

My body jerks around, as my hands clutch at the fabric of my shirt, covering my heart. “What the hell!”

The tall drink of muscular man-flavored water takes three steps toward me, swaying his hips in such a way that tingles run up my spine. Holy hotness. And just like that, he is forgiven for scaring me.

I watch stupidly, as he takes several more steps toward me.

Why am I not retreating?

I mean…the only thing that looks threatening about him is his attractive appeal. He probably has women passing out over his appearance.

I cannot be one of those ladies… No. I cannot.

Reaching out his hand, he looks expectantly at me.

“I don’t bite.” His eyes trail down my clothing, and suddenly I am questioning everything about my wardrobe selection. “Hard.”

“I, um…” My hand extends to meet his, submitting to the slight shake. “You must be—” I bite my bottom lip, stumbling back a step, until my butt collides with the wall. “You are?”

“Luke.”

“Luke?”

“Yes, Luke. Your new roommate.”

I shake my head. “No.” He must be one of those delivery guys that probably needs me to sign for a package or something. Having hot men carrying boxes is all the rage right now. People drop a lot of money to have some eye candy during a move.

Luke's hand scratches at the back of his neck, along where his dark hair curls upward, under a ball cap. "No? Is that any way to greet your new roomie?"

My jaw unhinges. "You are female."

His laugh fills the room, booming from his lips. "Did you look?"

"No."

"Not *yet*," he corrects, making a blush run up my body.

My eyes narrow at his unabashed boldness. "I signed up for a female roommate."

"Well, aren't you lucky. You got me instead. And I'm one hundred percent, all-beef dick, baby." Grabbing the zipper crotch of his jeans, he gives himself a squeeze. "No artificial meat and enhancement free. I'm organic."

What the actual hell? Who does that? "But"—I reach for my phone on the top of some cardboard boxes and open up my email app—"see, it says my roommate's name is Lucy." I just got notice about the name a couple of days ago, wondering when she would show her face.

"Oh, that was a typo."

"A typo?" My voice comes out louder than I expect. Who spells their name wrong and doesn't notice? "You didn't think it was worth going back and fixing the error?"

"And miss out on this momentous greeting? Oh, hell no. This is too much fun." Luke grabs my glass of lemonade I have situated on top of an end table and takes a sip. "Look how much fun we are having."

I can feel the muscles in my jaw releasing as my chin drops. "What—"

"Delicious. Tastes like sunshine."

"I—" My brow furrows. "What exactly do you do for a living?"

"Women."

I scoff. "Seriously."

Luke shrugs. "I mean, they want to when they see me perform. I work at the Boom Boom Club as a male stripper during the evening. I am VIP room material, granted. But there's no such place in the Boom Boom room. The boss claims the entire venue is the VIP room. Sounds gimmicky if you ask me and a waste of perfectly good sanitization products, as the entire customer space needs to be cleaned of all bodily fluids after closing, and not just the obvious places."

"Sounds like I need the VIP treatment in my life."

"Wow." He takes several steps back until his ass is leaning against the edge of some stacked boxes. "Let me savor this moment."

"What's the moment?" I ask stupidly.

"The moment where we just connected for the first time."

I sigh. "Shut up."

"You should come to the club, and I can show you around my lair."

"Hard pass."

Luke clutches his heart. "Ouch. You're a tease. No worries, though. My real talent lies in my"—he swivels his hips in a seductive way, gyrating his crotch when he comes full circle—"dancing."

"What the hell is going on?"

My eyes move behind Luke to find Collins standing in

my open door, carrying a large bouquet of flowers and a silver wrapped gift box. The huge bow on top nearly takes up the entire surface area of the lid, dwarfing its size.

"Collins?"

I haven't seen him in days, so it's extra surprising to find him in my entranceway, looking so angry.

He stares down at Luke's luggage and then over to him.

Why can't my new roommate stop looking so smug?

He won't when Collins bashes his face in like a soda can.

"Oh no, is this your daddy? Dads usually love me—well, sort of. Until…"

I spare a glance at Collins to know that he's about to lose it. Dammit. "No, not my dad," I say softly.

Luke's eyes travel between me and my bodyguard. "Oh, so he's the boyfriend?"

"No," Collins and I say in unison, our eyes never leaving each other's.

"Nice," Luke says, not buying what we are trying to portray. Except he doesn't say "nice" the normal way. No, instead he pronounces it—noice. "So you are single and ready to—"

"Nope. Not that either," I say in a hurry before Collins blows a gasket.

He doesn't like Luke. He doesn't need to confirm that with words. I can see the writing all over his grumpy facial expression.

Luke realizes this and it appears to spur him on. The dude thrives in drama and angst apparently.

Just wonderful…

“What are you doing here?” I ask, trying to ignore Collins’s eyes which penetrate through me like knives.

Sheesh. Don’t be angry with me! I didn’t do anything wrong.

Collins walks inside the apartment, shutting the door behind him with the flick of his foot. It slams a bit harder than I expect, and I shudder at the sound. He walks in silence to the kitchen, placing the flowers down on the counter. “I’m just bringing you a housewarming gift.”

“Thank you for our gift,” Luke says, apparently for both of us.

“It’s Penny’s.”

He puts his hands up in defense. “Got it. You don’t like the share.” Then he nudges me with his elbow. “I live here too. I’ll take the right side of the bouquet. That dude can pee on your side to mark his territory.”

“Just stop,” I whisper-hush him before Collins explodes. I can tell by his jaw tics that he’s on the verge, and that’s the last thing I need right now. Collins will be the first to break in this apartment—but with Luke’s head.

My roommate leans into me, and I swear I hear Collins growl. “Now that is a sweet gesture for a non-boyfriend,” he whispers a bit too loudly to me. “Just sayin’.”

I push him back, causing him to laugh. Shit. He’s making this worse. “Thanks for visiting me, Collins.” I push at Luke when he mutters “*us*” under his breath. “The flowers are lovely.”

Collins just stares at us. Well, damn. I feel like I’m doing something very wrong. What? I’m not sure.

Who would have thought that moving here would put me in the middle of some…

Pissing contest?

Which is weird because Collins doesn't want me.

"Can I speak with you in private, Penny?"

I swallow hard, rocking on my heels, all while Luke makes a dum-dum-dum-dum sound from deep in his throat, and then mumbles something about me needing to go to the principal's office. "Sure."

I follow Collins out into the hallway, saying a silent thank you that no one is out to witness this soon-to-be shitstorm.

Propping my hands on my hips, I wonder what Collins is going to lecture me about. I'm sure I did something to break a rule in his code of conduct book. I can already tell that whatever he's going to say isn't going to be what I want to hear.

"Not here."

My eyes meet his. "What?"

"We are going up to my place."

Butterflies populate in my stomach. "Why?"

Collins sighs. "Can you just be easy, this one time? I don't feel like having this conversation with you out in the middle of the hallway." He rubs his hand through his hair, tugging at the ends. "For heaven's sake, Pen, let's go."

My eyes shoot to my feet. "Um, I need shoes. Stay out here. I'll be right back."

I can't risk him going back inside and bashing in Luke's skull. The last thing I need is blood in our new place.

I open my apartment door and gently close it, leaving Collins standing alone in the hallway like a real bodyguard.

Like a magnet, Luke finds me and drapes his arm over my shoulder in a poor attempt at being nonchalant. "Finally, we are free," he says with a sigh, while giving me a side squeeze.

"Let's pull out the cognac, order us some filthy porn—the kind you pay for—and send sexy selfies to our exes."

Ducking out of his hold, I shake my head at him while laughing. "I need to leave."

"What? No." His words come out as a whine. "My carpal tunnel will have a flare-up without your supportive hand. Plus I don't trust you with him."

"Who? Collins?"

"Yeah. The man with the"—he taps a finger along his jaw—"umm…what's one step up from resting bitch face?"

I giggle. "Probably intentional bitch face?"

"Yes. That's a good descriptor. The man with the intentional bitch face…"

"He's not that scary."

"For a serial killer, sure…"

"Ha, he's not that bad. He can be nice." He just chooses not to be most of the time.

"Um, if you say so. That dude has the charisma of a robot and the personality of a hungry bear."

I turn to look at Luke. "Huh. You are right. That's oddly spot-on."

"See? This is proof that we need to cuddle on the couch together and bond."

Ignoring him, I slide my feet into my sandals and wiggle my fingers in a wave goodbye.

"You wound me. Don't you know that kicking a man while he's down just gives his eyes better visual access to your cootchie?"

My body whips around to stare right at Luke's. When he

sees me make eye contact, he quickly fakes looking sad. "It's fine, it's fine." He holds up his hands. "Go have fun with Mr. Grumpy Fish. I don't blame you. And in the famous words from Jimmy Letgo, 'Savor something good.'"

"Umm, isn't he the spokesperson for the fast-food chain, Rowdy Rowdy Chicken?"

"Oh. Yeah, I guess he is. But he is basically a philosophical genius."

"He's featured as a cartoon character," I deadpan.

"He is real!"

"I just can't with you right now."

When I make it back into the hallway, I'm nearly crying from laughter, which apparently is only adding to Collins's bad mood. He gives me the once-over, focusing on my sandals.

My toes are painted in a pretty shade of pink.

"Do you approve of my footwear, sir?"

Ohhh. Now I get a glare to match his grumpy face.

Lucky me.

Apparently I'm on a roll of disappointing everyone I encounter today.

"They will suffice."

I stick my tongue out at him. "My goal in life is fulfilled. Yay!"

His eyes crinkle just enough to imply amusement, but his lips refuse to submit to a smile. He wants to though. If anything, I am his entertainment for the moment.

I start to move toward the elevator bank, and Collins joins me. He hits the call button, and we wait in silence for the car to arrive. I just don't see the point of having privacy when he scolds me. At least if I have witnesses, he might dial it back a notch or two. Plus, why am I even putting myself in a position for it to happen in the first place?

The elevator dings and the doors open. Collins steps to the side, placing his hand into the opening to allow me to go first. But I don't move. I stay glued in my spot, wondering how I got to this place where I take orders like an obedient child.

"No."

"No?" he asks, his brow furrowing.

I shake my head. "If you want to talk to me, do it here." I prop my hands on my hips in defiance. Then I see a flash. "Hey! Put me down!"

From upside down, I watch as we enter the elevator. Collins hits the button for the eleventh floor and grips the back of my calves with authority. His touch is as commanding as his demeanor, never faltering, never uncertain.

"Who do you think you are?" I yell, smacking against his muscular back. I stretch my fingers, trying to mask the pain of hitting into solid rock.

"Your bodyguard."

"Well, you suck at it, because I feel like I'm not being protected from your egotistical tendencies!" I take a few deep breaths and feel the vibrations permeating from beneath my stomach. Oh, how dare he. "Stop laughing at me, you, you"—I smack as hard as I can onto his back—"brute."

When the car stops and the doors open, Collins just waltzes out into the hallway—like carrying me over his shoulder is the most normal thing.

Silently, I vow to learn my own self-defense moves of

what to do when someone is toting me over their shoulders like a rag doll to their man cave, because I can't trust Collins to be thorough.

Low-toned voices surround us, and I hide my head from any curious onlookers. I definitely don't need this attention now.

How embarrassing.

I know people see me propped up on Collins's shoulders like a sack of potatoes. How could they not notice? I stay silent as he carries me to his apartment, unlocks the door, and pushes it open with his spare shoulder.

Once he sets me on my feet, I snarl and take a step backward. "What has overcome you?"

"Would you like some water?"

"Seriously, what's your deal?" I demand, ignoring his first try at distracting me.

"Juice?"

"I don't need to quench my fucking thirst!"

"I got fresh-squeezed nectarine—no pulp."

My lips form the word no but the sound doesn't come out. Why is he softening me with juice, and why is it working?

Glued in place, I watch as Collins casually walks into his kitchen and grabs a glass out of the cupboard. He then moves to the refrigerator and pulls out the beverage container. Pouring some into the glass, he adds some ice and then strolls back over to me.

"Here. Drink."

And I do. Because when I'm here, I'm cast under some spell.

I take a sip. And another.

Oh my, this is good.

"Who is he?"

"Who is who?" I ask, scrunching up my nose. My exhale causes the glass to fog up. Then it dawns on me.

"The guy inside your apartment."

Did he just growl?

Yup. I think he did.

"Luke?"

"I care about his purpose being there, not his name, Penelope."

I make a face. He's extra testy. "Apparently my roommate."

"Did you sign up for a male roommate just to defy me?"

My jaw feels like it just crashed onto the floor. "Defy you?" I shake my head. "Really? Believe it or not, Mr. Stone…" I watch as his eyes darken but I continue my rant. I'm too invested now to back down. "My choices do not revolve around you. I am capable of going through life as I please."

He takes a step closer, causing me to back up. I feel the coolness of the wall behind me, but my body is full of adrenaline. I am charged, and the fire that starts in my toes ignites, sending shock waves of heat throughout my entire body.

"What's Luke's last name?"

"I thought you didn't care about his name."

"Tell me."

"Hell if I know. We literally just met."

Collins's eyes narrow. "You let a stranger into your apartment?"

"He had his own key, I am sure."

"What the hell, Penny? Have you lost your—"

Mind.

I bite my bottom lip, trying not to react. *Do not react.* I shoulder past Collins, making my way to the door I was tossed through, when I feel a light tug on my hand.

"Pen?"

"Hmm?"

"I didn't mean it that way. And I don't see you that way. It was just an expression."

I pull my hand from his. "We are done here."

This whole detour was pointless. I exit into the hallway and then make my way to the elevators. I slam the call button and then enter. Resting my butt against the handrail in the back of the car, I close my eyes as I think over how I'm going to handle rooming with Luke-whatever-his-last-name-is.

I never have cohabitated with a male before, so this shall be interesting.

I exit the elevator at my floor and make my way to my apartment. Pushing open the door, I stumble forward as I'm graced with Luke doing a handstand in the living room. He bends his knees, flicking them into the air, as he gyrates his hips. I stand dumbfounded as he flips himself over and then spots me ogling him. Licking his lips, he shoots me a satisfied look.

"Come to my show, and you will get the VIP treatment." Then he winks.

"I thought the entire club was VIP." My mouth feels like cotton is stuffed inside.

"It is, but there's always a way to make extra special guests feel"—his eyes trail over my flushed skin—"special.

I'll even throw in the free upgrade to the Princess Package."

"You are so full of yourself. You know that, right?"

"But you like it a little. I can tell."

Maybe just a little. Deep in my soul, I feel like Luke is harmless. He has good vibes radiating off him.

And at least now, I won't be lonely here.

Moving into the kitchen, I see the bouquet of flowers. They are beautiful.

I lift open the lid of the gift box, revealing a beautiful crystal vase. Well, that's perfect because I would have otherwise had no good place to display the flowers. Filling it up with water, I arrange the bouquet.

When I notice the card attached under the bow of the box, I rip it off and peel back the flap. Pulling out the card, in beautiful script, I see Collins's elegant but formal handwriting.

I hope this place brings you joy.
-The Bodyguard

I read the card three more times, trailing my finger over the words. I hope this place does bring me joy. Maybe it will, once I finally start settling in and making memories.

Turning my attention to Luke, I ask, "What is your last name?"

"Brawley."

"Luke Brawley," I say slowly.

"My stage name, though, is Lethal Luke."

"Sounds deadly," I grumble.

"That's because I"—his hands fly through the air in some type of karate move—"kill the competition."

"Catchy."

"It kinda goes with my whole bad boy persona. I know you women love a villain."

I nod. "That's actually true."

If Luke is one thing, he sure is certain of his appeal. I imagine the girls going wild over him. His personality can light up an entire room.

"Penny?"

"Yeah?"

"That man that showed up showering you with gifts and a broody temper… He likes you." Luke wiggles his eyebrows. "A lot."

"If you say so." I don't give his words much thought. I don't think Collins likes anything right now—let alone *anybody*.

And I'm certain he wants nothing to do with me in the romantic sense.

If the mortifying experience of me asking him for a kiss on the gym mats wasn't proof enough, then every awkward moment after that incident should solidify my conclusion.

"And if"—he holds up his hands to stop me from speaking even though I haven't said anything for a few seconds—"you want to make him jealous, I will sacrifice my body for the cause. You are welcome to use me at any time."

"Gee, thanks. But no thanks. It's complicated, but there's no way Collins and I will ever be a thing. He works for my two overprotective brothers. I'm basically a job for him."

"Um, you are the benefits package."

I laugh but allow his description to linger. I wish. But there's no way Collins would ever make a move on me even if he did want me—which he doesn't.

Luke holds my gaze. I can tell he's deep in thought. Shrugging, he walks toward our door. "I'm going to go grab some of my belongings from my car. Just for transparency sake, are we sharing a room, yes or no?"

"No!"

"Ball's in your court."

"No."

"You could have given it more thought, you know."

"Shut up and go get your stuff before I change my mind about living here."

I watch as Luke leaves, and then I let out a laugh.

What are the freaking chances that my roommate is a dude? I am in so over my head with drama, and I haven't even spent a night here yet.

I am so screwed.

21

COLLINS

I pull into the parking lot at an abandoned warehouse on the outskirts of town. If I want to meet up in a discreet location, this is where I choose to do business. There's no surveillance, and law enforcement rarely patrol this deserted area.

I kill the engine, undo my seatbelt, and then get out. Swallowing hard, I watch as a pickup truck pulls into the parking lot, blowing clouds of dust into the air. Placing my hands into my pockets, I rest my weight onto one foot.

For decisions as big as this, I usually feel a sense of direction—some type of inkling pushing me one way over another. To others, they may think my biggest weapon is my ability to shoot a target. However, it really is my intuition. I've learned to trust my gut feeling and proceed accordingly. Unfortunately, with this task, I'm having doubts already.

Maybe it's the guilt seeping in from knowing that I've failed Penelope Hoffman. Or maybe it's the fact that this girl is burrowing herself under my skin until she finds the location of my heart.

The truck door slams, and then I see Penny's potential bodyguard make his way toward me. He would be the guy who would demand a truck for his rental vehicle.

"Redeye," Chris greets, smacking hands with mine, which then turns into a hug.

It's been awhile since I heard my old nickname out loud. I just wish my memories of that era of my life had a happier ending.

"Good seeing you."

"Pardon me for being a bit surprised. I'm not used to being propositioned by the best of the west."

I chuckle. "I never expected you to leave your southern roots behind."

"I would have chosen sweet tea over anyone—except for you."

I place a hand to my heart. "I'm honored."

"Don't let it get to your head. The real reason I fully committed is because you finally got Rowdy Rowdy Chicken."

I let out a laugh. I forgot about Chris's obsession with fast food. "You know we do things differently up here, right?"

"Just because there's two ways to skin a deer, doesn't mean your way is better."

"Except it is," I joke.

Chris has always had a good sense of humor. We've known each other for years beginning during our military days. However, we went our separate ways when proximity no longer kept us in easy communication.

I got discharged. He stayed and retired with full veteran benefits.

But every time I think back to how things went down, I'm consumed with bitterness.

I was betrayed by the people I trusted.

"I do like this cooler weather, despite it being summer," Chris says, glancing around the open space around the warehouse.

It is cooler here. But it's also morning.

Despite going separate ways, that didn't mean I was completely out of the loop on what has been going on in Chris's life. I've seen his name tossed about in different social circles as being stellar at his freelance assignments.

"I hope your flight was smooth."

Chris gives his trademark big-grinned smile. "Only because you opted for the best seat on the plane."

I forget what I even assigned. Right after the self-defense lesson, I called up Chris and had him fly to Portland to meet with me face-to-face. I don't even remember what I selected outside of first class.

"You still hate the exit row, right?"

"I do."

"It's probably because you had to jump out of too many planes."

"No doubt. But you hooked me up with seat 1A, the greatest seat that ever existed on an aircraft."

"Your spoiled ass has standards, am I right? You're a bougie prick who probably ordered hot towels for a five-hour flight."

"Accurate."

We both laugh.

"Here's all the documentation you wanted," he says, handing me a stack of papers that can barely be contained inside a folder. "I didn't alphabetize them and color code them. So forgive me. I can see you never stopped being a picky bastard."

"I'm just trying to catch you in a lie."

"You never stopped interrogating either." Chris scratches his jawline, where his stubble is more than a five o'clock shadow. "Let's just get to the point. Why did you summon me here all the way from Texas?"

"As you know, I'm employed by the Hoffmans."

"Pretty sure there's a billboard advertising this. So yes…"

"Joking aside, I have to reassign myself from the guard assignment that I was given of watching Graham and Nic's youngest sister, Penny Hoffman."

Chris's eyes narrow. "That's not like you."

I shrug. "Part of being a good bodyguard is understanding the limitations and being able to identify if you are the wrong person for the job."

"How complex is the job?"

It's the hardest job I've ever taken on—hands down.

I look out into the empty field, where the sun is about to rise. It has been days since Penny and I spent time together. I miss her. Trying to respect her wishes, I've been watching from a distance—which is the most torturous part.

I stood on the sideline as she went shopping with her family—never intervening even when I knew her feet were hurting. I resisted helping her move into her new place, despite being available to get her settled in. I didn't even bring her lunch that day when I knew she skipped a meal.

I'm trying, yet every instinctive nerve in my body is screaming to protect her and to take care of her.

My urges want to do the very thing she is adamantly resisting…

I want to coddle her.

And now that I know there's an attraction from her side, I don't think I'll ever be able to be close to her and not want to rip her clothes off and fuck her against the nearest flat surface I can find.

So now, I have no other choice but to step back and allow someone else to provide the same protective services —but with zero emotional attachment. I've gotten too close to the mark, and it didn't take me much time to get there. That's the effect Penny has on me.

I've confused her, and I'll never forgive myself for causing her unneeded emotional pain.

"As long as you stay detached, you'll be fine."

"Huh," Chris says with a hum, "is that what went wrong?"

Part of our military training was anticipating events happening before they happened. I'm not surprised that Chris's intuition is kicking in. He's an insightful kind of guy.

"I'm not going to get into details. I can set up a discreet meeting with Penny for you to officially meet her and see what you think from afar."

"Okay…"

"I still will have to check out a few things and, of course, consult my boss about the potential change in assignment if I move forward with hiring you. I'm sure he'll want to meet with you, as well as his younger brother, Nic."

Chris nods, absorbing all of the information I'm giving him. "Sounds good."

"I'll be in touch, but don't worry. I'll cover all the living expenses leading up to the final decision. I have to do what will make the most sense for the Hoffmans."

"Understood. You need to be thorough. No hard feelings either way."

We smack hands again and then get into our vehicles. When I start the engine, a feeling of dread consumes me, as if I'm making a poor decision.

Am I?

Is this what's best for Penny, or is this what's best for me? I've spent the past forty-eight hours vetting potential candidates. While Chris was an add-on to the list, I think he's the best fit for his qualifications. I doubt he'll put up with Penny's stubbornness either. His no-nonsense personality might be exactly what she needs to keep her in line.

My phone buzzes from the cupholder and I see Nic's name, followed by Graham's, appear on the notifications list in a group text asking me if I am up for some sparring at the gym. The guys have been known to take their lunch break at the gym and blow off some steam, but this is very early for them to want the adrenaline rush. Right now, I feel pretty tense. I need to work through my aggression if I'm going to be mentally clear to make hard decisions. I text back with confirmation, backing out of the parking spot.

With Penny resisting my guidance, I'm trying my best not to smother her but still keep tabs—at least until I can get an official replacement figured out. When a final decision has been made, I'll fill her in. There's no need to cause her any more stress than I already have.

Penny is living life in a bit of a limbo right now, with the big transition into her new place and the start of her new job at Plus None. The other night was her first official time sleeping at her apartment, and I'm sure the moment was a bit bittersweet.

I know how much Penny loves her parents. Being away from them and not having any real friends in the city has to have her feeling the pangs of loneliness.

And now I'll be deserting her.

I am pawning her off to another qualified bodyguard who won't blur the lines and flirt with her.

When I get back into the city, I park in front of Ground Floor—the same coffee shop where Rex helped Penny carry a box of pastries out to my vehicle. It seems like a lifetime ago when she had her first Plus None meeting with the girls.

I exit the car and walk into the corner cafe, smelling the fresh aroma of ground coffee beans. When it's my turn in line, I order a nitro cold brew with foam and a cream cheese bagel. Plastered on the bulletin board, I see the speed dating event's information. I take a picture of the flyer, texting myself a reminder to add it to my calendar. There's no doubt in my mind that I'll find Penny there, and based on the date of the event, Chris may be officially on duty.

I should be relieved that I won't have to run surveillance at an event with a bunch of eager dickheads who are just wanting to get laid. Except I'm not.

Every time I think of someone other than myself watching Penny, I get this uneasy feeling in the pit of my stomach, screaming at me that this is not the best option—even though logically I don't have much choice. I either sever the entire relationship with the Hoffmans by overstepping an unspoken boundary, or humble myself to let them know that I'm not the best man for this job.

A glance at my watch lets me know that I need to get moving. Taking a sip of my drink, I exit the shop.

"You're getting weak," Graham says, jabbing me in my ribs. It isn't hard, but it's a sign that I'm distracted.

I duck as his other gloved fist comes barreling past my head. Grabbing both of his legs, I pull him down on his back. "At least my reflexes are still good."

I bounce back up on my heels. It feels great to get out some of my frustration, in a modified way. Graham is up and ready to fight again, as we circle each other. With Nic cheering from the sidelines, we go a few more rounds before rotating who's in the ring.

"Well, that was fun," Graham says, patting me on the back.

"It was," I agree with a nod. I catch the towel Nic throws at me, wiping the sweat from my face and neck. I sure got heated during the sparring.

"So, how does it feel having less drama in your life?" Nic asks.

Ha. If he's referring to his little sister, then he has her completely wrong. My life has been nothing but drama since I signed my name on the contract. "Like a vacation," I joke.

My leave hasn't been made official yet, and there's no point even saying anything until I fully vet Chris. I need to be certain that this is what's best for Penny before I make some rash decision.

With typical jobs that involve outside hires, there's also a trial period that the Hoffmans like to implement, especially considering past failures for hiring trustworthy people.

Graham laughs. "Well, don't get too comfortable. Penny's unpredictable. She always has been."

"Straight up facts," Nic concurs. "I'm still reeling from when she went to see fucking Tanner."

Graham growls, and I know his feelings without him ever speaking a word. He and I are similar in our rigidness. And if Penny was…

Mine...

If Penny was under my surveillance at that time, then she sure as hell wouldn't be trudging into a fucking prison seeing her abuser. Tanner better be glad his life was spared and that the authorities got to him before he could have perished in the fire. But his days are numbered if he thinks he can torment the poor girl from inside his barred cell.

Mark might be telling Penny that he will see her in court, but there's no way any of us want Penny to relive her trauma on the stand.

"But Collins has seen it all with Angie and Claire," Nic continues. "Can't get much worse than those two hellions."

I swallow hard. I honestly would have thought that from the sidelines, but I'm just a couple of weeks in on the job with Penny and already want to take a leave of absence.

"I'm just glad that Penny is out of the facility and is making progress at moving on. She is strong."

Graham and Nic nod, their eyes softening. I know they

love their sister. That's what this is all about in the first place—protecting her.

"Just keep her out of trouble," the eldest Hoffman says with a sigh. "I have my hands full with the wife. And to think I fell in love with her for her passion and independence."

Nic bursts out laughing. "That's the irony, isn't it? If I wasn't terrified of Claire's emotional state, I would lock her away for safekeeping and coddle the hell out of her."

"Pretty sure you are still doing the latter," Graham points out. When Nic starts to become defensive, he holds up a hand to quiet him. "Oh, I don't blame you. Trust me. If my Angie were to be in Claire's shoes, she best know that I'm not going to put up with half the shit I put up with now. My need to let her spread her wings only works when she isn't running herself into the ground. Someone needs to make sure that woman is taking care of herself and eating right. Drives me nuts."

I think back to the face Penny made when I made her eat breakfast on the way to her parents'. I swear all these fierce women are the same. They like to act like they don't need us, but in reality they totally do.

And if this dickhead of a roommate even thinks about making a move on Penny, I'm going to snatch her from this town and make the idiot she cohabitates with become part of a missing persons case. I swear life has a way of throwing curveballs my way that I never anticipated needing to catch.

I take a detour to the locker room to use the shower and clean up before heading home. At least I already ran a background check on the owner of the apartment building when

I first moved in, so the only thing left to do is keep a closer watch on this Luke Brawley. If he's like most guys his age, he'll reveal his cards soon, and I'll know just how much of a threat he is to my sanity.

When I exit the gym and unlock my car door, I see the shiny penny that I have resting in the center console. I remember seeing Penny's excitement over finding something that doesn't have much value, yet now holds special meaning to me.

I drive home in silence, just listening to my own internal thoughts. I allow muscle memory to take over, parking my car, exiting, and jogging up the stairs just like I have many times.

I unlock the door, de-arm the security system, and take off my shoes. I appreciate having a tidy home. However, I can't erase the image of Penny inside this apartment. She's not messy, yet I wouldn't describe her as a neat freak.

She is controlled chaos.

Despite her being in my residence just a couple of times, I still find little reminders that she was actually here and not some figment of my imagination. It's the simplest things too, like a hair tie left on a doorknob or the way she haphazardly hung the bathroom towel. Or it was the way the smell of fresh strawberries lingered, letting me know that I didn't just dream up the entire night in my head.

Making my way into my office, I lay out the file folder that Chris presented me with and go to work at verifying that he's the stand-up guy I knew back in my military days. It seems like a lifetime ago that I was being trained and working myself up in rank, and then that chapter of my life ended about as abruptly as it started.

When I graduated from high school and didn't have any clue what I wanted to do with my life, I did what many guys with my childhood upbringing do—I enlisted. It became obvious that I could endure the mental and physical stress without complaint, which were qualities that made me valuable.

I was good at my job and wasn't afraid of a little hard work—or a lot of it. I worked my way up the ladder fast, and looking back, probably too fast. Having a target on your back when surrounded by those who should all be on the same side of freedom isn't fun when the betrayal happens from within. It hurts more that way.

And the discharge that happened nearly crushed me.

I could put blame on others, but it all boils down to trusting the wrong people.

I refuse to ever make that mistake again.

Penny might not realize it yet, but we have similar traumas that have irrevocably changed the course of our lives.

And I'm trying my very best to prevent more trauma from happening to her.

When Chris's documents check out and nothing appears to be disproportionate or shady, I pile everything into the folder and lean back into my chair. Closing my eyes, I rub my fingers over my forehead, settling in at the bridge of my nose. The pulsing pain behind my eyes alerts me that I'm going to need to drink some more water. I am dehydrated.

I walk through my apartment, feeling the sting of loneliness. It's crazy to think about how having Penny here for just one night gave me a little taste of how things could be if I let someone into my life.

I'm a picky bastard, though. Not many women can handle my level of need for control and for things to be in their set place. I have an unhealthy level of OCD that gives me the ability to function with clarity. I am not sure I can handle anyone coming in and shaking everything up.

I open the door of the kitchen cabinet and pull out a glass, dropping it as my eyes connect with a huge spider at the bottom of it.

Except it's fake.

What the hell?

How did that even get there?

I toss the plastic critter into the trash and move over to the fridge to fill the glass with ice and then with water.

At least it didn't break…

I can't believe I forgot to drink something after working out at the gym with Graham and Nic. I rarely make those types of mistakes.

As the pulsing in my forehead elevates, I make my way into the living room. Settling in on the sofa, I feel the vibration of my phone alerting me of an incoming call.

"Hey, Graham," I greet, accepting the call.

"The legal team is breathing down my neck about prepping Penny for trial. Obviously, there isn't going to be a trial. Are you still on board with the plan?"

"Absolutely."

22

PENNY

After a week of nesting in my apartment, I'm ready to get out and socialize.

I thought living in the same building as Collins would be stifling with his overbearing tendencies, but he has been quiet for the last few days, and deep down I feel lost without his attention.

Granted, I'm pretty sure he is avoiding me like the plague now that I revealed my schoolgirl crush to him.

He's probably watching me still but definitely not making it known. That's what I wanted, right? Some independence and no smothering.

Glancing down both sides of the street, I don't see him, which isn't all that surprising.

It feels weird not to have a visible shadow on me. A very small part of me misses the attention.

I enter Ground Floor before I overanalyze any more things tonight and change my mind. My whole goal since getting out of Soulful Mind is to challenge myself and to step out of my comfort zone. I'm tired of being complacent. I'm tired of allowing circumstances to dictate my path.

No. Some things are definitely in my control.

Glancing around the space, I notice that the tables in the coffee shop are spread out more, but the intimate lighting is still the same. The place feels warm and inviting, with the smell of coffee still permeating through the air.

I fix the hem of my fitted black tank to rest along the waistband of my dark denim jeans. Being too afraid to have the girls help me get ready in fear my brothers would find out, I settled for Luke's very descriptive opinion of what a man wants, which could have been summed up in two words—skin and tight.

Apparently women that try too hard or wear too much makeup are a turnoff.

So, with his advice, I chose jeans and some mascara.

The fanciest thing on me are my shoes. Luke said men are whores for sexy shoes—so I went with the high-heeled ones. They were an emotional splurge purchase that I made after I got back home from visiting Mark at the prison.

I look down at my sparkling Cinderella esque shoes, knowing that not even their superficialness can change the fact that I'm a pathetic princess searching for her prince.

Maybe I need to lower my standards just to increase my fun. Perhaps I should be looking for a fuck boy to cope with all my horniness.

I mean, that's why I'm here doing the speed dating thing, right? No one really does these gimmicky things to actually fall in love. This is basically a dating app but in 3D.

Women don't go out on the prowl, signing up for speed dating events, if they are having success doing the traditional methods for meeting someone.

Nothing about this experience is casual. There's desperation written all over my motives for being here. Good thing is, everyone in attendance should be in a similarly constructed boat.

"Penny, you made it," a masculine voice says from behind.

I pivot and see the all-smiles Rex making his way toward me. I mirror his half hug, shifting my weight from foot to foot. "I'm here," I respond awkwardly. "You are too."

"I am."

I can only hope that by the time the actual dating starts, I'll have mentally perfected my usage of the English language. Because right now, I'm struggling to put the words together to form anything intelligible.

I forgot how awkward this would be already knowing someone present. The familiarity is bringing me anything but comfort. I might throw up.

"Well, I for one am very glad you came."

I fix my wavy hair over my shoulders, silently wishing I had pulled it up off my neck. I can already feel the sweat beading on my forehead, as more people shuffle into the shop.

"So, what do I do? I'm new at all of"—I sweep out a hand toward those gathering along the edge of the room—"this, and you look like a pro."

Rex smiles and moves over to a table set up along the wall. "Here," he says, handing me a white sticker with the number thirteen printed on it.

"Could you have assigned me a worse number?" I joke.

He chuckles. "I mean, I don't think the devil's number will be used, as the head count will break fire code. So, at least there's that. Oh, and here's your scorecard." He hands me a card with several columns listed.

"Okay…"

"It's pretty simple. Each guy will have a number assigned to him. Just rate them as a yes, no, or maybe. They will do the same. At the end, scorecards will be compared and you will be able to set up some outside dates with those with mutual interest."

I nod. "Sounds easy enough." I fidget with the hem of my shirt, hoping that my breathing can calm down enough to have a real conversation.

How am I supposed to socialize when I feel like hyperventilating?

"Oh, and I'm number one," Rex says with his megawatt smile.

I swallow hard. I knew Rex would be here tonight. I just wasn't expecting him to also be participating in the fun. Taking the pencil out of his hand, I start to circle the no for the first number.

"That's harsh," he says with a laugh.

I hand him back his pencil and then meander through the shop toward the order area. If I'm going to be starting off the night this nervous, then I better have something to hold in my hands to keep them from fidgeting.

"What can I get you?" the young female worker asks.

I scan over the menu. "I, um…"

She smiles at me when I am unable to complete a

sentence. "So, tonight, in addition to the coffee, we are also serving up some summer sangrias."

I shift my weight to the other foot. I'm not big into drinking when making decisions, but the thought of having a buffer to anything stupid I say is attractive to me. "Sure, let's go with that."

"Peach or berry."

"Berry, please."

I toss a few bills into the tip jar and pay for my drink. Making my way back to Rex, I spot my roommate.

"Penny, what are you doing here?" Luke asks.

I shrug. "Stepping out of my comfort zone. I thought you were working."

He wiggles his eyebrows. "Being around ladies is work. All the hidden messages and the deciphering needing to be done to even try to figure out what you all are saying… Yup. Hardest job around."

I smack his arm. "Why didn't you tell me you would be here? You literally helped me get dressed tonight."

"I'm shy."

"Bullshit."

"Well, you refused to tell me where you were going," he counters.

I shrug. "This is weird."

"Only if you make it weird. I mean, we basically bathe together."

I narrow my eyes. "Umm…no we don't."

"But we could. Easily."

"But we don't."

"Sure, but—"

I hold up my hand to stop him. "We are roommates who will never date—or bathe together."

Luke chuckles. "Only because I'm afraid to get my face bashed in by Meatball."

A smirk breaks on my lips. "By who?"

"You know…" He sighs. "Your life coach."

"I don't have a life coach."

I know exactly who he is referring to, and I'd be lying if I said I never thought of him tonight as I got ready. Collins most definitely wouldn't approve of any of this. He's been oddly quiet since I asked him to kiss me. Something changed that day in the gym, and I am still kicking myself for the role I played in the whole situation.

"But you have a gatekeeper."

"Well, getting your face bashed in should be a legit fear."

"I'm not on some kind of hit list, am I?" His eyes turn to concern. "Like, you would tell me, right? At least so I could get my funeral planned before the next economic depression?"

I think about the question, trying to keep the growing smile off my lips. "You're not on a list yet, but"—my head moves up and down several times—"yeah, I think I would tell you."

Luke pulls me into his side, and for a second I think he's going to mess up my hair, but instead he just embraces me into a half hug that screams sibling vibes all over it. Relief washes over me, as I find comfort in the friend zone.

There's no romantic spark between us, no matter how high he turns up the sexual energy. The feelings very much seem mutually platonic.

"If I get kidnapped by your stalker man and the police ask for a DNA sample, just get one from the couch."

"Ew. That's new!"

"Don't worry, everything dries clear."

"Yuck."

He better be kidding. I'll have to rush ship a black light just in case.

A deep voice comes on the mic, alerting participants to get a scorecard and pencil. The rules are explained and table assignments are done, with the women staying seated in one spot, while the men move through the lineup.

I take my seat at my assigned table, crossing my feet at my ankles beneath the surface. Wiggling my butt into the hard wood of the chair, I try to get comfortable. But I can't. My fingers twist a cocktail napkin into a deformed corkscrew, and then resort to fixing my hair neurotically behind my ears on repeat.

The once intimate space now feels claustrophobic. The tables are too small, and the thought of having to converse with someone I don't gel well with causes me anxiety—even if it's just for a few minutes.

My fingers curl and uncurl the edges of my scorecard, softening the cardboard from the sweat forming over my skin. Taking a sip of my sangria, I watch as other nervous patrons offer weak smiles and nods in greeting. I know I'm not alone, but I feel isolated, nonetheless. Maybe I'm just making this whole event bigger in my head than it needs to be.

Relax, Penny.

And as my therapist always asked, what's the worst thing that can happen? Sometimes facing some fears mentally head-on is the way to cope with the things holding me back.

It's what Margo has been telling me as well.

Sure, I could be seated across from a narcissistic jerk who only wants to talk about how awesome he is or some nerdy dude with an alphabetized stamp collection. So be it. I can just circle no, wait out the allotted time to elapse, and then hope the next person in the rotation is better than the last.

When I put it like that in my head, I think I'm ready to embark on this self-discovering journey.

I pull back my shoulders, take another sip from my liquid courage, and watch as the first guy—number five—takes his place opposite me.

"Hi," he says, reaching out his hand.

I relax my spine, take a deep breath, and offer up a smile. "Hi."

"How did everything go?" Rex asks, bumping me gently with his arm.

I laugh. "Better than expected. After we had our session, things started to pick up." So did the intake of my alcohol, but at events like this, I imagine some level of intoxication is expected. Granted, I'm just slightly tipsy. It's just enough to feel warm inside and a bit carefree.

Luke joins us, putting an arm around my shoulders to complete the man sandwich. "I just hope the fifteen hotties I circled yes for are matches."

"Fifteen seems like a lot," I comment, eyeing him for any sign of humor.

He shrugs. "It's all about increasing my odds."

Rex laughs. "Then why not just circle them all for yes?"

"Ew, I'm not a slut. Plus, I'm out of practice with this whole dating thing. I'm so used to showing my goods and then getting offers. This all seems backward."

I feel like this is the perfect opportunity for Luke to explain his line of work to Rex, but who am I to judge? I am living for these jaw-drop moments.

I make a face at my roommate. "You're a weirdo."

"Well, how many did you circle?"

"Nine."

Luke and Rex each step back to look at me and wiggle their eyebrows, making it awkward. I shake my head at them and then excuse myself to the ladies' room.

When I return, there's an energy moving through the venue.

"I got matched with six people," Rex says with excitement.

I know one of those people is not me. I'm just hoping that a handful of my circled men reciprocated their liking for me. I know of at least two guys who made it obvious that I was a yes by showing me their cards as they scored them.

Talk about an ego boost.

One of the male participants even slipped me a postcard looking thing and made me swear not to look at it until I'm home.

Who doesn't enjoy a little mystery and intrigue?

I turn to Luke, who seems to be busy doing math. "It's

just adding. Why are you acting like you are solving some difficult calculus problem?"

"Eleven," he says with the cheesiest grin. "It's basically an entire orgy if I invite them all over for"—he points to his groin—"introductions tonight."

I groan. "Ew."

Rex leans into me. "You better buy some stock in cleaning products. A solid sanitizing wipe can go a long way."

Luke shakes his head at us. "Don't worry, the chances are slim. I'd need them all to wear name tags, that's for sure. That all sounds like too much work. I'm in my lazy-lover mode era. I'm simple in the way that I just need one woman and both pairs of her lips."

When the host hands me my results, I look over the slip, trying to decipher what I'm actually seeing. This can't be right…

"Excuse me?" I say, causing him to turn around. "Is there some kind of mistake?" I lower my voice. "It appears that no one actually chose me."

He shifts his body weight to his other foot, glancing down to get a better look. "Huh. That's weird. That's never happened before, and I've been doing this event for nine years."

A warmth rushes up my neck to my cheeks, but the rest of me is chilled. Without another word, I pivot and move straight to the front counter, where I order another sangria—downing it with just a few gulps and nearly choking on the cut up bits of fruit.

This is so embarrassing.

A buzz fills my ears, causing me to shift on my feet. I grab the counter, straightening my body.

I need to get out of here. *Now.*

The air in here seems thicker, like I'm trying to suck mashed potatoes through a straw.

Reaching into my handbag, I pull out my phone, seeing that my ride isn't scheduled to arrive for another hour. Glancing around the space, I see couples chatting amongst themselves, probably setting up future dates. I thought tonight was going to go differently. I thought that I was here to banish some social fears and maybe start dating again.

Margo would be proud of me if I wasn't mentally spiraling into a full-blown freak-out moment.

The only thing I accomplished was to drink a little too much and to chip away more at my self-esteem. I keep building it up, just to break it down. If I don't have my brothers breathing down my neck, squashing all of my past dating possibilities, then I have my own insecurities creeping in through any crack in my exterior.

But really, who needs Nic and Graham to scare away guys, when I have a personality that seems to be doing the job equally as well?

Seriously though… What turned everyone off so I can keep that shit under wraps?

A pang of regret hits my stomach that is compressing into knots, after the surge of alcohol hit it. I shouldn't have come here. I shouldn't have put myself in this vulnerable position to get humiliated.

Making my way toward the exit, I push open the door and breathe in the fresh night air. I swipe my hair behind my shoulders and rock on my heels, thinking about where to go and what to do next.

It sucks not having friends in the city. I guess I could ask Luke or Rex for a lift, but they are busy flirting with their matches inside. Who could blame them? It's an exciting time—at least for those who have made mutual connections.

Calling Angie or Claire will alert my brothers, who will just crack down on more shadowing for me.

Looking down at my feet, I try to think of how tonight got so off course. I had really good conversations with so many of the guys. I wasn't shy, and I don't think I gave off any negative vibe.

But what do I know?

Obviously, nothing. I know nothing about the opposite sex.

Staring at my hands, I realize I no longer have my handbag, which has my phone and house keys.

Shit.

I must have dropped it.

Turning on my heel, I make my way back into the coffee shop to find it in the shadow of the door.

Looking up, I see a couple of the guys I expected to be matched with loitering in some sort of testosterone circle. We all had really good conversation, so not having any of them select me is really mind-boggling.

"Hey, Penny," one says, separating himself from the group.

I give a weak smile and a wave and then start to make my way back to the door. But before I can exit, I turn around and clear my throat.

"I just need to know"—I prop my hands on my hips—"why not me?"

The tall, dark-haired man frowns. "I was wondering the same thing about you. We had good conversation and I was shocked when we weren't matched. I figured you saw some"—he gestures into the air—"red flag."

"What? No. I never saw anything." But lately, I never do. I've been caught off guard so many times that I'm honestly questioning my intuition. "Well, that's weird."

When I go to leave, he follows me outside while I stand on the curb of the sidewalk.

"I most definitely said yes to you, Penny. You even watched me circle my response."

"When we weren't matched, I figured you just did that for show and changed your answer when I wasn't looking."

His eyes light up. "I would never do that. And I still say yes. Why not come hang out at my place? Not sure why the scoring system failed us, but I'd like the chance to get to know each other better."

Staring up into his eyes, I see the potential for an impulsive decision teetering on the edge of my tongue. "I don't know…"

"C'mon. Clearly we both like each other."

This doesn't feel right. It feels like I am betraying my own heart's desires.

Sure, he seems nice. But now that the adrenaline from the night is wearing off, I'm not so sure my feelings match what they were an hour ago.

"I just am—"

I stumble backward as his lips attach with mine, stealing my next words before they get the chance to be vocalized.

I've been kissed before by a guy, but this seems nothing like what I expected from past experience. This is rougher. A tad bit aggressive. And—

Where are his hands going?

No.

Stop.

Please stop.

I gasp for air just as his lips part so his tongue can go deeper.

It's slimy.

Ew.

Stop!

My handbag slips from my fingertips, as I struggle to keep my balance.

I squeeze my eyes shut, and I muster enough courage to push at his chest. "Mrrph…"

His moan comes out ragged, and the smell of alcohol on his breath lets me know that he was drinking heavily. His proximity burns my nostrils, making them flare as I try to push against him again.

But he's too strong.

His mouth crashes with mine, stealing from me my ability to consent verbally.

Tears fight for release at the corners of my eyes. "Staaa…"

And then suddenly his lips are ripped from mine. I suck in some air, flopping forward with my hands on my knees. And then I look up between my now soaked eyelashes to see *him* through my fog of tears.

Vibrant.

Enthralling.

Livid.

Collins Stone.

I blink to clear my vision and verify I'm not hallucinating.

"You came," I say in shock, my hands clutching at the fabric of my shirt over my heart.

My breathing is erratic, as if my lungs suddenly forget how to work.

The energy of Collins flows around me, coating me with the weight that can only come from someone with power.

"I will always come for you, Penelope."

23

COLLINS

I'm going to kill him. Straight up, on the streets in Portland, I'm going to gut the man alive and paint the city with his sacrificial blood just to send a message to anyone who dares to touch Penelope Hoffman.

All witnesses can be paid off. All security footage can be wiped clean.

Because right now, I don't think I've been angrier.

Or more dangerous.

He touched her.

He fucking *touched* her.

And all of the self-defense moves I taught to her just days ago went right out the window because she was paralyzed by fear.

Bastard.

I'm done with this game of tug-of-war with Penny where the only way it ends is by us both getting hurt. But dammit if I'll stand back and watch another man claim her soft lips or touch her smooth curves.

"Penny, are you okay?" I mean, how can she be?

Her silent nod is all I need to confirm that today's the day I wage war on this poor excuse for a man.

"She wanted it."

Turning my attention back to the kiss thief, I pull back my fist and drive it forward, connecting with the flesh of his cheek. He roars from the pain and stumbles to the concrete. As I pull back to go another round, I feel soft determined hands tug at me.

"Please, no, Collins," Penny pleads.

"He touched you," I say simply, as if that is explanation alone.

Does she not understand the severity of this? Because I'm about to show her what happens to assholes who overstep boundaries.

"I know. But I'm okay. Let's go before someone calls the cops for assault."

"He won't call anyone because the cameras on the store front will show him pushing himself on you first."

"I'm okay," she whispers. "Please…"

Relief floods through me that Penny is at least talking and not slipping into the dark hole she buried herself in most of last year.

My mind goes through my list of potential ways to make this look like an accident if he lays one more fucking finger on Penelope Hoffman—who is my responsibility to protect.

Just one more finger…

And then I'll end him.

For fun, I'll make him bleed slowly too. I know just how to prolong the inevitable if it means righting some wrongs. And this fucker made an unforgivable mistake.

That's how irate I am.

I can't believe he forced himself on her. She was not enjoying that at all.

I'd make her enjoy the feeling of being ravished—not abused.

Why can't pricks understand there is a difference between being dominant and being abusive? Every male wants to pretend he's an alpha, when in fact most are just insecure assholes who treat women as if they are expendable.

Penelope Josephine Hoffman is not replaceable.

She's a one-of-a-kind diamond in a mine of dull rocks.

My mood has been volatile all evening. And this… This is sending me over the edge, and if the abyss has this idiot's bones decaying at the bottom of it, I'll follow him down just to spit on his bloody grave.

He fucking touched her.

I should have been here sooner. Regret has already seeped into the shallow cracks of my dark soul. But I'm here now. And I will finish this fucker no matter how much cleanup it'll take in the aftermath.

Stumbling about on the sidewalk, the asshole bares his teeth toward me. "What was that for?"

"Never lay a finger on her again. Never look at her. Never come near her. Do you understand?"

Not saying a word, he approaches me for another round.

Let the fun begin…

I guide Penny behind me, as I prepare myself to unleash my wrath onto his face.

The kiss thief makes the first move, sending his fist barreling through the air. I catch it and drive it down toward the ground, as I punch right underneath his armpit into the ribs.

I hear a crack—and it's not my knuckles.

He crumbles to the sidewalk, weeping.

I pivot to check on a trembling Penny who is now tucked into a ball on the cement beneath her hugged arms.

But then in my periphery, the spud gets up and grabs for my knees, which I dodge.

Primal rage courses through me, as I grip the kiss thief's neck, dragging him up to come face-to-face with what he decided to set into motion.

"Straighten your spine," I hiss, "and face your demons like a man."

"Collins!"

My head feels like it's in a tunnel, and the only light at the end is justice for Penny.

"COLLINS!"

It's her voice. Her sweet, innocent voice…

"Don't hurt him," she yells from behind me, holding on to my biceps before I deliver another punishing blow. "Please."

Please?

"Sometimes lessons need to be taught. This idiot deserves to suffer for what he did to you. Throwing himself on you like that…"

"Let's go. Please."

There's that plea again. And just that one word is wreaking havoc on my conscience—something I didn't even think existed anymore.

I let go of the man, allowing gravity to take over. I want to solidify my point, yet I don't want Penny to have a front-row seat to my anger. She's been through too much and has experienced enough trauma tonight.

"She, ah, waa…" he stutters.

"Collins!" Penny squeals. "I'm fine. Let's go."

My eyes dart to hers, silencing her with what I can only assume is fear from my piercing gaze. "He touched you," I scoff, as if that should be enough reason for my temper. Why isn't she begging for me to annihilate him right now, right here?

Using the toe of my shoe, I kick at the fucker, getting him to roll over and look up at me. "There are twenty-seven bones in the human hand. So, if you touch her again, I'll break all twenty-seven and then rip both of those hands off, just to beat you with them. You dare to look at her again, I'll use a rusty sling blade to carve out those eyeballs of yours and shove them down your throat to choke on. And if you even think of coming within fifty yards of her, I'll saw through your femur so you'll never walk again. Do you understand?"

I watch as he throws himself off the ground and scampers off down the street to his car. Smartest thing the asshole has done all evening. I know he's had his eyes set on Penny. And if he thinks he can just charm his way into her panties, then he obviously doesn't understand the lengths I go through to keep her safe.

"Was that necessary?" Penny asks, gasping for air and pointing at the guy's retreating form. He better the hell scurry away before I neuter him. "Was it?" Her voice is louder.

"Yes," I snarl. Why are we even discussing this? The obvious answer can't be anything other than yes. Why is she now mad at me? "I spared him his life, Penelope. And that's something I never do."

"Why do you care? You don't even want me. Hell, every guy in that room"—she points behind her toward the coffee shop—"didn't want me." Tears pour out of her eyes in a cascading waterfall that I worry will never end. "Did you hear me? No one wants me!"

Oh, they wanted her. Who couldn't want someone as beautiful and flawless as Penelope Hoffman?

I grab her hand and pull her away from the coffee shop, trying to get space between us and the location where I almost took a man's life.

Dropping her hand, I rub my hands over the back of my neck.

I need time to cool off.

Even I know I have a temper that needs checked at times. But no matter how mad I get, I'll never lay a hand on Penny Hoffman. Unless, of course…

Dammit.

I need to get my head on straight.

But it's her fucking sniffles and her whimpering that are going to destroy all the self-control I've been trying so hard to maintain.

I glance over at her.

She looks so sad—lost.

I take a step closer, reaching up my thumbs to trail across her lips. "I want to wipe that disgusting guy's memory from your lips and make it so that the only thing on your mind is me."

"Then do it," she challenges.

It takes just a few seconds to weigh the consequences.

"I'll take you home, Pen," I say with finality.

I should take you home.

I've already exposed my hand to her tonight and my true feelings on the matter. She wanted me to kiss her at the apartment gym, but what she didn't realize is that I wanted to do so much more with her.

I'm in way over my head with desire for this girl, and the only way to fix it is to remove myself entirely from the situation.

Penny shakes her head. "No. I just want to stand here until I drown in enough self-pity to feel numb. Then I may think about going with you. But I'll decide—not you."

I take a step closer, just now realizing we have migrated into the alleyway along the side of the coffee shop. With hesitation, I extend a hand for her to take. "Come."

She lets out a demonic laugh and uses her thumb to point back behind her toward the coffee shop. "Nearly fifty men inside that place and not a single one got matched with me."

I clear my throat. None of those men deserve to even breathe the same air as her, let alone have a chance to score a real date.

Her hands fly into the air with exaggerated animation. "Like, am I really that repulsive?"

"Penelope…"

Her eyes study mine. "Answer the question."

"You shouldn't be here," I warn, almost sounding angry.

"But I am here. I'm here," she snaps. "And I am fucking tired of putting myself out into the world, just to feel the bitter sting of rejection. Just tell me what is wrong with me?"

"Not a damn thing."

The night is a dumpster fire. Why not just embrace the chaos and solidify my spot in hell—all in one day's time?

"But there is. There must be!"

I close the distance between us, allowing my need to prove her wrong to be my sole motivation. I feel edgier with every second that passes, and when I can't exercise any more restraint, I slide a hand to the base of Penny's throat, resting it gently against the pulse point.

Warmth coats my skin as I stand in her presence. It's like two souls meeting for the first time—and really seeing each other.

She is my stability, and her happiness is my strength.

My thumb massages over her sensitive skin, causing shivers to run up her body, all the way to her limbs where I see the telltale sign of my effect on her. "You are like the rarest, most exotic flower in a garden of weeds, Penny."

"Oh, wonderful," she groans, tilting her head up at the muted lights casting a glow into the alley.

The exposed column of her neck beckons me—taunts me. I want to bite it and then lick it better.

"What?"

"No wonder why no one wants to ravish me. I'm a freaking flower."

She pulls away from my loose hold on her, causing my hand to drop, and flops her head in defeat. Her come-fuck-me heels tease me.

I want her like no one I've ever wanted before…

I'm not sure if Graham and Nic have hired someone from the inside to tamper with her dates tonight. But if they did, I owe whomever a huge thank you.

Tilting her chin up with two fingers, I force her to look at me. "What's wrong with that? You are unique and one of a kind."

She shakes her head adamantly, placing both palms onto my chest. "I just wish men would quit seeing me as something that needs to be preserved and start seeing me as something meant to be enjoyed and experienced. No one wants to fuck a flower."

"You are a lot more innocent than you think. You need to be careful, or you'll wind up in a lot more trouble than you bargained for."

She makes a face. She does this a lot at me. "And how do you know?" She pushes up the hem of her shirt to reveal her navel, running her hand over her abdomen. "Are you keeping tabs on my sex life?"

My heart skips, and I can feel my nostrils flare. She's getting to me, and I'm allowing it. "Keep toying with me and see what happens."

A huff of breath deflates from her, while her eyes roll upward. "It can't be worse than what is happening now."

"And what is happening, Penny? Enlighten me."

"You are impeding on my fun just like everyone else in my life has done for the past year. I'm tired of being told when to sleep and when to eat and when to talk. I just want to live. Can you blame me? And if the answer even resembles something close to *no*, then please back down for just one time. Let me make some stupid mistakes. Let me get hurt."

"You did get hurt, Penelope," I snarl. "That bastard back there should be thankful he has full function of both of his hands."

"Maybe I want to experience pain if just to feel alive."

"Did getting manhandled in the streets of Portland by some asshole fulfill your needs?"

"No. But that's because I want *you* to do the manhandling. I want the same experience but with the right person. That's what went wrong tonight, Collins. He was not *you*. I want *you*."

"Penny…you've been drinking."

"No. I mean, yeah, I have been, but that isn't warping my true feelings on this shitty subject. So hear me out," she says, moving to poking her finger into my chest. "I'm tired of everyone around me putting me up on a shelf for safekeeping. I am not some expensive doll that never gets a chance to play. I want to play, Collins."

"You don't know what you are saying."

She takes a step backward, moving her hands down her body and then cupping her boobs.

Fuck.

What is she doing?

"I'm not a child, Collins. I'm a grown woman if you haven't noticed."

I choke on the spit pooling in my mouth, and then awkwardly swallow it down. "I noticed."

"Have you?" she questions. "Because to me, I'm constantly stuck wondering what is going on in your head—and every other guy's for that matter. And quite frankly, I'm not sure my ego can handle another man saying no to me tonight. I'm tired of not being good enou—"

In one fluid motion, I take Penny into my arms and push her back so her shoulders rest against the cold stone wall of the building. My hands rest on her curvy hips, playing with the belt loops of her painted-on jeans.

My touch is gentle, reverent—and every part of me holds back the beast inside that wants to show this girl exactly what I'm made of…

"What are you doing?"

"I'm about to enjoy the best taste I can imagine of forbidden fruit."

24

COLLINS

“Yes,” Penny hisses, spurring on every bad decision I’m about to make.

“But I know I shouldn’t. Because I’m afraid one taste won’t be enough.”

“We don’t go through life holding an umbrella just in case it decides to rain. You must take risks.”

My eyes focus on her lips. The way they press together… The slight glossy shine they have in the lights filtering in from the main street. “If this doesn’t put me on the fast track to hell then there may be redemption for me after all.”

A whimper escapes her lips, as my vision blurs.

My thumbs reach up and trace a soft path along the outline of her lips, wiping away the touch from the past. And then I feel it—Penny’s tongue—licking the pads of my fingers and then sucking them inside her warm mouth.

Closing my eyes, I roll my head back slightly as the blood rushes to my cock, providing it life.

Dammit, that feels good.

All the bad decisions I've delayed making are on the edge of the cliff I've been too afraid to leap off—until now.

So I jump.

And without warning, my thumbs slide out of her mouth and my own lips crash into hers, as Penny's part to let me in.

That's a good girl.

I devour her.

I lick and taste and probe and…savor.

I get drunk off her innocence, and indulge in the taste of sin and betrayal. And in this one moment in time, it's as if our hearts collide, sending energy through my entire body and into hers.

Our frames mold to each other, as if we can't get close enough.

Penny breathes into me the life I didn't know I wasn't experiencing, opening for me and giving me permission to fill in her voids.

My arms wrap around her, molding her to me and shielding her body with mine as I binge on her sweetness.

I can't think.

I can't breathe.

But I sure as hell can feel. And in this moment—right now—I feel on top of the world.

All this time, I thought I could resist her, but my craving is just too strong. Knowing that she feels the same way is what is making it impossible to keep my emotions in check. She wants me like I want her.

The rigidness of my cock rubs against me through my pants, fighting for more friction.

"Is this proof enough of my desire?" I growl, while sliding my hands over the sides of her waistline.

My teeth bite at her, demanding that she opens up more for me. I want her to give in to the passion that I'm inflicting on her wanton body. I suck air into my lungs, making me feel alive, while one hand grips her hair and the other digs into her ass.

Lifting up her leg, I wrap it around my hips, allowing the other to join. I grind my cock against her pussy, causing her kiss to become more…

Assertive?

No.

Impassioned.

I lean my weight against the wall, resting a hand by her head, while my entire body shields hers by its sheer mass. My thumb from my other hand grazes against her cheekbone, tracing along the curvature of her jaw, and then slowly it makes its way down to her neck.

"I wish I knew what you were thinking," she says softly.

My eyes hood, while I maintain a firm grip on her body to keep her stable. "I'm thinking about how I'm going to burn for every dirty thought of you running unrestrained in my head."

She smirks. "How dirty?"

I study her. Why is she not running away from me? Why is she not fighting against me? Why does she feel so content in my arms?

But she doesn't know… She'll never know…

"You have no fucking clue how depraved my mind and my tastes are."

Leaning forward, she pushes her shoulders off the wall

to get closer to me. "What…happens…if…" she says, kissing me between each word. "I…want…dirty?"

My body hardens against hers. She feels like a dream. It's as if she'll just float away if I don't hold on to her tightly.

She's my weakness and my strength—in equal parts.

But the consequence of us being together could eventually send a ripple into this moment in time that could cause catastrophic damages in the future.

I pull back after licking her sweet lips, sucking in air through my teeth.

"You don't know what you're saying."

"Why do you keep overthinking everything?"

Gently placing Penny back onto sturdy ground, I take two steps away from her, while running my hands through my hair. "Dammit, we shouldn't be doing this."

"And why not?"

She looks genuinely confused. Why is this so hard for her to understand?

Penny shakes her head. Her breathing picks up, causing her chest to rise and fall like rolling hills. "You are valuing sex too much. Quit making it into a big ceremony or something. Just put it in"—she pauses her monologue to add hand movements—"swish it around a few times. Bam-o. Done."

I can feel my mouth gaping, as I take another step back.

"What the hell, Pen? Is that how you view sex? This isn't like making a freaking cocktail. There's a bit more finesse." My fingers run through my hair.

"I'm simply saying that it doesn't need to be more than what it is. I don't need special."

"You deserve special, Pen." I know she's been drinking, but there's still some truth to her description, and a part of me is upset that she lacks the self-esteem to wish for something grander. And dare I think it—a little more special.

"I need a release. I need someone to notice me and to want to be with me. And I'm starting to get antsy and desperate. The next guy that shows me any interest will probably find himself inside my squishy pussy before he can use his safe word."

"Fucking hell, you don't know what you're saying."

"I'm not some little girl who doesn't know what sex is, Collins."

"You deserve more than to get railed in the backseat of some loser's car."

I close the distance between us.

My fingers dig gently into the softness of her hips, and for a second I worry I will bruise her. She has all the right curves, and I love having something to squeeze on to…

Except I shouldn't. I shouldn't be touching. I shouldn't be sampling the forbidden fruit, no matter how tempting she is and how persuasive her depictions are. Yet, my eyes can't stop focusing on her beautiful body or how her breasts look extra plump when she is breathing heavily.

Penny is equal parts sweet and sassy—and I can't decide which I like best.

I sigh. Why am I the only one who understands the implications and the fallout that will ensue if her family were to find out I made a move on her? "You are the baby sister of the two men who entrusted me with your care."

"I never asked for a guardian, Collins. I didn't ask for anything."

"That doesn't change the reality of the current situation."

"Well, then quit," she challenges.

"I'm older by sixteen years. I should know better. It's too big of an age gap, little princess."

"So."

"It's wrong. And I'd be evil for pursuing it."

"Oh, please save my ears from filling them with the innocence garbage. I'm a grown woman—one who is rejected yet again tonight. And this stings the worst, because you showed me what it could feel like to be with you. And I fucking liked it!"

I can't even look at her. I can't be near her and not want to rip her clothes off.

She's the source of all my agony—all my torment—and to downplay this life-shattering decision to merely just a rejection is careless.

"This isn't a rejection, Penny. This is self-reflection. Because crossing over the line a little is still crossing over the line. There's no gray area where you are concerned."

What I want to do with Penelope Hoffman is wrong on all accounts.

But I'm lacking the strength to resist, and the way her lip is pouting out, I don't think she realizes just how much I yearn for her.

"We are attracted to one another. And I consent to whatever you're willing to give to me."

"But this is wrong, Pen. I know it. You know it."

Her nose flares, and I brace myself for the fire. "Then why does wrong feel so right?"

"Because you are intoxicated."

“Am not!”

I glance down at her plump curves, while wrapping her blonde locks between my fingers. “You are an angel with the purest heart, and I’m a monster desiring to commit my next sin. I’m not good for you, Penny. And this is wrong going against your brothers’ backs.”

“Please don’t mention my brothers right now, Collins. Not now. Not while I’m being vulnerable in front of you. You think you have dirty thoughts flooding through your brain right now. Well, you haven’t seen mine. They will rival yours—guaranteed. If I’m an angel, I’m a dark one. Don’t let the innocent facade fool you. I know what I want. And I’m prepared to go through the flames to get it.”

I believe every word she speaks. I know that just having the Hoffman last name gives her a certain amount of power. The problem is, her brothers have way more of it. They run this city with their connections and wealth. The last thing I need is to be on the opposite side of their good graces.

I’d much rather be an ally than an enemy.

And touching their one and only sister will be the ultimate betrayal to sever any bond I’ve spent years trying to nurture.

Sure, I can hold my own. But why would I want to spit in the faces of my bosses?

Penny is determined. And if I’m not careful, I’ll either fall for her or suffer at the hands of the men who hired me to keep their sister safe.

“Come,” I say, taking ahold of her elbow. “I’m taking you back to your place, before I make the biggest mistake of my life.”

“How noble of you,” she gripes, trying to pull away

from me. She bends to pick up her handbag and tosses a few items that poured out onto the street back in.

Ignoring her saltiness, I guide her to my SUV and open the passenger side door, helping her inside. I take a few deep breaths as I round the front and enter into the driver's side. I snap on my belt and spare a glance her way.

"It's not that I don't want you, Pen. Trust me, I do."

"But not enough to actually act on it."

"It's best for the both of us if I don't. I've already overstepped enough."

"Because I'm not like all the other girls…"

"No, you are not." Doesn't she realize that men don't actually enjoy the easy girls, as much as they enjoy the chase? "But that's not a bad thing."

Penny picks some paint off her fingernails, looking out the window as I start to pull out onto the street and into traffic. "Are you going to go to jail for assault?"

"It'll be worth it."

Her head whips over to me. "Collins…"

"No, Penny. I won't be going to prison. That fucker won't be pressing charges."

"Why are you so certain?"

"Because he has an open warrant in Washington state and won't be drawing any more attention to himself."

Her eyes blink a few times, probably trying to decipher first if I'm telling the truth and then second how I'm privy to these bits of information.

"Just take me home," she says in exasperation after a long pause. "I'm ready for some battery operated toys and a new day to start. Who needs a man to stumble around trying to please himself in my flesh when I have silicone and my own hands to do the job?"

My greedy-as-fuck cock jerks in my pants as if it just hit puberty and can't keep under control. The sass on this girl. She knows exactly what to say to elicit a reaction out of me —albeit this time I'm able to stay quiet about it.

She has no clue just how good being with me would be. What she doesn't need is some boy in need of a road map to locate her erogenous zones. No. Instead she needs a man who can work her up to the edge and then send her over it in a rush. She doesn't need someone to satisfy her. She needs someone to devour her.

But I'm not the man.

I can't be that man.

We drive in silence back to Sky View Apartments. I'm used to the quiet and yet there's something so bothersome to me about all of this.

I keep my eyes on the road, afraid that if I glance over, I'll give away every emotion running through my body right now—many I haven't even deciphered quite yet. There's a large part of me that knows my torrid thoughts are going to get me sent straight to hell.

Yet, there's a more aggressive part of me that knows that every stirring sensation I am feeling inside is in direct relation to the happiness Penny brings into my life. She makes me want to be softer, more yielding.

Don't get me wrong. I'm demanding as fuck. It's just that now I'm considering how my actions will make her feel. I don't want to scare her with my intensity. If anything, I want to make her feel so comfortable that if she ever has a problem, I'll be the first person she'll lean on.

A foreign feeling rushes over me. Is this what jealousy feels like? I already feel like an idiot comparing myself to inanimate objects—like her silicone dildo—when clearly I can supply her needs better than they can.

But that's what this whole night has been about, beyond just protecting Penny.

It was about jealousy.

If I can't have Penny, no person or object can…

And that there is the shittiest revelation of this entire journey.

I finally glance over at her as she fidgets with her handbag, opening and closing about two inches worth of the zipper on repeat. "I think I'm broken."

"You aren't broken, Penny. Don't say things like that."

She shakes her head adamantly. "How else would you describe it then, Collins? I'm twenty-two years old and have only experienced one orgasm in my entire life. And I think it was just a fluke anyway. It wasn't anything like the magazines describe it as."

Oh. I was not expecting this. Damn.

And then she sighs. "And now I'm questioning if I ever even experienced one in the first place. And it definitely was by my own doing if it was genuinely one, because there's no way a man could ever be responsible enough to handle that endeavor."

Well, at least I know that Penny is an open book when she has some wine running throughout her system. She's providing me more insight into her past experiences than I've known up to now.

"What makes you question yourself?" Why the fuck am I even asking? What benefit would result from knowing this highly inappropriate information? I'm her bodyguard for fuck's sake—not her sex coach.

"Because the euphoria I felt when you kissed and ground against me in the alleyway was so potent that I know I've never felt that zing before in my…"

Now she's being shy? What's changed other than possibly having a chance to sober up?

I nod, not because I'm agreeing with anything she's saying, but instead because I'm trying with everything I am not to sport a freaking hard-on in these close quarters with her—when all I need to do is draw a firmer line. And then actually not cross it.

"Pussy."

Fuck. Is she trying to kill me? Is it the alcohol that just dissolves her filter or is this the real Penny all along?

I know Graham and Nic want to keep this angelic vision of Penny preserved in their minds, and I don't blame them one bit from all she's endured from Mark Tanner, but this woman is not the innocent little girl they see.

No.

Penny is a seductress.

And every naughty word spilling out of her perfect little mouth causes a primal response deep within me.

To claim.

To worship.

To own.

There's no path out of this situation that won't lead to hell. I am literally delaying the inevitable.

I slipped up tonight, and while I promised myself I wouldn't do it again after sending Penny mixed messages during our self-defense session, I know I'm a liar. I know that if this girl keeps dangling her forbidden fruits in front of me, she's going to unleash the hunger inside me that won't be quenched until I make her completely mine.

If Penny only realized how dark my desires for her go, then she would understand why a rejection by me is the best thing for her right now. She isn't ready for what I have to offer, and she sure isn't ready for the baggage I bring to the table.

When we get up to her place, she unloads the contents of her handbag all over the floor outside her apartment, most likely looking for her keys.

"Why do you have plastic spiders in your bag?" I ask, growing very suspicious she's the person who placed one into my glass the other day.

"Oh, no reason."

It's amazing how much a small rectangular bag can hold.

I watch as this firecracker of a girl sifts through all her belongings, excited to find the key that should never have taken three minutes to locate.

By the time she stands to insert it, she notices my own in her lock.

"That's obnoxious, you know?" she says with a glare. "I guess I need to change the locks."

"And I guess I'll just need to make a new key then."

"That's breaking the law."

"Report me."

She sticks her tongue out, turns my key, and pushes open the door in a huff.

"Fuck!" Luke calls out over his shoulders.

I shoot daggers at him as he stumbles about the place,

covering up his freaking dick with the palms of his hands, while some girl pouts her lips that she had to stop giving what appears to be a blowjob.

Penny's mouth completely gapes, as her eyes stay glued on the situation. "Shit," she slowly whispers, her voice sounding throaty and raw.

I pull her away from her place, slam the door without a care for anyone on the floor within hearing range, and usher her back down the hallway.

She tugs on my arm, but I keep moving, pulling her toward the elevators and away from her horned-up roommate.

"What is happening?" She lets out a strained giggle, as she tries to look back to where we just left. "What did I just witness?"

Anger bubbles inside me. That idiot. "That there was your dog of a roommate getting it on with some eager participant. How often does he forget you live there too, Penny?"

She shrugs, watching mindlessly as I slam the button on the wall. "I, uh, not often."

"So this has happened before?"

"No. I mean, unless my mind is blocking out the trauma."

"Fuck."

"I'm sure he is clothed now and his cock has simmered down to a lukewarm state."

And then she loses it in a fit of laughter over her little joke and play on words with his name.

"You are staying with me."

I glare down at her doubled over form. Is she really

making light of this situation? And does she really think I would escort her back to that whorehouse of a residence? Luke better be glad I don't toss his entire body into a freezer to cool down.

Straightening herself up, Penny places her hands on her hips. Oh great, now comes the defiance.

"I want to go back and at least grab my toys."

What the actual fuck? "No." Is she for real? How will I be able to maintain a professional relationship if I know she is masturbating a room away from me down the hall in my own residence?

The elevator car arrives, and I usher her inside before she can think to protest further.

"You don't even want me," she snaps, as the elevator doors close, securing us inside.

"I want you safe, first and foremost. And if that means doing my fucking job, then so be it. But going against what I'm hired to do is not in either of our best interests." No matter how horny this princess makes me. "And there's no way in hell I'm allowing you in your apartment while your roommate is entertaining some chick while nude."

Luke needs to contain his hobbies to his own bedroom. I'll be damned if I'm allowing Penny to go back to that scene. Her entire place is going to need disinfected.

"Well, I'm not staying with you."

"You are staying somewhere," I challenge. "And it won't be your apartment."

Penny twists her fingers, while rocking on her feet.

"Let me go get my clothes at least."

"You aren't walking back into that fuck fest."

"Huh…"

"What?"

"A fuck fest sounds amazing right now. Maybe there's room for one more."

Oh, hell no. "You better be joking."

She shrugs. "You'll never know."

I stay on guard in case she decides to make a run for it when the car arrives to the designated floor. "I have clothes at my place. You're staying with me."

"Can I expect a fuck fest?"

"No, Penelope."

"You are boring."

25

PENNY

I wake the next day in Collins's guest room with a migraine from hell. Pinching the bridge of my nose, I try to get the pounding to subside.

That's what that bitch, sangria, does to me. She is a sneaky thing whose company is enjoyable at first, but then out of nowhere, she gets hostile.

Despite drinking way too much the night before, I have all the essential events carved into my brain. The humiliation… The jealous rage… And the disappointment of wanting someone who will never choose me.

Despite the kiss and petting session, Collins doesn't want me. He just likes toying with my emotions. Hot and cold. One minute we are making out. The next he's pushing me away. Sure, I get his motives for wanting to keep everything business, but my brothers don't dictate my life.

If it wasn't for the memory of our kiss burned on my lips, I would have thought I dreamt the whole thing up. But based on the friendship vibe I got right afterward, I doubt I'll ever get to experience it again.

I'm a job.

I'm also a mistake.

There's a light knock on my door. "Penny?"

"Yeah, come in."

I pull my comforter up to my neck, trying to sit up in the darkness.

With just a shift of the blackout curtains, Collins has the light spilling into the room, coating the entire space in a golden hue.

"Turn it down," I moan, pressing my palms into my eye sockets.

"What—the sun?"

"Yes. It's too early for this type of offensive behavior."

Collins chuckles. "Penny, it's noon."

"Oh."

He sits on the edge of my bed, causing it to dip slightly. "Feeling pretty bad, yeah?"

"Yup."

"Hope you learned a lesson."

I give his snideness a mental middle finger. "Oh, I did. But it's only to be extra sly when I try to ditch you next time."

"I had eyes on you and knew where you were the whole time."

"That's super creepy." I push my hair off my forehead. "Surely you can agree that your level of surveillance over me is stalkerish."

"It is."

"See?" I point my finger at him. "You admit to it!"

"I do."

Sliding out of bed, I stumble into the bathroom, wincing as I need to turn on a light or risk falling into the bathtub instead of the toilet. With my foot, I kick the door shut.

When I exit, Collins has vanished but has placed a bottle of water on my nightstand with two ibuprofens and a sandwich.

Why does him taking care of me cause me to smile and stomp my foot at the same time?

His personality is a dichotomy between knight in shining armor and unhinged stalker.

Both sides of Collins drive me equally wonky.

I throw myself back into bed and take a bite of the sandwich.

It is perfection.

I drink my water and swallow my medicine without the hovering of my bodyguard to make sure I do all the steps correctly.

See—I can be a fully functioning adult.

Reaching for my handbag, I remove the slip that states I had zero matches from last night.

How humiliating…

And then I find the postcard thing that one of the men—I can't remember his name—handed to me.

Turning it over in my hands, I read the description written in elegant, printed font.

Glow Night - July 25th
444 Fine Oak Lane

Wow. Tonight.

If I had been in a good headspace after the speed dating event, I would have pulled out this postcard last night and inquired further about it with the person who actually handed it to me.

It's just that everything surrounding it is fuzzy. I know that if my memory was clearer, I would be more excited for it than I am now.

However, I'm too devastated and butt-hurt over my loss of hope that someone—anyone—would have wanted me beyond the five minutes we were assigned to chat.

So why would I think going to a public event again will pan out in my favor?

It seems like if I attend, I'm essentially a masochist, which in a way I've already confirmed.

So what's the harm in submitting myself to even more humiliation? It really can't get worse—can it?

I read the card again.

But it does sound fun…

And if I deserve anything right now—it's fun.

I'm doing it.

And Mr. Collins Stone doesn't need to find out.

After breakfast—which is essentially lunch at this point—Collins walks me back to my place and enters first to assess what I assume would be the scene.

"Any cocks or vaginas?" I ask, peering around his side dramatically and a tad bit hopeful.

I can't believe we kissed last night, and it was by far the best one of my life.

But it's obvious that Collins's hard exterior shell is in place as he's in work mode.

He grunts out what I assume is a no.

Something is on his mind. I can tell by the way he isn't offering even a smirk at my attempted humor.

"I need to be away the rest of the day."

"Okay…"

"Typically I wouldn't make this known, but I am since you have the tendency of getting drunk off your freedom. The last thing I need is to come back here and find you in the middle of—"

"A fuck fest."

"No," he snaps. "I was going to say…trouble."

"Why are you telling me this though?"

"Because I will have tabs on you and don't want you to be alarmed if you feel the presence of someone watching you."

"Okay. I'll probably just mope around and beg for your safe return so we can cuddle on the couch and watch movies."

"Penny…"

"What? Oh, let me guess. You find that offensive too?"

"What happened in the alleyway was wrong." He clears his throat. "The kiss… I was wrong. I knew better, and I took advantage of you."

"Can you do it again?"

"No," he snaps, his jaw dropping just a tad before he regains his composure.

I let out an exasperated breath. "And why not, Collins? I'm a consenting adult. I consent to your hands roaming up my body. I consent to your mouth devouring me. I consent to it all. I want more." The desperation can't be removed from the tone of my words. I'm needy and whiny—and I also don't care.

"Never again, Penny."

I take a step closer to him. "You are horrible for my ego. You know that?"

"I never want to hurt you."

"Well, I'm hurt." It's the truth too.

"I'm looking for a replacement."

"A replacement for who?"

"Me. I can't keep guarding you."

It's like the breath is taken from me at just the sound of his words. "If not you, then who?" I demand.

"That's what I'm trying to figure out."

"And I get no say yet again?"

"That's correct."

I'm angry that he's giving up on me. And I'm angry that I'm upset over this.

For weeks, I've resented Collins for being in charge of my safety. Then when I finally start enjoying his company, he wants to desert me and pass me off to someone else.

Pushing at his chest, I try to get him to move. "Just leave. Bye. Go enjoy your time away from me."

A sadness hits his features, but he doesn't argue or defend himself or his choices. When Collins exits my apartment, I shut the door and lean my back against the smooth surface.

I feel emotionally drained.

Closing my eyes, I rub both hands behind the back of my neck, trying to ease the building tension.

Knock.

Knock.

Knock.

Startled by the sound, I push myself off the door and take a look through the peephole, expecting to see Collins. Instead, I see the delivery girl from the other day when I confused her as my roommate, holding a balloon with a teddy bear attached.

Opening the door, I sign off on the gift she hands over to me.

"Thanks," I mutter, not in the mood to make small talk.

Examining the gift, I see no card or anything attached to help me determine the sender.

The balloon is shaped like the number two which is bizarre and making me wonder if the previous occupants of this apartment unit had a small child.

"Two," I whisper, placing the bear next to my bouquet of flowers from Collins.

Nope. That's not confusing at all.

I migrate into my bedroom, flop onto my mattress, and remind myself that a man doesn't need to be in charge of my happiness. I have the power to decide for myself how I want to move forward from the collective humiliation of the last few days.

Collins doesn't need a girl throwing herself at him. He needs a woman who can be emotionally stable and who doesn't require as much maintenance as I do.

That's why he's distancing himself from me.

It's because I'm a freaking train wreck.

Who could blame someone from wanting to steer clear of my destructive path?

Rolling onto my side, I find the postcard for Glow Night

at the mysterious address that is listed underneath the description.

And right here… Right now… I decide I am going to attend.

Hearing movement outside my door, followed by some aggressive singing of what I can only distinguish as the Rowdy Rowdy Chicken theme song, I am confident that Luke is out there alone and not with a girl—or multiple girls.

I drag myself out of bed and go in search of the obnoxious singing.

My ears do all the work, and I don't have to look far.

"Hey, Luke," I say, making his body jerk around.

"Oh, hey, Sunshine. Rough night, eh?"

My eyes narrow. "Do I look that rough?"

"No…"

"So…"

"It's just that Meatball kidnapped you and dragged you back to his lair."

I let out a laugh. "Yeah, pretty much. But it's nothing of what you think."

"Oh, I rarely think." Luke pauses at my giggling and then scoffs. "Stop laughing. That's not what I meant to say."

"I was wondering if you could help me out."

"And you forever owe me a favor? Sign me up. I love IOUs. Just name it, and I'm game."

"I need you to help me flirt."

Luke's hands fly up to his face. "Oh no. This is some kind of setup with the police, isn't it? I'm being framed."

"No, you goof. I simply need help trying to entice men to want to take a chance on me and not scare them off."

"This sounds like a rebound. Are you sure this is what you want?" He stares intently at me. "This is about last night?"

"Yeah, pretty much, yes to all of that."

Luke does a bow with praying hands in front. "I'm at your service."

"I knew you would make this weird."

26

PENNY

If there's one thing I learned in therapy, it's to push myself a few inches past what I think I can handle. It worked in my favor taking the leap of faith on this apartment, so it may work again. Sure, Luke is extra, but at least he seems harmless. If anything he's predictable in his over-the-top sexuality.

And right now in this stage of my life, predictable is comforting.

Plus, he supplied me with some great pointers on dance moves, as well as the cat-and-mouse game that men seem to like. It's not like I've ever had free access to the male brain from someone so willing to dump whatever is on his mind.

And with Luke, there's no reading between the lines. He says it how it is, and I kind of like that.

But despite all of the mental prep work I've done for tonight, I still find myself twitchy, since I clearly do not know what to expect from the actual Glow Night event.

There's a lot of really fun clubs in and around Portland.

Well, so I've heard. I've never actually had a chance to fully experience any of them.

Angie and Claire have been known to cause quite the ruckus at a few of them. It's no wonder my brothers keep them surrounded by a whole security squad. But I don't want that tonight.

And as much as it would be fun having Angie and Claire be a part of this, I need to not use their company as a security blanket.

So I'm on my own tonight, just as I've been on my own most nights for an entire year.

While it does feel sad not to have anyone to lean on, I do find it oddly refreshing not to have anyone to watch me be awkward in a social situation.

Granted, the goal is to blend in and not stand out.

I spent a couple of hours online, analyzing descriptions and images, trying to determine what the theme of Glow Night really entailed. Luckily, the little boutiques in town have a delivery service that makes everything super convenient to come up with a last-minute outfit.

Honestly, this is where not having a female roommate is really an inconvenience. At least then, we could possibly share clothes.

Figuring that white lights would be present, I opted for a white miniskirt and a white halter top. I also got a cute neon light-up necklace that has a pink glowing flower as the pendant.

Tonight is my opportunity to face some social fears and try to expand on my friends list which just happens to have one member right now—Luke.

Grabbing my journal, I try to manifest the hell out of any positive energy circulating around me.

It's time to cross off another goal from my list. Who knows, maybe even a couple will get accomplished all in one outing.

Making my way to my own closet, I pull down the outfit I had picked out specifically for tonight from its hangers. I steamed out the wrinkles but have yet to try it on.

I strip down, tossing my lounge clothes into the hamper, and slip on my white panty and strapless bra set that is made of silk and lace. It always makes me feel special to have nice undergarments—even if I don't have plans for anyone to see them.

I slide on the halter top next, tying the strap around my neck into a bow. The front rides up, completely revealing my navel and abs, and there's not much I can do to stop that either—unless I tug it down and expose more cleavage. My boobs are basically counting on the tie not to fail, otherwise the top would be rendered useless.

When I eye the matching miniskirt, I know my booty is not going to fit.

How did I not notice its length so I could find a backup outfit?

The skirt is basically panties without the crotch.

This is all entirely my fault for buying something last-minute and expecting it to work out. But it's not like these things typically get tried on in a store anyway.

Sticking to the theme of the night, I have no choice but to pull them on and wiggle my tush inside without ripping the seam.

At least the material stretches to accommodate my

curves—and I have them. I'll just have to be extra cautious if I need to bend over to pick something up.

Opting for modesty, which is almost like a running joke going on in my head, I slide on a pair of thigh high panty hose, a garter belt, and then secure the clips into place.

One glance in the mirror has me cringing. I don't look bad per se. I actually think the outfit complements what I've got. It's just that I'm basically highlighting the fact that I'm looking for fun.

Collins's disapproving voice cuts through my thoughts. Too bad he's not my keeper for tonight. And honestly, his opinion doesn't matter.

I am angry that he pushed down his walls enough to kiss me, but then erected them back into place—and with stronger material—before I could offer one back.

He's a good kisser.

That's another reason I'm pissed off.

It's as if the universe is playing one big prank on me by dangling the perfect man in front of me and then snatching him away with his conscientiousness to do the right thing.

And if his words were true, then he will soon no longer be my bodyguard, and that probably ticks me off the most.

Just when I was getting used to him and accepting his role, he is going to bolt.

Figures…

I move into the attached bathroom, pulling out items and setting them onto the vanity. My hair is still wet from my previous shower, so I comb through it with some leave-in conditioner. I plug in my dryer and turn it on to max, allowing the heated air to whip through my hair.

When I decided to go blonde, it was more of an impulse.

I wanted to reinvent myself, and doing something as simple as dying it seemed like a symbolic moment for me. Now that I've had time to get used to it, I think I want to keep it.

Using a curling iron, I curl the ends of my hair, making spiral ringlets. Taking my brush, I gather my locks into a high ponytail, securing it into place.

Glancing in the mirror, I frown. I think I look more "cute" than "sexy." If I want guys to even consider talking to me, I think I need to work on the latter, although Luke did teach me that being flirty means being friendly. And I at least look friendly—approachable.

Grabbing my makeup palette, I line my eyes with black eyeliner. I dust on metallic shadow, blending it into place. Mascara finishes my look, causing my eyes to pop.

Taking down my hair, I fluff it over my shoulders. I then take half into my fingers, and then pile only that portion high on my head with a tie.

I can't leave the room looking like this and risk sending red flags out to whoever Collins has potentially watching me in the building, so I throw on a white wrap dress. I don't need my plans for tonight derailed before they even start.

Now that my blisters have mainly healed, wearing high heels is no longer painful. I settle on the three-inch, white satin ones that have ties that wrap up around my calves and cute little bows on the sides.

When I exit my room, I nearly knock into Luke who is coming out of his room looking like he just spent eight hours at the gym.

"Sorry, Penny. Didn't mean to startle you."

"No problem. Are you okay? You seem"—I gesture with my hand in a circle—"worn out?"

Luke runs his hands through his hair. "As much as I enjoy being man candy, it does get exhausting. I actually just got up from a nap. I start my shift in an hour."

"Wow. What time will you be home tonight?" I knew he was working but never can remember his schedule, as it constantly changes.

"Not tonight," he chuckles. "I'm there until closing at three in the morning tomorrow."

"Sheesh."

His eyes trail down my body. "You look nice. Where are you headed? Not-the-boyfriend's room?"

"Definitely not going to be hanging out with not-the-boyfriend." Because he basically declared himself never-gonna-be-my-boyfriend.

And once he finds a replacement, he'll really be able to go through life with the title of Not My Bodyguard.

"And why is that? He seemed pretty angry that you like me more. I volunteer to help you make him jealous if you want to poke the bear to see if he'll pounce."

Laughter bubbles out from my throat. "Thanks for the offer. But I'll pass." The last thing I need is Collins to interfere more than what he already is doing.

He already told me he would be gone today but that I'll be watched. Too bad for whoever is in charge of the bodyguard duties for the day… I'm good at sneaking away.

"So what has you looking so"—Luke taps his finger along his jaw—"promiscuous?"

I giggle. "I'm just going to a thing."

"A thing?"

"Yes."

"Will you be utilizing my flirting lessons?"

"Hopefully."

Luke reaches out his hand. "Give me your phone."

When I don't instantly obey, he makes the gimme gimme hand.

"Why do you need it?"

"I need to program my number into your contacts in case you ever need something."

My lips curve into a smile as I hand it over. It's the sweetest thing he's ever said to me. Despite the oversexualized shell he likes to hide under, at his core Luke is a sensitive guy. And the more we interact, the more I'm coming to learn this about him. "Thank you."

"I added myself and texted from it, so now I have your number."

I nod, and then glance down at my phone. "Super Hot Roommate?"

Luke manages to look offended. "Make it a statement and not a question."

I roll my eyes, then head over to the main door. Taking a few cleansing breaths, I open it and swallow down all of my fear.

Baby steps.

Knowing that Collins has at least one person watching me, I decide to take the elevator to the lobby and then walk to the boutique where I had my outfit delivered.

The last time I was in the shop, I noticed that there are back door exits.

Using my phone, I schedule my ride with a female driver—and this time from a researched and known company. I then gather some outfits in my arms and pretend to shop, while discreetly checking my phone to see how far away the car is.

When my driver is just a few minutes from the boutique, I make my way into the dressing room and text her to meet me at the back of the store.

"If you need anything while in the dressing room, just ring the bell," the worker instructs.

"Actually," I lower my voice while cracking open the door, "I think some creeper is following me. Can I escape out the back and visit tomorrow to try on some clothes?"

"Oh, yeah, of course. Should I call the police?"

I shake my head. "I think it's probably just my paranoia." In a way, I'm not lying. It's not like I actually see anyone following me—I just assume.

"Okay, come with me."

She opens the heavy metal door, and I step out into the fresh air.

The car waiting to pick me up is idling, so I wave goodbye and settle into the backseat. I remind the driver of the address that I have tucked into my handbag on the folded-up postcard and relax my head against the cushioned headrest.

This wasn't so bad. At the very least I should be able to have an hour of fun before Collins's minion finds me and makes me return to my fortress.

However, the more time that passes on the trip, the more I fidget in my seat—crossing and uncrossing my ankles on repeat. I can't tell if I'm more nervous about being found or about the event itself.

We drive the entire way in silence, passing through the city of Portland and then finding ourselves on the outskirts where the stars start to become more visible with the lack of light pollution.

"It's beautiful out here," I mutter, cutting through the silence. Normally I don't mind the quiet—I actually savor it—but the more time that passes without anyone speaking, the more worried I grow over the driver falling asleep behind the wheel.

The road that once was dotted with some lone houses now turns into one cutting into a forest. The moon peeks through on occasion between the canopy of leaves, but there isn't a light post or street sign in sight.

All these years I've lived in this state, and I can guarantee I've never been to this part of the suburbs.

The driver glances at her phone, to what I assume is a GPS.

Leaning forward, I ask, "How close are we?"

She puts on her turn signal, shifting us all the way into a sharp turn.

Shit. We are here.

"Close," she says with a friendly laugh. "I think this is the address?"

Her hesitation makes the butterflies that were just fluttering in my stomach turn into a manic sea of wings.

"This is fancier than I was expecting," I admit, glancing around at the nicest parking lot I've ever seen. It's illuminated by subdued glowing lights, and I imagine this place would shine with beauty in the enhancement of the sun.

My google search earlier didn't produce pictures that represent this view, but I'm sure things look different at night.

When the driver parks the car, I stay seated.

Dammit.

This is my now or never moment.

And there are a ton of cars in the parking lot which bodes well for social proof that this is a legit establishment.

I mean, I did try to check it out online, but it wasn't like I found anything of value other than the address verification and that there was a club on site.

"Here's my business card with my name on it." The driver hands it to me. "You know, just in case you need a lift back tonight."

"Thanks."

I hand over my money and double-check that I have all of my belongings, which aren't much. It's just a handbag for my phone and essentials.

Stepping out into the night's air, I take a deep breath, recite a silent motivational chant to my scared self, and shut the door.

I watch as the driver pulls away from the parking lot.

And just like that, I no longer have a ride.

Now there's no way for me to chicken out, and I'm too far from home to go back on foot. The only logical thing to do now is walk inside and hope I recognize someone from the speed dating event.

I watch as clusters of people exit their cars, taxis, and even limos. Everyone is dressed similarly to me, except I still am wearing my wrap dress.

Glancing toward the building, I take in the sights around me.

I'm not sure what I expected, but what I see is not what I thought I'd find.

A luxury mansion takes up the focal point of the entire

plot of land and looks as nondescript as any other billionaire's abode. I mean, don't get me wrong, the place is gorgeous with huge concrete pillars, a balcony, and intricate designs that are carved into the stone siding. Several lit-up waterfalls make the place look enchanting, as if I should expect to find royalty inside.

It very much has the appeal of the mansion my brothers use for their business events and the location of the wedding, but since it's so dark out, it's hard to draw any adequate conclusions.

I take my first steps toward the entrance that is bustling with energy as herds of people enter. It's hard to know if this is the normal volume or if this is something special.

My feet propel me a few more paces, and then I feel a hand touch me. Whipping my body around, I snarl as fragmented images from the dark abyss of my mind flash in front of me.

Mark. Touching me. Standing over me. His sinister face mocking me.

And then like a warm blanket, Collins's voice cuts through the chaotic darkness, reminding me that I have the ability to fight. Recalling the lessons taught with the blindfold on, I break free from the hold this stranger has on me.

"Back off," I say, fully detaching myself with a step backward.

"I'm sorry. I'm sorry," the man says, holding up one hand in arrest. "You dropped your bag. Here."

I shake my head, trying to calm my heart that wants to escape from my body. It's pounding that hard.

I'm always dropping things. I should be accustomed to others picking them up for me. Yet I'm not.

Every touch feels foreign. Every touch causes me to panic.

Except for Collins…

His touch is different, and no matter how hard I try to provide reason, there's really no valid explanation other than I trust him.

Collins is my safe space.

But he doesn't want me and will be avoiding me soon.

I need to move on.

And I guess in a way, being here is me moving on.

"I'm…" I stare into his kind eyes. He's visibly shaken from my outburst. "I'm sorry too. I thought you were someone else."

"I'm literally here tonight to pretend to be someone else," he says cryptically. "Here."

I take my handbag from his palm. "Thank you."

Slowly, my breathing returns to normal as the man departs and enters into the mansion without any formal introduction.

When will I stop being a freak?

Removing my phone from my bag, I find Margo's number and type out a text.

Penny: I keep having these episodes…

Margo: What are you most afraid of?

Penny: Going back to the facility.

Margo: You can't keep living your life with that fear.

Because you wouldn't be living…you'd just be waiting for the shoe to drop.

Penny: I know…

Margo: Hang in there. You already took big first steps. Be proud and celebrate all the little victories. ;) OH, and don't miss another session with me. I'm keeping track for your report card.

Penny: Fine.

Penny: Thank you. :)

Placing my phone back into my handbag, I focus my eyes back on the mansion. The crowd has dwindled in size, having already been granted access.

Taking a deep breath, I marshal in every butterfly wreaking havoc on my nerves, ready to evict each one from my stomach before I vomit.

I can do this.

I take a step. And I take one more.

As I approach the door, it is then that I notice a couple serving as what I assume are the host and hostess. The male is dressed all in black—from head to toe—while the female is in all white. In fact, now I'm starting to notice that all the guys entering are in black. Hmmm…

As I move closer, I see that the woman is wearing a diamond-encrusted white collar around her neck. I swallow hard as I follow the attached chain until I discover that the man is holding it in his left hand, the excess loosely wrapped around his fingers.

Holy fuck.

This is one of the most erotic things I've seen in person, and I worry that my staring is being seen as rude.

I can't imagine the woman didn't choose to have this detail added to her ensemble. Her gentle smile says she is having a good time. Oh, I bet she is. Just the way that man looks at her with adoration is enough for me to connect the dots that they are smitten with each other and into the kinky stuff.

"Come closer, little one," he says, motioning me with his free hand. He has a gentle warmth about him, yet appears very confident. "You'll be safer inside than out here."

I glance down at my feet and realize that they aren't moving. How long have I been immobile and just staring? I look behind me and see that the parking lot is full of vehicles, but I'm the only one out here. Surely I'm not the last one to arrive.

I've been out of the social loop for a while now, but nothing about tonight feels like I'll be entering into a normal gathering. Something feels different. Like the air is laced with electricity, charging everyone into an edgy state of being.

"Come, little dove," the man encourages. "You obviously are new. Who is accompanying you tonight, and is your paperwork complete?"

With uncertainty, I force myself forward. If I don't make a move, I'll just spend the rest of the night regretting it.

"I'm here by myself, and I don't have any papers."

Glancing down at my outfit, I look conservative compared to the woman in the collar. Granted, I plan on taking off my wrap dress at some point and shoving it into the recesses of my handbag—if it will fit. I only wore it to get out of the building without looking like a hooker. I didn't need to send off warning bells to a crew of watchdogs. I'm sure my brothers have the lobby attendants watching my every move as well as Collins—in addition to whoever else he hired while he was away from the job.

I know for a fact they don't trust me.

But I also don't trust myself.

What happens if I have another episode where someone touches me, and I freak? The whole point of coming tonight is to step outside my comfort zone. But what if I'm just pushing myself too hard or too fast?

"Don't be frightened. Come," the host coaxes, his kind eyes luring me.

With feet that feel like they're walking through drying cement, I take a few steps forward, toward the couple. I watch in awe as the man whispers something to his woman, and she immediately kneels down at his feet.

Holy shit.

I've only read about these types of power dynamic relationships in a few books that Angie left at the house when she visited for holidays.

I'm not a big reader like she is, but I couldn't help myself with my curiosity.

It's vastly different witnessing this in person.

Nothing about these two looks fictional.

The host reaches out an arm to welcome me and I walk forward, allowing him to embrace me in a one-armed hug.

His cologne smells so good, making me want to cuddle closer, but I resist. The last thing I need is to make the woman mad at me before I even enter the dance party. Stepping back, I take stock of the expensive five-piece suit that he is wearing. He looks regal, and by the feel of the fabric, I imagine it cost a small fortune.

"What's your name, little one?"

"Penny Hoffman." My words come out choked. Maybe I shouldn't have said my last name. I'm the worst over-sharer at the most awkward times.

"Welcome. My name is Michael, and this"—he looks down and pets the head of the woman who is kneeling so patiently at his feet—"is Daphne."

I give them each a smile, not knowing where to rest my eyes.

Michael looks around me into the dark parking lot. "Who brought you?"

"I was dropped off." I clear my throat. "Well, basically."

"How did you learn about us, little one? And locate us?"

Why does he keep calling me that? I know I'm on the shorter side, but I still think of myself as average.

"I was at another social event yesterday and"—I dig in my handbag and pull out the folded-up postcard—"someone handed me this."

"Hmm…" Michael hums, unfolding the card and looking at the information that is written on it. "Interesting."

Suddenly I feel uncomfortable—like an intruder. Maybe I should have never come here. Being scrutinized under Michael's penetrating gaze before I even go in to dance or whatever they do here on Glow Night is causing my palms to sweat.

"I'm sorry," I mutter, looking down at my feet, feeling the overwhelming need to apologize. "I think I'll"—I pivot my body and take the first step—"go now." My driver won't be all the way back into the city and can just turn around.

"Stop, little dove. Come back."

And I listen. Just like that. For someone who likes to break the rules, I am captivated by his verbal demands. I spin around and take the step that was once in retreat back to the intriguing—albeit overly sexual—couple.

Playing with the tie on my dress, I let out a half laugh. I'm pretty sure squirrels have more composure than I do right now.

I watch as Daphne, with her eyes still cast downward, reaches up a hand to touch Michael's.

"You may speak, pet," he says softly, his tone controlled but kind.

"I was once new here a year ago. It may take several visits to not feel so frightened."

"That's very presumptuous, pet, that Yuri will accept this unapproved visit in the first place."

Daphne licks her lips and trails her eyes up my legs. "He'd be a fool not to."

"I see you're in the mood for"—Michael smirks at his woman—"fun tonight."

There's a twinkle in her eyes, and it's as if they are playing a game that has secret rules. "It would be a shame to come all this way and not get the chance to discover what you came here for." Her eyes search mine. "This place is like therapy for me. If you know what I mean."

I nod. I know a lot of people who use dance as a stress reliever. "Makes sense."

"Daphne?"

"Yes, sir?"

Michael's fingers touch under her chin, coaxing her to stand. "Do you think you can show Penny around the venue?"

"It will be an honor."

"Make sure you check in with Yuri and get her to sign any required forms and prove her identity first."

"Certainly."

The tension in my shoulders releases, as Daphne waits for Michael to unhook the beautifully polished silver chain that is secured to her collar. I was wondering how she would be able to dance without choking.

I can't help but be drawn to the couple's dynamic and vibe. They definitely match each other in terms of attractiveness. Both are stunning.

Michael leans into his girl, bites at her ear, and then whispers, "You may have some freedom tonight, but that doesn't mean there aren't rules to be followed. Know your role or accept the consequences."

Michael winks at me, knowing that I heard his message to Daphne. Heat hits my cheeks first as I look away to hide my blush. I'm not sure what his cryptic message means, but by the smile on Daphne's face, it is being received well.

"Understood."

"And don't piss off Yuri," he states, his tone serious and unyielding. "I won't stick up for you if you go against his cardinal rules."

27

PENNY

When Michael dismisses us, Daphne links arms with mine, and we enter the huge wooden doors that lead into what can only be described as a palace for the elite. My eyes take time to adjust to the lack of adequate lighting.

"Wow," I whisper, taking in the shadowed light in the lobby. Black sconces are arranged on the walls, with light flickering from the geometric shapes cut out of the sides.

"I love this place," Daphne says, glancing around. "It calms me down when I'm feeling stressed out and isolated. I hope you love it here as much as I do."

I nod. "I hope so too. It's been awhile since I was at a dance club."

She gives me a quick look, shakes her head, and then narrows her eyes. "You really know nothing about our club?"

"Not a thing. Well, except that it is glow night."

"Interesting… And someone gave you an invite?"

"Yeah. I was at another event, and I was handed a postcard. I forget who the person was who handed it to me."

"I'm assuming you never caught their name?"

"That's correct."

Okay, this is weird. I'm about to start asking why she's asking all the questions when she claps her hands together in excitement.

"Assuming you get approval from Yuri, you are free to explore the venue on your own, but I would love to walk you around."

It's easy to relax around Daphne. Her soft-spoken words calm down my pulse that keeps wanting to accelerate. "I would love that. Thank you."

"Good, because I've been let off the leash tonight. I'm free," Daphne chants joyfully, playing with the loop on her collar. "So let's go be rebels."

I turn to her. "That sounds very dangerous. I'm pretty sure your man isn't the type that allows you to break too many rules."

She giggles. "I'm teasing—well, kind of. Plus, rules can be fun to break. I just need to be strategic about it or suffer all the consequences. But really, I know better than to piss off Master Michael. That man knows how to dole out the worst punishments. Kinky fucker."

My mouth seals shut as I don't know how much to take seriously with Daphne. She's hard to read, despite being verbally expressive.

She gives me a look from head to toe but her eyes lack judgment. "I have a feeling you're going to cause quite the stir…on the *dance* floor."

I teeter on my heels. "Is that a good thing or a bad thing?"

And where the hell is this dance floor? Why all the bureaucratic procedures just around me showing up here tonight?

Daphne shrugs. "All depends on what you came here to accomplish."

"Honestly, I just wanted to take a risk and accept an invite to something I may normally have declined. I wanted to step outside my comfort zone. If you couldn't tell already"—I let out a few puffs of laughter—"I'm shy when it comes to some social situations. Maybe even a bit awkward."

"I think you'll do great here. Master Michael would not have allowed you to pass through the doors if he didn't give his seal of approval first. And that man is picky as fuck. Oh, and he is super good at reading emotions. It's creepy." She giggles. "In the sexy sense."

"Gotcha."

I follow her as she leads me to a room with lockers. "If you have anything you'd like to secure inside, feel free to do so. It is a strict rule that all cell phones are either left in vehicles"—she rattles the metal door to one of the lockers—"or placed inside one of these."

Weird. "Alright."

Is someone famous in attendance tonight and they are worried about leaked photos?

"Oh, but Master Yuri will want to hold on to your driver's license."

"I don't have one."

"Oh shit." She turns to direct all her attention toward

me. "Are you underage? Please tell me no. I mean, of course, tell me the truth. But—"

"No, no. I just celebrated a birthday and am twenty-two." I dig into my handbag and pull out my identification card that proves my age. "Here. For Yuri." Whoever Yuri is. I am assuming he is the owner? If so, that would make Michael the gatekeeper.

"Okay, great." She takes the card from my hand and gives it a good look. "That's a relief. For a second, you had me scared."

"Oh, sorry."

"No worries. So, I recommend actually leaving your entire handbag in the locker. No phones allowed at all past this point."

"What about my money? I assume there will be a place to order drinks inside…" And I could easily use one right now as the nerves start to take hold. But I rarely drink.

"It's covered. Just don't go overboard on the alcohol since it's free. Master Yuri does not take nicely to anyone becoming belligerent—no matter how cute you are."

"Got it."

I inwardly cringe over the word "cute." That was not the intention of my outfit selection tonight. Grabbing the ties on my wrap dress, I start undoing them, revealing my sexier ensemble. I gently place the folded dress inside the locker. Daphne shuts the door and hands me the key, which I tuck into the tiny pocket of my miniskirt.

"I love your necklace."

"Thanks," I say joyfully, holding the pink flower that glows brightly in this dimly lit alcove.

"Everyone here has been vetted"—she makes a little

laugh—“well, most people have.” She is referring to me. “And Master Yuri takes security very serious. No one will mess with your stuff. You are safe here. Have fun. Explore. And if you have a problem, find a monitor and report anything that makes you uncomfortable.”

“Thank you,” I mutter, slowly feeling the pressure I once had on my shoulders release with each minute I’m here. The hard part is over, and at least I have Daphne to walk me through the venue so I’m not so freaking scared.

A few women dressed in head-to-toe white latex outfits enter the locker room while we exit. Some people take themes to the extreme.

Daphne leads me across the hall into a private office space.

“Master Yuri likes to personally check in with all new guests before they hit the main part of the building, but he doesn’t appear to be available right now nor was he expecting you.”

“Oh, ah, sorry.” Why do I keep apologizing tonight?

“Oh, it’s fine. He’s probably working the floor or tending to a matter.” She takes a notepad from the top of his pristine desk, rips off a page haphazardly while sprinkling frayed pieces onto the polished surface, and then scribbles out a message. Plopping my ID on top, she pivots and makes her way toward a filing cabinet. Opening it up, she pulls out a file and then hands me a piece of paper. “Sign this.”

I glance over the form. “An NDA?”

“Yeah. Just for protecting the authenticity of this place.”

“Okay…”

"The gist is…whatever happens here stays here. Don't go blabbering about how amazing this place is to others."

"Alright." I scan over the bulleted items, and when I see nothing too shocking, I give it a sign. "Um, did someone break the NDA by giving me that postcard the other night?"

"Yes."

My eyes snap to Daphne. "Seriously? Should I leave?"

"Absolutely not. I think Master Yuri will love making this exception."

"Okay…"

"Come. We'll catch up with him later."

I follow Daphne out of the room, down the hall, and when we get to a series of doors, she reaches for my hand to give it a squeeze.

"Are you ready for the real fun to begin?"

Why would I say no now? This whole preamble has only made me crave what mystery awaits me from behind those doors.

"Yes. Bring it on."

And with my affirmation, Daphne pulls open the doors.

Wow.

When the lights and music hit me, the entire atmosphere changes in the venue. I feel like I'm part of a huge indoor block party. Everyone is having a good time.

Along the back wall is a huge bar that's made of glass and brightly colored translucent balls floating in water. It basically looks like a rectangular lava lamp.

A DJ mixes songs along the side, the attention placed on the music, rather than on him. On the dance floor couples sway, shaking their bodies to the rhythm of the music.

Several couches are set up throughout the space, encouraging social engagement.

"This is so fun," I say, trying to make my voice loud enough so Daphne can hear over the buzz from the crowd.

"Is it what you were expecting?"

I turn to her. "Yeah? There's a bar, a dance floor, and music. Seems like the typical young crowd social scene."

"Oh, just give it time. Everyone is just warming up."

Several men make eye contact with me from across various parts of the dance floor, and I can't help but smile what I hope isn't a cheesy one back.

I say a silent thank you that no one approaches me. I'm not sure I can talk with the butterflies migrating their way into my throat.

It's an odd feeling of being excited and nervous at the same time. It comes in waves. Some moments I'm relaxed and seem to fit in, and other moments I'm a bundle of anxiety and thinking I don't belong.

As the song merges into the next, I start to feel it—the building tension in the air. Even the crowd swaying on the dance floor seems to shift rhythms. Sultrier. More intentional with the hand placement on their partners.

Then the black lights come on, making all the girls in white glow like stars in the darkness. I glance down at my outfit and love how fun I look with the effect turning me into a night-light. Even my necklace has an added brightness to it.

"Here, take these," Daphne encourages, passing me some glow rings to put on my wrists and one around my waist in various neon colors.

Beach balls with lights inside get tossed into the crowd,

followed by a stream of bubbles blowing down from the ceiling. It is so fun. Enchanting.

And then—

Oh, damn.

"Is that what I think it is?" I ask, wondering if I'm just hallucinating.

Daphne's eyes follow my stare. "Five people grinding together? Yeah. They can get pretty horny."

"I, uh…"

I turn my gaze away, focusing now on the other side of the venue.

At the bar, a man slides his hand down the naked back of a girl who is dressed like a disco ball in silver glittery sparkles. When he squeezes both globes of her ass, I can't get myself to look away.

A shiver runs through me, as I imagine being desired to that level by a person of the opposite sex. Would I even know what to do with the attention if the roles were reversed and I was the one being ravished?

When his hands completely disappear out of my line of vision, and I'm pretty convinced he is doing more than just rubbing her *assets*, I turn back to the dance floor just in time to see one girl being covered with so many hands that it looks like they are a part of her.

Wow.

I wonder what it feels like to be that desired—by so many people? She seems to be living her best life.

I get lost in stimulation overload, overcome by the lustful atmosphere. My body tingles with a need from the possibility of something more happening here tonight. I won't be reckless, but a little fun wouldn't hurt—right? It's so unlike me to even think these thoughts, especially when physical touch can cause such an adverse reaction from me.

"Take it all in, Penny."

"I'm trying to, but everywhere I look seems like I'm imposing on a private moment."

Daphne lets out a boisterous laugh that has a sinister edge to it. "At Limit-X, patrons know it is basically a playground for all of their naughtiest fantasies. Everyone here being watched chooses it. Desires it. It all just adds to the fun."

"Limit-X? This is more than just a social club, isn't it?" The words get stuck in my throat, as I take in the entire scene.

If arriving and seeing Michael hold a leash on Daphne wasn't enough giveaway…

I really am that naive and inexperienced girl that I crave to evolve out of…

"As long as socializing with body parts meets the criteria, then I think this place would pass inspection," Daphne giggles. "But remember, you are not allowed to breathe a word about what happens here to nonmembers. I mean, technically you aren't a member yet anyway." Her eyes crawl up from my feet to my eyes, taking stock yet again of my body. "But Master Yuri will want to lock you in, I'm sure. You're his type."

Before I can ask for more clarification on what she means, my attention gets pulled across the room, where I see a man giving a woman oral sex while she writhes around on a chair. And then I see the silver wrought iron cages elevated off the floor by chains hung from the ceilings.

“How did I not notice those before?”

“Oh, those just got lowered a few minutes ago. Look fun?”

“This is wild.”

“I’ll go in one with you. Surprisingly the floor is super comfy, and they are sturdy and don’t swing around like you might expect.”

“What’s the point of going inside?”

Daphne can’t stop giggling. “I mean, some people fuck each other’s brains out inside…”When I make a face, she laughs even harder.

Tugging me along, we go explore closer to the dance floor.

I’m being naive—clearly—and I think she’s enjoying the whole experience of giving me the grand tour. At least my shock is entertaining to her.

The song changes and we start to sway to the music, when her attention is on the man approaching us. “Hold on to your thong, because things may get a little wilder for you.”

I look between the man and Daphne. “What?”

“If you’ll excuse me for just a moment,” she says, closing the distance between us and the man.

I can hear her mumble something to him and then within seconds, she is down on her knees, undoing his belt, button, and zipper. What the hell is happening? And when—oh, I don’t know—some number of inches springs free from his boxer briefs, I know this is my cue to get the fuck out of dodge.

“I, um, I’ll go grab a drink at”—I look around the room

to see if I can find one place where I won't be a blatant observer—"catch up later."

"I'm thirsty as well," I hear Daphne say, but I refuse to look at her.

I pull myself from the awkward situation, as she proceeds to mutter unintelligible words to me, while her mouth must be stuffed full of some man-who-is-not-Michael's cock. Damn. Nothing about tonight is what I expected. This place is intense.

I stumble backward before pivoting and turning toward what appears to be the bathrooms and then—

"Ouch," I gasp, rubbing at my head. "Sorry."

"My apologies," the long-haired blond man says, rubbing at his chest. He dips his head in greeting, giving me the once-over on the way back up to my eyes. "You must be Penny."

"I, um…" My eyes stare up into crystal-blue ones. They are warm. Inviting. I could get lost in them if I wasn't so intimidated by his stance and demeanor of power. "How did—"

"I am Yuri. And Michael informed me after Daphne failed to inform me that there was a little fawn loose in the club."

"I, uh, oh." Then realization dawns on me. I'm the little fawn. "I'm sorry. She left you a note on your desk. I didn't mean to—"

"Little fawn, you need to stop apologizing for everyone else's bad choices. Daphne could have looked harder for me. She likes to get in trouble, because she treats the attention as a reward instead of as a punishment. You didn't do anything wrong. Now, tell me what brought you to the doors of the most elite and private club in the state of Oregon."

"I thought this was an open house at a fun dance club. I was handed a card at a dating mixer event in the city, so I thought this would be a fun way to step outside my comfort zone and meet new people."

I watch as his face changes form but gives nothing away. I swear every time I mention open house I get the most bizarre responses. "Obviously I stumbled into a porn dungeon instead."

Yuri runs a hand down the side of his neck and then slides it up to scratch at his chin. "Porn dungeon?"

Shit. Why did I say that out loud? My mouth needs a muzzle. It's as if this place completely dissolved my filter. "Sorry. That wasn't what I meant."

"It sounds like I need to change the description on our member portal. Porn dungeon is pretty catchy."

I laugh and then sigh in relief that the owner seems nonthreatening.

"Has Daphne been treating you well,"—he looks around to find her—"when she doesn't have her mouth full?"

"Very well."

I have a hopeful monogamous heart, so seeing people enjoy more than just one partner causes me to be twitchy, but that's probably just because I haven't been exposed to anything outside of the movies I find on QuickFlix. Oh, and Hallmark. Call me crazy, but the thought of pleasing more than one person at any given time just seems—

Excessive?

Or perhaps, too overachiever-ish.

I can barely manage my own mood, let alone the moods of multiple partners.

But by the look of the patrons filling up the floor, I think the value of fun trumps any sort of committed relationship. That's the appeal this place has for me. I can come here and have the freedom to be anyone I want to be. If I want to be shy, I can be shy. If I want to be outgoing, then that is fine too. There are no expectations—other than to keep it safe, sane, and consensual.

"Yeah," I whisper, realizing that I've been silent for a while and should fill the space with some comment. "Daphne was giving me the grand tour until she got—"

Yuri laughs. "Sidetracked."

"Yup." Does Michael not care that his pet is with other guys? I think about it while I look at other groups of people gathering around us. Hmm…he might actually enjoy the thrill.

Yuri places an arm around my back, sending shocks of warmth up my spine. I'm thankful that his touch seems nonthreatening and kind—protective. But why is every little caress of his hand causing me such a stimulating response? Maybe I should have done some self-care prior to coming here, so I'm less charged and ready to ignite at the first graze of a hand or brush of a body.

I've never been this on edge. While it's fun for me to have these moments where I'm moving past the toxic pain of my past, it's also alarming that I could potentially put myself out there too much and in return be in a state of vulnerability that makes me easy prey.

Sure, everyone is vetted here. Well, except any of the newbies like me.

What if someone wants to take advantage of me here, just because I am so inexperienced?

Uninvited, the apathetic side of my subconscious suddenly chastises me with a myriad of scenes, flashing in a montage through my mind as a reminder of all of the hours of therapy I needed at Soulful Mind.

Trusting the wrong people…

Putting myself into scenarios where I had the potential to be hurt…

Allowing Mark to convince me he was a good guy…

And ending up in a therapy center, alone and detached from reality.

Will I ever learn to trust anyone again? Can the walls I've protectively built around myself be chiseled away?

Or will I allow any man who doesn't make me repulsed at the feel of his hand into my life?

I guess I should be thankful that I'm not freaked out more while being here. But will my inability to see people for who they really are make me an easy victim?

"I can tell you're nervous about being here, Penny. But I assure you this is a safe space for personal growth. Members have been vetted, background checked, and have signed NDAs. Whatever happens here, stays here, just as I hope Daphne has told you upon entry. You are free to explore your boundaries with the safety net of having staff blending into the crowd to oversee and make sure that everyone is complying with the rules."

I nod. I can do this. For one night, I can be normal and let down my guard enough for me to free myself of the personal responsibility of keeping men at arm's length.

I may not have come here tonight expecting to discover

Limit-X, but it found me—and probably when I needed it the most.

If I'm going to move past my intimacy hurdle and conquer some of my short-term goals, then there's no better place to explore my limits than right here.

I may have arrived here as a caterpillar. But I can still leave as a butterfly.

I just need to take that leap.

28

PENNY

"Give me your wrist, little fawn."

With large eyes, I look up into Yuri's with confusion but do as I'm told. It's actually difficult not to do as I'm told when he states things with such calm authority. "Okay…"

"This is for your own protection, as well as anyone else who tries to"—he appears to struggle for the right word—"*play* with you." He then proceeds to snap a white band onto my wrist. With the flick of a button, it illuminates into the dimly lit room the color of red.

"What's this for?" I ask, no longer able to keep my curiosity at bay.

"Since you're new, we need to ease you into some of the…amenities here. This band restricts you from certain areas of the building, as well as alerts den monitors that you are testing the scene and that you might need some extra eyes looking out for you."

I guess I should be thankful.

"Hey, Penny," Daphne calls over the loud music. "Sorry about that, um, detour."

I laugh. "No problem. I actually caught up with—"

"Oh, damn." She snaps her mouth shut, placing a hand over it for added protection. Her eyes turn mischievous when Yuri's gaze holds hers. Is she with him too? I can feel the sizzle between them, similar to how I felt when she was around Michael.

Keeping remarkably calm, he pulls Daphne to him without any warning and whispers something into her ear that causes her to shiver. Turning to me, he allows his demeanor to soften. "Miss Daphne only has about fifteen minutes before Michael is going to start to *hunt* for her. And he is extra feral tonight. So, I suggest you use your time with her wisely, because I doubt she'll be"—he taps a finger along his jawline—"in the *mood* to sit around and chat with you later."

I nod with the overall understanding—I think. Granted, there were a lot of hidden messages.

Once Yuri makes his exit and disappears into the sea of people, Daphne turns to me with sparkles in her eyes. "So how should I spend these last few minutes of freedom?"

An upbeat song starts playing through the sound system, with the bass thump-thumping in the undertone of the rhythm. "Do you want to dance?" It would be a waste not to utilize some of Luke's advice.

Excitement beams from Daphne's eyes. "Oh, yes. Yes, I do!"

This time it is me tugging her toward the dance floor that is full of x-rated shenanigans. Some women are topless.

Some men are bottomless. And some are basically having sex—right there for us all to see.

When the white lights turn on intermittently, it reveals hidden body messages that must be painted on the skin of some of the members on the floor.

All yours.

Mine.

Brand me.

Open season.

I like it hard.

It's my birthday.

Pick a hole.

Suck me.

Seeing what is holding my attention, Daphne calls over what appears to be a floor monitor and asks for something I can't quite make out. When he hands her a pen, she looks like she just won the lottery.

"Close your eyes and give me your arm. Trust me. This will make the evening more interesting."

I comply but not without apprehension. What is she going to write on me? The feel of the pen gliding against the skin of my arm tickles, making me laugh.

When she is done with my other arm, she turns me around, moves my hair out of the way, and uses the bare span of my back as her next canvas. I am so distracted by the feel of the cool pen on my warm skin that I can't keep track of the letters she is pressing into me.

"Ta-da," she says with pride. "Here's to hoping I didn't jack up the spelling."

I look at my arms, not able to see anything—at least not

until the light changes again back to white. We sway and dance to the music, and when the beat drops, a darker feel hits the room like a ghostly shadow. And then the light comes back on, revealing just how naughty Daphne can be.

"Really?" I ask, looking down and reading what she decided to write on me in the visible locations. "Angel in disguise? Villain era. Good girl with bad girl vibes…"

"Hey, I kept it super innocent this time. Be glad I didn't draw pictures. One of my many talents is my stick figures with penises."

We laugh and joke, enjoying each other's company.

"It's wild here," I call out over the music.

"But fun though, right?"

I nod eagerly. I'm surprised at how relaxed I am. I'm also surprised I made it inside without getting stopped by my security detail.

Maybe Collins doesn't have eyes on me like he claimed and was just bluffing.

But I'm also not doing anything wrong.

I didn't come to get naked, yet those who are aren't doing it to cause a spectacle. This has way less of an orgy feel than how porn makes these types of clubs out to be. I'm sure there are less stellar venues in existence, but it's refreshing knowing that some place more upscale is available for self-exploration.

I feel a presence behind me and the feel of strong fingers gripping my waistline. I suck in a deep breath as every worst-case scenario flutters through my mind.

Dammit.

This is what I've been trying to avoid happening, and

yet no matter how hard I try, my past seems to still sneak through the cracks that have been partially repaired through therapy.

I shiver and sidestep from the touch, causing a cacophony of things to happen. Three men in black shirts surround us, remove the man from the room, and then one asks, "Are you okay, little bunny?"

I nod slowly. "I'm fine." My words tumble out of my mouth in trembly syllables. "I'm sorry that caused him to be kicked out."

"He was on his last warning. Him touching you when you are wearing your wristlet just helped to hurry things along. He knew better but still chose to break a rule. Do not accept responsibility for a man who clearly knew what he was doing."

I give a weak smile, trying to take off some of the guilt that is stacking up in my heart.

Daphne moves to stand beside me when the monitors disappear back into the crowd. "You froze up there and looked like you were caught in a bad dream."

A nightmare…

"I just…"

"Are you okay?"

No. "Yes."

"You're sure?"

I look back over my shoulder, feeling gravity's weight of embarrassment. Rejection sucks, and I did it blindly without even giving him a chance and caused him to be removed from the premises. "I just have some baggage, that's all."

"Don't we all?"

"Mine might be heavier than someone else's though," I say, mostly as a whisper.

"Hey. Whatever you are dealing with, this is a wonderful place to work through it. But can I give you a bit of advice?"

"Sure. Go on."

"Just be honest with the men. I think a lot of people here welcome the luxury of a temporary connection. However, some are here to find a partner outside of Limit-X. The last thing you need is to want one thing and find someone who wants something different. Then it gets…"

"Complicated."

Daphne nods. "Yup. And that's where my problems start. I just can't choose one man. I love the species entirely too much. If only I had more holes in my body to offer up."

I laugh, although she has given me so much to think about in such a short time frame. From across the dance floor, I see Michael making his way toward Daphne. I assume he knows she had another man's dick in her mouth within the past sixty minutes, but it isn't my place to ask those types of details.

Right now, I need no-strings-attached. I'm not good girlfriend material anyway. I need to work through my own kinks in my plan.

Maybe flooding my system with the thing that scares me is a strategy for desensitizing myself. I just need time and the space to process the fact that not all men are Mark Tanner.

And perhaps I can explore that type of healing process right here.

When Michael gets to us, he nods in greeting and opens his arm to welcome me inside. "How have you done so far, little one? Hope nothing scared you."

I watch in awe as he wraps one arm around me and with his other one attaches the strap of the leash back onto Daphne's collar with the flick of his wrist. I need to ask her more about the meaning of all of this. Yet, I don't want to be too intrusive. I mean, really, how does one go about asking why the guy she seems to be dating is leading her around on a dog leash?

"I asked you a question, little dove."

My eyes snap up to his and for a second they get lost. Blinking, I mentally try to form words together to make a sentence. "I'm trying to get used to everything."

Michael nods. "I imagine your senses are a bit overwhelmed. You are very brave."

"Everyone seems really nice, though. And there was only one altercation."

His gentle eyes turn to ones of concern. "What happened?"

When I don't answer, Daphne puts me out of my misery. "Someone got grabby. He was thrown out."

"Good," he says, releasing his hold on me. "I hope you weren't too shaken up."

"I'm fine. Really."

He studies me, analyzing me for whatever unknown truths my body wants to broadcast. "Will you be alright for a bit? I need to take my pet on a little excursion upstairs."

I feel the rush of blood make its way to my cheeks. Daphne gives me a look, letting me know she most definitely is excited about going to some place upstairs that I have yet to explore.

"I'll be fine. I think I'm going to go grab a drink at the bar."

"Okay," Michael says. "Just make sure you stay hydrated—with something other than alcohol."

"Will do," I mutter.

I walk over to the lava lamp bar, finding a man there enjoying what looks to be scotch or whiskey.

"Hi," he greets, causing yet another rush of warmth to race through my body.

At this point, I know I'm just horny. It is obnoxious. And I bet everyone who looks at me knows it too.

"Sit." He clears his throat. "Please."

I hop up on a bar stool, sucking my bottom lip into my mouth.

"What will you have?" the bartender asks.

With the exception of the already-prepared sangria last night, I can't remember the last time I really had an actual drink that wasn't celebratory champagne or a dish made with cooking wine. In therapy, we focused a lot on keeping a clear mind. I'm just not sure now is a good time to be exploring my alcohol tolerance—especially when I have no clue what to actually order.

"Do you have juice?" As soon as my words escape, I realize how lame they sound. What am I—five? "I mean, um…"

The bartender smiles. "Orange, pineapple, cranberry, or mango?" He glances behind him at the arrangement of fresh produce. "Or I can make you apple, peach, or pomegranate."

My head dips. "Pineapple, please. But with something" —I gesture to all the bottles lined up behind him—"fun added to it."

"Now that sounds enticing," the man says, pulling my attention back to him. "I'm Neil, by the way."

"Nice to meet you."

He clears his throat. "I pride myself in having impeccable manners and not allowing my impulses to take over. You have me so distracted by your beauty, I forgot to even ask you your name."

I smile. "Penny." Maybe I'm not the only one who's nervous.

My pineapple juice cocktail arrives. It is garnished beautifully with a piece of fruit cut into the shape of a star, balancing on the sugared rim of the glass. It seems unnecessarily fancy and decadent.

"How is it, Penny?" Neil asks, watching me take my first sip. His eyes are trained on me, watching with such reverence as I do something so mundane. He might be flirting—or trying to—but I'm too inexperienced to know for certain to reciprocate.

"Best I've had."

His eyes catch my wrist, seeing the red glow of the warning light that alerts everyone here that I'm fresh to the scene. "What brings you here tonight?"

I think about the question, wondering how I should answer it. I don't want to say I am here for open house because I get the weirdest reaction when I do. So I settle for a reversal question, if just to give my mind more time to think of a viable answer. "Do you want the honest answer or the expected answer?"

"Both?" he laughs.

"I came to prove to myself that I can be normal." My eyes meet Neil's. "In reality, I should just be here for fun, right?"

He shrugs. "First, normal is overrated." He raises his eyebrows. "And boring. Second, if you haven't had much fun yet, then we need to go take a look upstairs."

I take another sip of my juice, savoring the taste, all while wondering what this mysterious place upstairs is all about and why Daphne hadn't told me about it during the tour. I have heard several mentions of it already, and I'd be lying if I said my interest wasn't piqued. Knowing that Daphne escaped with Michael up there gives me the impression that it will be wild.

I glance around the room, looking for a set of stairs or an elevator. "How does one get invited to go upstairs?"

Neil's eyes light up. "One simply has to ask. Are you asking?"

I nod, as adrenaline rushes through me. "I'm asking."

Neil slides from his stool, offering his open hand for me to take. Before I can change my mind, I accept, allowing him to help me down from the stool. My eyes catch my wrist and I notice my band is gone. I glance around on the floor, not spotting it. Oops.

We walk holding hands to the hallway on the other side of the bar, where there is a hidden staircase. A few guys smirk at my arms when the lights change, illuminating Daphne's script on my skin. Several people say hi to him as we pass.

"Aren't you popular," I mutter, turning my head to catch his expression. He really is handsome, but in a rugged manly way with a full beard. His impeccable manners are in direct contrast to every stereotype I'd have pegged on him. Maybe it's the tattoos or the gruffness to his voice.

"I've been a member here for some time. I accumulate a lot of acquaintances."

Like trophies? "So it seems."

We ascend the stairs, as my heart rate climbs with each step up. I don't even know what to expect, except that whatever awaits us will surely be worthwhile. How can it not be? Everyone has basically suggested as such.

When we make it to the top, Neil squeezes my hand and studies my face. I know my cheeks are flushed from the exercise, as well as the anticipation.

"You have a particular interest in mind?" he asks.

"Interest?"

"Preference as to where you would like to start," he clarifies without actually revealing anything.

I wrinkle my nose. "Neil, I have no idea what you are talking about. It's not like I got an informative brochure or a map before entering the club. This is literally my first time here."

His smile is warm, not condescending. I feel so new—inexperienced. "Come. I'll show you then. Some things are best explored through action."

I follow along, until we come to a wall of glass. My hand rests on the handrail underneath the panel, gripping the cold metal as I gaze inside the room. Holy shit.

"You okay?" Neil chuckles, looking down at me. "You aren't going to pass out, are you?"

"I feel like we are intruding," I mumble, but can't take

my eyes away from the threesome that is happening before us—just a wall of glass away.

"That's the vibe here at Limit-X. Some people like to be watched. Almost as much as those doing the watching."

In a muted haze, I ignore everything and everyone around me, as I take in the scene between the participants in the room.

I stare in awe as the two men sandwich a woman under the spray of the open, wall-less shower. Slick bodies slide against one another, in an erotic water dance. And sticking with the theme of Glow Night, the men have lit-up bands wrapped around the base of their cocks.

I can't look away, yet I know I should. The girl turns and catches my eye, winking as the men around her devour her and bring her to orgasm.

I take a step back, bumping into Neil, who steadies me.

"Ready to move on to the next exhibit? We can find a booth that is more interactive."

"In-ter-act-ive?" I ask, dramatically separating the word into syllables, as if I'm not proficient in English.

Neil smiles. I think he actually likes how naive I'm being. Maybe that's his kink. "Where viewers can make suggestions for the"—he gestures toward the glass enclosure—"acts."

"Oh."

"Think of it as a guided theater performance. Come." He pulls me along the main walkway. "We can meander through and see what interests you before settling."

"You make it seem like we are working our way through a museum."

Neil stops and scratches at his jawline covered with his

beard. “In a way, this is very similar. Admiring art and beauty in its natural form.”

The corners of my lips curl up. It’s true. I allow him to guide me to the next section that has a similar viewing area of glass. This time, I get to witness two men making out on a huge four-poster bed that is adorned in red satin and wrapped in strings of lights. I bite my bottom lip as I watch their chemistry in full technicolor.

Damn.

The next room has a massage table set up to look like a typical spa. It’s so sensual watching the woman getting massaged by this burly man.

I can’t help but stare. I can’t help but fantasize.

And this is how Neil and I spend our time upstairs, walking along the hallway and bearing witness to a plethora of sexual acts. It is energizing. It is unfiltered. It is beautiful.

“Now that your thirst is quenched”—Neil brings his fingers to my chin, tilting my head upward to meet his eyes—“are you ready for the main course?”

I swallow hard, feeling lightheaded. “Care to give me a little more detail?”

“Perhaps something a bit more”—his eyes move suggestively down my body—“hands-on?”

I look down at the floor to see if my chin is there. “Involving me?”

“Is that an offer?”

No? “I, um, I don’t know.” What is he suggesting? What am I suggesting?

He analyzes me for a few seconds. “How about we test the water with something a bit more *hardcore*?”

My hand sweeps out in a half circle. "Than this? Because watching people have sex is pretty kinky to me."

He gives a one-shoulder shrug. "There's a spare room. We have the option of fogging or defogging the glass to be open or closed—if that makes a difference."

But I don't even know you. A thrill runs through me, and I can't tell if it is from excitement or trepidation. He has been so kind to me all night, and we've been having a lot of fun just exploring this part of the club together.

Was this the ultimate expectation? Is this what the equivalent dinner and a movie eventually ends up with—a trip home for sex?

It seems selfish of me to end the night right now, without even seeing what some alone time with Neil involves. I'd be lying if I said I wasn't a tad bit curious. This would be one way to cross off some items from my goal list in my journal.

But I don't know him.

And I can't tell if that is the problem or if my hang-ups are deeply rooted in how Mark Tanner violated my trust in all men.

Do I just force myself through the barrier that is holding me back from experiencing a real connection with a man?

Do I throw myself into the pool heart-first and flood my senses with the thing that scares me the most?

Neil coaxes me forward, toward the opposite side of the hallway where a little green light is lit up on the wall outside the door. I guess this is a signal that it is free.

I enter the room, gambling on some notion that my mind and body are collectively healed from the trauma of my past.

Taking initiative, Neil fogs the window, giving us some privacy. I'm not sure if that helps my nerves or just revs them up even more. I can't tell what emotion is winning right now, I'm that mixed up.

I turn toward him, watching as he starts to remove his shirt. Unlike a lot of the men at this club, he has on a decent amount of clothes. It's definitely a disproportionate feeling when compared to the scraps I decided to wear.

I clear my throat, trying to push down the knot forming. "I think I should probably tell you that—"

"Shhh…"

My eyes grow big as his finger lingers over my lips, silencing me before I can even finish with a warning about my sexual experience. Maybe he has gotten the wrong idea with how I'm dressed. Perhaps just entering this club has already stereotyped me into being a certain type of woman. Shit. What have I gotten myself into?

I fidget with my fingers, as I pivot to take in the rest of the room. Like most of the space upstairs, the room is dimly lit yet fitting the theme with the option of turning on the black light.

It seems welcoming with all wrought iron furniture and linens in soft hues, yet sterile with the lack of any decor.

Can I even go through with this? It seems so out of character for me. I mean, it's not like I have to do anything more than kiss.

I never was one to rush things in the past, despite giving my first time over to someone who didn't deserve it at all. I don't need to make more bad choices just to prove to myself that I can have a normal sex life.

I see a shadow on the wall in front of me, reminding me that I'm not alone.

All of these little details were missed by me when we first came upstairs together. I think my mind was just elsewhere. And maybe this whole time Neil didn't find my naivete cute—he found it essential.

I quiver at the feel of fingers on the straps of my top, gently tugging each side down, causing my hands to grasp the material in front to keep it from falling. "Calm down and relax, little bird. Just trying to make you more comfortable."

I'm tired of being a little forest animal.

A fawn. A dove. A bunny. A bird. An awkward squirrel…

I make some sound that registers as foreign even to my own ears. I can't settle my mind.

My heart rate quickens, as Neil's whisper tickles my ears. "If this is all too much for you, we can leave. But I think you just may enjoy yourself." His fingers trail down my neck, fixing my wavy hair over my shoulders. A tingle runs up my spine, from either his touch or the anticipation of finding out what will happen next.

Then my vision blurs with flashes of Mark Tanner's face. His sneer. His sinister laugh. They are the same visions I have rehearsed in my head on loop for months, guessing at how the night I was drugged went down. Did he touch me? Did he take pictures of me? Did he snicker and gawk over my inebriated state? Did he get off afterward to how helpless he had me?

Does he get off now in the cell of his prison with thoughts of me?

I shudder.

He may not have raped me at the time…but he is raping my mind now. He is infiltrating it with every known evil.

His lips are on me. Dousing me with his hatred.

No.

Stop.

Please stop!

"No!"

Even my own voice causes me to startle. I turn and glare at Mark, as he morphs back into Neil, who is shockingly naked. When did he even remove his clothes? There were so many of them.

"What's wrong?"

"I can't do this." My words come out choked. I need to get out of here.

I am so deeply retracted into the life I once lived that all those months of therapy can't even compete with how lousy I feel right now at this very moment. I don't belong here. I don't really belong anywhere. It's as if every single lesson ingrained into me from Soulful Mind has resurrected from the hallows of my consciousness, just to get obliterated and sent back into hell.

Therapy only prepared me for hypothetical situations. But right now is real…

And it is clear that I still have a lot of work left to do.

With awareness of my surroundings sinking into my thoughts, I scrape as much self-preservation as I can muster up, just so I can find the free will to escape here before anyone else intrudes on my misery. That's the thing with embarrassment. It shows no mercy.

I guess the silver lining of this whole debacle is that now

I know. Now I know that no amount of makeup or designer lingerie can mask the fact that I'm not okay.

I wasn't before.

I sure as hell am not now.

And the once glimmer of hope that I had walking into this place has been burnt at the stake and turned to unharvestable ash. It was a pathetic belief that a place like Limit-X could change the damage that still exists inside of me.

Sure, I didn't know walking in tonight to this building that this was a kink palace. But prior mental preparation would not have changed any amount of damage that I carry around like scars.

I feel so freaking stupid. Stupid for trusting that I'm strong enough. Stupid for coming here in the first place.

I frantically fix the straps of my outfit, tugging them up so hard that I scratch my neck. Then I make my escape, leaving a naked Neil behind without another word.

I mean, what else is there to say? Pretty sure he'll never talk to me again if I ever possess the courage to come back here. That's assuming I'm not blacklisted from the entire property if he speaks with Yuri about my erratic behavior.

When I get into the hall, I turn and run to where I think are the stairs but find myself passing through another section that I've never seen before. How did I get so turned around?

The space is muted from the dimmed light coming from wall sconces. It reminds me of the lobby, yet has an entirely different vibe.

There are no windows to allow in natural light, and it's fitting, because nothing about this room feels inviting.

Several groups of people are gathered, spectating on

what I can only assume is something a bit more X-rated. I stand on my tiptoes and crane my neck. I can feel the sexual energy stirring amongst the crowd, as those watching shift on their feet and keep their eyes straight ahead.

SMACK.

What.

SMACK.

The.

SMACK.

Hell?

29

PENNY

My body retracts, as I stretch up to see where the noise is coming from. And then the crowd surges, pressing forward to get a closer look. I feel the masculine energy of several men behind me, molding their bodies to mine. I feel claustrophobic, the air becoming too thick in the small space.

Steadying myself, I anchor my feet to the ground, careful to not be pushed over in the excitement.

SMACK.

I shiver at the sound of flesh meeting flesh.

A few men in the group of spectators chuckle, grabbing their crotches and pulling on their dicks. A hiss slips out through my teeth. Are they for real?

Just as I'm about to call an end to this blind show, I hear a familiar voice cut through the crowd.

"Stop. Please, I can't take anymore."

The sweet feminine voice of panic just makes the men surrounding me even hornier. If this is what a sausage party is called, get me the hell out of dodge. They make me want to be a vegetarian.

The room is becoming too warm. Too…sweaty?

Too many ball sacks…

"I'm sorry. I'm really sorry. I won't do it again."

I'm sorry.

I know that voice.

Dammit! I know that voice!

I pull away from the crowd and push through the wall of concrete standing in front of me, urging them to let me to the front. The barrier of men parts ways, allowing me through, and it is then that I get a front-row view of the fiasco.

SMACK.

I flinch. But the victim endures it—leans into it.

Why is she not fighting and thrashing and cursing?

And then I see the restraints.

Bastard.

My eyes glare daggers into the back of his skull, as I plot his murder. There will be a lot of witnesses, that's for sure.

The perpetrator rotates the bench to show the work of his hands. It's as if I'm seeing myself lying helpless on that bench, with not a soul brave enough to help me.

Color blooms along her backside, as the abuser circles his hand along her reddening flesh.

Her inflicter manages to angle himself to remain anonymous to those watching, never turning to glare out into the crowd.

Coward.

And then the people around me roar to life again with reckless excitement as another hollowing smack cuts through the buzz from the audience.

The bench turns again and my eyes soak in the harrowing scene.

Holy fuck.

"Daphne?" I call out, but her name gets stuck in my throat. My mouth feels raw and dry, as air gets sucked in violently.

Hair sticks to her forehead that is covered in a layer of sweat, and her lipstick-painted lips are slightly parted, as she pants. Her facial features are distorted as she appears to endure the pain being doled out to her.

She is beautiful but broken.

Mascara tears streak her cheeks as her head flops to the side, giving us onlookers a better view of her features. She whimpers and writhes on the bench, trying to get away from the one causing her pain.

Her eyes pale as some half-naked man stands before her, as his back remains turned toward the crowd of spectators with their dicks hanging out like red flags—enjoying the sight of her misery.

Sick fucks.

Every single one of them.

Daphne shakes her head no, but the man just raises his hand and smacks it against her ass, so hard that it makes me quiver along with her.

A wail escapes her lips, causing her to flop forward. Her chains rattle along the bench's underneath side. When her face falls to the padded cushion and a look of defeat hits her blank eyes, I lose it.

That's it, dammit!

The energy running through me is vibrating, to the point that I'm trembling. Here I stand before a stranger I'm so spitting mad at, that I'm seconds away from doing something I'll regret.

SMACK.

"Get your hands off of her!" I bellow.

Without even thinking, I hop over the half wall, glad that there isn't any glass here to separate the audience from the scene like in the other spaces. Daphne flies up to her knees on the padded table, her hands still secured at the top, keeping her from moving her upper body.

Glassy eyes reach mine, and then pure horror washes the color out of her face.

Her abuser halts his movements and growls blindly at who I can only assume is me. "It's against—"

"Stop, you brute!" I bark anyway.

"Oh, no," Daphne says with an exhale. "You shouldn't be here."

Without thinking, I pull back my right fist and smack it into the space between the shoulder blades of her abuser. But I don't stop there. I pound and pound.

Like a whip, the man turns his attention behind him, letting out an animalistic growl. Pivoting away from his victim—poor Daphne—who must be traumatized, he moves away from my flying fists. His gaze comes to rest on me, his eyes growing as they fuse to mine. The spark of recognition ignites, causing my heart to fail, just as my breath catches in my throat.

Static fills my ears, and then the only thing I hear is my erratic breathing.

Holy.

Fucking.

Shit.

Everything I expected from tonight free-falls to the floor, casting light on the fact that I know nothing about this man. The man who I just witnessed in a compromising moment. The man who is now ending his scene and taking long strides toward me. The man who I no longer trust.

No.

I must be hallucinating.

My feet push me back.

And back.

Until I bump into the partial height wall, stumbling backward.

My breath stills, as if I'm in a weird dreamlike state, causing my heart to stop beating.

I see him.

Collins.

Virile.

Masculine.

Collins.

And I see him with her. Hitting her…

In just a few seconds, my life splinters apart, as a rush of realization coats my body, sending chills of coldness up my spine.

"You bastard," I hiss. I rub at my eyes. "*Collins*?" It can't be.

A buzz forms in my ears, morphing into the sound of water crashing into a pit. I take several deep breaths, my legs wanting to buckle beneath me. This can't be happening.

Staggering against the half wall, I lean my ass against the surface, clutching my heart as I suck in air through my teeth.

This cannot be happening.

If there ever was a turning point tonight, this would be it.

The moment when the stable rug that was Collins Stone gets pulled out from under me—revealing a side to himself that I know he'd want to remain hidden.

Who are you?

"What the hell are you doing here, Penny?"

Collins's words bite like venom, making me seethe. And just like that, the strong current between us becomes deeper —*wider*—forcing me to either swim or drown. It's as if the world stops spinning, causing my feet to plant and take root in their spot.

I am frozen as my mind tries to comprehend in this moment what the hell is happening. How does one solve a puzzle when all the pieces are missing?

Collins's sigh of disapproval and frustration fills the space.

If anyone should be mad, it should be me, dammit. Like who the hell does he think he is?

"Penny, I asked you a question." His words are a growl, and in no way should this man be pushing his anger onto me. I'm not the predator here. I'm simply the witness.

Ignoring him, I move to Daphne, who is now burying herself in a fluffy beige blanket. I didn't even realize she was naked—or released from her hold on the table. I am just glad to see her free.

"Are you okay?" I ask her. "I can't believe he tied you to the bench and beat you. I am"—the words get stuck in my throat—"so sorry."

I shouldn't be fucking apologizing for the bastard. Yet I feel responsible because I simply know him.

"It's okay, Penny…"

"It sure as hell *is not*." Why is she being casual about this? "Do you need to file a police report? You can mark me down as a witness."

"Dammit," Collins sneers, rubbing at his temples.

I glare at him. "Shut it."

"It was by choice," Daphne whispers. "I chose for it to happen."

My jaw loses all muscle control, dropping from gravity. "What?"

"I asked for it."

"You are a victim," I correct. "No one deserves to be beat."

"Fuck, Penny. Did you follow me here and sneak in?"

My body twists around to stare at him. "Oh, how dare you!" I rant.

Collins doesn't back down. He maintains eye contact right back. "Can we discuss this someplace else?"

"Oh, that would be really convenient for you, wouldn't it be?"

"I assure you, it was consensual," Daphne says softly, the look of embarrassment reddening her skin. She doesn't need to be ashamed for a man's evilness. "You may be in trouble for interrupting though. And I don't think I can even defend you on this one."

"What?" Why would I be in trouble?

When I look back at the spectators' area, it has completely cleared out—except for Yuri who is making his way toward us. Oh, shit. He does not look happy.

"Miss Hoffman," he says with disapproval. "Where is your wristlet?"

"I lost it. It must have fallen off." But why does he care? I haven't been wearing it for some time.

"That explains why you weren't stopped from being granted access to this floor. But you've broken a cardinal rule here at Limit-X. You mustn't interrupt any scenes."

"But…"

"No buts."

"She was getting beat."

His eyes glance to Daphne's, and he can't help but smirk. "The wench does love her drama. Is this enough excitement for you, Daph, or do you want another round—but this time in my personal dungeon?"

Daphne swallows hard. What is happening? Get me out of this twilight zone.

Turning his attention back to me, his eyes go stern. "If you feel as passionately as you did during any scenes, the correct protocol would be to hit the wall button or find a guard to assist. We have safety measures in place for that very reason. However, being overwhelmed by any scenes does not justify interrupting them."

"I…"

"We know each other," Collins says to Yuri.

Yuri looks from me back to Collins. "Is this true?"

I can only nod.

Collins rubs at the back of his neck. "I'll take care of it and make sure it never happens again."

My eyes narrow at him. Am I the *it*? Then I watch, frozen in place, as he grabs a folded robe off a nearby shelf and attempts to drape it over my shoulders.

"Save it," I say.

I can tell he disapproves of my outfit based on how his face can't stop from looking angry at my refusal. And to think I'm one of the most modestly clothed people in the building.

When he tries again, I toss the robe onto a bench. I don't need warmth right now. Right now, I need an explanation.

"Penny…"

But I can already tell he's not going to talk. Men like Collins rarely do. They dole out information in breadcrumb portions, never handing over a full cracker.

With my anger and embarrassment so fresh, I do what I do best. I turn and retreat.

"Penny…"

I don't turn back. I just keep moving my feet, through the door and through the glass hallway of voyeurism. I pass by Neil, never giving him more than a dismissive wave.

A nearly nude waitress carrying a tray of drinks shimmies through the narrow crowd of one of the booths, and before she can notice, I grab one that looks enticing and down it with a few gulps.

The burn hits my throat last, as the bitterness settles on my tongue as an aftertaste.

Hell.

This is another reason I don't drink much. It tastes awful.

Who actually enjoys the flavor of liquidized leather? Yuck. Not me.

But I need to dull this ache inside, and society has proven to me that alcohol can numb all sorts of problems.

As much as I hate to admit it, seeing Collins with another woman has done things to me that I wasn't expecting. Sure, I'm still butt-hurt that we kissed the other night and then he rejected me, but I'm also mad he chose Daphne to perform a consensual act with…

Daphne…the girl who got more action in one night than I have in my entire existence on this planet.

I thought we were friends—or would-be friends. I don't know. Do I even know how to make one?

It's just all kinds of fucked up no matter how I slice it.

Collins might have wanted to escort me home, but I can't be around him right now. I'm on edge. There's a nervous energy buzzing through me, ready to ignite at the first sign of heat.

Am I jealous?

Probably. But I'll never admit it out loud.

I'm such a fool for coming here, especially without really knowing what I was getting myself into—physically or emotionally.

Why was tonight the night I tried to be brave?

Silly fool.

I feel raw. Gutted at the seams. My mind races at how to get out of this pornographic maze as fast as I can, while my jumbled thoughts about what I just witnessed play on loop in my head.

I don't turn back to look, but I know I have a couple of people hot on my tail, as I weave between patrons. I fly down the stairs, run past the bar, and through the orgy of people bumping and grinding on the dance floor.

I hope Daphne is okay. I can try to get her contact information and check up on her later. But right now, the only thing I want to do is get out of here.

I want to erase the feral images of Collins Stone in primal, masculine glory from my memory.

30

COLLINS

Never in a million years would I have expected to find Penelope Hoffman at Limit-X. I mean, technically she found me—but that's beside the point.

This refuge is for people who want to get their rocks off in a safe environment, and often without being bogged down by commitment. It's meant for people who have demons to exorcize and for those that want a space to explore fantasies that aren't societal norms.

It's for people who have been background checked, vetted, and held to the high standards of a club's contract.

This place is not meant for sweet girls like Penny Hoffman, who happen to walk in and suddenly fill the space with more warmth than it has ever seen.

Darkness and Penny do not go together. Seeing her here, on my turf, in my safe place, is fucking with my head.

Dammit.

Has she lost her ever-loving mind?

What was that girl thinking?

And to stop a scene mid-act…

Yes. She most definitely has lost it.

Every time I think of the way she looked at me, I feel my blood boil. Of all the places to come trotting inside, why did she pick my one and only refuge?

Sure, I haven't visited in a while. But this place is definitely more mine than hers.

Yuri prides himself on keeping the venue off the radar of outsiders. It has an invite-only membership protocol. Yet, Penny comes waltzing in, looking like a beautiful flower in a field of weeds.

I hope she enjoyed the establishment while she did, because I sure as fuck never want to see her here again. Yet, it's going to be impossible for me to erase the image of her standing innocently in front of me, wearing the sexiest outfit I've ever seen, from my mind.

Does she even have a sliver of self-preservation in her body? So many bad things could have happened tonight from her reckless behavior, and I never warned anyone here to stay the fuck away from her.

She's going to be the death of me.

And if her brothers were to find out… They may put her on house arrest and conveniently lose the key.

I throw on my shirt, not even bothering to turn it the right side out. I just need to get to Penny before she hails a cab or does something equally as stupid—*yet again*—putting herself in harm's way.

Where the hell was Chris, who I hired to watch her for the night?

That man prides himself on being able to handle

anything and literally went into battle during our military days, but can't handle the princess for a few hours?

How did she even get inside?

"Do you want to talk about it, man?" Yuri asks me, while tending to the redhead, who seems unfazed by any of this.

I mean, she shouldn't be fazed. I've seen her make her rounds multiple times in this place. I just never bothered to learn anything more about her. I know she likes things rough and is good at following directions. By the glazed expression I elicited from her, I know she was having a damn good time under my control, as most women that enjoy this kink do.

I was giving her what she craved, and in exchange I got to release some endorphins. It was a win-win exchange of power that was mutually agreed upon. I came here tonight to blow off some steam and relax. And I was, until a fiery blonde flower got in my way. Now she's the only thing I can think about as I shove my guilt into the back of my head.

My motive in accepting to have a scene with the redhead was strictly a logical one—and definitely not an emotional one.

I lead with my brain, not my heart.

The heart gets you hurt.

So I wanted someone who could handle my moodiness, while still getting off. And I also owed Michael a favor.

Doing this "public" scene was the favor.

And I'm pretty sure I'll be owing Yuri one just to keep the princess from this establishment in the future.

"She's going to need aftercare," his voice cuts through the silence.

"Then give it to her," I snap back. Sighing, I glance to the redheaded girl who is coming down from her high, in need of the comfort I can no longer provide to her.

It makes me feel shitty. But I need to get to Penny.

Turning my frustration to Yuri, I bark. "When did you start letting in nonmembers, and doesn't that shatter the entire privacy clause?"

"She got an invite from another member apparently. I just don't know who extended one to her when clearly that breaks the rules."

What the fuck… I shake my head at his smirk. "And you couldn't resist telling her no? You always had a thing for strays. Always wanting to rescue some baby butterfly who has hurt her wings."

Yuri chuckles, obviously not fazed by my momentary lack of respect. He might own the place, but we always treated each other as equals. And with that comes a certain level of filters that get taken down when we are around each other. "Take that up with Michael. You know how he loves trying to control things."

"Well, he chose to let in the one girl who can't be controlled. Trust me, I've tried."

Yuri's eyes narrow. "So that's what this is about? Some domestic dispute?"

"Just shut it."

I'm not so unattached from my emotions not to realize how moody I sound. It's just that I never got the release I came here for and am still teetering on the edge of simmering need. I'm so tightly wound up that going to Penny now would not be my best move, yet it's the only one I can think about making. I need to make sure she's okay and cannot count on anyone to have her best interests in mind like I do.

Dammit.

I had everything lined up so I could have a night to clear my head. Now things are cloudier than ever. The only thing tonight accomplished was making Penny distrust me even more, which shouldn't matter now that I'm stepping down from being her bodyguard.

Yet, how can I trust anyone to watch her when I can't even take a break for one evening and have the fill-in have success?

I mean, what are the fucking chances she would be here? She's never come here before. How did I miss this necessary information?

Ever since we shared that kiss outside of the coffee shop, I've been reliving that scene over and over in my head on repeat. Which is good, because prior to that I was reliving the devastation all over her face when I rejected her at the apartment gym.

Since then, I have questioned my decision to pull away from her and to step down from being her bodyguard.

That's why I showed up here tonight.

Being here was about throwing myself into a scene and trying to forget how cruel life's circumstances can be.

I was trying to forget the fact that Penelope Josephine Hoffman would never be mine.

But she showed up tonight and completely flooded my brain with tantalizing images of taking my own sexual aggression out on her—the cause of all my agony.

I've never been this tightly wound up.

When Graham and Nic hired me to watch over their

little sister, it was never meant to be twenty-four seven surveillance. Yet, with her track record so far, I don't know how it won't turn into something of that nature.

It's not like I can even bring the topic up with them without causing alarm or their curiosity to flare, and I've been unable to convince myself that anyone other than me would be perfect to guard Penny.

The Hoffman brothers may take overprotectiveness to the next level, but I'm worse when it comes to protecting those I care about. And Penelope Hoffman is currently under my care, no matter how many times I've contemplated over the last few days of passing her off to someone else.

Clearly, I can't trust anyone with her if she managed to infiltrate my once safe haven and scattered my thoughts even more.

So she will yield to me.

Her brothers need to know no part of what happened here tonight.

Airing out her dirty laundry would in return air out mine. While I respect Penny enough not to share this little discovery with others, I'm banking on the notion that she'll give me the same courtesy.

"I need to run," I say simply, earning a nod from Yuri. He knows I'm not overly empathetic. I turn to the girl. "Sorry the scene ended."

She's shaking, and I can't tell why other than she may have hit her happy place faster than I would have expected from the average scene. We had barely gotten into the action before we were interrupted.

"Get her another blanket and a snack, man," I say to Yuri.

He shakes his head at me but goes to tend to the girl.

A shiver runs through her. "Just make sure Penny isn't mad at me."

Of course the two of them would be buddy-buddy. Penny has that small-town charm and girl-next-door appeal.

"Got it."

"I didn't know you guys were—"

"I'm sure someone will gladly step in and take over where I left off if that's what your body still needs. Perhaps…"

She waves a hand at me, a blush hitting her cheeks. "No worries."

I know the girl is making assumptions about Penny and me, but that isn't anything I can control or have the patience for right now to set her straight.

With only one mission in mind, I take off into a jog, exit the room, and then weave through clusters of people. It's getting pretty late, and the club goes from mild to wild rather quickly, thanks to alcohol and bad decision-making skills. I take two steps at a time on the descent, propelling myself forward toward the locker room to grab my belongings.

How did I not see this coming? Seriously. This could have all been avoided if I had my head on straight and not trying to pawn Penny off on someone else while I used my own needs as a distraction to cope. I'm more disciplined than this, and yet I have no one to blame other than myself.

When the warm summer air hits my face as I exit out

through the main doors, I scan the premises in hopes I can find Penny. Then I hear it—her scream.

Not having any time to retrieve my gun from my car, I take off running toward the panicked sound of Penny's high-pitched voice.

"Let me go!"

I will carve the skin off anyone who dares to hurt her.

My calves burn as I charge toward her attacker, feeling the air flying in and out of my lungs as I pick up the pace.

When I make it to the scene, I stop dead in my tracks. Chris is dodging blows coming from Penny's fists like he's a blow-up punching bag, while he squeals like a little baby.

Granted, she's extra violent tonight.

Sheesh.

I made her this way. It's me who set her into a feral tail-spin as she distanced herself far away from me.

She's repulsed by me and who could blame her?

Turning to shoulder some of the force, my hired henchman looks to be stressed and shocked over her outburst.

Not even war prepared him for anything like Penelope Hoffman.

Poor guy.

"I'm not going to hurt you."

"Says every freaking kidnapper"—she smacks him with every spoken word—"that has ever existed."

SMACK.

Shit, she can be fiery.

"I mean it."

SMACK.

"I mean it too, you brute!"

"Owww, you have heels on! Stop!"

Chris's eyes connect with mine, silently begging me to bail him out of this shitstorm, as he tries to keep Penny off of him. He better the hell not let her hurt herself. Then he'll be sporting more than just bloody shins and some bruises.

That's the thing though with men like Chris. They are trained on how to deliver pain, not prevent someone from getting hurt while attacking them.

"Penny, I hired Chris," I call out, trying to catch her attention before she gives him a broken nose.

I wish I could take credit for her self-defense moves, but I can't. Besides, this is a full-blown attack. Her life isn't at risk, but my ex-military friend's is.

When my words finally register to her, she stops suddenly and whips her body around to glare at me. She hasn't changed her outfit, and I can't help but feel jealous that the entire club has seen her like this.

She is a vision in white.

The sexy scraps of material are in contradiction to her purity. I know Penny hasn't had a chance to fully date. She's barely been out of the facility to make deeper connections. Plus, the few guys that she was interested in while there didn't pan out. And by that, I mean they were shut out fast and efficiently.

Penny can do better than them.

And she can do better than coming here to prowl for who the fuck knows what.

She points behind her but keeps her eyes trained on me. "*He* is your hired guard?"

"Hey!" Chris scoffs. "I'm standing right here. I take offense."

I ignore his hissy fit, having eyes only for Penny.

With her foot tapping against the pavement, Penny props her hands on her slender hips, which only elevates her breasts even more. Her gaze rakes over me, while her temper flares. And then she charges toward me, fists blazing.

"Calm down," I snarl, actually concerned she's going to get hurt this time.

She smacks against my chest. "You are a barbarian!"

"And you are defiant!"

"I can't be defiant if I don't answer to you!" She hits me again, but this time I catch both fists into my hands, immobilizing her.

"But you do answer to me," I say simply. I glance back at Chris who is rubbing at his sore leg. Surely he's been through worse, but the way he is pouting like a pansy, I'm really questioning if he can handle sweet Penny Hoffman.

Based on tonight, my instincts say no he can't.

"I'm mad at you."

"Did you bruise your hand?" I ask, ignoring her anger. I rotate her wrists, looking her over.

"What about my body?" Chris whines from the sidelines.

"Quit being a baby."

"I need a Band-Aid."

He's a tulip.

"Penny, did you get hurt during your tirade?" She seems fine, but I want her verbal verification. "And what did I tell you during your lesson about where to keep your thumb's location during a punch?" When she doesn't answer, I remind her. "Well, you don't tuck it in unless you want to break some bones."

Chris makes eye contact with me. With a nod to my chin, he retreats and moves away from us, happy to get away to sulk and nurse his wounds, I am sure. He may be trained for stressful situations, but Penny takes everything up a notch. And nothing about tonight has gone to plan.

"I hate being followed."

"I warned you that I would have eyes on you. You should not have tried to sneak away. It's unsafe."

"No," she snaps. "Having a guy jump me in a dark parking lot is wrong."

I sigh. "I told you that I'm vetting a potential guard for you, since we aren't working out." Granted, said guard is acting like he can't handle a paper cut.

"That's very fastidious of you." Anger bubbles in her eyes as she comprehends my train of thought.

"Seemed like the most logical next steps."

"You followed me here?"

I shake my head. "I had no clue you would be here." I glance toward the mansion. Even if she had no clue what happens on the inside, why would she risk going into a new place alone? This is equivalent to going into someone's van because they are claiming to sell cheap designer purses.

"Okay. I didn't know you'd be here either."

"I hired Chris just for the night. He probably saw you leaving Sky View and followed you. He probably got stopped at the doors here and prohibited from entering—just as you should have been."

"That is so beyond creepy. And the fact that you don't see it as such makes me extra angry. But please, keep enlightening me. Maybe if you throw me enough crumbs, I'll be able to paste them all together to actually understand the inner workings of your damn mind."

Shit, she is pissed. I take in a deep breath, slowly exhaling. "I came here to let off some steam, Pen. I had Chris monitoring you while I took time off to figure out my next steps. He's probably been in his car waiting for you to exit the building most of the night. It's not like he had a good way of contacting me, when I too don't have access to my devices. But why are you here, Penelope?"

"It's not your concern."

Her sass is giving me the start of a migraine. "If I'd known you were coming here, I would have surely stopped it."

She lets out a huff. "Of course you would, Mr. Always Knows Best."

"This isn't a place for you, Pen."

"Is that so?" Her eyes look back at the building that is buzzing with vibrating energy. "Seems very double standard-ish, if you ask me. But that's the thing, Collins. You never ask me. You just assume to understand how I'm feeling or what is best for me. And you are slowly and methodically driving me to my breaking point. So, tell me, Collins. When did you develop a kink for beating up defenseless women?"

My teeth clench together. "It was consensual, Penelope."

"That's what any abuser says."

She's pushing me, and if she does it any harder she will find out what darkness lurks at the end of my threshold.

"Why Daphne?"

"Who's Daphne?"

Her hands fly upwards. "You don't even know the name of the person you were striking?"

"It was consensual spanking, Pen." Why do I need to keep reminding her? "I would never do anything to someone who wasn't begging for it."

Her hands get animated again. "Don't you dare try to twist what I saw to suit your narrative. As if you were doing her some grand favor. My goodness, do you even hear yourself?"

"I was doing Michael a favor. And in return he better grant me one with never allowing you to step foot back into that building."

"Well, if I wasn't welcome here tonight then they shouldn't have been handing out invites."

"Penny, whoever told you this venue was open to nonmembers lied to you."

I watch impatiently as she paces back and forth, teetering on her sky-high heels. She's going to twist an ankle. Why does she continue to wear such impractical shoes? I mean, they look sexy as fuck, but they are dangerous.

Then, without warning, she starts walking farther away from me.

It's my eyes that chase after her first, because my brain can't get my feet to cooperate.

"Where are you going?" I call out.

"Home."

"Penny!" I yell, forcing myself to move.

"Collins," she mocks in an obnoxious voice that has never been used with the saying of my name in the past.

I break out in a jog in order to catch up with her. "I'll drive you home."

"Nope. Not interested."

"I wasn't asking."

"I'm still not accepting."

"Let me give you a ride," I try again.

Turning, she shoots me a disgusted look. "I don't take rides from strangers."

"Except you do, literally every fucking time you need a ride."

"I thought I knew enough about you, but it's all been some deluded construction of false details I construed in my own head."

Her words sting. It's true that there's a lot about each other neither of us know, but if she thinks I'm going to let her walk home, then she doesn't know me at all.

"Penny, be reasonable."

Rounding her shoulders, she stands tall. "It's a beautiful evening for a walk."

She can't be serious. She's testing me. There's no other logical explanation as to why she thinks walking right now is appropriate. "It's fifteen miles. At least."

"I'm in the mood for some exercise."

"Then I'll drive you to the gym. Oh, and what do you know? We have one at our apartment building."

"Oh, and some peace and quiet that the dark night can offer me."

She is pushing against my patience, seeing how far she can take me before I lose it.

I reach for her arm, at the exact time her body whips around. Her eyes hold all her secrets, and right now, she's not being shy about how angry she is at me. I get it. Neither of us expected to find the other here tonight. I'm still in a bit of shock. And I'm sure—once I've had time to process everything—I'll be a bit embarrassed that she caught me in a compromising position…with her new friend, nonetheless.

It's one thing being confident in yourself. But it's another thing allowing people who are present in your life to witness those insights—especially when it's of the sexual nature.

Her hands grip the hem of her halter top, tugging it down to conceal some of her abdomen, and the only thing it does is give me a better view of her perfect breasts. I hate how exposed she is and am thankful that we seem to be the only ones out here.

I'm sure Chris is lurking somewhere. He's three times her size, and he couldn't stop her from beating him up? The first sign of tension, and he folded like a first-timer gambling in Vegas.

I shouldn't be surprised. Penny has a long running history of ditching her guards and causing chaos, and I'm starting to wonder if she would do this reckless behavior with anyone that wasn't me.

Because pulling these stunts with me won't fare well for her… And maybe deep down, she knows it.

"You're going to get blisters walking anymore in those deathtrap shoes." I gesture to her feet. Her ankles look so small and feminine. "And your outfit is—"

"Slutty. Just say it," she calls to me, her words slurring a bit. "No need to sugarcoat your feelings now."

"I wasn't going to say that, Pen."

"But you sure were thinking it."

Feeling like my patience is dwindling, I try again. “Come, I’ll give you a lift.”

Turning, she continues to walk away from me, making her way to the edge of the parking lot near the access point to the road. Her hips sway, as she takes long strides, stumbling a bit as she tries to separate herself from me.

Sassy little thing she is.

Dammit.

She has some nerve thinking she can openly defy me.

Without thinking, I run to catch up with Penny and scoop her into my arms, cradling her to my chest. Her protests are adorable, making it difficult for me to resist laughing. She would not like that I’m finding humor in this situation.

“L’me down!”

How much has she been drinking? “I will when we get to my car.”

Her hands smack at my back. Without any hesitation, I take long strides to my car, open the passenger side, and deposit a flailing Penny inside. Reaching across, I snap her into her seat, despite her trying to escape. In the confined space, I smell the telltale signs of alcohol on her breath. That’ll be a chat for another day. This girl could use a lesson in respecting some limits.

Penny mutters under her breath. “Ever the gentleman.”

“You seem angry,” I state the obvious, stifling a laugh, as she flips around to shoot me with her volatile temper.

“Angry?” She points to herself. “Who, me? Nah, this is just my ’ormal perwonality.”

Yup. She’s slurring.

“You haven’t seen anythin’ yet. You er kidnappin’ me and holdin’ me hostage.”

I let out a growl. “Call it whatever you want, but if you move from this seat, we will have problems.”

Her nose flares. “Is that so?” she huffs out. “What’ll you do, spank me like you did Daphne?” She exaggerates the name into more syllables than it has.

Bending down, I look her straight in the eyes. “No.”

“And why not?” she challenges.

“What I will do to you will actually be punishment. Besides, call me old-fashioned, but when I spank someone, I prefer it to be consensual and with agreed-upon terms.”

Her eyes widen and fill up with tears. “You would hurt me?”

“Of course not, Penny. How could you ever think that?”

“So what you were doing with Daphne was for both of your pwea”—she stumbles with the word—“pleasures?”

“Yes.” Why are we dwelling on this—again? “But mainly hers. I’m actually not big into the impact play.”

“Well, then what’ll you do to me as punishment?”

“I will just tighten security on you. Embed a tracking device under you ”

“NO!”

I smirk. The last part was a joke to test out how drunk she really is and to cause a healthy amount of fear into her if she thinks she can dictate to me how to keep her safe. “Okay, Penny.”

“Besides, isn’t that what you’ve already done by hiring that baboon who manhandled me?”

I have had enough of this conversation. I’m not going to stand here outside of a sex club and go ten rounds with

Penelope Hoffman on how I value her safety, despite how little regard she has for her own well-being.

Double-checking that her limbs are safely inside, I shut her door, round the front, and am about to open my driver's side door when I catch movement from my side.

It's Chris.

"Should I run anymore surveillance?"

Looking back through the window, I see Penny stewing. "Nah, I got it covered tonight."

"Oh my goodness…"

"What?" I hiss. He looks too smug to have anything of value to say.

"I never thought I would see the day."

"Just get on with it, you fucker."

"You have no freaking clue how to control her. Your entire adult life you have learned to read people, study them, and anticipate their actions. Except her… She is the free-spirited woman who is going to drive you insane. And it's all because she is unpredictable."

His tone is laced with amusement. He is enjoying himself, and I am planning out how I am going to recover after I pummel his ass into the ground.

"Just go back to your car."

"Aye, aye, Redeye."

I roll my eyes and watch him walk along the shadowy border of the parking lot back to his vehicle. And he's fucking humming, having way too much fun.

Reaching for my door, I feel the car shake and see the flash of blonde hair whisking through the air, moving toward the front of the mansion.

"Dammit, Penny!"

31

COLLINS

I take off running after Penny, just as Chris jumps out of the shadows and stops her from going any farther.

At least he didn't fumble this play.

"Everything okay, Redeye?"

My eyes dart between Penny, who is struggling to stay still, and Chris. "It will be."

Reaching out, I grab Penny under her arm—firmly but not enough to hurt her—and escort her back to my car.

"Don't you think this is a bit overkill?"

"You best be glad that my desire to protect you right now is eclipsing the fact that I'm raging inside at you."

I open up the backseat and gently guide her inside. At least now I can hit the childproof lock on my key fob and keep her secure. I shut the door and watch as she tries the handle, smacking her hand on the window.

Taking a couple of deep breaths, I brace myself for the ride back to Sky View Apartments.

Because it's going to be a long one.

When I get behind the wheel, Penny is climbing over the back of the seats to get to the passenger side.

"Really? This is necessary?"

"Yup," she says with a giggle. "I was lonely back there."

I think I would prefer anything over Angry Penny, so I welcome the sudden change.

Sprawling herself out like a lazy octopus, her smaller frame manages to take up the majority of the space. In my periphery, I watch as she hikes up her leg and rests her foot along the seat near her ass.

"You can't sit like that."

"Why not?" She scrunches up her nose. "It feels naturally comfortable."

"You can't, Penny." My words come out stuttered, which is an unconscious sign that I'm anxious.

She spreads her legs wider, and I know because now I can't stop staring. "Is it un-la-dy-like?"

Yes.

I help her snap her belt into place because she's clearly incapable of taking care of herself right now.

"It's because of the fact that if we are in an accident, the pressure from the airbags exploding will cause your femur to snap in half."

"Okay, Boy Scout. Always going straight to da worst-case scenario."

My eyes twitch over the usage of a childhood nickname that she'd have no way of knowing was assigned to me at a young age due to my resourcefulness.

"Do it, Penelope."

"Fine, fine."

If I wasn't certain by the way Penny is slurring her

words that she is drunk, then it is abundantly clear by how she is finding humor in everything.

What is she doing?

Why are her legs spreading like that?

What is she doing?

"Collins?"

I'm not sure how my name has evolved into having four syllables, but Penny seems to enjoy her nonjoke, so I don't try to act like she is out of sorts.

I ignore how Penny's skin ripens to the softest shade of pink when she laughs.

I ignore the way her voice heightens in pitch when she giggles.

And I ignore the fact that I can see the lace of her fucking panties every time she shifts in her seat.

Please shut those delectable legs.

"Yes, Penny?"

"I want you to touch me. Right"—she spreads her legs wider and cups the mound of her pussy—"he—"

"I know where!"

She readjusts herself in her seat. "Why are you yelling at me?"

"Sorry." I clear my throat to try to remove some of the hoarseness. "I didn't mean to raise my voice."

"Do you think someone could die from horniness?"

What the actual hell? Is this a real question? And why has she deemed me the expert? This is going to be the longest twenty-seven minutes back to Sky View Apartments.

I swallow the saliva pooling in my mouth, keep my eyes trained on the other parked cars surrounding us, and manage not to choke on air.

"I was just thinking"—her leg kicks up and soon her foot is dangling into my side of the vehicle—"how sad it would be to not be thoroughly fucked and then to not make it until tomorrow. Tra-gic-c."

Lovely. She is getting extra creative with her mispronunciations, which just lets me know she has had way too much to drink tonight. Reaching into my center console, I pull out a bottled water. "Drink." My one-word directive comes out hoarse.

"Ever the sex muffin of a Boy Scout. What else you packing up there in secret? But quit distracting me. Let's get us back to dying of horniness… Thoughts?"

I take a deep breath, not sure if I should even contemplate answering, but Penny saves me the trouble of deciding by filling the space with more drunken word vomit.

"I mean…there's only so much comfort a toy can provide a pussy cat before it craves the real cream. Do you agree?"

"I don't have a pussy," I blurt out, not realizing how fucked up I sound even partaking in this exchange.

"Do you like creaming in pussies, Collins?"

I can feel my face wrinkling. "What the hell, Penny?"

"But it's not like my pussy has seen much action. I kinda feel bad for it. Is it an it? She? Her? Scaredy pussy. That's what I should name it. Neil got close to it and then my scaredy pussy overreacted. If only I could shut off the doom flashes. Then I could get laid."

Reaching for my phone, I send a quick text to Chris.

Collins: Find out who the fuck Neil is.

Chris: Aye, aye, Captain Redeye.

I honestly don't remember Chris being this annoying. But he is.

Turning to Penny, I take a deep breath and brace myself. "Who the hell is Neil?"

"Oh, he's the one that calls me a little woodland animal. Um, little fawn? No, that was Yuri. Oh, um, little dove. Nope. What is with men calling girls forest animals?"

She's trying my patience. Does she normally talk this much? If I didn't have to take her home to sober the hell up, I'd hunt down Neil and make sure he stays away from Penny Hoffman. She is off-fucking-limits.

Limit-X is *off*-limits as well. If she thinks she'll ever step foot in this club again, then she miscalculated how headstrong I can be.

Starting the engine, I back out of the parking spot and pull out onto the road.

Penny's giggling makes me nervous.

"Just as long as these men don't run out of options and resort to calling me a farm animal name. 'Come here, little heifer' doesn't quite get the juices flowing in the southern hemisphere. 'Or come here, ya little mule.' Sexy, eh? Little billy goat."

I stifle my own laughter. She really can be quite entertaining.

"Collins!"

Darting my eyes to her and slowing down my speed, I ask, "What? What's wrong?"

"The trees are moving!"

Oh, my goodness. “Penelope,” I snap. “It’s us that is moving.”

“Oh, ha.” Now she can’t stop giggling.

Great.

“Keep drinking that water.”

“Collins?”

I brace myself. “Yes?”

“Can I ask you a personal question?”

No. “Do I even have a choice?”

“No.”

“Go ahead.”

“What are your top three porn searches?”

“What? Why are you asking me this?”

“It’s a get-to-know-you type of question, and I feel like that is a major way of getting to know someone.”

I mean…she’s not wrong. “I’m not answering that.”

“Challenge accepted.”

I rub at my temples and try to steer the car to stay on the road as Penny mentally tries to derail me.

“Do you think anyone will want to touch me”—she spreads her legs and points between them—“in my—”

“I know where,” I say in a rush. Why does she keep using her fucking pussy as a landmark? “And yes, someone will.” But they better plan on their fingers being broken if I have any say.

“But not you?”

I allow my lungs to deflate. “That’s correct.”

“Because why?”

“Because you are under my protection and because I’m sixteen years older than you.”

Penny crosses her arms. “Well, with age probably comes experience…”

Where is she going with this?

“And wouldn’t my pussy benefit more from someone of your expertise than from some twenty-two-year-old stumbling around trying to pin-his-finger-on-my-clitoris blindly in the dark like a birthday party game?”

She does have a point.

“With age comes responsibility. And I know better.”

“That’s my point. I want someone who knows better than someone my age who won’t make my”—she spreads her legs to awkwardly point to the spot as if I could forget—“pussy feel good.”

It’s a miracle I can drive with a hard-on.

It’s an even bigger miracle that I arrive to town without pulling over to the side of the road and fucking Penny so hard that she will be sore for weeks.

Because I’m not a gentle man.

And it’s that realization that continues to keep that wall between us intact.

When I get to our street, I hit every freaking red light. It isn’t until I’m pulling into the parking garage, cutting off the engine, and helping a clumsy Penny from the passenger seat that I relax.

I survived this awkward trip home—barely.

Rounding the back of the vehicle, I pop open the trunk and say a silent thank you that I have a rain jacket tucked into the side compartment. There is no way in hell I would have allowed Penny to walk into our apartment building wearing scraps of white fabric—even if there was a minimal chance of someone catching sight of her.

And she is a sight.

Her body would have demanded everyone's attention, and I don't have enough energy to fight off anyone who would have looked at her twice. And they would have looked. I'm having a hard time myself keeping my eyes off of the straps of her heels and the way her calves flex and relax as she steps forward.

The girl is gorgeous.

"No thanks," she says sweetly, as I try to help her into the jacket.

"Too bad."

"I don't need help," she insists, stumbling into the side of a parked vehicle.

"Right," I mumble. Then I do what I do best—ignore boundaries and provide assistance. "Too bad you are getting it anyway."

She tugs the side panels to her chest, crossing her arms in the process. "Is this what biggie bro and less biggie bro pay you for?"

Not exactly. But clearly, they should. Not that it would have changed anything, but I wish I had some warning that Penny can't handle alcohol and also has the interest of a teenager when it comes to sex. I can't predict what she will say n—

Turning her bright blue eyes to me, she stops my heart and my inner monologue. "Do you think I'm sexy?"

Yes. Shit. No. I, um…

"It isn't going to benefit the situation for me to respond to your questions, Penny."

Letting out a huff, she taps her foot. "Your nonanswer is your answer, Collins."

It takes everything in me not to hoist her over my shoulder and give her a spanking for how dangerous tonight could have been for her if our paths hadn't crossed.

Sure, the club is a safe playground for exploring fantasies, but Penny would have been easy prey to anyone who would have noticed her condition.

And Chris couldn't have done a damn thing about it—even if he did want inside the venue.

Neither money nor words would have given him access. I know this because I know Yuri and Michael, and I made sure that it was safe for someone like me, who values privacy and all things security, to enter.

I'm not shocked that Penny was allowed inside without any contract or vetting period. That's the effect she has on others. She enchants them and lures them in with her sweet innocence.

Something tells me I may need to pay Michael a special visit. If he was enthralled enough to grant Penny access without a personal invite from a staff member, then he might have had ulterior motives.

She is off-limits.

She is not to be anyone's little anything.

I shake my head over her drunken speech about pet names. I never really had a reason to call anyone an endearment before, but just listening to her rant, I can see how that can be counterproductive—and confusing.

I hold Penny's waist firmly, as I escort her through the parking lot.

"You don't need to walk me to my door," Penny says with irritation as she watches me hit the button for her floor, while never pressing the one for my own. "It's not like we will be fucking."

I ignore her, making her stew even more, while we both exit the elevator. I just don't think she quite understands that keeping her safe is my top priority—whether I'm getting paid for it or not.

Ever since I discovered that Penny was drugged, it became my personal vendetta to seek revenge for her. In a way, I'm living vicariously through her justice, as I was never able to receive it for those that did me wrong in the military.

Helping Penny not make stupid mistakes is a segment of that. I was naive back then too, but it was life's cruelty that taught me to trust less and question more.

I follow Penny to her door and watch as she teeters on her heels. She tries the doorknob and then knocks. After several tries, she leans her back against the door and then slides down to the floor, crossing her arms over her chest and settling her face against her knees.

"Quit looking at me like that," she snaps, making my lips curl into a half smile. "I'm just going to wait here until my roommate gets off work soon. I, unfortunately, left my keys and phone in the lockers at the club. Oh, and my dress."

"Phew, at least you had more fabric to your outfit at one point."

She growls at me. Actually growls.

As for her belongings, I figured as much on our way here. I know the rules of the club, and knowing how fast Penny wanted out of the place, it was easy for her to bypass the lockers.

I reach a hand down for her to take. "You are not waiting out here in the hall."

"Luke will be here soon."

"No, he won't."

Her eyes dart to mine, and the action causes her to flop her upper body onto the carpeted floor. "What?"

"He gets off work around three. Then he showers and with travel, that tacks on another hour. And that's assuming he doesn't crash at a coworker's place, which he's already done about sixty percent of the time."

"Oh, my goodness." Kicking her feet up the wall, she looks like she is doing Pilates while staring at me from the floor. "Do you hear yourself? Your stalker tendencies have no boundaries."

Call me crazy, but when Penny hurls insults, I find it cute.

"Stay at my place."

"No."

"Make good choices, Penny."

"Just use the key you had made and let me inside my place."

I look away to hide my smirk. "I forgot to bring it."

She rolls her eyes and then ignores my hand in offering, getting up unassisted like a deer learning to stand.

"I will just walk to Nic and Claire's place and sleep in the guest room."

"It's after midnight."

"So?"

"I'm pretty sure your brother—no matter which one you turn to—will lock you up forever with an outfit like you're wearing." I wait for that to sink in to her drunken head. "You are staying with me."

"Don't you have some place to be or some work to do to occupy your time?"

"You are my work, Penny."

Realization lights up her face. Has she really forgotten my role in this whole chaotic madness?

"But, my stuff…"

She knows that I'm equipped to offer her comfort. It's not the first time she's spent the night at my place. I open up my hand and motion for her to walk to the elevators. There's no point hashing something out where there's only one real logical option.

"I need to get my phone and purse," she pleads.

"I'll have someone retrieve them." I don't tell her that I basically have her items in my possession. Chris retrieved them and texted me during the drive here that he has them. I need her with me tonight to make sure we hash out our issues once and for all. The best way to do that is to be forced to spend time together in close proximity. If she gets her phone and keys back, then I have no reason but to let her go. "But until then, we are going to go to my place."

"So bossy," she says, a bit higher pitch than her normal angry tone.

"So insubordinate."

Penny playfully smacks me on the arm. "Keep it up, and I will run again."

Anger sizzles under my skin. She better damn well never run from me again. "Keep it up, and I will haul your ass over my shoulder and never let you leave."

Her body goes rigid as she stares at me, searching for

sincerity in my words. "You wouldn't," she snarls, placing her hands on her hips.

The front panel of the rain jacket pops open, showing me ample view of her cleavage. I swallow hard as I take in her stance, the way her breathing seems to pick up, and how her fingers curl and uncurl at her sides. Her long blonde hair is sticking to her neck, with some tucked into the collar of the jacket. She is beautifully disheveled—a chaotic force I have no power in stopping.

"I would," I deadpan.

Her eyes twitch as she studies me, hopefully finding zero ounce of flexibility. Her safety matters to me most, and the reckless way she continues to go about her life is proof that she needs a keeper.

"Lead the way to your place, caveman."

Penny and I walk to the elevators, enter when the doors open, and then remain silent until we exit onto my floor. Since the last time Penny stayed at my place, I decided to be a bit more prepared this go-round—just in case.

I unlock the door, disarm the security system, and turn on the lights. The apartment building is calm and quiet for a weekend night, which is part of the reason I love this place so much. I can find peace here. Few people get rowdy or make asses of themselves.

"Why did you go to Limit-X tonight, Pen?" I bend to remove my shoes, placing them in their resting location on the shelf. "What were you trying to prove?"

Penny wrestles with the ties on her heels and then kicks them at me to catch—one at a time.

"Why were you hitting a woman, while masking it under the category of pleasure? Really, Collins?"

Her eyes are vacant, as if the sunshine I once saw is now eclipsed by the realization of how big of an asshole I am.

I walk across the living room to the wall of glass windows. The city is so serene at night, with the lights reflecting off the water.

"I am not a good partner for anyone, Penny. I've not had the best past experiences to carve out how I choose to live my future."

"Well, neither have I."

My body turns to find Penny stripped of the rain jacket, standing in the middle of my living room, in nothing but her tight white strips of fabric. I saw her in this outfit already tonight, and yet, having her in my space, without the backdrop of chaos and noise, makes her appear so…

Fucking sexy.

32

PENNY

"Put some clothes on," Collins snaps.

The spark of disapproval simmers in Collins's features. It begins in his eyes and then works its way down to the tic of his jaw, followed by the rigidness of his stance. It's like he's playing a waiting game—trying to decide when to light the fuse and turn this into a full-blown lecture on my wardrobe.

Good girls wear modest clothes.

Good girls carry themselves with poise and respect.

Good girls always…avoid going into unmarked mansions that happen to be sex clubs…

Well, I'm tired of being a good girl. I'm tired of doing what everyone expects of me. And I'm tired of being told what to do by one overbearing, overprotective, overcritical bodyguard.

Yet, no matter how hard I try to hold my ground, a part of me still strives for approval from others and, right now, especially him.

"I don't have any clothes, remember?" I say, my voice shaky.

My skin feels warm and sweat beads on my forehead. Maybe I'm dehydrated. Or perhaps the deflated feeling is just me coming down from the high I was having at the club.

Collins storms past me, down the hall, calling for me to follow him. Sheesh, he can be so moody. I make it into the guest room, the same place I stayed during the night of the storm, shocked to see him pull out a pair of pink pajamas from the closet. Does he just have women's clothes lying around? I want to ask more, but his demeanor tells me he's not in the right frame of mind for a discussion.

And my head is starting to hurt too much to analyze this further.

"Get dressed."

I snatch the clothes from his extended hand, grumbling a few words as to his bossiness under my breath. I watch as he moves into the bathroom, flicks on the lights, and steps out holding a white tube.

Our eyes meet, and it's like seeing each other again for the first time. The way his bottom lip twitches as he studies me just makes me retract under his scrutinization. It's like he has something to say but is too disciplined to actually say it. I shift my weight from foot to foot."Why do you keep looking at me like that?"

I should expect Collins to ignore my question like he does, but it's still annoying. My eyes search his, inviting him to say something—*anything*. Why does this man frustrate me so much, more than anyone who has ever frustrated me before?

He hits my panic button.

I have two older brothers who have no boundaries, and yet this one man standing before me is owning my attention. Owning my anger. And owning my ability to control when to hide within myself.

He is peeling back layers of vulnerability in me, making me want to punch his mute button until it shatters into a million pieces.

The silence is killing me.

"Here," he says, passing me the tube.

I accept it, glancing down at his offering. I scrunch up my nose. "This isn't toothpaste. This is face wash."

"Wipe it off."

"What?" I look between the tube and Collins.

"Your makeup."

"What?"

"You don't need it. At least not to the extent you thought was appropriate."

It starts in my shoulders—the trembling—and then moves up to my lip that quivers. Tears fill up my eyes, and I suck in a breath to try to keep them at bay. He is crushing through so many boundaries that I'm starting to wonder if they ever existed in the first place.

Sensing my imminent meltdown, Collins wraps me into a hug, pulling me close to him and cradling the back of my head in his hands.

"Penny, what's happening? Why are you crying?"

"I'm not crying!" I shout, pulling back to no avail.

I feel stupid. Petty. *Insignificant.*

"Yes, you are." He continues holding me, while I tremble in his arms.

"You think I'm"—each word is followed by a sniffle—"over-the-top?"

Collins pulls back to look at me. "I wasn't trying to hurt you, Pen. It's quite the opposite. You're naturally pretty. I just wish you'd quit messing with what you've been blessed with."

"You're calling me a clown."

"What? No. I didn't say or mean that."

"You implied it!"

He mutters a curse word under his breath, cocooning me more thoroughly in his warmth.

The press of his lips against my forehead is almost more intimate than the way we made out on the street outside the coffee shop.

It feels good to be wrapped up in Collins, but I feel stupid for having his disapproval affect me this much in the first place. What is wrong with me? I hate feeling like a ticking time bomb of emotions.

His hands move to my face, gently feeling the skin of my cheeks. His thumbs coast down, swirling against the dampness that I don't want to acknowledge is there.

Guiding my chin to force my eyes to look at him, he sighs. "You are beautiful, Penny. I'm only saying that you don't have to try so hard."

Tears continue to run down my cheeks as I look away. "I do if I want anyone to actually see me."

"I see you."

"But you don't like what you see—clearly."

"Listen," he says softly. "I suck at words. I'm"—he takes a step back and runs his hands over the back of his neck—"ah, just going to give you some privacy."

As soon as I hear the sound of the door shutting, I fall to my knees onto the floor. How did everything go wrong tonight? The night started out so differently and ended in such a blazing disaster.

After who knows how long, I pick myself up off the floor and stumble into the bathroom. One glance into the mirror lets me see what the world sees of me. No wonder Collins handed me face wash.

I do look like a clown.

I squirt some into my hands, lathering them up underneath the warm water from the faucet. Massaging circles over my blush-stained cheeks, I move upward to the mascara that has run under my eyes. I scrub at my eyebrows that have glitter stuck in them, and then swipe over my lids.

I rinse and dry my skin, patting my eyes that still hold some of the caked-on makeup. I didn't realize how thick I applied it. After another round of soap, I am satisfied that I got most of it off and look less like a raccoon.

Finishing up my routine, I strip and slide into the softest pair of cashmere pajamas. I'm thankful they are long-sleeved, as Collins likes his place to be on the cooler side.

I move back into the room, looking at the nightstand for my phone. Dammit. I keep forgetting it's in the locker at Limit-X. I feel a bit lost without knowing what time it is.

The apartment is so quiet. I don't even hear Collins moving about his space. What is he up to? Is he asleep already? I need to stay clear of him right now. He's not good for my nerves. When we are around each other, I feel like my heart stops and then starts again—but at a completely new rhythm. He makes me uneasy.

I quietly walk down the hall and into the kitchen, where

I can see the time displayed on the oven. Luke won't be back for a couple more hours, and that's assuming he isn't going to crash elsewhere.

Pulling open the fridge, I take a look. My eyes scan over all of the contents. You can tell a lot about a person by what they store inside, and I'm getting a healthy dose of information right now.

It is immaculate. Organized.

Every fruit, every vegetable, and every protein has its perfect spot. I've never seen a fridge so…

Clean?

No, that's not the right word. So…

Deliberately OCD?

I'm afraid to touch anything and jack up the order that Collins has obviously tried to achieve, and yet the bottles of juice lined up so eloquently with all the labels facing the same way has me feeling parched.

And he has tangerine juice…

Who is this man?

I pluck a bottle from the second shelf. Looking at the lineup, it feels so unbalanced. I have to fix this. Stretching my hand back, I push the bottles in back toward the front, bumping into the neighboring columns of pineapple and cranberry juice. I never expected anyone to like juice more than I do, so this is a fun revelation.

It takes me entirely too long to be satisfied enough to stop fussing over the arrangement and step away from the fridge. Leaning my butt against the countertop, I crack open the bottle, busting through the protective seal. The first sip tastes so good that I ignore the acidic jolts hitting my taste buds.

I keep drinking until the bottle is completely empty. I seal the cap and then toss it into the recycling bin.

Seeing a permanent marker in a cup on the counter, I go back into the fridge for a little fun.

When my work is done, I meander into the living room, taking stock of the little details I missed the last time I was here. The soft blanket draped over the couch is folded perfectly and without wrinkles. It looks too pristine for me to be convinced Collins actually uses it. The coffee table is polished and smudge-free. The plush area rug is aligned and situated exactly in the middle of the room.

I'm too much of a hot mess to ever fit into his space.

Despite everything having a firm place in Collins's home, he sure knows how to pick out comfy furniture. I plop down onto the couch to rest. It has been a long day. I unfold the blanket, kick out my feet to stretch its length, and tuck my toes into the soft folds. Getting off my feet lets me know how badly they hurt. I just need a bit more time until Luke is home and I can sleep in my own bed—where my body belongs. At least out here I'll be able to watch the clock better.

I melt into the cushions of the couch, loving how warm my cocoon has become. My eyelids feel like paperweights, pushing down and blocking out the city lights coming in through the blinds. I pry them open and stare at the wall.

Stay awake, Penny.

I drift again and allow my mind to become void of the emotion that once coursed through me. I allow the tension in my shoulders to relax. I just breathe. And drift. And breathe some more.

The fear of falling jolts me from my slumber, forcing me

to sit upright. It takes me several seconds to realize I'm in Collins's apartment. I push myself up off the couch and walk into the kitchen. Squinting, I look at the clock.

Luke should be home. If I wait too long he'll be asleep and might not even hear the doorbell. I'd better go now.

I grab my shoes and slip them onto my feet, tying them just enough not to risk tripping over them.

Maybe if I'm quiet enough, I can get back to my place without Collins noticing. His job was basically over for the night as soon as he brought me to this building. I can take it from here.

Making my way to the front door, I take one look back to make sure I didn't forget anything. Ah, the blanket is all balled up. Oh well, I'm sure his compulsiveness will push him toward giving it a fresh wash and folding it into perfection once again, if that's how he wants to spend seventy-five minutes of his time. It's best that I don't try a task that I know I'll just mess up anyway.

With shaky fingers, I unlock the deadbolt and pull open the door. I hear the vibrating countdown of the alarm system, instructing me to type in the pin code. Shit. I need to be fast.

I rush out the door, slam it shut, and dash down the hallway toward the elevators. I sigh in relief when the door opens as soon as I press the button. I enter, hit my floor's number, and say a silent *thank you* for not running into anyone in my bra-less and panty-less state of being.

If I learned anything this evening, it's to be more prepared and to think about a worst-case scenario. Forgetting my house keys and my phone was a major flaw in my plan. I still can't believe I did that.

The ding of the elevator startles me, making me fidget. When the doors open, I walk quickly to my unit.

Please be home, Luke. Please.

I ring the doorbell and follow it with a series of three knocks. Why isn't he answering? C'mon!

My mind races at the possible options. I can either go back to Collins's and sleep there, or I can sleep on the floor here in the hallway. I don't even know which one sounds better.

I give another pitiful knock, and I smack the doorbell. Leaning my forehead against the cold metal of the door, I close my eyes in defeat. Then I hear it—the sound of the knob.

I jump back as Luke pulls open the door, looking freshly showered and exhausted.

"Penny," he says smoothly. He gives me the once-over, most definitely noticing I'm not wearing undergarments. "Is this an unannounced booty call? I love surprises."

I push him back, laughing. "I live here. Remember?"

"So, we are friends with benefits. Either way, I very much approve."

"Being friends is still up for debate," I tease.

Luke grabs his heart. "Ouch."

I shake my head at him as he shuts the door and hits the lock. "I don't have my keys or phone. It's been"—I expel the air from my lungs—"one of those nights."

Luke scratches the back of his head. "Yeah, I hear you. Has your man made any more moves on you?"

I allow his words to penetrate my brain. "Which man?" I don't have a man.

"You know," he says, circling his hand into the air. "The

guy with the one facial expression." Then he demonstrates with a look of indifference. "He has a perpetual scowl on his face, like this."

Oh my. He's good at this.

"Collins?" I bark out into a laugh, making Luke nod. "Oh heavens, no. He is basically the opposite version of what I'm looking for." As soon as the words leave my lips, I know I just told a lie. At least that's how it feels. Have I been fooling myself all this time? Could someone like Collins want a girl like me?

Sure, we kissed… And ground against each other… But that could have been chalked up to heightened hormones from both of us.

I'm nothing like Daphne.

But Collins didn't seem all that into her either considering he couldn't even remember her name. And Daphne is pretty memorable.

"I've seen the way he looks at you."

"And how is that?"

"Like he's the Little Mermaid and you are dry land."

I laugh. "I guess that's better than me being a flower."

"Oh, you can be that too."

"But then I'll always be treated like someone who is delicate, when all I really want is to be ravished."

Luke blocks his ears. "TMI. Sheesh, we just met."

Smacking his arm, I giggle. "Stop it. I'm basically moonshine in the Abolition Era."

"Now that sounds fun…"

"Until my brothers find out. They would lose their minds."

Luke makes a face. "Sounds like they have anger issues."

"That's putting it mildly. You have no idea."

"So how did you wind up trying to beat down the door to our place?"

"I forgot my key."

I hope he doesn't ask any detailed questions, because I have been sworn to secrecy about keeping Limit-X hidden from others.

I'm already mentally planning my next excursion there —if Yuri lets me back in—so I need to be extra careful to stick to the rules.

"Well, lucky for you, I just got out of the shower and was about to go to bed." He wiggles his eyebrows like a cartoon character from the nineties. "And I own a queen."

My eyes take stock of his wardrobe choice—or lack thereof. Wearing just a pair of black boxers, the man looks good. How am I only realizing this now?

"But you won't own this queen," I say, all smiles.

"Oh, that's good. Offer still stands."

"Thanks for letting me in," I say meekly, ignoring his lazy proposition.

Luke gives me a once-over. "Glad I could help."

His answer is serious and a bit sobering for my mood. Maybe we can be good roommates. So far he seems harmless. At the very least, I plan to laugh a lot while I'm here.

KNOCK. KNOCK. KNOCK.

Oh shit.

Luke's eyes meet mine. I don't know what to say, other than to shrug. He walks over to the door and peers out the peephole. Turning back to me, he snickers. "You order a tall, broody drink of water from GiveMeNow? Because I don't think there's refunds."

I shake my head. Stomping toward the door, I round my shoulders. "I'll handle this."

"Alrighty. But if you need backup, I'll be in my queen bed cozying up to my favorite porn."

"Ew. Gross."

"Everyone does it."

"No, they don't."

"Well, everyone should do it," he counters, walking backward away from the door. "And if they did, they would lower their standards on how they expect men to act in real life."

"You are impossible."

"Whatevs. Good night."

"Good night, Luke."

I take a deep breath and count to three. I can do this.

"Penny!" Collins's loud voice calls out in the hallway. He's going to wake up my poor neighbors or get security called on him.

"Go away. I'm sleeping!"

I hear his laughter. Then, I see the lock move and the door opening.

"What the hell, Collins," I yell, covering a hand over my chest. "How did you get in?"

"I have a key," he says, holding it up for me to see.

My eyes catch the keychain attached, and then I feel my pulse pick up. "For starters, that's my key. Second, have you ever heard of boundaries?"

"I've heard of them. I just don't respect them."

"That much is obvious!"

"Keep your voice down. You'll wake the neighbors."

"No, you'll wake them!"

His eyes have a brightness to them that I haven't seen before. Is he enjoying this showdown? Oh, he better not be. I snatch the keys from his finger, and then notice my handbag in his other hand. When I go to reach for it, he pulls his hand back, keeping me from my belongings.

"Why did you leave?"

"What?"

"You snuck out, set off my security alarm, and didn't say a word."

"Oh. I just really wanted to sleep in my own bed. I figured my roommate was home to let me in, which he was. See?" I motion up and down my body with a hand, making Collins follow with his eyes. "I'm safe and sound."

"I don't like it."

"Don't like what? My body? My independence? Not getting your way? There's probably a plethora of things that piss you off at the moment, so please enlighten me."

"You walking alone in the hallways at night."

"I live here, Collins. Better get used to it."

"I don't like it, Penny."

Propping my hands on my waist, I pop out a hip.

It takes me glancing down one time to quickly cross my arms over my chest.

You can see the outlines of my nipples through this fabric. Eek!

His eyes darken, and my sudden modesty is now fueling his compulsion to stare.

"Quit treating me like a client, one you don't even act like you like. It's so cold."

Collins's eye twitches. "You are a client," he points out matter-of-factly.

How could I forget?

"Well, how do I get out of an agreement that I never signed up for in the first place? Huh?"

"Penny…"

"Aren't you tossing me to the brute in the parking lot anyway? Carl?"

"Chris."

"Fine, Chris. If so, why are you here?"

His eyes turn to anger. "I'm still furious that you took it upon yourself to go to a place like"—he lowers his voice—"Limit-X. What were you thinking?"

"The same thing you were," I mutter, my eyes cast downward, shamefully. Although I had no clue what I was getting into, other than to attend a party and meet new people.

After several agonizing seconds, I sigh. "Please don't tell my brothers." I mean, what would they think? I imagine they would tighten security on me, probably thinking I've gone wild. My teeth gnaw at my lip, as anxiety builds in my stomach. I feel ill, lightheaded, and weak. "I was trying to—"

"Check off fuck goals from your to-do list?"

My eyes dart up to his. "What did you say?" I feel the pulse in my neck ticking with fervor, as if my blood is suddenly too thick. I can't possibly be hearing him correctly.

"You heard me."

I look down at my hand and then up to him. "You

snooped through my bag? How dare you! What is wrong with you?"

"I could ask the same thing about you, Pen." He takes a step forward, closing the distance. From my hands, he snatches my handbag, unzips it with ease, and removes the copied list I have folded into a square. Unraveling it, he stares at me. "You want to be tied up? Blindfolded? Make out with a stranger?" He glances down at the sheet, scanning over my inked words.

I reach out and grab at the paper, only for Collins to pivot and avoid my attempt. "Give it to me." My words come out labored, as I struggle to take in enough oxygen.

Collins spares me from further humiliation by stopping there, and not reciting the goals of having sex and visiting a sex toy store. When I made my goal list, I never expected anyone to find it—especially not my bodyguard.

It was for just me.

How am I ever going to look this man in the eyes again without subconsciously thinking back to this very moment in time where he has invaded my privacy and crossed a very clear line?

"Are you happy?" I ask point-blank.

He tosses the handbag he's still holding onto the counter in the kitchen along with my portable goal list. "Happy with what, Pen?"

"Happy humiliating me? Does it make you feel good? More of a man?"

"Fuck no," he snarls, taken aback by my anger. How did he expect me to react? "I'm simply pointing out how reckless you're being. Why can't you see that?"

"You overstepped, and now you're trying to make this

look like it's my fault. Isn't that the definition of gaslighting?"

Turning my back, I walk deeper into my apartment, ignoring his presence behind me.

"Penny, just listen, please."

Keeping my stride, I call out, "No, Collins. For a man who uses minimal words, the ones you do string together suck. Get your head out of your ass and come up with a better plan for us to coexist, because right now I'm so heavily pissed off you better be glad I'm not running to my brothers for an intervention away from you. Bye now."

33

COLLINS

If Penny is trying to tick me off, it's working. I'm at my wits' end with that woman.

Sassy.

Fiery.

And stubborn as hell.

She is testing me, and I am failing miserably. From the moment she saw me at Limit-X, to the way she fought me on giving her a ride in the parking lot, to how she set off my security system without a second thought, to now…

Dismissing me?

When the hell has anyone dismissed me and gotten away with it?

I watch as Penny's ass shimmies while she saunters away from me, in an outfit I know is lacking any undergarments. Should I be purchasing these items for her to have on stock at my place?

Apparently, yes, I should.

It's just that I never considered these types of dilemmas

before when I have had to pick out clothes for others when an emergency arose.

However, something is different with Penny.

And knowing her, she'd refuse to put them on out of principle.

Enticing little wench.

When I got her belongings delivered via Chris—who I'm shocked took the initiative—and looked through to find her phone, I was livid to find her goal sheet. I knew she had a list. I did not know she had a mission to be promiscuous.

Sure, she alluded to doing so while at the Japanese Garden, but I honestly thought she was bluffing.

Hell, I would have refrained from giving her a new journal for her birthday if I thought it would be turned into her own personal sex documentation system.

Fury burns through my veins as I think of some loser touching her. I imagine this is how Graham and Nic feel when their women are around other men.

Shit.

My situation is different…

Penny isn't mine. She's no one's. And if I have any say, then she will remain that way.

She doesn't fear punishment because I can't do anything other than threaten to lock her up. Even if I did, she'd need to plead one time, and I'd cave.

That's her unrelenting effect on me…

I'm screwed.

I should be thankful that the transparency of Penny's plans has been revealed. However, the only thing I can't stop myself from thinking about is some asshole running his hands over her body. She deserves better than anything Limit-X can offer her.

Penny deserves to be worshipped and not in a semi-private setting.

Fuck!

So many horrible things could have gone wrong tonight. What would have happened if our paths didn't cross?

It's my fault I took a night off. So much for attempting to have a relaxing time blowing off some steam. Instead, I got an even more jacked-up situation with a passionate blonde girl, who knows exactly how to push every single one of my buttons.

I mean, I do see her point over Limit-X. It's hard for me to scold her for being there, when I went for my own reasons as well.

For her to think I would tell her brothers is also frustrating. I'm not some type of middleman. I'm simply her bodyguard—and turning out to be a lousy one at that.

If she would just do as she's told…

When my body can no longer handle her dismissal, I follow after her, gently taking her hand in mine and halting her retreat. Her skin feels warm and smooth, probably from living a pampered princess lifestyle.

Turning her body, Penny moves until she is standing before me. Her bottom lip is tucked into her mouth. I imagine her tongue running over the soft tissue, and the tremor running through my lower half at the mental image lets me know that was a bad decision.

"What?" she asks defiantly. "You plan to snoop through my bedroom nightstand while you're here? Confiscate anything that doesn't meet your standards? You can disguise it under the subtitle of not-breaking-and-entering. You know, a technicality, since the door will still be intact? Here, I'll help you out," she rants, moving erratically to the side of her bed and using her foot to pull open the bottom drawer. Bending down, she grabs an item and tosses it onto her bed. "I haven't even used it yet. So no need to gather any potential DNA evidence to ensure it's mine."

Her smart mouth sparks excitement up my spine, as I stare blankly at the tiny box that contains a little bullet vibrator.

I can feel my lips curling up into a smile. For starters, that device would barely be a whisper along her clit. I highly doubt something so small could bring her to orgasm without a ton of other types of stimulation.

If she is going to invest in a toy, she better immerse herself in a little research—and get something that is waterproof and with a decent motor.

"Don't you dare do that."

My eyes move to hers. "What?" I genuinely want to know.

"That smirk thing you do. We are having a fight, so play fair."

I can't help but shake my head at her. She is something. "This isn't a fight, Penny."

Propping her hands on her hips, she straightens her posture. "Oh no? Then what is it?"

"A discussion," I say simply.

"Then let's discuss how you are violating all sorts of boundaries."

"And let's discuss how you are not going to make any more lists, Penelope. No more silly games. No more—"

She rounds the bed and shoves me against my chest, catching me off guard. "You may be my bodyguard, but you sure as hell aren't my boss! I will fuck whomever I want and kiss the face off any man I—"

My hand tugs hers until her core is pressed up against mine. Warm breath expels from her lungs and hits against my neck.

Jealousy floods through me, making me livid and irrational. I'm tired of her bragging about her future conquests before they even happen. She did it at the Japanese Gardens and she's doing it again now. Those imaginative scenarios she concocted in her head won't happen anyway—at least not while I'm standing there watching.

Hell, no.

"Maybe I haven't made myself clear," I growl. "The games stop tonight. I'm done listening to you challenge me with all the reckless behavior you can dream up. I'm done, Penny."

Her eyes twitch and her lips part. I can tell she wants to say something, but like I've felt many times before, she doesn't know how to communicate her thoughts. There's no need really. I'm not open to negotiations—at least not on this subject.

"You don't even like me, so why are you so invested? Seems a bit extreme if you ask me. Are you bored? I imagine my brothers don't consider me in danger right now, so why all of the obsessive attention?"

Penny has some valid questions, I'll give her that. Sure, guarding her is different than when I was watching Angie and Claire. Penny's right; there's no immediate danger and my job should simply be maintenance really. However, there's something deep inside me that can't see her self-destruct and sit back and watch.

I know Penny is trying to be independent. However, sometimes that drive to break free from those who care could put her in a position to be taken advantage of.

This past year has been hell on her and her entire family. I can't allow her to fall into the trap of believing in the wrong people and potentially end up in an equally tragic situation.

She may have trust issues. But so do I.

"I wouldn't have to interfere as much as I do, if you would stop putting yourself in harm's way."

Her hands toss up into the air. "Oh, yeah, the highly guarded, members-only club was very *dangerous*." Her fingers make air quotes around the last word, wiggling them above her head.

"Stop mocking me." My voice goes an octave deeper, as I try to deal with her constant sass.

"Fine."

The Penny I encountered a year ago is vastly different from the one I am seeing in front of me today. Maybe she hasn't changed at all. Maybe she is just starting to shift back into the person she always was.

"You don't belong in a place like Limit-X, Pen."

"Oh, and you do?" She lets out a huff, turning her shoulder to me.

"Girls like"—I pause, not knowing how to complete the sentence without adding more kindling to the fire already blazing inside of her—"you, Penny, shouldn't be prowling the floors of a place like that. Trouble will find you. Trust me. Membership or not, the innocent girls always seem to get swallowed whole by the snakes."

I watch in silence as her body whips back around, while stomping predatorily toward me. I can see the heat in her eyes, the way her chest rises with each breath, and how her jaw tics.

She is radiant.

If her temper wasn't directed at me, I might be able to enjoy it more. Except right now, my only focus is on what her next move will be.

"Look at me, Collins," she demands. "Look at me, dammit!"

My eyes search hers. I am looking at her. Why does she think otherwise? "I see you."

"Do you? Because from everything that just spewed out of your mouth right now, you don't see me at all. You see some fragile girl who you were hired to protect. And I'm sick of it. I don't blame my brothers for being detached from reality. But you? I expect someone as neutral as you should be to have some type of realization and rational thinking happening to understand that this is my life we are talking about." She takes a step closer, making my heart stop for a beat. Stretching up on her tiptoes, she places a single hand on my chest for balance, as her lips move to my ears. "And I'll let you in on a little secret," she whispers.

Her warm breath tickles my neck, as the smell of strawberries permeates my senses, with such an intensity that I swear she bathed herself in the ripened fruit. I stand as stiff as a board as her upper body molds to mine. I can feel her pert nipples graze against the fabric of my shirt. She is a freaking temptress.

For fuck's sake, don't move your hips.

"I'm going to shatter your misinformed view of me. You just watch and see."

She takes a step back, running her hands down the hourglass form of her body, from her chest to her hips. Biting her bottom lip, she gives me a smirk. This is where something indeterminable has changed. I can see it in her eyes. I can tell from the way her body hums with the knowledge that she is now in control.

And I'll be damned, but will admit—it turns me on.

"Penny…"

"Remember this moment, Collins." She marches out of her room and over to the ripped-out piece of paper that holds her goals. Taking a pen off the counter, she jots something down onto it. "Here," she says, passing me the note.

Staring down at her elegant script, I mumble the words she added to the bottom of the list. "Become a member of Limit-X." I look over at Penny, who looks absolutely smitten with herself. "Maybe I'll make a *friend* there."

Oh, hell.

Penny is definitely speaking in code, and I'm hearing her euphemism loud and clear.

"If you expect me to stand back and watch you self-destruct, then you obviously have underestimated me."

"If you expect me to be locked in this"—she waves a hand through the air—"gilded cage and play the sweet girl in this story, then you obviously don't understand that the harder you try to stop me, the more reckless I'll be."

My jaw twitches as I allow her words to soak in.

I can tell by the gleam of commitment in her eyes that this isn't a bluff. If I'm going to continue guarding Penny

—and how can I even stop now given her declaration?— then I have to act like what she's planning to do won't affect me. Maybe if she thinks she has some control, then she won't be hell-bent on trying to dangle herself in front of the first available taker.

This is something happening psychologically within Penny. She fears that every time she gets close to a man she'll see Tanner, so she's planning to counterbalance it by flooding her system with as many men as she can to desensitize herself.

It is reckless.

And it won't work in her favor.

Someone is going to go too far with her, thinking she is "asking for it," and I'll have to come up with a burial plan for the unsuspecting idiot.

I can talk with the staff at Limit-X. A lot know me from my days of working there. Now is about the right time to call in a few of the favors owed to me.

I feign a casual shrug. "Listen, Pen," I say casually. "Your brothers gave me strict orders to watch out for you, not dictate what you do every second of the day." Although if I were to give them any hints as to where little sister wants to spend all of her energy, they would for sure construct that gilded cage and conveniently lose the key.

Her lips curl into a Cheshire cat smile. "Good." Wiggling her fingers, she waves goodbye. "Have a good night, Collins."

I watch her obedient facade, not buying the act at all. Every part of me wants to jerk her toward me and make her promise that she'll be a good girl. I refuse to back down—but neither will Penny.

I walk to the door backward, watching as Penny retreats deeper into her apartment. Is she going to lock herself in? Hell, I guess I can use the spare key I made. There's no way in hell I'll walk out of here and not even provide some level of security to her unit.

Running a hand through my hair, I exit, turn the lock into place, and then rest my back against the door.

How in the world am I going to survive the next few months when Penny Hoffman has a choke hold on my self-control and my libido?

I can no longer keep things professional, and I doubt anything could happen to make me flip the switch.

And in this moment, I know that I won't be able to voluntarily let Penelope Hoffman go.

34

PENNY

I can feel the anger seeping from my skin as I walk briskly down the sidewalk toward Nic and Claire's apartment. It almost feels like I have freedom, but who the fuck knows where Collins is or how he's watching?

I would have worn something he'd surely disapprove of just to piss him off if I wasn't trying to avoid his attention as it is.

I'm mad.

I've been fuming for days over Collins snooping through my belongings to discover my goals sheet. That man is unhinged if he even thinks that's normal.

Next up, he'll be retrieving my latest pap smear results and digging up my third grade spelling bee rank.

I'll put nothing past him and his intrusive tendencies. He has no boundaries—just like my brothers when it comes to their women.

But I am not Collins's anything…

Well, other than the pesky brat who won't allow him to bulldoze over my entire life.

Hence, why I'm going to gift him the ultimate gift for being such a giant dick—just in case he's not sure of my true feelings over that stunt.

I've been running on popcorn and pineapple juice for days and can't think straight, so I expect some fun and vibrant bad choices to be made. I'm twitchy and in need of a solid distraction.

That's what Collins does to me. He makes me want to be bad.

I walk into the building and wave to the lobby attendant who immediately escorts me to the elevator as if I can't possibly take the twenty steps to arrive there myself without getting lost. It honestly makes me wonder just how much my brother pays to have all these extra details.

When I get inside and hit the button for the correct floor, I send Claire a quick text that I'll be there in a minute.

Ringing the doorbell, I wait patiently. This may be the last time I visit this place. Soon the deliriously happy couple will be moving into their newly constructed custom-built house prior to the baby arriving, and I can't wait to see it. I'm sure Nic spared no expense to give his fiancée the forever dream home she deserves—and never had growing up.

I hear some rustling and then Claire appears in the doorway, all smiles and looking adorably pregnant.

"I need a dick cake," I blurt out without any preamble.

"So do I…" she exaggerates all the syllables. "I'm always starving for dick cake. I'm at the horned-up phase of the pregnancy where my hooters hurt and my hoo-ha wants action."

"Not for us to eat, but for me to send," I clarify.

She nods eagerly. "Also, yes, please. That sounds fun too."

It's obvious she's on board with this idea, without knowing any detail or who it's for. Claire's the ride-or-die type of friend, and slowly I'm starting to see her as more than just my future sister-in-law.

"I want a *giant* dick cake."

"A colossal cock…got it." Claire steps back to allow me to enter, welcoming me inside. "I know the best bakeries in town."

"I have zero doubt."

I follow her inside, and we settle on the sofa in her living room, facing each other.

"Or we can make one ourselves."

My shoulders lift. "Whatever you think is best."

Reaching for a notepad resting on a side table near the lamp, Claire turns back the cover and pulls the pen from the spiraled binding. "Let's get to work."

How is she able to maintain professionalism when I'm in a desperate state of mind to send Collins Stone a message? I still can't believe he snooped through basically a private journal entry.

"I appreciate this, Claire."

She holds her hands to her heart. "It is my honor that you thought of me first when you were in your time of need. You know I sent your brother a massive dick cake for being a massive dick when he messed up the good thing we had going on?"

"Oh, I know. I saw it in the fridge once when I was visiting. My eyes can never unsee."

She laughs. "Trust me, he deserved it."

"Oh, I bet. Punk always deserves what you choose to serve up."

"Okay"—Claire claps her hands together—"back to business. We have a lot to discuss, but I'm going to warn you about something…"

"This sounds ominous…"

She pulls up a bent leg onto the couch cushion and gives me a smirk. "I'm in my Revenge Era, so I might enjoy this more than you."

I'm not sure what that means, but all of her previous eras were epic. So I trust that Claire will rock this one as well.

I almost feel bad for my brother…

She is so fierce, and I admire her strength and resilience so much.

"Fair enough."

"But be warned. If some guy did you wrong and your brothers find out, they won't hesitate to let Collins know and rid the world of his existence. Granted, I'm not supposed to know any of these things, and technically I don't have proof. But, let's just say that I can read between the lines well when it comes to those possessive men."

I swallow hard. She's right. Well, except *Collins* is the one who did me wrong.

"I even vetted a few custom bake options, hoping your brother would mess up and warrant a tasty dick cake 2.0. But the man has been nearly perfect and by far the best thing that's ever happened to me."

"That is just too sweet." I knew my brother would take a while to settle down, but I'm thrilled he has done it with Claire. They are the perfect match. Seeing them together makes me want what they have.

"Okay, let's talk details. Realistic or cartoonish?"

I laugh. "Excuse me?"

"This is a serious question, Penny. Stop laughing. Are you looking for veins and varying colors of pink and purple, or are you wanting exaggerated hair and googly eyeballs and a mouth? Ohhh, or a chlamydia outbreak for funsies? The options are pretty endless, really. Actually, do you have a dick pic? Like a real one and not a stock image." She does the give-me-give-me hands. "That would be very helpful."

I suck in air through my teeth, trying to keep myself from irritating her further by giggling. I don't think I've given this whole revenge gift enough thought—obviously. From the cake she once sent my brother, I know she is the right person to help me with this task. I just never thought there would be this much to consider. "Umm, cartoonish?"

"Pierced or not pierced?"

"I, ah…"

"Oh, you haven't seen his dick yet?"

"No." Well, I felt the impression of it and it's intimidating as fuck. What is happening? Why am I so overwhelmed? "Okay, maybe no piercing."

"Well, with cartoonish, anything goes. So…" Claire taps her finger along her jaw. "You could include one as like a threat?" She giggles. "That actually sounds fun—yeah?" Before I can answer, she continues, "It's really just a personal preference."

"Surprise me."

Rubbing her hands together as if casting some special spell, she takes a deep breath and cracks her knuckles. "Your wish is my command. This is going to be so good."

"What are you girls up to?" Nic says, his voice cutting through our laughter. He eyes us both suspiciously.

Claire tosses the notebook where she was writing all of the details, including cute little penis doodles, behind the couch. "Oh, nothing." She busies herself with a bottle of pills that are on the end table, which I assume are her prenatal vitamins.

Nic intercepts her container and passes her another one from a pharmacy bag that he happens to be holding. "Take these instead."

"Why?"

"More folic acid."

Claire turns to me and cups a hand to her mouth as if Nic can't hear her. "See what I'm dealing with?" She nudges her elbow toward him as if he isn't in the room. "He knows more about how to carry a baby than I do."

"Oh, trust me. I get it." Punk hired Collins to shadow my every movement and not actually tell me about it. So, nothing surprises me with him.

"It's a full-time job micromanaging his expectations."

I spare my brother a glance, and he manages to look innocent.

Faker.

"You both done ganging up on me?"

Claire shakes her head no and stands up. "This boy"—she pokes him in the chest which gets him to smirk—"made me an online profile so he can use my account to garner fake likes and support on social media."

"Oh yeah? What is your screen name?" I really should make popcorn for this.

"Oh, he kept it totally classy. Wait for it… Notyomomma."

"Wow."

"It helps me stay relevant and up-to-date with all the parenting trends," Nic defends.

Claire gives me a look. "He needs a hobby before I make myself a fake profile just to stir up shit and red flag all his lame-ass posts."

"You wouldn't," Nic says with a scoff.

"I would."

"She would," I agree.

He lets out a sigh. "I'll get blocked. Those hormone-fueled admins scare me."

Claire shakes her head at him. "You called a bunch of moms self-cannibals for eating their placentas."

I choke on my own spit.

Yup.

Nic straightens his posture. "I said what I said."

"It was a step too far," Claire says, looking resigned. "Just stick to your lane, Nic Hoffman."

He holds his hands up. "Fine, fine."

My brother has gone from overprotective to overbearing with this pregnancy. I can tell he is worried over his girl, but he needs to lighten up some or risk Claire feeling suffocated.

I think some of his fears for his girl are also exaggerating his fears for me. He has a huge heart, and not being able to control every single situation probably eats at him.

Making sure the people he loves are protected—the way he sees fit—must give him the freedom to live his life.

Men like Collins and my brothers thrive on this control.

They need it to function.

But Collins overstepped majorly by blatantly snooping and has earned himself a custom cock cake as a consequence. He can try to cockblock my goals however he wants, but he needs to learn that there are invisible boundaries that should never be crossed.

At least it will be a tasty lesson…

I watch as Nic places his palm under Claire's chin to guide her gaze back to his. Leaning down, he gently kisses her nose, shakes out a pill into the palm of his hand from the new Nic-approved bottle, and then rests it against her bottom lip. When she opens, he slides the little orange soft gel onto her tongue and then retrieves the oversized canteen of water he conveniently has filled.

I swear every time I see her, the water bottle gets bigger and bigger.

"Sip. More." He sighs. "More, Claire, so your stomach lining doesn't peel away."

"So dramatic. Like that probably only happens to five percent of the population."

When he is satisfied with Claire's hydration, he turns back to me. "Penny, are you staying out of trouble?"

"Always."

"Liar."

"Well, I'm sure you would get a report if I was breaking any rules, am I right?"

Nic gives me a look. What's up with all these looks being shot my way? He has to know I know about Collins's position, and while neither of us had a discussion about it, there's no way that I can't know.

I guess since I haven't run away yet, or at least haven't been successful at my attempts, he's happy with the outcome thus far. I've been known to ditch my secret guards in the past. Obviously, Collins wouldn't have shared that I was able to sneak away and get to Limit-X without much fuss.

Standing up from the couch, I stretch my arms over my head.

"I appreciate your help, Claire."

Her smile is warm. "I'll text you later with the final sketch and details for your bakery delivery," Claire says.

Nic gives me a half hug. "Can I give you a ride back to your place?"

I shake my head no. "I'll just walk."

"I would prefer you to be escorted back, Penny."

"Then just message my henchman."

His mouth opens and then quickly shuts.

"Never mind, I'll just do it myself." Pulling out my phone, I pretend to send a text to Collins.

I give one last wave and step into the foyer only to be confronted with my broody bodyguard.

"You scared me," I half scream, holding my hand on my heart. "What were you doing—just waiting for me all this time?"

"Yes."

"Why? It sounds boring."

"It was convenient." He looks me up and down. "You should have texted me"—he holds his hand up when he sees me about to interrupt—"*and* then wait for me to get here."

"Oh, I pretend texted you and then discovered I didn't need to wait at all."

Collins gives me a *look.*

I am fucking done with these looks.

Everyone can just stop looking at me.

Collins sighs. "Luckily I decided to wait here for you, on the off chance you were too mad at me to be reasonable."

I let out a huff. "I'm always reasonable. I texted you, well, in theory, you brute."

"How many days do you think you need before you stop being mad at me?"

I shrug, giving it some thought. "Probably eternity."

35

COLLINS

The worst part about my job assignment is feeling like a fucking traitor every time I'm around the Hoffman family. It doesn't help that Nic called me into his home today to check in with how things are going with Penny.

She didn't even know I was there because she and Claire were planning something and needing that girl time.

But that's what I do. I slither in unnoticed and am there to eliminate as many threats to the welfare of the entire Hoffman family as I can.

After discussing in generic terms Penny's inability to see danger, Nic and I agreed that putting a couple of extra tracking devices on her wouldn't be a bad idea. Graham isn't a huge fan of this idea and has made it clear to just leave him out of these little decisions. He'd much rather keep his sister under lock and key and probably would if he didn't have his wife's wrath to consider.

Claire, Angie, and Penny are the definition of "girl power." And while Penny might not quite understand how loyal the other two are to her, she would just need to attend one family discussion to realize their influence.

While the placement of these trackers won't be directly discussed with her, based on prior knowledge of her brothers' capabilities and past methods alone, they shouldn't surprise her that much. Justifying my behavior to myself makes it feel less of a violation. But if Penny were somehow to find out the extent we would all go for her safety, I have a strong feeling she would take out her anger on me—versus the source giving me the orders.

I can handle her—sassy defiance and all.

And she is defiant as fuck.

I knew Penny walked here, because I got a call from the front door security worker at Sky View. I was already headed out, so I followed her discreetly, several paces behind. Not once did she notice my presence.

Sure, Portland is an overall safe city. However, when it comes to protecting my target, I don't like to make assumptions. Assumptions get people hurt—or worse, killed.

From the cold shoulder Penny gives me in the elevator, I know she's not a fan of being escorted back to our apartment complex. At this point, I don't very much care. Finding Penny at Limit-X has solidified every preliminary thought that she isn't ready to make healthy choices for herself unaccompanied. Pair that with her trip to see Mark Tanner in prison, and let's just say there's no way in hell I think her brothers are overexaggerating their need for my services.

I swallow. But Penny doesn't need a shadow as much as she needs her ass tanned and the image of my hand print seared firmly into her memory. For a second, I allow the fantasy of her being mine to flitter through my limbs, causing my hands to twitch. If she thinks I'm hardcore and rigid now, then she'd be in for a shock if she had me as a…

Fuck.

A lover? *Really, Stone.*

"I'm still mad at you," she mumbles, pulling me from my thoughts.

"I can see that."

"Did you meet with my brother?"

She's perceptive. I'll give her that.

"Yes."

"Why?"

"Business."

Penny makes a face, and then follows it up by sticking her tongue out at me. I can't help but find her disdain for me cute. There's no part of me that isn't absolutely enchanted by her courageous passion for trying to piss me off.

Trying.

Because it sure as hell isn't working. She's too adorable for me to actually be upset, but she doesn't need to know the effect she has on me. Revealing a weakness will just get me caught with my pants down, thrusting into her tight…

Fuck.

Now she's wiggling her tongue back and forth, while I can hear her mental thoughts taunting me with a na-na-na-na-na.

"Put your tongue back in your mouth, Penny." My words come out more as a threat than a warning. It's still a failed attempt. Penny isn't scared of me.

"Aren't you close to retirement?"

I tip my head back and laugh. She really is quite funny.

"Not quite yet. I still got a few years before I'm too old to work." It's more like decades left, but who's counting?

When we get to the lobby, we exit to the main street. Penny looks down both directions of the sidewalk. "See? No axe murderers prowling the street today. I think I'm safe now to make my way home without your overbearing company."

"I'm going that direction anyway. We can walk together. I insist."

She scrunches up her nose, remembering we both live in the same building. She's probably thinking I'll concoct a plan to be on the same floor as her—for security purposes, of course. The idea did cross my mind.

We walk in silence and maintain a semi-brisk pace back to Sky View.

Except when we get just two blocks away, Penny decides to take a detour down a perpendicular street.

I don't question her. I just follow.

She's not in the mood for small talk, and I'm not a fan of using words to fill space that is content in the silence.

But Penny does have me curious.

It takes us about fifteen minutes and several crossed streets to wind up at the gym where her brothers and I often spar.

"Taking me into the ring?" I ask in an amused tone.

"Yes."

She really is pissed at me.

I jog ahead of her and open the door, granting her first entry.

And I follow.

"You're going to hurt yourself."

"Then you're a poor teacher," Penny slings back at me.

Her words sting and make my jaw twitch.

What is this girl doing to me? Never would I allow anyone to talk to me how she so freely speaks.

Our previous self-defense lesson feels like a lifetime ago, as so much has happened between us since.

"You need to know where your target is, but more importantly any other threats nearby." I bounce on the balls of my feet. "Keep your eyes moving and protect your head. Protect the soft tissue."

But all of this advice is useless because Penny is becoming my attacker, charging for me with all her might.

"Ahhhh!"

And it's me who is trying my best to protect all of her vital organs—as well as mine.

"For fuck's sake, Penelope!"

But she commits and thrashes about me, hitting me and taking out all of her aggressions.

And I let her—within reason.

I dodge her kick but can't avoid her slap. "Ouch."

Penny's using all sorts of creative moves that would never hold up in a true fight, but she doesn't seem to care.

When she charges toward me again, I squat down and hoist her up above my head and then send her down toward the blue mat, all while cushioning her fall.

Lying on top of her, I use my legs to immobilize her and pin her wrists to the mat.

"What in the world, Penny?" I huff out, trying to catch my breath.

She thrashes underneath my weight. "Get off of me!"

But I don't allow her to move. I just press her into the mat and give her the space to struggle without hurting herself.

I hate that she is this fired up, and for what? I have no clue.

"I'm mad at you!"

My eyes search hers. "Fine. But at least tell me why."

"No!"

"Yes. Tell me what has you so upset."

She twists and turns, trying to shoulder her way out of my hold.

But it's useless.

And that part actually scares me.

"If you ever have a man on top of you and you need to get out of the hold, I'm going to teach you the steps. But I need you to be calm enough to listen."

So I wait. I scoop an arm under her lower back, and I wait.

I wait for Penny's breathing to get back to a nonpanting status.

I wait for her face to become less flushed.

And I wait until she stops trying to push me away.

"Are you ready now?"

I watch as the heat that was once so present in her eyes fizzles out to lukewarm. But behind those pretty blues, I still see the fight she has inside of her.

Penny nods.

"I need your words."

"I'm ready."

Compliance must taste horrible on her tongue if her facial expression is any indication of her true feelings.

I want to laugh, but I also value full usage of my genitals. So I resist.

And for the next thirty minutes, I teach Penny the necessary steps on how to get out of a hold if someone is undesirably on top of her.

"Are you still mad at me?" I ask, handing Penny a small white sweat towel.

"That's pretty much my permanent emotion at this point."

"Good to know."

She gives me a look. "Is it?"

"Yes. Now I'll know not to try to get your impression of me to change—yet."

I get another look and a small smirk. I might not even have noticed it if I wasn't so tunnel-visioned toward this girl.

Then I hear her stomach growl.

"Let's get you some food."

Penny shifts her weight to her other foot. "I'll have to go back to my apartment first. I forgot to bring my purse with my money."

"I have it covered, Penny. You don't need to ever worry about money."

"But I can pay for it with my own money. I don't need yours."

"True. But if you pay for it now, I'll just add it back into your account later. This saves me a step."

Penny starts to talk but then quickly closes her mouth. And then she opens it again, but never says another word about my revelation.

We exit the gym and walk into a little cafe just a block from Sky View.

"What are you in the mood for?" I ask, scanning the menu.

At least Penny doesn't seem to have many hang-ups when it comes to food options. She always seems to find something she likes.

"Umm, maybe the…"

An odd feeling hits me all at once, and I glance around the venue.

Something is off.

And if there's anything I've learned in the past, it's always to trust my instincts.

Reaching for Penny, I gently pull her by her arm to me.

"We have to go."

Her eyes dart to mine. "What? Why?"

"Something doesn't seem right. I need you out of here."

Reaching for my cell, I call Chris. "Corner of Birchview and Norris."

Wrapping an arm around Penny, I guide her outside and onto the sidewalk. We are really close to our apartment, so I opt to just walk her home.

"You are scaring me," she says softly.

My eyes keep moving, looking for anything even slightly out of place.

We pass by several groups of walkers.

Why is it so crowded at this time of the day?

When I get us into the lobby at Sky View, I motion for a worker to come closer.

"I need you to make sure Miss Hoffman gets inside her apartment."

"Understood."

"I can get there myself," she whines.

"Not now, Penny. Go."

Her eyes fill with panic, and it takes everything in me not to press her to me and comfort her.

"Everything will be fine. Just go to your place and wait for me. I'll be there soon."

When they walk away, I text the head of security for the building.

Collins: Make sure Penelope Hoffman doesn't leave the building and no one arrives to her floor without identification.

Then I send a group text to Graham and Nic.

Collins: Checking surveillance at Rose City Cafe. Something seems off while there.

Graham: Gather info and meet at my place in an hour.

Nic: Okay. Is Penny okay? Was she with you?

Collins: She's fine. I have her back at Sky View. I'm being overly cautious. Could be nothing.

Graham: When have your instincts ever been wrong?

I swallow down the knot forming in my throat.

Collins: Never

Graham: Exactly

Nic: I am working on getting tracers put on cells for prison guards. The last thing we need is a double dipper.

Collins: I can share any credit card, phone, and social media records I've collected when we meet.

Graham: See you both soon.

36

PENNY

For the last week, I've lived inside my little bubble of an apartment, not really doing much other than wait for the imagined threat that caused us to leave the little cafe abruptly to get resolved or silently hope Collins would pay attention to me. But he's been missing in action ever since that day. He's also made it very clear that I need to lie low until he figures things out.

But I am lonely.

Even Luke has a more active social life than I do, which isn't all that shocking—but still. I guess his personality is more conducive to making friends.

But I'd be lying if I wasn't curious what has my bodyguard spooked. Something happened in that cafe that is directly impacting my solitary life right now.

In true Collins form, he never brought me out of the dark, and I doubt he will based on historical data. Instead, for days I've been thinking of every worst-case scenario and following his wish of me staying in hermit mode.

Well, I'm done.

I've watched all the series. I've online shopped for all the unnecessary items. I've ordered all the takeout meals. And I've created five different mock-up subscription box ideas for future upcoming months—my favorite being the Revenge Box and the Make Him Jealous Box.

But I miss the office. I need people in my life and not just words on an email.

Because Claire will be going on maternity leave with the new baby, I've been learning some of the marketing responsibilities she typically manages. I love channeling my brain in a different direction, so this has been a lot of fun for me.

It helps that Plus None's business model is designed to appeal to the modern woman—at all stages of her life. The company wants to expand, and with that expansion comes the need for more ideas. So my vision for a box theme might differ from Claire's, but it could still work.

And I am freaking excited to show the team and founders my ideas.

But in person…

I can't do any more virtual meetings. They are lame, and I look like I have hydrocephalus every time my big head pops up on the two-dimensional screen.

At this point, I don't even care if Collins escorts me to the office on his own. Granted, he's the inspiration for the boxes. He definitely put me in a mood during the birth of those ideas.

I can't do another cottage in a field puzzle or watch another infomercial on making custom-flavored sodas with just the push of a button. I'm never going to make sourdough bread or be a homesteader, and yet I went deep down the rabbit hole midweek thinking I could be it and wasted three hours learning how to make a starter.

Boring.

I'm bored.

Now I need some excitement in my life.

If there was a threat six days ago, then surely it's gone now. I can't live like this anymore.

So I do something super reckless. I leave my apartment and take the elevator to Collins's floor.

Maybe if I pretend to play by the rules, then he'll be more inclined to get me out of this slump. Knocking on his door, I silently pray that he answers.

"Can I help you, Miss Hoffman?"

My body whips around to find Collins's sidekick—Chris?—standing just a yard away. He really can be sneaky despite being much taller and far more muscular than I am. I didn't even notice he was following me.

"Yes. Yes, you can," I say confidently.

Chris tips his head. "How can I be of service?"

"I am going to Hoffman Headquarters today. I need to get out of this building and enjoy life. I'd like to go in the next three minutes."

"Alright, let's do it."

I don't know what I was expecting when I showed up here, but it wasn't that. Chris is being way too compliant, which makes me uneasy.

But I can't be too picky today or smack the gift horse in the chompers. I'll take what I can get. If it means being escorted through the city by a friendly ogre, so be it.

So I walk beside Chris as he leads me to the parking garage and silently celebrate my little slice of victory.

Because freedom tastes delicious.

"These ideas are amazing," one of the marketing team employees says, glancing at my portfolio and mock-ups for the boxes I created over the last week. "Truly innovative and fresh."

"Thank you." I beam with pride.

I couldn't have asked for a better response, but glancing over at one of the other team members, Jill, I can tell she has a few things on her mind.

"Do you have any thoughts?" I ask her. I'm not a confrontational person, and yet I can't help but wonder what her pushback would be. I don't mind adapting or altering things. It's not like I'm not flexible.

Jill leans back in her chair. There are six of us having a conference in one of the rooms that is made mostly of windows. We have the blur feature activated that can allow for privacy when needed.

"Yes, please, Jill. Share your thoughts with Penny," another teammate encourages.

I mean, I am super curious as well.

"It's just that," she starts, shuffling through my sketches and write-ups, "these seem a little immature and vindictive, don't you all think?"

Silence fills the space, and instantly I'm taken back to elementary school when I was called into the office over an issue with another kid that I clearly shouldn't have been a part of, but because I was unable to defend myself, I took the blame.

While not the same thing, I won't be that shattered, quiet girl who sits back and just allows someone to walk all over me.

"I value everyone's opinions, as this is in the early stages of the planning process. However, I've done a lot of research on the target audience for these box themes that I'd like to share with you all."

"A Google search can't be counted as research," Jill says, partially under her breath but loud enough for everyone to hear.

A few workers glance my way. Their eyes are kind. I imagine Jill talks to them this way too and that it has less to do with me being new and more to do with it just being her personality. I guarantee if Angie or Claire were present in the room, I'd be treated differently by her. But I don't need to be rescued all the time. I can try to handle some things on my own.

Reaching into my bag, I pull out my data sheets that I constructed and consolidated to make it easier for my peers to see my efforts. It's not enjoyable to try to prove myself, but I also understand the need to establish myself to those who don't know my work ethic well enough yet.

"Here are the top one hundred videos that have been trending on three social media platforms over the last six months." I spread out the graphs so everyone can see. "Across the various platforms, there's a correlation in content topics among viewers aged twenty to forty. Granted, I filtered and focused on the videos where females were the creators."

Several teammates lean over to get a better look.

"This is fascinating, Penny," one says.

"Great job researching," another compliments.

"Well, what is in common?" Jill says in a hurry.

"Several things, actually," I say. "First off, there's a social epidemic of women being cheated on. And then there's a strong desire to find the right man."

"So, you used those trending ideas to construct box themes?" a worker asks.

"Exactly," I confirm. "And I wa—"

"But social media is constantly changing," Jill interrupts.

I nod. "It is. I agree with you, Jill. But so is Plus None. This is not a stagnant company but an evolving one. It is a cool, modern subscription business that strives to create products that appeal to the everyday woman in the *now*, which means staying on top of trends or predicting them before they go viral. And what better way to know what those trends will be other than to use these massive platforms to gather our data and study the market?"

Several people clap their hands together, making me blush, and making Jill look like she could use some Retinol serum for her scowl.

"Well done," Angie says from the doorway, beaming with pride.

I didn't even know she was there witnessing some of our discussion.

When the meeting is over, I join my sister-in-law in the break room for a snack.

"Thank you for giving me this opportunity, Angie."

She gives me a side hug. "You are shining in this fluid role, and I couldn't be more proud."

We hang out at the table, snacking on some cheese slices and fresh fruit that gets delivered weekly to stock the fridge.

I pop a strawberry into my mouth, savoring the taste of summer. "I could get used to this."

She smiles. "I hope you do."

"You have created such an amazing company with Claire." I glance around the lounge. "It's truly a dream to work in such a welcoming place."

"Thank you. I'm just glad that Jill didn't get to you. I know she comes off harsh, but she's going through some things right now."

My smile dims. "I'm really sorry to hear that."

"It's no excuse, but she could use some grace. Heaven knows I needed grace in my life at one time."

I'm relieved that I chose the high road earlier and didn't get snippy like my instincts sometimes suggest in the heat of the moment. I really do hope that whatever Jill is experiencing gets better.

We are all in this life together, just trying to figure things out.

When I leave the Plus None office space, I'm met with Chris apparently waiting for me.

"I don't need an escort."

"Oh, I need one. I forget how to get back to Sky View."

He starts walking with me, which just makes me groan.

"Then use a GPS."

"A what?" he asks, but I know he's teasing.

I shake my head at him. "Never mind."

Then he smirks, and I just allow him to usher me onto the elevator. But instead of hitting the button for the lobby, I hit the one for Graham's floor.

"Going to pay a visit to big bro?"

I look up at Chris and narrow my eyes. I know Collins wouldn't ever trust me with someone incompetent, yet this guy does not fit the mold of a powerful bodyguard.

But what do I know when it comes to all things security? The only thing I focus on in that regard is how to slide under the radar.

Graham's assistant waves to me and uses her extended hand to show that my brother is available to see me. I must have caught him at the right time.

Walking into his office, I also find Nic.

"Two for one special," Chris says jokingly.

He's odd, and that's saying it mildly.

"Hey, Penny," they both greet.

They get up from their seats to give me a hug.

"What brings you here?" Graham asks.

"What happened in the cafe the other day?"

"Nothing," Nic says quickly.

"Liar."

"Nothing for you to worry about," Graham clarifies.

I fold my arms over my chest. "You know when you say *not* to worry, it makes me worry."

"Well, you should work on that," Nic says, unhelpfully.

"Gee, thanks, Punk. I'll get right on it."

My phone starts vibrating in my hand, drawing my attention to it. Typically, workers have to check in all electronic devices down in the lobby. However, keeping mine is the added benefit of having two older brothers who run this entire building.

Looking down at the screen, I see the caller ID and nearly drop the device.

It says it's from *my* number…

Me.

But I know that is impossible. I am obviously not calling myself.

"Penny, what's wrong?" Graham asks, moving closer to see what has me so off-balance.

He looks at the screen and sees the words—Penelope Hoffman mobile.

I hope my mind is just playing tricks on me, but something tells me the person on the other line is a known person and one who is evil.

Taking the device from my hand, Graham slides the bar to answer and then steps away from me. Nic joins him and they both lean into one another to listen to the call meant for me.

"Who was it?" I demand when the call is over.

"No one," Nic snaps, not at me but at the situation. Then he quickly says an apology. "I'm sorry, Pen."

"Have you received any calls like this in the past?" Graham asks, pacing along the windows in his massive office.

"No."

I can tell he's scrolling through my missed and recent calls anyway, but it doesn't bother me.

"Okay," he says softly.

"Was it Mark? He was calling me?"

Graham looks at Nic, and just like that a message was passed between them without a word spoken.

"Everything will be fine," Nic says, trying to comfort me.

It's not working for obvious reasons. For starters, the world could be burning to the ground, and I swear my brothers would have a positive way to spin it if just to attempt to keep me calm.

"I can't be locked up again. I could barely take this last week." My words come out frantically.

"It won't be that bad," Graham says. "Just go back to your apartment and wait until we tell you it's safe again to resume normal responsibilities."

"Okay," I say, but only to keep them appeased.

There's no way I'm staying inside anymore.

No. Way.

37

PENNY

I'm getting pretty good at escaping my fortress undetected. I simply needed to go to the lobby to check my mail and use the main floor's bathroom. I waited until all of the workers were busy greeting the dinner crowd and slipped out the back exit without a fuss.

And my scheduled car was already idling as planned.

It was too easy, and it's in that ease that guilt sets in.

I know Collins has some stress in his life, but he doesn't need to worry over me.

I'm fine.

Plus, it's Margo who wants me to keep making personal goals and working toward them. I'm doing exactly that tonight.

And tonight will be different. I'll be better prepared, and I'm trying to channel my inner brave girl.

I am safe. I am fierce. I am loved.

My gaze looks out the window as the building comes

into view. Instantly—and despite my self-initiated pep talk—my nerves multiply and wreak havoc on my system before the car even pulls into the drop-off lane at Limit-X.

How is it possible that I'm more nervous tonight than I was my first time here? I thought knowing what to expect would have its benefits. However, it's just adding to my apprehension.

Like a flood of emotions, all my fears come barreling through me.

What if I go inside and no one wants to hang out? It's not like I made any real friends while I was here the last time. Nope. Instead I probably painted a self-portrait for everyone of myself titled "Freak."

What if someone touches me and I spaz out? What if I can't recover as quickly as I'd like?

My driver slowly pulls along the damp asphalt, his headlights casting a golden glow in the darkness of the night. The mansion is lit up only at the door and the path leading up to it. I know they want to appear nondescript, and I think they've mastered that objective.

"Have fun in the dungeon," the driver jokes, making me cringe.

If he only knew how true his teasing really is. "Thank you," I say, handing him a bunch of bills to pay for my ride.

He stares at the money. "Thanks, hun! If you need a ride back home"—he hands me a business card—"consider it done."

"Thank you. Have a good night."

Closing the door, I take a step back and scan over the cars. A shiver creeps up my spine.

The last time I was here, I ended the night being accosted in the parking lot. Here's to hoping that doesn't happen at the start of it.

Michael greets me with a big smile when he sees me trekking up the long pathway. He really does have the ideal view of the parking lot.

"What a pleasant and unexpected surprise," he says, meeting me halfway and taking my hand in his. His dwarfs mine, making me feel petite and feminine. "I'm so glad you decided to give this place another chance."

I can't hide my smirk. "Hi."

"I'm *really* glad, Penny."

"You remembered my name," I mutter, not knowing if that is a good or bad thing. Being memorable could have double meanings. Was it because I had a monumental freakout moment the last time I was here, catching Collins doing wicked acts with Daphne?

"Of course, little dove. Come," he coaxes, as we ascend the stairway. "And at least you chose a fun night, with Testing Your Limits."

"Yeah, about that, the website description was vague."

Michael tilts his head back and laughs. "That's exactly what Master Yuri was going for. He's such a mysterious bastard."

I bite my bottom lip and rock on my ridiculously too high glass heels. "Is it going to be as scary as it sounds?"

His eyes soften and level with mine. "No one should scare you here, and if they do, they are at fault. Unless, of course, being scared is your kink…"

"It's definitely not."

"Well, then…" He reaches into his pocket and pulls out a white bracelet. "This should help keep you safe, but you have to not lose it this time."

Motioning for my hand, I watch as he snaps the bracelet onto my wrist and then hits a side switch that makes the bracelet change colors. Red, green, and yellow.

"What do the colors mean?"

Michael smiles. "Each color represents a limit preference. Tonight in the upstairs rooms, there will be many scenes going on. I know you got yourself acquainted with the vibe happening up there the last time you were here."

Air catches in my throat. "I, um…"

"I'm not here to reprimand you, little one. I am just stating the obvious."

"I'm sorry," I whisper.

Michael nods but doesn't look upset, and that is comforting to me for some unknown reason. "As you watch what unfolds, you can hit your color to represent your comfort level—or *limit*—for that particular type of play."

"Okay…"

"So red is a strong no. Choosing red means you only want to watch. Green means that you would like to be invited to participate. You can end the scene at any moment, but green basically gives those around you access to openly explore more with you. And yellow is for uncertainty and means you are intrigued by what you see, but whoever is in charge of the scene should still proceed with caution. Your limit would be more of a testing the waters approach."

I nod as I absorb all of this new information. I'm familiar with the upstairs scene rooms. That's where I caught Daphne and Collins doing their thing. The mere thought of them causes my temper to rise inside thinking about the two of them together. I mean, Daphne had a thing going with a bunch of other men—Michael included—so who knows if she actually likes Collins or just likes what he can give to her.

"If you need assistance at any time tonight, there's a hidden button on the inside of the bracelet that you can push and either myself or Master Yuri will find you. Lockers are available for your personal items. Remember, no phones or recording devices—no exceptions. Open bar is available but don't overdo it. Do you understand?"

"Yes. Thank you."

We part ways, and I walk through the huge door. The lobby is dimly lit just as I remember from last time. I find the locker area and place my belongings inside, securing the lock into place. I make a mental reminder to myself not to forget them when the night is over.

Taking three deep breaths, I try to calm my nerves. If I just want to be an observer tonight, I need to keep my light at red. No one will bother me. I can still have a good time and not feel any pressure. If I want to push my limits, I can choose to do that at my own will—on my own time.

I got this.

What could go wrong?

Ugh, probably a ton of things I just don't want to analyze right now. I'm here, so I might as well enjoy myself.

Despite feeling the pangs of inadequacy, I want to explore and overcome my fears. I owe it to myself to try for that personal growth. If this past year taught me anything, it's that life is too short to wait for the perfect time.

My feet transport me to the main floor where there's dancing, the huge bar, and people mingling in a variety of outfits. My leather shorts and fiery-red silk halter top seem conservative in comparison, but I don't feel comfortable taking everything off to reveal the panty set underneath just yet.

My heartbeat thumps to the rhythm of the music, as I watch dancers grind and gyrate against one another. It's a sultry wave that beckons me to ride, knowing that if I'm not careful I could drown.

I've always loved to dance. But do I just jump into the crowd? I missed some of the parties and clubbing adventures in my limited college days, so I don't know what's good etiquette or not. The last thing I want to do is feel like an intruder.

If Luke was here, he'd tell me that dancing is ninety percent confidence and ten percent skill—and just to go for it.

So I go for it.

Making my way to the center of the dance floor, I feel the touch of a hand on my elbow, causing me to turn around and look into Daphne's eyes.

"You returned," she says sweetly.

I shrug. "Yeah. Figured I'd try this place out again." I play with my fingernails, worried that I'm being awkward. The last time I saw her, Daphne was getting her ass beaten by Collins. Maybe tonight I can resist rescuing anyone who doesn't need saving.

"It's my favorite night." Her body seems to be humming with excitement, and her energy is helping my own.

"Oh yeah?"

"I'm all about pushing the boundaries, and this night is dedicated to just that."

I twist my fingers together. I don't really know what to say.

"Look," she starts. "I didn't know you had a thing going on with Collins."

"A thing? No. We don't have anything going on." I mean, I can't very well say that he's my bodyguard that my two overprotective brothers hired—can I?

She looks at me with confusion. "Oh. Well, umm, you sure?"

"Yeah. I'm sure. You're free to explore him or whatever it is you do here together."

No sooner are the words falling from my lips, than I am wanting to shove them back inside. I don't mean it. I'm just bitter with them both.

I am jealous that Daphne is living her best life doing whatever the hell she wants, and I'm jealous that Collins isn't walking through life feeling as defeated as I am right now.

Maybe carrying my heart on my sleeve just to be plucked away and stomped on isn't an enviable quality to have. If I can't protect my own heart, then I can't expect anyone else to want to.

"I was given strict instruction to stay away from Collins from Master Yuri. Our limited contract was terminated, no discussion, no questions allowed to be asked. So even if I wanted to, it's now considered forbidden and very distasteful. I just have to accept that."

I feel my jaw release muscle control as my mouth drops. "Contract?"

Daphne's hands slide up to her mouth. "Oops. Forget I just said that. I think I must be confused or high or hungry… Or just plain stupid. Fuck." She draws out the swear word and starts to walk away.

I gently grab her elbow. "Stop. Please. What contract?"

Daphne turns to look at me, and from the way her skin pales to an alabaster shade of white, I know she is regretting her slip of the tongue. But now I know there's some sort of contract, and there's no way to undo this tidbit of information.

"The membership contract."

"Bullshit," I hiss. "Stop lying to me. I can tell all over your face that you are hiding the truth."

"Just ask Collins. You obviously know each other. But please don't mention me. He'll be furious that I told you. It's nothing special between us. I don't even know if he remembers my name. And if word got out what I just revealed, I may get kicked out of here for breaching the confidentiality agreement. But that's what I do; I get my mouth into trouble. Ask Master Michael, and he will verify that the only time it shuts up is when I'm swallowing a cock."

I try to mentally sieve through all of Daphne's monologue words. "Okay, fine, I won't mention you. I would never intentionally get you in trouble."

"Thanks, Penny."

Daphne spots Michael and makes her way toward him,

as I scope out the overall vibe of the club and reacquaint myself with the layout. Despite being here once before, the theme for the night is giving this place a dangerous, electric feel.

Members are dancing closer. The music is darker, more suggestive. Even the bar's decor is more gothic and symbolic of a dungeon.

The downside of having my hair secured up high on top of my head in a curly blonde waterfall is that I cannot use it as a shield to hide behind. I have a wide lens on my surroundings, and knowing that I don't have anyone to use as a social crutch is a bit terrifying to me now that Daphne is occupied.

I mean, I can't be the only one who decided to come alone. Yet, everyone seems to know one another. Making my way to the bar, I decide to splurge and get a drink. Maybe it will calm my nerves wreaking havoc in my stomach.

It didn't exactly help last time I was here. But lightning doesn't strike twice in the same place—right? Surely tonight will go smoother.

"What'll it be, miss?" the bartender asks, eyeing me up. He seems more than just a bartender, and I assume he partakes in a scene while off duty. There's an aura about him that I can't put my finger on, yet the darkness of his eyes alludes to having a dominant side.

Or I could be completely wrong.

That's the thing about this time around… Everyone I look at, I silently wonder what kink they are hiding. I also wonder if I'm the most vanilla person here.

Vanilla is the number one ice cream flavor for a reason. It's delicious.

"Miss?"

"Oh, sorry. Um, I think I want…" My eyes scan the bottles of alcohol.

"Want me to surprise you?"

I look at him with hesitation. "How will you know if I'll like it?"

The corners of his lips move up into a big smile. "Trust me."

"Okay…"

He studies me for a moment and then pivots to start pulling down bottles of liquor from the various shelves. He adds several into the mixing container and shakes. Then he pours the contents into a clean glass over ice.

"Try this."

With hesitation, I take a small sip and feel my lips pucker in the best kind of way from the sweet and sour mixture. "Wow, this is really good. What's it called?"

"Burst of Sunshine."

I smile and take a few more drinks. "Thank you. I hope you can replicate it when I want another one."

His smile is genuine. "Just know your limits and adhere to them." He tips his head forward. "The pleasure was mine."

I feel a presence at my side. Turning, I look into the grayish-blue eyes of a walking sex god. He is dressed in just a pair of black jeans, although his chest and arms are covered in an abundance of tattoos. From the way he carries himself to the confidence he has in his knowing grin, the man oozes sexual energy. I feel it radiating off him in copious amounts.

He looks like the kind of trouble that most women would lose their clothes for…

"What's your name, little one?"

Oh great, he sees me as prey.

"Penny."

He reaches out a hand, and without thinking, I join his with mine. I watch in awe as he kisses the tops of my fingers, one by one—never removing his eyes from mine.

Dayyyyum. Maybe being prey has its sexual perks.

"My name is Wesley. What brings you here tonight?"

I take a sip of my cocktail, feeling the buzz starting to form in my head and in my limbs. Or perhaps that is just attraction. "I came tonight to step out of my comfort zone. I was here once before and didn't accomplish what I set out to do."

Wesley orders a drink from the bartender as he thinks about my answer. "What are you looking to accomplish tonight in terms of limits?"

I shrug, while playing with the cocktail napkin collecting the moisture under my glass. "I'm actually not sure. I know there are scenes in the upstairs rooms, but my feet are too scared to venture up there without some liquid courage."

He laughs lightly. "There's nothing to be afraid of here. This place should be a safe haven for anyone who wants to have their fantasies played out." His hand touches the back of my chair, while his thumb grazes against the exposed section of my shoulder blades. "Your bracelet allows you to control the flow. If you want to watch only, that is your choice. If you want to experiment, then that is fine too."

"It sounds simple enough in theory," I say with a laugh, trying to keep the mood light. If I get too much inside my head, I'll just make a beeline for the exit and then regret what could have been.

Wesley studies me for a moment, his hand rubbing along the side of his cheek. I wonder if he's going to fill the pause in our conversation with small talk, when he clears his throat and lifts his chin in confidence. "Would you like to dance?"

I look out at the area where bodies are mingling. I was out on the dance floor already tonight, but I never actually did any dancing before running into Daphne.

"I, um…"

Before I can change my mind, I find my head nodding. My hand joins Wesley's offered one, allowing him to pull me off the stool and guide me to the center of the room. Facing each other, we sway to the upbeat music.

I missed the stage of my life—often experienced during college—where clubbing is the norm. I'm out of practice and not even sure I'm doing it right. Would I even know if I was?

I always feel weird, no matter how many times Luke has assured me that dancing is awkward for everyone.

So I just go through the motions and try not to overthink everything.

Wesley's fingertips play with the hem of my halter top, tickling the skin underneath the fabric, as he draws me closer. I wish I felt more for him than he seems to for me, because he is nice and attentive. Yet, there isn't anything sparking between us.

Sure, he's attractive. But I need more than that.

I need comfort.

I need safety.

And I need someone who makes my toes curl just from the thought of him touching me.

And unfortunately, that isn't Wesley.

He leans in closer to me, his mouth taking the lead. His lips part, and I can smell the alcohol on his breath, he is that close. My spine stiffens, and I tilt my head to the side to feign oblivion.

But then I feel it. His fingertips, pulling my chin up. And—

Oh shit.

His lips. They are on me.

I struggle and hear him moan. It is a deep, guttural sound. My mouth stays rigid, and my heart feels like it will beat right out of my chest as I panic.

Thoughts of Mark Tanner touching me flitter through my system.

His sinister smile is so vivid. The way his voice turns evil is so clear.

It's those talons of memory that stalk my hope for happiness and claw at my inability to fully move on. I'm trapped in a maze of mirrors, unable to get out unscathed, as haunting images race through my brain like a nightmare on loop.

My mind shutters as hands roam over me.

It's as if I'm witnessing a scene play out where I'm the main star, and yet I'm simply a bystander.

Was that all I ever was to Mark Tanner—collateral damage? I was just a naive girl who fell for the guy who promised to make her modeling dreams come true.

Shoving my fragmented memories into the shadowy vault in my brain, I squeeze my eyes tightly shut for a few seconds and think of a way out of this unwanted petting session. Placing my hands on Wesley's chest, I try to push him away, but he takes it as playful reluctance and just teases my waist with his fingertips. Moaning.

Why is he enjoying this so much?

I push—*hard*—and do not stop the pressure until I am released. Out of breath, I pant, flopping forward a bit and placing my hands on my knees. "I…am…not interested…" My words come out raspy.

He grabs my arm, yanking me to him. "It's not nice to tease."

Using the techniques taught to me, I get my arm free. Righting myself, I glare at the menacing eyes of Wesley. How did he just flip the switch like that? Jerk. "I…"

Then I feel a looming force behind us before actually finding proof of his existence, as his aura fills the room like a protective fog.

Collins.

My eyes scan the crowd, ignoring Mr. Handsy, and search for the one man who seems to have a choke hold on my lungs—and my heart.

Then I find him standing with venom in his eyes directed right at the man who stole more than just a kiss. He stole another opportunity for me to be near a man and it not end in re-traumatization.

Last visit, Neil triggered me. On the street outside of Ground Floor, it was the guy from the speed dating.

When will this stop?

When will I be able to be with someone and it not be a horror scene inside my head?

And then I remember how the man who is here to rescue me made me feel.

Collins is safety.

Collins is comfort.

Collins has my toes curling as I predict his next move.

It takes him three long steps to close the distance between us to be face-to-face in front of Wesley, who basically looks like he's seen a ghost.

38

PENNY

"Touch her again if you want to deal with the fallout," Collins threatens, his tone pure venom.

I quiver back and feel my shoulders curling forward as I take in the scene. Adrenaline races through me, as I struggle to try to deescalate the testosterone showdown happening before my eyes.

Again.

It's like I'm living some Groundhog Day alternate reality—where Collins fights men but doesn't fight for *me*.

Wesley looks like he might pee his pants.

"Sir, I didn't know she was—"

"She's mine," Collins says with unwavering certainty.

He almost sounds like my boyfriend and not just my bodyguard, and that is playing tricks with my head and my heart.

Wesley turns back to look at me with horror. "I'm sorry. I didn't know you were Mr. Stone's…" His words trail off, with an unspoken expectation for me to complete the blank.

Mr. Stone's what?

My eyebrows move inward at his sudden turn in personality.

"Okay," I whisper.

Turning back to Collins, he looks like he might throw up on his shoes. "I have a wife and baby at home. Please don't hurt me."

"Then go the fuck home to them and stop prowling for young girls here."

He's married? Ew, gross! Then why is he here?

Wesley glances at me and quickly diverts his attention. "I'm sorry about Penny. I'm really sorry. I'll never approach her again."

Does Wesley think I'm Mr. Stone's property? It feels that way in this moment, and yet knowing what Daphne slipped telling me earlier, I know that it isn't even remotely close to being the truth.

I am Collins Stone's nothing. At least not anything of importance.

I'm not his girlfriend.

I'm not his side chick.

I am just a girl he happens to guard without my permission.

If I didn't love my brothers as much as I do, I would have put a stop to this a long time ago. However, I understand that they are still healing from what happened to me when Mark Tanner drugged and almost raped me. My entire family is still healing from that trauma.

And no matter how many sessions I've had of private and group therapy, I'm still trying to heal as well.

Without another glance, Wesley exits the dance floor,

leaving me with an angry Collins. Actually, angry seems too mild to be the accurate description.

Livid?

Furious?

Murderous?

Damn. How do I keep finding myself in horrible positions yet again?

And if looks could kill…

“All the trouble of scaring off a man just so you can dance with me?” I say sarcastically, trying to lighten the mood. Clearly, he doesn’t have a joking bone in his body right now. “Was that even necessary? I mean, really, Collins. It’s not like you are”—I gesture to his immobile body—“trying to act normal.”

“I don’t dance.”

“Of course you don’t.”

“I thought you could behave and not try to sneak away from my watch.”

“We’ve been through this. I don’t need a bodyguard.”

“Clearly you do.”

“Why are you here?”

His eyes darken. “I belong here. You don’t.”

“Yuri disagrees.”

“Yuri has a kink for hurt fawns.”

I scrunch up my nose and make a face. “I’m not a hurt fawn.”

“You are as close to a female Bambi as they come, Princess.”

I’m sure I am scoffing. How can he be so annoying? “Great. Now everyone sees me as damaged goods.”

He takes a step closer.

I'm not scared, but I sure am intimidated. Why does he have this effect on me?

"There is nothing damaged about you, Penny. Except for your faulty view of safety. You aren't safe here, and I want you to leave."

I prop my hands on my hips. "The website states otherwise." Well, it was rather vague and a bit cryptic.

"Let me take you home."

I keep my stance. "No."

"Penny…"

The man is so tightly wound up that he could make a friendly game of hopscotch turn violent, and in turn he's making me want to hit him.

"I *need* this place."

"You need to be home."

"You don't know what I need! You just don't get it!"

"Explain it to me then, and maybe you'll one day realize that we're more alike than you think."

"Doubtful."

"Try."

"I'm broken, Collins. There's no amount of therapy that can fix the damage that was caused the day Mark drugged me. So, please, just go. Step aside and allow me to repair whatever is salvageable on my own."

"Here, Penny? You think you will find some sort of healing here—in a kink club with a bunch of strangers?"

"At least I can test the waters and won't have the hovering guilt of disappointing someone by not being enough. Here, I can be anyone I want to be without the fear of commitment."

"Not here, Penny. Find somewhere else to work through these gnawing fears."

"Don't you realize that the darkness whispers to me no matter what light the day brings? It finds me. No matter where I am. No matter what I'm doing. It finds me! I can't look at a man without thinking—if just for a second—how he can hurt me. And you know what the sick thing is? I actually want that pain. At least with the pain, I can feel fucking alive and not this numb, hollowed-out shell. So I keep finding myself here or in other compromising places, hoping to welcome that exhilaration and not hide from it."

"Getting together with random men who *can* actually hurt you—physically or mentally—and playing chicken with your memories to see if you have flashbacks is not how you should be spending your evenings, Penny. You are playing a game with psychological flooding, and it's a game you'll continue to lose."

How does he know I was doing that? How does this man seem to keep figuring me out before I can even articulate what I'm doing in the first place?

But that's what I'm doing…

I'm playing chicken.

I'm testing myself to see if I can be with a man and it not trigger me into an out-of-control spiral.

"I'm lonely." My words come out as a whimper. And when the man who I once found comforting offers nothing back to me, I start moving toward the bar.

Collins is hot on my tail. "What are you doing?"

"I need a drink."

"Penny, you shouldn't drink at a place like this."

"What?" I point to the bartender. "Why is there a huge bar then?"

"Decoration. It adds to the ambiance."

"That's silly. Pretty sure I see a ton of people drinking. And I know for a fact I consumed some prior to hitting the dance floor."

I mean, I probably shouldn't drink, considering I once got drunk on champagne vinaigrette that I used on a salad. But I'm too committed in proving my point to admit he is right.

"Drinking on limits night is asking for trouble. You shouldn't be here."

Ignoring him, I confidently round my shoulders as I eye up the bartender that served me just minutes ago. "Can you please make me one of the sunshine drinks again?"

His eyes move to Collins who is hovering behind me like Eeyore.

"Sorry," he says with a frown. "I'm not able to do that."

"What?" I ask stupidly, and then whip around to glare at the man who probably put a stop to the flow of fun. "Really? You are really doing this? The sober mountain is the one you are going to die on right now?"

"You shouldn't be here. Let me take you home."

I dig my heels into the floor, shaking my head. "No. I'm staying—if just out of principle and spite."

I walk toward the restrooms, knowing Collins is right behind me. We enter into the hallway, away from the crowd of people.

"I'm sorry you are upset with me."

I look into his eyes, willing myself not to get lost in

them. “Let me get this straight. You don’t dance. You don’t drink. Well, not often at least.”

“That’s correct.”

“Are you a Mormon?”

“No, Princess.”

My eye twitches at his usage of my apparent nickname. The way the tone of his voice massages every syllable of the name causes my equilibrium to falter. He’s the only one I’ve been allowing to call me that, and right now I want to revoke his special privilege.

That’s what this man does to me. He shakes me and makes me question if I’m woman enough for him—even in my depraved fantasies. He causes me to wonder how things could be if he wasn’t the hired henchman of my two older brothers.

Would we ever stand a chance together?

Because the only way to fix this frustration between us is to fuck it out of one another.

“Are you sure? I mean, that would explain your dedication to rules and how you”—I bite my bottom lip and sway to the thumping sound of the bass—“can resist sexual temptation. Or maybe I’m just not sexy enough. Is that it?” I play with the hem of my halter top, lifting the fabric to reveal my navel. I feel the buzz from my previous drink running through my veins, giving me the courage to attempt to be flirty—although I’m not sure it’s even working.

Collins is too disciplined to be seduced, or maybe he just lacks the sex drive to cave to temptation.

"You are, without an ounce of doubt, the biggest mistake I’m ever going to make.”

“*Mistake*,” I repeat. “Well, you haven’t made it yet.”

"But I will."

I sigh. "You act like it's inevitable."

"I'm starting to think it is. That no matter how much I resist, I will forever be drawn back to you. You are like a rubber band. The harder I pull away, the more forceful the attraction toward you is."

"Now that sounds like fun." I click my tongue, trying to lighten the mood.

"It won't be fun if your brothers ever find out the"—his hands move to the back of his neck—"carnal thoughts running through my head of you."

"Quit treating me like a stain on your perfect record. And for heaven's sake, please stop thinking about my brothers. This is my life to live and not their life to control."

His eyes smolder, hooding over as he takes them on a lazy stroll down my body. "I would ruin you."

"Wouldn't that be best done by you and not someone else who wouldn't necessarily have my best interests in mind?"

"It's not that simple, Pen."

"But it is." Tilting my chin up, I whisper, "If you want me, come and get me. Unless, of course, it goes against the rules."

His eyes twitch and before I can take my next breath, his lips are on mine.

We've kissed before in the alleyway, but this time is different. It's like he is sucking the oxygen out of my lungs and making it hard to breathe.

He is my life source, and I want to drown in that gray area between right and wrong.

Because the only thing I know for certain is that I want Collins Stone—and I want him now.

Collins's hands entwine into my hair, as he presses my back up against a wall. I gasp for air and get a reprieve only because his attention gets shifted to my neck. I moan and grind into him, wanting to get as close as I can without completely suffocating myself from the pressure of my face in his hair. I inhale his clean, masculine scent, breathing him in, wanting to commit every detail to memory.

This man commands my body to be his puppet, and I'm too weak and impassioned to give a damn.

I want him, and I finally believe him when he claims he wants me too.

"Are you still doubting my feelings toward you?" he asks, breathlessly.

My hand moves up to my lips, feeling their newfound plumpness. "Hmm, no. I think you made yourself clear," I say with a hum. "It just took you an eternity to get here."

"You're a light in this dungeon of darkness. You shouldn't be here." His finger toys with a strand of my hair. "This club isn't for girls like you."

"Then turn me into the girl that would belong at an establishment like this. I have needs that I need to fulfill or I'll implode. What better place to try some things out than here, where activities are monitored and fantasies can be explored?"

His eyes darken to nearly black. "You aren't trying out anything with anyone," he growls.

"Then you better be the hero of this story and intervene on my sexual desire's behalf."

He shakes his head. "How can I be the hero when I've been given the hand of the villain?"

"Quit trying to complicate everything. You either want me or you don't." I thought we already established this…

"I want you," he says without hesitation.

"Then start taking care of my needs before I start seeking out other takers. And trust me, Collins, I have wasted enough of my time working through my problems in the therapy facility to squander any more time trying to get the attention of someone that is emotionally incapable of giving me what my body desires."

"Penny…"

I look around the room as couples gather at the bar. A group watches a scene playing out in one corner. People dance on the wooden platformed floor, enjoying the thump thump of the bass, while the elevated cages are full with patrons engaging in group activities.

Something tells me I won't have a problem finding a for-now taker. However, I came here tonight to continue to break down the barriers keeping me from fully embracing the idea of being with a man.

When I turn to look into Collins's eyes, he awakens something deep inside me.

"You are the sister of my bosses," he reminds me—as if I could forget. Graham and Nic would probably slice him up into pieces if he were to hurt me.

But what if I want to be hurt by him? What if I want the risk of getting my heart smashed—or my ass? It isn't like I'm making this decision lightly. I've given it a lot of thought.

An agonizing amount of thought…

But Collins is my safety net, and the best person to guide me into the darkness of my mind to explore my most vivid fantasies.

I trust him to see to my best interests.

I trust him to take care of my needs.

I want to feel the burn from Collins digging his fingers into my flesh.

I want to feel the sting of him playfully smacking my ass…and maybe a bit not-so-playfully.

"And you are my bodyguard," I say, almost absentmindedly. "We would both be crossing the arbitrary boundary that only one of us is willing to cross."

The hand against the wall works its way into my hair, pulling my head closer to him. His other hand caresses my lower back, eliciting a moan from deep in my throat.

"Everything about this is wrong."

"Too bad my body doesn't care."

His thumb moves to my lips, pulling the bottom one down. He rubs his pad against the sensitive skin, lazily trailing it along. "But I care about you, Penny. I don't want to be the reason for any more tension in your life."

I take a step closer, and his body turns tense against mine, not because he doesn't want me. No. Every firm inch of him pressing against my core lets me in on his little secret. Collins most definitely has a thing for his bosses' little sister. And the thrill of knowing how much I affect him is giving me a newfound pleasure from blurring the line that we both know we shouldn't cross. We are pulled together by an invisible string—neither of us strong enough to resist its force.

"You make me want to be a bad girl."

Taking my hands, Collins secures them above my head. His eyes are dark with hesitation, yet his free hand roaming my body is full of promise and certainty.

He wants me. I just hope it's as much as I want him.

I stand on my tippy toes to try to get to his lips.

"Tsk, tsk," he teases. "One thing you'll learn is that I thrive on being in control. I call the shots—not you, Princess."

Swooping down, Collins captures my lips, biting and sucking the air out of my lungs.

It is intense.

It is forbidden.

My body molds itself to his touch, silently praying that he doesn't stop like he has in the past.

I pull against his restraints, trying to tug my hands free so I can touch him. Collins's mouth moves to my neck as he gnaws on my sensitive flesh at the base of it.

With each passing second, he's exploring me and helping me to discover my own body's favorite spots.

"Fuck," I hiss, feeling my bones melt into a gelatin.

Whatever he's doing to me, I like it.

"You can't keep putting temptation in front of me and then expect me not to sample a taste. I've wanted to show your body from the moment you walked into this place just who owns it."

"Ahhh…you followed me?" I gasp.

"You knew I would. No matter where I am, I keep tabs on you. I'm obsessed with your safety, Princess."

Princess.

Coming from anyone else's mouth, I would cringe. But

Collins makes me feel special—adored—with that simple two-syllable word.

"I thought you were taking a personal day."

Collins smiles against my cheek. "Seems like I'm utilizing my personal day in the best way possible."

"Good."

"But you aren't safe here, no matter what the website or club description says."

"Well, then aren't you glad you made your grand arrival…"

Collins's eyes level with mine, searching for what, I'm not sure. "You aren't safe with me either, Penny. I'm—"

"Dangerous," I finish, interrupting his bullshit speech.

"I am though. And I'd be very irresponsible to not—"

"Warn me."

His hand goes to my chin, giving it a possessive squeeze. "Yes, dammit. As much as I'm a giver"—his thumb finds my bottom lip and pulls it down—"I'm also a taker. And the last thing I need is to take something that doesn't belong to me."

"Maybe the danger helps me to feel alive."

Releasing my wrists, he grabs my ass, lifting me up and pressing me harder against the flat surface of the wall. His eyes keep searching mine for any reservation.

"There's nothing more that I want right now than to dirty you up."

My ankles dig into his lower back. "No one's stopping you."

And just like that, the glimmer of hope is shadowed by the doubt. Releasing me, Collins runs his hands through his hair. "Fuck. You can't keep making me lose control like this. This is wrong, Penny."

Trying to find steadiness on the ground, I growl in frustration. "We want each other, Collins. That much is obvious."

"But we can't act on that want, Pen. It's not fair to either of us."

"Then why not let me into one of the contracts like you have with some of the women here. What is it, a sex contract?"

His eyes turn livid as his jaw tics. "You want to be my whore? Is that what you're saying? You are considering going against your brothers to enter into a forbidden contract with me? You don't comprehend what you're asking of me."

"If it means eliminating this feeling of whiplash every time we start to get close, then sign me up, please. Because I'm about to get the equivalent of a man getting blue balls."

"Fuck, Penny, you have to have more self-esteem than this."

"Every time you reject me, I lose more than I gain. I'm not sure how much of this I can take."

"How the hell did you find out about the contracts?"

I shrug, fixing my shirt. "I have my ways. Why not have that type of arrangement with me? I mean, at one point, we were meeting in the Japanese Gardens to discuss something similar."

"This is a completely different proposition."

"Yeah, it is. And it's one I think I'll actually approve of."

He runs both hands down the back of his neck. "You don't know what you're saying."

"Just listen. I will behave and be your loyal damsel in distress who needs your bodyguard protection. I'll follow the rules and let you boss me around. And in return, you service me."

"Service you?"

"You know," I say with a nod of my chin. "Sex." I lean in closer, trying my best not to cause myself to fall. "Like really good sex. I want you to teach me what I should have learned by now. I want to do that with you and not someone else."

"Damn."

"We both want each other. This would be temporary. We would agree on the terms of the contract, and I promise that I will submit to whatever you want in regard to guarding me. I won't run away. I will let you do your thing without any more fuss. Hell, you can even put a leash on me and an ankle tracker—whatever helps you sleep at night. I may draw the line though if you want me to sleep in a cage under your bed. Hmmm…if it wasn't for the fear of not being able to roll over, I might actually be on board even with that. Anyway, we can work out the kinks later. Ha! I meant to say *details*."

"Fuck, Penny."

"Oh, I sure as hell want fucking to be at the top of the to-do list."

"Everything about your proposition is going to solidify my villain status."

"Not if I sign the dotted line willingly. I will consent to it all. Isn't that what you've wanted all along—to protect me from whatever imaginary evil you think there is?"

"Penny…"

"You win, Collins. And I know how much you love to win. Listen, I'm simply asking for a sexual relationship in return. No feelings. Just sex. Straight up, fuck me in my vagina sex."

"I'd be fucking you a lot more places," he bites out.

"Okay, that too. We can put it in the contract."

"There is no contract, Penny!" he snaps.

"But there can be."

I can tell he is mulling the idea around in his head. In a way, I'm relieved he hasn't completely shot down my idea. Plus, this is one of my better ones. "I'm at the point where if I don't satisfy my urges, I'll end up with some jerk again who doesn't know my belly button from my clit and will need some lengthy road map drawn to locate it. I don't need some egomaniac to jackhammer my pussy with his fingers thinking he's king of the harem."

Collins shakes his head at me, but I can't tell if he is frustrated or amused. "You have no clue my sexual preferences."

"Enlighten me."

"I can be demanding…"

"So?"

"I like it rough."

"How do you know I don't?"

"And I like being in control."

"I can handle it."

"Can you?" Collins challenges.

I pivot and start to walk away. "You'll see."

"Where are you going?"

"Upstairs to test my limits."

Collins catches up with me. "Fucking hell, Penny. What has gotten into you tonight?"

"Not sure, but I can say with one hundred percent certainty that it isn't a dick."

"Seriously. You are scaring me."

"I'm deprived, Collins!" My hands fly out in exasperation. "I've spent the better half of a year trying to dig myself out of an emotional abyss, just to finally think I was connecting with someone who worked there, and then to have my brothers—it had to be them—scare him off."

"He was an asshole."

I glare at him. "So you scared him off."

"He wasn't good enough for you."

I let out an exaggerated exhale. "Then I went to a speed dating event and no one chose me. No one. You know how humiliating that is? Then, I went from that hellish revelation, just to go outside and make out with you and then have you reject me. And I know you want me. I can feel it"—I motion with my hand back and forth between us—"so denying it no longer works. So either do something about it or watch me walk right upstairs and see if anyone has the balls enough to play with me. Because I came to *play*. I'm done treating life like a spectator sport. And I most certainly don't need your permission—or anyone else's for that matter. If you don't like it, call for backup. You and whoever his name is can watch me live my best life. Just save me some popcorn. I'm a slut for popcorn."

When Collins says nothing, I keep walking. I move through the crowd, past the bartender who will no longer serve me, and sidestep Daphne who appears to have her mouth stuffed with some guy's cock.

Yeah, I'm still a little bit bitter she and Collins had a thing. It might have only been a contractual thing, but it was definitely still more commitment than I ever got from him.

When I get to the stairs, I propel myself up them, despite feeling my feet hurting from all of the walking.

Why did I choose these heels? They hurt so badly.

I feel Collins's presence behind me, without even having to look. Everywhere I go, he isn't but a few steps away. Yet, there's a distance between us that I doubt will ever lessen.

Push and pull. That's what we do.

"She told you, didn't she?" he asks.

When I get to the last step, I turn and glare. "Who?"

He motions to Daphne down below. "She told you about the contracts?"

I look away, not wanting to get Daphne in trouble. She was convinced if Collins were to find out that she would get kicked out of Limit-X. "I found out on my own, and I'm curious how many women you have arrangements with while here, since you claim not to use your Sky View apartment as a fuckpad. Or was that all just one big, orchestrated lie? And I know people will lie for you. You probably scare the shit out of them."

"I never lied to you, Penny."

"Withholding the truth is basically the same thing!" I snap. "All you men are the same."

"Quit deflecting."

"I would have found out on my own. I'm not some stupid, young girl. Eventually I would have been brought out of the dark, so don't start thinking about retaliating against the person who just sped up the process."

"This place isn't for you, Penny."

Defiantly, I tilt up my chin, as he takes a step closer. "Then who is it for, Collins?"

"People who have a thirst for the dark."

"And how do you know what I crave when I don't even know my own limits?"

"Go home, Miss Hoffman."

"Go to hell, Mr. Stone."

39

COLLINS

If I'm going to lose my mind, it will be tonight. From the moment I realized Penny was heading toward Limit-X—unaccompanied and without protection—I have wanted to yank her out of here as fast as I can.

Trust me, if she was mine, her ass would be raw by now, and a reminder not to cross me would be branded into her permanent memory bank.

Since finding her in the presence of other men enjoying her tight, little body, I've been twitching with an electricity to fight, as jealousy slithers around me, taking root and growing with an undeniable force.

Her innocence plagues me, haunting me through the darkness of my desires.

Just seeing her grinding bodies on the dance floor caused a stir inside me to protect her from Wesley. I'm sure he meant no real harm—except for the fact he's married and has kids—but just watching him paw her ample curves was enough to make me see red.

And now I can't see any other color other than it.

I'm starting to think that Penny secretly hoped I would show up. I think she likes it when I go a bit crazy.

From the way she is dressed in tight leather shorts to how her fiery-red halter top accentuates her breasts, I'd think that she wore this number solely for my viewing pleasure.

And my eyes are pleased.

Fuck, she's beautiful.

But it's more than just me watching her. Nearly everyone we pass gets a second or third glance at her over their shoulder—regardless of sexual orientation and regardless of who they actually walked in with. Penny has that appeal. She isn't like the others.

I would know, because I've been with quite a few *others*.

Sadly, they're all the same—eager to please and easy to pleasure. It sounds good in theory, of course, but in reality I got bored.

I am—*was*—bored.

While I never thought of Penny in a sexual nature while she was healing in therapy, I most definitely can't prevent my mind from drifting to the darkness now.

She makes it impossible to not see.

Now she's taunting me into arranging a forbidden sex contract between us, and I'm seriously considering it—only because I don't think I can keep resisting her. Getting things in writing might help me maintain some level of professionalism, while she thrusts her sexual prowess at me every chance she gets.

Every time I witness her legs moving, I want to grab her luscious ass cheeks and sink my teeth into them.

I want Penny to wear my mark.

I want to dirty her up and make her so needy for me that only my touch will soothe the burn.

But can she handle a man as demanding as I am? I'm not an easy person to be with, and any of my previous partners will share that I'm controlling as fuck. It's not something I pretend to hide or soften with flowery language or society's kinky labels.

I need to be with someone who knows the score. I like what I like. And I'm not afraid to vocalize it. This is why there are contracts in place. So both parties consent to the activities willingly and without the risk of coercion.

But this is Penelope Hoffman.

And she doesn't deserve to be treated in the same clinical way as I have any partnership over the last few years.

Yet I know if Penny doesn't get her fill of the experience tonight, she will just insist on coming back here again and again. She is determined and stubborn—two qualities that I admire but also struggle to accept.

Limit-X is not designed for a girl as straightlaced as Penny Hoffman. She is soft and feminine and needs to be cherished—not thrown against a wall and felt up in public.

But that's what's happening to us, and the guilt of not giving her more than what equates to an alleyway grind session is messing with my focus.

Our desires can't possibly align because she hasn't lived long enough to discover her preferences—and I doubt I could be the man to walk her through the journey.

I'm not the hand-holding type.

But can I stomach the idea of someone else doing the job?

No. Definitely not.

There's no part of me that wants Penny to explore her sexual awakening with anyone else—that much is clear. While I don't know details about her past, I can tell she doesn't have very many amazing experiences to pull from and is probably searching for someone to fill that void.

I hate myself for how easy she makes me lose touch with reality. She is a temptress, trying to get me to give in to this notion that she thinks she wants.

Penny doesn't know what she wants.

She wants to test the waters and explore, and I'm not sure I can give her those experiences without taking more from her than she is prepared to give. Another perk of having sexual contracts with my partners is that there are no misunderstandings and that when the contract ends, so do the expectations for more.

I don't do *more.*

I do what is mutually agreed upon and nothing extra. There is no bonding and definitely nothing romantic about the arrangement. There are no dates and no dinners. No one texts except to confirm meetups here. All signatures on the contract consent to a sexual union only.

Having the finality of ending relationships is the driving force behind the appeal of us both signing on the dotted line. Not to mention the nondisclosure aspect that keeps my personal life free from my professional life.

On the other hand, if Penny and I were to have that type of arrangement, everything would get murky. How could it not? Penny would then be part of both lives, and the separation once the line is crossed would be impossible to fulfill.

I'm her bodyguard…

And I don't want to die via the wrath of her brothers…

I stare at Penny as her hands reach behind her and start undoing the tie of her halter top.

Shit.

Why is she doing that? It's as if she has no idea what she does to me—and yet is calculated in her moves. Baiting me. Luring me in to her with my weakening self-control.

She is chiseling away at me, and there's no way possible that she doesn't realize her effect on me.

I look up at the viewing booth we happened to stop next to and notice that the sign suggests that the test for pushing boundaries is clothes. No wonder Penny is trying to remove her top. She is testing more limits than just her own. She is testing mine.

Slowly, she is pushing back the boundaries, stretching them to blur the lines between going too far and not going far enough.

If I don't help her with her fantasies, I run the risk of her finding some sleazeball who simply wants an easy thrill. If I do comply, then I basically go against the code I live by—the one I tell myself separates me from the assholes in this world.

But can I give up on the girl who is making a home for herself inside my heart?

"Penny…"

Turning around, she points to the back of her neck where her fingers are struggling. "Can you help me with my knot, please?"

"What? No. Fuck. Penny, you aren't going to take off all your clothes at some club for everyone to see."

Spinning around, she pouts out her bottom lip. "It's dark and no one will even notice me." Her eyes plead with me, as her fingers continue to try to work out the knot.

"Every man in this place has been eye-fucking you long before you walked upstairs."

"Fine, I'll just get someone else to help." She hits her bracelet's button, turning it green.

"The hell you will," I growl, grabbing her wrist and switching the color to red. If she's not careful, I'll remove the entire thing and slam it against the wall to make it stop working entirely.

"You've got quite the temper, Mr. Stone."

"You keep toying with me and you are going to find yourself pressed up against a wall with my cock pumping inside you. That's what you want, right? A quick and dirty fuck in a public place for everyone to see? You want to be degraded, Pen?"

"Maybe."

My fingers grip her chin, careful not to squeeze too tightly, but rather just to hold her attention. "You want to crawl on your knees and have your hair yanked?"

I watch as her throat swallows, and I can't tell if she's turned on or appalled by my non-sugarcoated words. The truth in her eyes is that of expectation, longing, and desire.

Rolling her shoulders, she continues to untangle the knot of her halter top, finally making progress. Her silence is what unnerves me the most. I can't tell what she's thinking or how far she'll go tonight. Sure, the theme of the evening is about pushing the boundaries, and I'm about to lose all of mine with her.

For someone who strives to be logical and consistent, my mind is racing right now with torrid thoughts as Penny's halter top slides up over her curves and neck, revealing a strapless red and black bra.

Penny has never looked hotter.

And I'm going to bash in every guy's face who happens to notice her seductive striptease.

She is mine.

We may not have a contract in place right now, but there is no way I'm allowing anyone else to take her home.

Maybe Penny is right that having an arrangement where we both get what we want—where I can control the situation—will be the best solution to scratch these itches that keep tormenting both of us. Perhaps at the end of the time frame, we go back to being professional—at least until her brothers trust her without a shadow. As long as Graham and Nic don't find out, everything will be as if it never happened.

Why can't we have our cake and eat it too?

Penny's fingers slide to the button of her leather shorts and mine intercept hers to cause them to halt. Turning her around, I press my front to her back. I pull off my shirt, tossing it to the side where there are benches aligned against the outer perimeter of the viewing space. I join Penny's warmth, moving my arms around her to squeeze her tightly to me. My fingers splay against her bare stomach, trying to conceal as much of her as I can with my own body.

Mine.

My mouth kisses at the side of her neck, down her arm, and then back up again.

The crowd around us fades like a moving wave that is getting farther in the distance. In this moment, it's easy to get lost to the buzz of not-so-innocent touches, but I can't help but fully submerse myself in Penny.

My fingers tease her belly button, as our hips sway side to side to the muffled music coming from the downstairs dance area. We move like the breeze, matching each other's energies.

"They are so sexy," she says with an exhale.

My eyes focus in on the people in the showcase room, stripping and dancing around ceiling-to-floor mounted poles. It's erotic to be here with Penny in my arms, viewing the same scene and enjoying it with a new lens.

I've never gotten into scene observing, yet there's something about sharing this with Penny that feels different than the dozens of times I've been here without her.

"You're so sexy, Penny."

She is on the verge of a sexual awakening, and I have the luxury of being a part of her journey. She is the forbidden fruit that I shouldn't want, yet it's everything I crave.

Slowly, I unbutton the top button of her shorts, and then the next one. Leaning her head back, Penny's lips search for mine. I unite with hers, sliding my tongue deep into her mouth, taking whatever she is willing to give—and a bit more.

Now that I already crossed one, I want to push all those boundaries. I want all of her.

Every single inch.

Sliding down the zipper, I work a hand into her skin-tight shorts, moving it lower and lower, until I can palm her lace-covered pussy.

And I do—hard.

"Yes," she says breathily, leaning on me for support.

I rub upward, causing Penny to lift to her tiptoes to mirror the movement. Her body melts into mine, and I feel and smell the arousal trickling out of her and soaking into the fabric.

"Yes, Princess," I coax, while massaging my free hand up over her bare stomach. "You like the feel of my hands on your body?"

Relaxing her stance, Penny moans her approval, and it's those soft sounds of pleasure that are coming from deep in her throat that coax me to continue.

I'm the devil possessing the angel, staking my claim on her and crossing the line that can no longer be seen.

This is wrong, and yet I have no power left in me to stop it.

With the heel of my foot, I push open her legs to widen her stance to give me better access to the hot spot between her thighs.

The hand massaging over her bra takes a detour underneath, enjoying the way her nipples are hardening just from my touch.

"You are fucking perfection."

Penny shifts her weight from foot to foot, wiggling her bottom into my crotch as she squirms from the pressure I'm applying with my hands.

"I want…"

"What do you want, Princess?"

I widen her stance further with another kick to her heel. I know what she wants before her brain can even comprehend it. I can feel her desires trembling through her.

But I want her to say it. I need that verbal consent when this is still so new to both of us. I need that reassurance that I'm not entirely a monster.

"I want your hands"—she wiggles her delectable ass against me again—"inside my panties."

Fuck, yes.

Moving my hand up and out of her shorts, I rest it on her stomach.

She is soft in all the right places, and I want to savor this moment and commit it to memory.

With concentrated slowness, I peel back the waistband of her scrap of panties and slide my hand inside the warmth radiating between her legs—all while pinching her nipples and alternating sides.

"Hmmm..." Penny hums, resting more of her weight onto me.

Her soft tuft of hair gathers stickiness from the liquid leaking out, and a part of me can't wait until I can shave her bare so that every touch I give her will be exaggerated in feeling.

"You are primed and ready."

"Yes..." She allows the ending sound to linger.

I can feel Penny's pulse quicken as we press against one another, every curve of her delectable body fitting perfectly with mine like a puzzle.

My lips move to her ear, as I nibble on her lobe. "I'm going to have so much fun making you mine."

"Hmm... I want to be yours. And you mine."

Flashbacks of memories flitter through my vision, and I push them away. I need to stay in this moment—in present time—and not think back to the last person I thought was *mine*.

Because if my mind fully goes there, I'll remember just how damaged I really am.

Penny rotates her hips in a rolling motion, humping herself on my hand, as her ass cheeks tease my cock that is hardening to a painful level behind her.

I feel like a teenage boy who can come in his pants if she continues these simple but effective movements.

Curling my middle finger, I press it against her opening.

"Do you touch yourself here, Princess?"

"Yes."

"Do you use your fingers or your toys?"

Her breath hitches. "Both sometimes. It depends on my mood."

My finger lingers at her entrance, barely inside her heat. "How many fingers can your little pussy swallow?"

She pauses as she leans back farther into me. I bend my knee to use as a seat for her backside. "Just one."

"Just one?"

"Yes."

"And why no more?"

"Because I'm too tight."

I swirl my finger at her opening, stretching her gently. "Yes, you are tight. And we're going to have to work at getting you to accept more. Okay?"

"Okay. I'll try."

"That's my good girl."

With gentle precision, I slide my finger deeper inside,

groaning over her tightness. Using my other hand, I massage and knead the fleshy globes of her tits, making her feel good.

Penny's leather shorts have shimmied down her thighs, making her lower half immobile.

And I'm not complaining.

I love her like this. Warm and relaxed and pliable.

Moving my finger in and out, I push along her pussy walls, testing their elasticity.

"Your pussy feels like a vise on my finger, Princess. You sure you want my cock to stretch it out? Because once I have a piece of you, I'll demand access to your honeypot all the time."

"I don't want anyone else to take me. Just you."

In an instant I go from being overcome with pleasure to being overwhelmed with jealousy.

"I will bury anyone that dares to try to steal what I have claimed as mine. So, heed my warning over any desire inside you that thinks it's funny to tease me over something I refuse to share."

"What happens if my sexual appetite is stronger than yours?"

I huff out a laugh. "Doubtful."

Shifting against me, Penny kicks her shorts off from around her ankles, discarding them against the wall of the viewing area.

Placing her foot on the bench, she silently urges me to go deeper. "It feels so good, Collins. I want more than just a finger. I want to be stuffed full."

"Fuck," I hiss. She has no freaking clue what she is

doing to me right now, other than annihilating my self-control.

My finger pumps inside her a few more times, before pulling my hand out of her panties, helping her back into her shorts, and buttoning her up.

Facing me, she lets out a pant. "What? Why did you stop? I, um, I—"

I place my still glistening finger against her lips, silencing her. Then I trail my tongue along the length, sucking up all the juices and ending at her lips. I encourage her to do the same with the other side, joining mouths in a kiss so deep I think I might suffocate.

When we finally detach, I suck in oxygen and try to steady my breathing. "Tonight is about testing limits, and I plan to learn all of yours. Come," I say, tugging her hand and leading her to the next viewing area that features several threesome acts in session.

When I turn to move to a new area, Penny halts my movements. "I want to watch."

"Do you now?" I ask, captivated by her unveiled interest.

Perhaps this has always been a fascination of hers, and I'm just learning it now. Something tells me I'll be learning a lot about Penny. I can honestly say I don't know much about her sexual preferences, except that she was intrigued by the spanking scene I was doing with her new friend. I'd be lying if I said I wasn't itching for the opportunity to leave my mark on her ass cheeks, making a stinging reminder for her to know where I've been.

My cock stirs at just the thought, as Penny stretches up to kiss me. I savor her taste on my tongue. She is a sensual goddess who leads with her heart, when she isn't using her sassy personality to mask her fears.

I might put up with her boldness right now, but I won't allow her to dictate things in the bedroom. I'm too much of a demanding bastard to give in to her pouting lips and sad eyes.

I won't allow her to skip meals or mistreat her body. Getting enough rest will be a requirement, and seeing her therapist regularly will be nonnegotiable.

Being with me is not easy—even on temporary terms.

"Care if I join?" a masculine voice asks.

"Sure," Penny says to the male, as I feel my temper rising.

"No," I answer gruffly.

Why the hell is he initiating and engaging with us?

My eyes size him up, wondering why he is even interrupting our private moment. "We are just watching." My words come out as a snap, and it's then that I notice both my bracelet and Penny's are lit with a green glow. I capture her wrist in mine as the guy scurries off to find another couple to join, his face looking a bit confused.

"Bummer," Penny whines but I know it's a facade.

"You're a sneaky little thing, aren't you?"

She has the nerve to feign innocence. While her experiences may be limited, she knows exactly which buttons of mine to push to get me to react. And it's working, because I'm about to turn her over my knee and tan those supple ass cheeks that keep bumping into my cock at every chance they get.

"Just trying to have fun," she simpers, watching me as I change both of our lights to red.

"Your independence and resilience are commendable. But don't deliberately try to defy me, just to test my reaction. You won't like it. And if you think I wouldn't dare make a scene out in public just to prove my point—you are wrong." My eyes level with hers. "Oh, and Penny?"

"Yes, sir?"

"I don't share."

"Then why did you participate with Daphne of all people? She has had a taste of every male here I imagine."

I scratch along the side of my cheek. "Let me rephrase. I won't share you."

"But you will exercise double standards? That's some strong, toxic male energy you have harboring, don't you think?"

"I won't share myself either," I clarify.

"So, we have a deal?"

"No." I suck in a breath. "Not until we at least go over the terms and understand all the pros and cons. This isn't something I jump into impulsively."

Penny nods and bites at her bottom lip, clearly deep in thought. She looks so freaking adorable, despite the rest of her body looking like it needs to be worshipped and dominated all at once.

"Well, when are you going to enlighten me?" Craning her neck, she trails her tongue up my neck, settling her lips at my ear. "All of this sexual energy in this place is making me"—her voice turns gravelly with need—"*horny*."

And on that note, I grab Penny's hand and walk us back to where we removed our shirts. My body shields hers, preventing any members from getting a look at the girl who is chiseling away at all the walls I've built around myself.

I help Penny into her halter shirt and tie the straps at her neck extra secure. Then I pull my shirt over my head. We exit the viewing booth, walk down the hall, and descend the stairs. I guide her through the orgy forming on the dance floor and into the locker room where we both grab our personal belongings.

"How did you know I'd be here tonight?" she asks quietly.

"I knew from the look in your eyes the last time you were here that you didn't get your curiosity quenched. I figured round two was in order. Plus, I know that you have a few items on your goal list that you want to knock out."

"You should have never looked at that private document."

"I know." It won't stop me the next time though. I'll just get better at not making it known to her that I did it.

"So you came to spy on me?"

"The last thing you need is to be trusting some stranger here to fulfill a fantasy that you may think you want in theory, when in reality you get freaked out by it."

"And you are having me watched by that other guy too."

My eye twitches. "I always have backup plans. So, yes." I don't even deny it, as there's really no point.

"That's really creepy."

"It's really necessary. Just trust me. And I haven't hid the fact that I'll be continuing to do just that."

"Well, the person needs to seek out an ophthalmologist because they suck. I was able to get here and inside without being stopped yet again."

"And that reckless behavior will actually have a deliverable punishment if you pull a stunt like that under a contract —if we have one."

"Fine."

"And that mocking tone will as well."

"Fi—" And then she stops and glares at me when it finally sinks in.

"You've made a lasting impression on Yuri and Michael with your charm. There's no way they'd be able to turn you away from here no matter how many threats I make."

"Well, maybe you just aren't that scary."

I feel the corner of my lips rising with a smirk. Then I laugh. "Maybe."

Penny allows me to lead her to the lockers and then out of the building, where we are greeted again by Michael.

"Leaving so soon, little dove?"

Penny gnaws on her lip and looks down at her feet. "Appears that way," she says quietly.

Where did my sex vixen go? She can't possibly be getting shy—can she?

"I'll see to it that she is home safely," I confirm, and then guide Penny toward my parked car.

On our way there, I nod my greeting to a few members who just arrived.

"Why do you know everyone it seems at the club? You have sex with all of them?"

"No, Penny," I say with a chuckle. She really is hung up on who I have and haven't had sex with. "But you have quite the imagination."

"Well, then what?"

I motion back toward the venue. "I'm an employee there."

40

COLLINS

Penny stops in her tracks, leaning her back end against the bumper of my Tesla. "Well, damn."

I'm surprised I flat out admitted my employment to her. It's not like I've really told anyone else about it. I definitely would never add it to my resume under the title—job experience.

"It's not full-time, and the infrequency about it makes me not even want to classify it as part-time." I shrug. "I basically fill in on occasion. And once in a while I get pulled into decision-making meetings as a security consult."

I can see she's pondering over this little piece of information, and I'd be lying if I said I wasn't curious as to her thoughts on the matter.

"Well, this does make sense."

She's going to need to elaborate. Her lack of words is making me uneasy.

"How so?"

"It's just that I know you like to fuck 'em and forget

'em. And working here would definitely make it easy to have that constant flow of fresh pussy available for your prowess."

I shake my head at her. Where does she come up with these wild sayings that fly out of her mouth?

"You make it sound predatory, Penny. Most nights, even after working a shift, I stayed celibate."

"But why?"

"Because I found pleasure in an instructional scene or two and didn't always need to go further." I clear my throat. "I also don't like to complicate things."

Penny lets out a laugh. "Oh, the irony. Because things are just about to get super complex."

"This is true."

Looking back at the venue, Penny watches as clusters of patrons flutter out of the mansion in droves.

"What do you do in there?"

"I mainly work security. You know, monitor scenes and occasionally intervene when necessary."

"Oh, like I intervened with you and Daphne."

"No. What you did is called an interruption, and it breaks club rules under almost all circumstances."

Penny makes a face at me. "Are you working tonight?"

"Only to keep you safe as your personal bodyguard but not here."

Penny nods, as she absorbs this tidbit of information. I've never really shared with others my side jobs I took on after leaving the military. I had some anger to work through, and it was best that I stayed as busy as I could. It helped to keep my head out of the darkness by deliberately walking into it of my own free will.

"I imagine you had a whole buffet of women there to enjoy. You know"—she shrugs and pretends to keep it nonchalant—"on your breaks."

"You have this vision inside your head that I'm some type of man whore."

She crosses her arms over her chest. "Well, just how many women have you been with?" Making a face, she glances away when I don't immediately answer. "Wow, that many?"

I sigh. "It's not like I cataloged every single time I fucked someone, Penny. How can I possibly give you a number without you thinking I'm withholding the truth?"

She shrugs, appearing not to know how to move past the unknown. "At least you don't have any of my ex-boyfriends to worry about. Spoiler alert…there are none."

"No. But I have a whole list of current ones to keep watch on."

Penny scoffs. "That's so far from the truth it's kind of depressing. No one will even notice if I'm temporarily off the market, as we explore a sex-only arrangement. Once we get our fill of each other or the contract ends—whichever happens first—I doubt a single male specimen will even notice I'm back on the playing field again."

I unravel her hair band from her ponytail, freeing her locks to cascade around her face like a waterfall made of silk. Her long moan makes me wonder why she tortured herself in the first place.

"Your cluelessness about just how attractive you are is what draws me to you the most. It's as if you have no idea just how"—I struggle for the right word—"*alluring* you are.

The fact that you will soon be mine is even more impressive." Holding her chin, I bend down for a kiss.

"I love when you kiss me like that."

I can't help but smile around this girl.

"I just need you to be sure that you want what I have to offer. I'm not a gentle lover, Penny." I grip her ass and set her up higher on the hood of my car. "I'm going to train your body to submit to my intentional touch. Nothing I do to you will be an accident. I'm going to devour every part of you."

"I want that, Collins."

"You sure?"

She nods eagerly. "I want to be all those things for you. But you are going to have to be patient with me. I don't have the experience you seem to have, and as much as I'm excited to try new things, I'm a bit scared. I'm intimidated and worried that I won't be enough for you."

I shush her with another kiss on the lips, taken aback by her vulnerability but not shying away from it. "You are enough, Penny."

I breathe in her strawberry scent and shove down the feelings of trepidation deep into the pit of my conscience. I've tried to resist her. Really, I have. But catching her twice at Limit-X has made it clear that it would only be a matter of time for Penny to give herself over to some stranger who could do with her whatever he wanted and might not take her authentic consent into consideration.

Yeah…that's not going to happen.

Yuri prides himself on creating and maintaining a safe playground, but bad shit can happen anywhere—no matter what security measures are in place.

My job is to protect Penny. Maybe being with me will be the lesser of two evils.

Penny has already been emotionally scarred from Mark Tanner. The last thing she needs is for another man to crash into her life and cut through the scars again or make fresh ones. By having a contract, we both can work through what we want from our arrangement, so there are no surprises. A clean break can be worked into the deal when our time is up, and expectations can be negotiated, so it is mutually beneficial for the both of us.

"Collins?"

"Yes, Penny?"

"Are you willing to teach me? You know…"—her cheeks warm to a beautiful shade of pink—"how to pleasure you."

I kiss her forehead, tucking her head into my chest, while running my hands over her back. "Of course, Princess." But she already has pleased me. "I'll train you how to be my good girl." And have a damn grand time doing it too.

Just the thought of having Penny as my trainee has me feeling the electric buzz of anticipation snaking through my entire body that I've missed in all of my other partnerships. All the other women have had some sort of experience. Most knew how to suck a cock and get me off in a clinical sense.

But none possessed the sweetness that exudes from Penelope Hoffman.

And it's her innocent words and uncertainty that are making my cock come to life.

I help Penny down from my car. As much as I want to

thrust into her while she has the backdrop of the shiny paint behind her, I also need to go over my nonnegotiables with her prior to us having sex. If my personality never turned her off, then those very well might be the final straw.

And it's better to work that out before I am balls deep in fresh, young pussy.

Fuck.

Am I capable of going through with any of this?

Even if we both spell out all of our expectations, will either of us fully understand the depths at which we are exploring?

Opening the passenger side door, I watch as Penny slides into her seat and clicks her belt into place. I close it and round the front, just as I've done a dozen times with her in tow.

But this time feels different.

Everything about tonight is more amped.

Sliding into my own seat, I can feel her eyes on me, and I know that she senses the magnitude.

"I want you to teach me how to drive," she blurts out.

"Okay…"

"Just letting you know that I want that added to the contract."

I eye her, as I start the engine and shift it into drive. So we are making a list it seems. "Fair enough." I planned on giving her some lessons anyway. Ever since her brothers gifted her a car, she must be eager to try it out. "Anything else?"

"Can you teach me some more self-defense moves?"

I pull out of the parking lot and onto the dark road. "Of course."

Turning in her seat, Penny twists her fingers into her lap. "I also want you to blindfold me."

"I already have at the gym."

"But I was thinking in more of an intimate setting."

This desire is featured on her goal list, so I'm not too surprised. "Why?"

Her legs fidget, as she kicks up the floor mat, burrowing her shoes under it. "Well, because it freaks me out and is a fear of mine."

"So you want to face that fear?"

"Only with you. You're someone I trust to not take advantage of me in my vulnerable state. Can we try at least?"

If I learned anything from guarding Angie and Claire, telling a woman "no" is basically like cementing the idea into their permanent memory bank in their brain, at which they will relentlessly pursue it at all cost.

My teeth grind together. "I'll consider it."

I'll be doing a lot more than inhibiting her one sense. And I know all too well about doing things to face your fears. If we follow through with this arrangement, it will be uncharted territory for the both of us.

I'm nervous about it too. All of my previous contracts have had very simplistic stipulations. But with Penny, I think there needs to be way less gray area involved. I don't want to hurt her in any way—unless she consents to some pain-pleasure. In that case, I'll be happy to oblige.

"And I want you to take me to a sex store for toys."

"Can't you buy them from a website?"

She shakes her head. "No. That's boring. I want a real

sex toy store, not one that is masquerading as such. I want one with those little rooms and the wall holes."

"Wall holes?" What the hell is she talking about now?

"Gory holes?"

"Fuck, Penny. They are called glory holes, and those places only exist in porn movies or skeezy places we will never visit."

Penny bursts out laughing. "I thought the name was gory because the guy's erection thickens and it gets stuck in the hole, and then blood. Lotssss of—"

"Got it," I say in a hurry, wanting to shut this part of the conversation down fast.

I'm not sure what kind of porn she's been watching, but it sure isn't the commercial shit that is plastered on the bigger sites. She must have found something super niche.

I continue driving, trying to keep my composure, when I know Penny's mind is cooking up even more ideas for this contract. She seems to be having fun in the process, as I catch her stifling giggles and covering her mouth to contain her giddiness.

She is a seductive angel all wrapped in a sinful fantasy I never knew I could have.

"Collins?"

I can feel the tension running up my spine to my shoulders and neck. "Yes?"

"I want to make a sex tape so I can watch us going at it anytime I want."

"What the hell, Pen?"

She shrugs. "I think it would be hot."

No doubt about that. But I would have to put that

footage in a high security lockbox. No way in hell I would chance someone else seeing us in action.

I can't tell if this is just who Penny is or if the buzz of the alcohol from the club is still in her system, making her mouth and brain filters disintegrate at the expense of my self-control. Regardless, I'm not sure how I'm able to drive the car with a hard-on.

"Any other stipulations?" I grind out. She sure is full of ideas tonight.

Penny stares out the window, as I get us closer and closer to the city's limits.

I remind myself that the contract will have an end date. I've ended contracts early, and there's usually a clause allowing that occurrence. However, I've never once extended the termination date—ever. Surely, with a time table set, I can work through Penny's laundry list of to-do items. Minus the *gory* holes. That's a hard limit—for sure.

Ever since Penny left the therapy facility, she's been adamant about accomplishing her goals. By the look in her eyes, she's conjuring up a few more to add to the already lengthy list.

She turns to look at me. "Are you into kinky stuff, Collins?"

If I had enough spit in my mouth, I would choke on it. Instead, I cough into my elbow, desperately trying not to wreck the vehicle. "What's with the third degree, Penny?"

"I'm just asking."

"But why are you asking?" I counter. Surely, she has some motive as to why she is asking in the first place.

"Well…" She twists her hands in her lap.

"Just ask." I can't take any more of her writhing around

in her seat before I pull this car over and steal another touch from her delectable body. She has no freaking clue just how badly my cock is straining against my jeans. How can she not notice how tightly strung she has me?

"Would you be willing to tie me up?"

Fuck.

Thoughts of her chained to my bed run unfiltered in my head. We could start with silk ties and work our way up to something with a bit more bite. Her breasts would look lovely—I am sure—squeezed between some intricate rope work. I want her to wear the indentations of my handiwork.

Her body would make the most beautiful canvas.

Would she let me drip hot wax onto her curves?

What about spreading her out and feasting on her with the bite from my teeth?

Damn. When I agreed to the contract, I never expected Penny to be this sexually open. For someone who claims not to have much experience, she sure has a dark side—and one I'm eager to explore.

The Hoffman princess is a dirty little thing, isn't she?

This new discovery makes me want to own her—all of her.

There's only so much sweet persuasion I can endure before the monster inside me unleashes.

But what price will I be willing to pay in order to have Penelope Hoffman in my bed, under my control?

And will the potential fallout be worth that risk?

41

PENNY

"Did I say something wrong?"

"No, Penelope."

It sure feels like I did. I may be lacking experience around guys—especially the silent types like Collins—but I know when I've hit a wall. His entire demeanor has changed, including his breathing. Sheesh. I'm going to derail this train before it even exits the station.

"Obviously I did."

"No, you didn't."

"Then why are you being so quiet? I must have said something—"

"I'm trying to drive us home while my cock is so rigid in my jeans that I think it may cut through the fabric."

Laughing, I reach over the center console. "Wow, that sounds painful. Here, let me help."

"No!" he snaps.

"Chill," I try to calm. "I was just going to try to get it to settle."

Collins shakes his head at me, as if I'm clueless—about what, I don't know. He sure is moody. "There's no settling it, Penny."

"Why are you so tense? Let me help."

"I'm trying to get us back safely and not crash this car because your hands are touching me."

"Oh. Okay, sorry." I turn and face the front windshield.

"There's no need to apologize. We'll be back into Portland soon."

I feel so inadequate compared to the other women at the club who have probably all had a piece of Collins Stone. The thought actually makes me sick to my stomach. If I use them as a level of standard, I'll never add up.

"What if we start to have sex and you change your mind and think I'm not doing it *right*? Or just suffer through the event in misery…"

"That's not going to happen."

"You say it with such confidence."

"I am confident." He won't even look at me.

I twirl a piece of my hair to use my hands to hopefully distract my mind. My nerves are getting the best of me, and we haven't even done anything. "I could be really horrible at sex. You've been warned. What happens if—"

"You won't be bad at it, Penny. That I promise you. It's impossible."

I shift my weight to one hip, bending my knees to lean into the center of the car. "How do you know?"

"Trust me."

I sigh. He's not getting it. "Will you teach me?"

"Teach you what? I already said I would."

His words come out rushed. He's flustered with me.

I need to get this conversation back on track… "Teach me how to fuck like a bad little cum slut?"

"What the hell, Penny?"

I read an article once that stated that men love when girls talk dirty and refer to themselves with vulgar names. Apparently Collins is immune to such antics. I better kick it up another notch. "I'm serious. I can be your cum dumpster if that is more your jam."

"I don't know how you can possibly be so fucking sweet and then talk like you are put on this earth just to torment me and challenge my control."

"Ew."

Collins glances over at me with his brows scrunched together. "What?"

"Don't call me sweet."

"But you are sweet."

"No, no, no! Sweet girls don't get railed and defiled."

"That's what you want from this arrangement?"

I think about it for a moment. "Umm, not exactly. It's just that…when I say I'm inexperienced, I *really* mean it. I am not a"—my words come out as a stutter—"virgin. But I basically am since I made the guy stop as soon as he put it inside. It was my one and only time during my college days, and I basically go through life trying to forget it ever happened. It was that horrible. But I now use toys. The ones that I can penetrate my—"

"What made it so bad for you?" he blurts out.

I thought I was tense; Collins's spine looks like a steel flagpole.

I make a face. "It hurt. And not in the good way that

porn videos try to portray." Finally, I'm spared a glance—barely. I let out a sigh. "There was nothing sexy about it. He didn't get me ready. It felt like he was slicing me up like deli meat. I felt unpleasantly sore afterward. And then I really didn't want to do it again, so I didn't. Flash forward a few years, and I'm horny as fuck."

"That's the difference between fucking a boy and fucking a man. A man will know when you are ready versus when you aren't. Trust me to know, Penny."

I nod, allowing his words to settle. "Yeah… I wasn't ready mentally either, and I sure as hell wasn't ready physically. But I'm ready now. Or just plain ol' horny and deprived."

"That's not a good combo."

"You're telling me. It's the worst. Try living with it."

Collins runs a hand down the back of his neck, looking visibly agitated. I'm messing this all up. It feels like I'm killing the mood and then beating it again with my embarrassing past.

"You're mad."

His hands white-knuckle grip the steering wheel so tightly that I worry he'll rip it from its post. "I'm not mad."

"Frustrated, then?"

Collins sighs. His back is rigid, as his eyes stay focused forward on the road. He's obviously feeling some type of emotion, despite his lips staying sealed in a stern line. "No."

I toss my hands into the air, bumping them against the ceiling. "Well, it would be helpful to know what you're thinking, as my mind races with every negative thought I can possibly conjure up. And trust me, your silence is only adding fuel to the flame of self-doubt that burns through me. I know I'm going to disappoint you. That much is obvious."

It's so quiet inside the car that I can hear the straining beats of my own blood pumping through my heart. Collins pulls into the parking garage at our complex, cuts the engine, and is walking toward my door before I even have a chance to undo my seatbelt.

With calculated efficiency, Collins opens the door, unhooks my belt, and pulls me out of the car so fast that I don't even have a chance to overthink what is happening.

I start to break the silence with another bout of word vomit, and his lips are on mine, sucking the words from my throat before they ever get a chance to hit our ears. My back presses against the cool metal and glass of the passenger side door, as his hands dig into the fleshy part of my ass cheeks. I gasp for air in between him kissing my neck and then traveling back to my lips. It's a full-on assault—in the best possible way—as he reverently worships me with his physical touch, letting me know that my body is desirable to him.

Pulling away, he catches his breath. "Is this clear enough to you how deep my attraction is?"

"I need another reminder." I start to giggle when he growls, and then quickly shut my mouth.

His fingers move to my sides, and he starts to tickle me.

"Stop, please"—I inhale and exhale, frantically trying to catch my breath—"I'll pass out."

When I break free, I make a dash for the elevator, laughing as I hear Collins's cursing behind me as he races to catch up.

I knew it was a mistake to try to escape him from the first two paces, but I'm too invested now to stop.

So I run and run, as my lungs burn from the exertion.

There's something very feral about having Collins Stone hunt me down. And I know without a doubt that I'll be caught, and I will be punished.

Because the man can run…

Damn. He really can run.

I make it three more paces before arms bind around me. Like I'm a sack of potatoes, Collins picks me up and hauls me over his strong shoulders.

It takes one smack to my ass to make me yelp.

"Don't you know that running away just makes it all the more fun when I catch you?"

"Maybe that was my plan," I say cheekily, getting the perfect upside down view of his ass cheeks. I can't resist and smack my hand against one, feeling the burning pain hit my palm.

Okay, I won't do that again.

Why is he so fit? I thought men get in worse physical shape as they age, and it seems like Collins is only improving himself with time.

"You'll hurt your hand, Pen," he warns, shifting me so I'm cradled to his front.

He hits the call button for the elevator with ease and it opens within seconds. Once I am safely inside and he presses the button for his floor, Collins places me on my feet and backs away.

"You're going to be the death of me, my dirty little princess."

I lean my butt against the cool metal handrail, as I catch my breath.

Hearing Collins call me his dirty little anything makes me feel a gush of wetness between my thighs. There's no place for it to go other than to collect in my panties, because my shorts are so tight they need to be peeled off.

This man may not say too much, but when he does talk, it's like an erotic arrow straight to my pussy.

Just watching Collins's chest rise and fall, and the way his jaw tics, makes me want to jump him. Masculine energy radiates off him, and I know that whatever he plans to do with me in the bedroom will be spectacular. I won't need to have experience or know everything there is to know. I can just let him lead the way and hope not to completely botch up trying to be sexy.

That's assuming we ever get to the bedroom. It's definitely not a requirement. I'm not picky either. I'll settle for this elevator floor, his kitchen countertop, or even the wall outside his bedroom.

I clear my throat, maintaining eye contact. "Can you add elevator sex to your mental list of *my wants*?"

"You are insatiable, and we haven't even started exploring each other. I am going to have so much fun with you. I mean, I might as well, since I'm going to hell anyway."

I shrug. "You sound dramatic. No one is going to find out about our *arrangement*. Anyway, I can't wait until we sign the papers, so if I give you blow jobs with my teeth only, you just have to deal with it."

Collins shakes his head at me, as if I'm somehow lying. I mean, I have a lot to learn. I just hope he has the patience to teach me. There's only so much being an observer at a kink club can do for me, especially when I only have frequented it twice. Relying on porn as an instructional tool doesn't seem very practical to hands-on learners.

Despite my original fear coming across in a joking manner, I'd be lying if I said it wasn't a genuine concern. When my ex and I met in college, I thought he would be understanding that I was a virgin. He acted so sweet and caring until he managed to get my pants off.

My first time was not even a real experience, unless you count the two minutes he was inside me. Everything hurt like hell, and my body repelled his entry like a foreign object that didn't belong. It didn't matter how hard he pushed on my clit—as if it was the magic button to get me to come—I received zero pleasure. He made what could have been a memorable experience just be one I spent years vowing I'd never repeat.

I bled afterward and stayed bruised for over a week.

It's no wonder Mark Tanner's charm attracted me to another horrible situation soon after.

It was like I was feeding my trauma with more trauma.

Maybe in some demented sense, the identification of the trauma was the comforting component that allowed me to continue the cycle.

I was vulnerable then, but I'm done being the naive girl that falls for the flowery words that are only meant to manipulate me. No, instead, I'm tying myself to a man who blatantly tells me this is a horrible idea every chance he gets. And I believe him, because deep down inside I can't help but wonder how this will all end.

And there will be an end, because that is the entire point of having it in writing.

Unfortunately, I can't make myself not attracted to Collins. There's something undeniable between us, and by the look of wonder in his eyes, I think he feels it too.

I may walk out of this with my head held high, taking with me the added knowledge that comes from being with someone more experienced. Or instead, I might have to crawl my way out of the ashes of another heartbreak and hope the next time I involve myself with another person, it won't be as damaging.

Can I keep this arrangement strictly professional—as a way to fulfill each of our needs?

When the elevator stops, we exit and make our way down the hallway. I have yet to see anyone on this floor and wonder if anyone even lives here. Maybe he chose this location for the quietness it brings. I would feel peace right now if I wasn't voluntarily walking into what now seems like the lion's den.

I've been to his apartment numerous times and yet this visit just feels different. It's like once I cross the threshold, I won't need some paper promises to tie me to the one man who can knock down the walls I have strategically built around myself for protection.

Collins disarms the security system for his unit and guides me inside. I'm glad he is content being at his own place, because I wouldn't be able to trust Luke to keep his big mouth shut whenever the girls or my brothers pay me a visit. The less he knows, the better. He is the only one who thinks he's discreet—when in reality he is blatantly obvious about anything he does. I also can't risk him asking to join in. He's obnoxious like that.

Collins helps me out of my heels and then curses at the sight of my angry blisters. "You need to stop abusing your sensitive skin like this," he scolds, rubbing his thumbs over the sore patches.

I nod, gesturing toward my shoes. "But they look so cute on."

I honestly didn't even realize I had blisters until he pointed them out.

He removes his own and places them perfectly on the rack beside the door. "They look fucking fantastic on you, but I don't need the view at the expense of your comfort." He scoops me up and starts to carry me toward his bedroom.

"I take it I'm not welcome in your guest room anymore."

Smiling down at me, he kisses me on the nose. "You are welcome in every square inch of my place, but I much prefer to have you in my bed tonight. The cage for underneath is arriving next week."

"Oh my g—"

"Teasing."

"You better be." I snuggle in closer to Collins's chest, loving the feel of his muscles against the side of my cheek. "Can you add spooning to my list of wants?"

Collins chuckles, dropping me into the center of the bed with a bounce. "I will add whatever clause you want to the contract, assuming you can follow my three main rules."

"And what are those?" I bite at my bottom lip, as I watch him slowly remove his jeans.

His lips curl into a half smile. "I'll tell you tomorrow."

I cross my arms at my chest and pout out my lip. "Why the suspense?" Seriously, why is he being so secretive?

"If I show you my cards too soon, you'll have time to think of some strategies to get you out of complying."

I'm so confused. "So you're going to fuck me but then drop a bombshell on me tomorrow with your demands?"

He shakes his head. "No, Penelope. We're not having sex tonight."

I feel my jaw unhinging. "And why not? Isn't that the point?" It's like he's speaking another language—one in which I have zero foundational knowledge.

"For one, you've been drinking."

"Barely," I grumble. I'm not even slurring my words. At least I don't think I am. Well, damn. Maybe I am?

"I'm not having you making life-altering decisions while you've been under the influence of alcohol."

"Well, you rejecting me—yet again—is pretty sobering."

Ignoring my mini-rant, he sighs. "Second, I want us both to understand the terms of the contract to every last detail before engaging in a sexual relationship that can muddy the already murky water."

"Yeah, we wouldn't want me to take advantage of you or anything," I say, my tone mocking.

"And third, we will both get physicals tomorrow with a physician of my choosing, and not someone you type into Google to find."

I sit up straighter on the bed. "So this is what it's going to be like?"

"What?"

"Where you dictate what is going to happen, and I listen and obey like a good little girl?"

A smile beams across his face. "Now that sounds like music to my ears."

"I mean it, Collins!"

"That's the incentive you threw my way, isn't it? You allow me to be your bodyguard without any fight, and your sexual appetite gets satisfied."

I huff out a breath. "Your cock better be worth the wait."

"And your sassy mouth better be glad I don't put a ball gag in it."

Well, that silenced me.

From his tone, I don't think Collins is joking—even in the slightest. Now that the secret's out that he has been a part-time employee at Limit-X, I'd be lying if my ass cheeks weren't a tad bit intimidated.

He's probably had a lot of practice wielding the whip.

I mentally shudder. I can't do whips.

Stretching out over the bed, I try to reach the bottom drawer of his nightstand.

Collins chuckles. "You can't even wait until I leave the room to start snooping?"

"I need to examine the size of the ball gag to determine whether my sass is worth the consequence."

"You are going to be so much fun to tame. But don't worry, I want you to keep that zesty spirit about you. It just makes this all extra fun." There's amusement in his timbre.

Ignoring his commentary, I stick with my focus. "I can only imagine the armory of sex toys you have stored in your bottom nightstand drawer. Who needs a store when I can shop here for free? You can learn a lot about a man by what he has hidden."

"There are none, Pen."

Sitting up, I bring my knees to my chest. "So, you just use the good, old-fashioned hand, eh?"

His lips curl up into a smirk. "You really do have a very active imagination."

"It's overactive most days."

"No doubt."

"Prefer hotel rooms?"

He sighs. "I prefer public places with rules set so both parties know what to expect."

I make a face. "Seems clinical."

"It's logical," he counters. "At least for men like me."

"What does that mean?"

"I treat arrangements for what they are—a way to satisfy sexual urges for both parties."

"A business…"

"Sure, but without any money exchanged."

"Got it."

"It'll be best if you try not to attach strings to fleeting things, like emotions. Things will end between us. It's inevitable—finite. The more we both accept that fact, the better in the end."

I think about his answer for a moment. I've always known Collins to be a man who valued his privacy. However, going through life specifically looking for an emotionally detached relationship seems…

Lonely?

And here I sit, about to embark on a similar journey. It

makes me cringe inside, because I'm probably just a number in his list of clients. No one special…

I'll just be a warm body that serves a specific purpose. And when I'm done, I'll be discarded and will have to go back to pretending that Collins is just my bodyguard.

Can I even do this?

I remind myself that this was solely my idea. Collins can do his job by being my bodyguard and not having to fight with me to comply. In return, I can fulfill some of my goals without the fear of being taken advantage of in the process. It is a win-win situation.

I trust Collins.

He's not intentionally going to cause me harm, and it is all on me if I attach strings that don't need to be attached.

Sure, he has this idea in his head that he is betraying Graham and Nic, but my brothers never once consulted me about having a bodyguard. I was never part of a negotiation or even the bare minimum discussion on the framework around Collins's requirements. Instead, they took it upon themselves to figure out what they thought was best for me, when all I need to do is to push forward with my life and leave my ghosts in the past.

Maybe they are punishing me for visiting Mark in prison. Perhaps they are still coping with everything that happened to me. I know my parents are still struggling. Just the extra details Momma added to my birthday celebration was indication enough that she is trying to make up for lost time.

But no matter how special you make the present, it's the past that is the haunting reminder of just how volatile time is. One day you think you have all the time in the world.

Then the next months pass by and you can't even remember them.

As much as it unnerves me to be left out of the choices made about my well-being, I know that Graham and Nic have good hearts, and that their decisions are a direct result of the evil they have encountered when I was drugged.

Mark Tanner causing me harm has had a huge impact on so many lives, and I'd be a fool not to acknowledge that. I don't blame my brothers for wanting to protect me, but I'm an adult. I am twenty-two years old, and need to continue to make my own mistakes and learn from them.

I'm not perfect.

But I also am not stupid. Sure, I don't have a college degree, but I am perceptive and resourceful.

"Penny?"

My mind snaps to the present when Collins starts removing his shirt over his head and unbuttoning his jeans.

I dampen my dry lips with my tongue. Then I remember his declaration earlier about no sex tonight.

"Are you"—I motion to his crotch with my hand—"changing your mind? I mean, I won't object." Shit, I sound like a deprived teenager on the verge of puberty.

Collins stares at me, stopping his zipper's descent. "No, Penelope. I'm simply getting ready for bed and so should you."

I point a finger into the mattress underneath me. "I'm staying here?"

He continues to slide down his jeans. "Yes."

My eyes zero in on his black boxer briefs. They make his body look even more fit.

I can't help but imagine his strong legs straining as he

pumps inside me. Or using them to anchor me against the wall while he thrusts up into me. Yep, I'm not sure I can sleep comfortably knowing that he'll be practically naked beside me.

"You're sure we can't activate the Bodyguard With Benefits package tonight?"

"I'm sure."

"Can we at least spoon?" It's a simple question. "Why are you smirking at me?"

"Probably because you've already asked me so many questions, and I can't help but admire your desire for an interrogation." He shrugs. "Maybe I find you utterly adorable."

"Ew, no. Stop."

"What?"

"Adorable equates to butterfly kisses and dry humping."

"Wha—"

"And I want something rougher and passionate. Puppies and looking for cloud shapes in the sky are adorable." Running my hands up my body, I toss my hair over my shoulders. "I want to be the girl who makes you break your rules."

Collins crawls onto the bed, threading his fingers through my hair as he tugs me closer. "What if I find you equal parts adorable and sexy?"

I close the distance, bringing my lips to his. And we feast and explore.

When I can take no more, I pull back to catch my breath, as my lungs pant for air.

"I would say that I'm okay with it, as long as you don't treat me like I'm fragile. I want to be broken in a little. I want to know what it feels like the day after you take me."

"Hmm…"

"Part of me is excited to be a little sore, but only because I trust you to make it"—I pause to think of the right word—"memorable. And worth it."

"Penny," he exhales. "I'm struggling to control myself."

"Good."

"Not good—reckless."

"Now *that* sounds like a good time."

Sitting back, Collins seems to be battling internally with his next step. Then, suddenly he helps me untie my halter top. I think he's completely shifted into gear, but then he starts to move away.

"You are giving me whiplash," I huff out an exhale. "What is going on with you?"

"I'll go get you some of your clothes from your room and—"

"No." I pull on his arm to stop him from leaving. "Can I just wear your shirt?"

Collins smiles and slides off the bed to move into the closet. "Sure."

When he returns, I move my hands up to my breasts, inviting his eyes to the banquet.

I will be his. He just needs to take me.

But it's just a fantasy—a wish—that he would make a move and stop leaving me dangling from the cliff of my own self-doubt.

"Not tonight, Penny."

My hope deflates with the sting of yet another rejection.

I turn my back to him and strip down until I'm just

wearing a scanty pair of panties, discarding everything else into a pile on the floor. His warming presence is what I feel first as he presses his front against my back.

"Lift your arms."

I raise them above my head and watch as Collins's soft, faded gray T-shirt slides over my naked torso, ending with the hem at midthigh.

"And you're certain we aren't having sex tonight?"

"Yes, I'm certain, Penny."

"Challenge accepted."

"No challenge. At least not tonight."

Fine. "Good night, Collins."

"Good night, Penny."

42

COLLINS

I can't sleep.

Every part of me is wide awake and overthinking the biggest decision I'm ever going to make with the Hoffman princess lying right beside me.

What alternate universe am I living in to think that this won't blow up in my face?

I know Penny is insecure over her inexperience. However, I'm the one who is experiencing multiple firsts ever since she pried her way into my life.

She is a lioness dressed up as a lamb.

In hindsight, I never stood a chance against her. In a way, it almost seems silly thinking that I could have resisted her at all. The moment I was officially assigned to her was the kiss of death on my self-control.

Sure, I've spent many hours in Seattle watching over Penny's treatment regimen and caretakers. I was always making sure I checked up on her progress and overseeing the facility when they didn't know I was watching.

But nothing prepared me for officially being Penny's bodyguard and the adrenaline rush running through my bloodstream right now.

Never once have I invited a partner to my bed—let alone my apartment. Never once have I spooned with anyone or actually lain beside someone with the intention of just sleeping.

Yet, here I am, snuggled behind this beautiful enchantress, who is so freaking sexy wearing nothing but my T-shirt and her lacy panties.

How in the hell did the stars align in the universe that granted me this one moment in life?

I know where our relationship is heading, but the forceful desire I feel in this single blip in time to rip her clothes off and rock my body on top of hers is almost more than I can handle right now.

Just being in the same bed as Penny is agony enough. Yet there is nowhere else she belongs more than right here with me.

But this is close to straight-up masochism.

Especially with how Penny is moaning as I rub her arms and hands. She enjoys my touch, and a sense of relief rushes through my veins that she isn't freaked out over it. The last thing I would ever want is for our pending arrangement to cause her any harm—or a setback on her mental health progress. She's been through a lot of trauma. I don't need to make her continued healing worse.

And that's what she's doing—healing. Perhaps our union can lessen some of her pain and insecurities over her own self-image. I damn well will try to tell her and show her just how beautiful I find her, because I do find her irresistible.

"That feels so good. I love to be massaged," she coos, relaxing her head back against mine.

"I didn't mean to disturb you."

"It's not a disturbance if I crave everything your touch can deliver."

I breathe in her sweet scent.

The smell of strawberries will surely be all over my sheets, and I will undoubtedly regret the moment they'll need to be washed.

I place gentle kisses to her neck and then to her ear. "Sleep well, my princess. Because tomorrow, after we go through our formal expectations, you'll officially be mine."

"Hmm…" Leaning her head back at an angle, her eyes find mine. "I'm not tired."

"You need sleep."

"You aren't sleeping."

She has a point. "I'd much rather watch you sleep."

"That's creepy."

I laugh. "I'll try to be less creepy."

Penny thinks about it for a minute. "You sure you don't want to break the rules?"

"If you only realize just how many rules I've already broken with you."

She rolls her eyes. "Rules are meant to be broken, Collins."

"Not in my world."

"This whole abstinence thing you have going on"—yawn—"is the biggest surprise of the night."

I chuckle into her hair. "I can't wait until your pussy is

in a constant state of being sore. You'll have multiple daily reminders of where I've been. So, enjoy your rest now, because this bed will soon become secondary to sleep."

Wrapping my arms around her, I close my eyes and listen for her breathing to change, before I allow my own sleep to overtake me.

If Penny realized I would cave to her every demand with her pouty bottom lip alone, then I'd be in serious trouble. The woman is ruthless when it comes to getting what she wants. For weeks she has tormented me in ways I didn't consider a turn-on prior to her input.

Never once did I think a girl wearing my shirt would cause such a profound territorial reaction inside. Yet, the sight of her lacy panties peeking out of my tee, as she reaches up into the cupboard to pull down a mug, is one sure way to get her fucked on the countertops before four in the morning.

Apparently I'm not the only one who can't sleep.

My mouth fills with saliva at the thought of getting lost between her legs. Even just watching her fill her mug up with water is tantalizing.

I can't keep my head clear when she's around. Every other cloudy thought is of a sexual position I'd like to twist her in. She is like a closed tulip that just needs the right nurturing to open up and bloom, and I have an overwhelming sense of pride that I'm going to be the man to help her see her full potential.

Her innocence is a gift—one I don't take lightly.

Sure, Penny is not a virgin. But being with a boy versus a man are two vastly different experiences. To me, she's never been intentionally touched with her pleasure as the focal point. From the little responses she's given me thus far, I know her body will react explosively.

And the excitement of that coming to fruition is causing all my nerve endings to ignite.

"Do I even need to get a physical today?" she asks, sensing my presence behind her. She takes a sip of water before shifting her attentive gaze back to me.

"You couldn't sleep anymore?"

She shakes her head, casting dancing shadows on the wall from the dimmed light of the lamp she has on from the other room. "Too much on my mind."

"Like the physical?"

"It's not like I've been with anyone since college."

She slices up a lemon into wedges and then adds one to her cup. Stirring vigorously, she manages to spill some onto the counter.

"And before I was admitted to Soulful Mind, I'm pretty sure I got some type of examination in the Emergency Room where blood was also drawn. Then there's the delivery guy from Seattle who tried to shove his hands down my pants and—"

"Do you want me to find him and fuck him up?"

"Whoa, what? No!"

"Because I will and harbor zero regrets."

"Easy there, killer." Penny backs her ass up against the counter, and quickly adjusts her shirt, probably from the coldness hitting her exposed skin. Crossing her arms over her chest, she gives me a stern look. "And to answer your question—no."

"You shouldn't be letting anyone—especially strangers —put their hands down your pants, Pen. For fuck's sake."

"I do recall your hand being down my pants last night at the club."

"I'm not a stranger."

Turning, she grabs her mug and takes a sip. "And neither was the guy."

I look at her skeptically, feeling the anger bubbling inside. She is being deliberately vague, even though she has to realize I already know exactly who she is referring to. Her brothers made it very clear to handle the problem, and I was all too happy to follow the order. Penny deserves so much better than to be felt up near the vending machines. "If you can't even recall his name, then he was a stranger." Why are we even arguing about this right now? "The fucker didn't deserve you." And he should be glad I didn't break his hands for even touching her.

Her lip curls up into a smirk. "And all this time I thought you didn't care or even see me. You have a jealous streak, Mr. Stone."

"And you have a defiant streak, Miss Hoffman."

She busies herself by filling another mug with water and then offering it to me, which I accept. I could get used to her serving me, with her sassy smile and creamy smooth thighs.

"For you, sir."

My eyes narrow on hers. I'm starting to learn that Penny thrives on playing games and driving me wild. "I could get used to you being my little servant."

She huffs out a laugh, obviously finding my comment

fun. Her upper teeth gnaw on her lower lip, drawing my attention to the sensitive flesh.

"You'd fire me the first day for not taking orders."

My lips curl into a smile. "Or punish you for your disobedience."

"It's not a punishment if I like it."

I nod, thinking about the possibilities for the near future. "True." Maybe fucking the brattiness out of her in feral lust will do the trick then.

"Anyway"—she takes a sip of her drink—"it was just a few times at Soulful Mind when we were messing around."

Okay, we are back to the fucker again…

"No fluids were exchanged, but that's because I wasn't ready for that kind of commitment. He got pretty mad that I wanted to take things slow." She shrugs, obviously thinking back on the situation. "Huh, well, maybe that is why he called me a prude the one time we were making out, and I wouldn't give him a hand job."

I clench my mug so tightly that I worry I might shatter it. It takes everything in me to resist the urge to relocate the asshole and verify that he knows never to contact Penny ever again. It's not like he hasn't already been threatened to stay the hell away from her—by numerous people. Sometimes a broken nose just adds necessary punctuation to the message.

Penny deserves a man, not some boy looking to scratch an itch.

"I would prefer to not use condoms, Penny," I say, trying to get back to the point of this whole thing.

"Okay…"

"Thus, it's best to talk with a professional about a birth

control schedule and to make sure that both of us are healthy."

"I'm pretty sure no one actually has this talk when they hook up after a night out partying. Just sayin'."

"Well, this should be the normal and responsible thing to do before starting any sexual relationship. It's also the difference between being with a man versus a man-child."

"I'm pretty sure we are in the minority, Collins."

"How so?"

"Well, most people enter into relationships for the romance aspect. And nothing about a sex contract screams hearts and flowers."

"At least it will offer protection in the aspect that we both will know exactly what to expect. Plus, you'd be surprised what people do behind closed doors. We might not be as much in the minority as you think."

"I don't need the romance. I just need the rapture. I don't need a Hallmark card love story, Collins. What I want is a slam-me-against-the-wall fuckfest."

"Bloody hell."

"And right now, this teetering along the edge of right and intensely wrong is making me feel all sorts of temptation." She fixes her hair behind her ear. "I don't want condoms."

"Good. We are in mutual agreement."

"And I've been getting injections periodically for years to help with cramps. So I'm good to"—her eyes meet mine—"go. So let's get it on."

"Patience."

"Do you like her?"

My blank stare eats its way through every nerve ending,

sparking an electricity through me that only puts me more on edge. “Who?”

“Daphne.”

My eyes twitch. “Why are we talking about her right now? And no. At least not how you are envisioning.”

“Rate her pussy from one to ten, with one being a dumpster and ten being a penis paradise.”

My lower jaw goes boneless. “You can’t be serious.” Is this Penny’s version of an anxiety-riddled self-sabotage episode?

“You had to find her hot enough to have a kinky spanking scene with her. Are we going to have a public scene at Limit-X during the contract’s duration?”

“Hell no.”

She props her hands on her hips. “And why not?”

“Because I respect you too much.”

“But you don’t respect those other girls?”

I let out the breath from my lungs. Where is Penny going with this? I’m not used to someone so sexually inexperienced being so sexually bold. It’s like she is taunting me with both her innocence and her dirty mouth at the same time, and I can’t tell which one is winning the battle. “Because I don’t want to share you. I *won’t* share you.”

“Even if I want to be part of an orgy?”

“Fuck, Penny.”

“Just teasing,” she giggles. “I was just testing you. Don’t worry, you passed.”

“You keep testing me with that smart mouth of yours, and I’ll put it to better use.”

Her smile is contagious, well, until she doubles over into a fit of giggles. I don’t see her face for a solid minute, and when she finally recovers, she bats her eyelashes at me like a temptress. "Maybe that's been my plan all along."

I shake my head at her—which I seem to be doing a lot this morning. She does seem to have this running list of all the things she wants jostling around in her head. Never in a million years would I have been able to predict the turn my life is now taking, with this gorgeous girl who I know wholeheartedly I shouldn't touch. Yet I can't stop thinking of all the ways I want to dominate her.

Penny doesn't make me want to be a better man. She makes me want to be the villain. And something deep inside me makes me wonder if she doesn't want the same thing.

She sparks my darker side, making me territorial and a predator to her. Yet that's what she seems to desire.

Penny is equal parts temptress and princess, all wrapped up in my oversized T-shirt that she is now lifting above her—

"What the hell, Penny? Why are you—"

"Shhh…" She places her finger over my lips. "I just think that having a contract before actually having sex is silly. What happens if we aren't compatible?"

With any other woman, I would be able to see her point. However, just the way my cock stirs every time this girl is near it is indication enough that we will certainly have fireworks whenever we finally submit to the act.

"And if we aren't compatible?" I challenge, mostly because I want to hear her next steps.

When I can sift through all the extra words, I can usually find the truth. Motives guide actions, and I'm certainly interested in what drives Penny.

"Then, I will still allow you to bodyguard me."

I resist snickering over her use of the word *allow*, as if her approval is governing my ability to do my job.

I may have been looking for my replacement before, but so much has changed since our almost kiss in the gym.

Since then, I've had numerous samples of the forbidden fruit, and there's no part of me that doesn't crave a more substantial taste.

Our attraction for one another is undeniable, and I now know that it's this magnetic pull that makes me cocky enough to realize I'm by far the best person for the position. I will lay down my life to protect her—whether she approves or not.

"But I can have a fuckboy on the side," she adds quickly.

A growl erupts from my diaphragm. "Never." She has to be joking…

"Then you better put out now so I can sign with confidence later."

"So you want a trial run?"

"Like a sample snack from the snack shack."

Now I'm a snack? What am I going to do with her? That's the bigger question. "Okay," I agree with hesitation. I at least understand her point. "And when do you want to have your snack?"

Her eyes trail leisurely down my body as her fingers play with the waistband of my boxer briefs. Turning her head, she looks at the time on the stove. How is it after five in the morning?

"Now." Her eyes move back to mine. "I'm famished."

"I'm breaking all the rules with you."

A smile plays on her lips. "Fun, isn't it?"

"Dangerous."

"My tests are all clear, Collins. I actually have had a recent physical. I can provide you a copy of the results. I have them saved on my phone. I have been taking a reliable form of birth control for years, albeit for something unrelated. You know—since I wasn't actually fucking anyone during that time."

"I had a physical done recently as well and have not had intercourse with anyone after it."

"Wow."

"Surprised?"

Her eyes trail down my torso, lingering on my crotch. "I hope you still remember how to use—"

Penny's yelp makes me laugh, as I fling her up into the air and carry her back to my bedroom. I lay her on my bed and soak in the magnitude of this moment.

Penny looks good in the moonlight seeping in from the windows. Soon it'll be the sun.

I had envisioned how our first time together would be in my head numerous times. I've spent most of this past night fantasizing about how I'd take her. However, there's only so much teasing and taunting I can endure before completely snapping and resorting to my genetically-dispositioned caveman tendencies.

Within seconds our clothes are discarded.

"Collins?"

"Yes?"

"You'll go slow, right?"

"Of course, Princess. I'm going to prepare you to take me. You don't need to worry about that, okay?"

And she will take me—all of me.

Her head nods, allowing my promise to permeate what I assume are her fearful thoughts. "Okay."

There's no turning back time now. She set this all into motion when she triggered my overprotective instincts and provoked me with her curious questions about the contract.

This is what she claims she wants, so who am I to deny her? When it's daylight she can start obeying me. Right now, I'm a loyal servant to her needs.

I have tried to resist her innocent stares and her alluring personality. I have tried to stop myself from tasting the forbidden fruit, knowing that I'd get sent a one-way ticket straight to hell. I tried…

Trust me—I tried.

But I failed.

With concentrated precision, I reach for her ankles and pull her down the bed to a standing position. Steadying her stance, I splay my fingers over the sides of her hips.

"I'm obsessed with your curves."

"I just don't want to disappoint you," she whispers, looking down at her naked toes.

"I don't want you to overthink this." I kiss her on her forehead.

Then I take my seat in the armchair, leaving her standing in her nakedness in front of me.

"Dance."

"What? Why?"

"Because I eat with my eyes first." And because I'm fucking jealous of every man—and woman—at Limit-X who got to experience her on the dance floor.

Now it's my turn to indulge.

After several long seconds and the prediction that she won't follow through, Penny starts to perform.

Her hips swivel and her head tilts back up toward the ceiling.

I can tell she isn't fully confident, and that alone sends blood to my cock. I like her innocence. I like that she isn't some porn star replica.

Much preferring her softness, I find Penny absolutely enchanting.

"You're doing amazing, Princess. Keep dancing. Show me what will soon be mine."

She moves to the music in her soul and enchants me with every shift her body makes.

When she gets close enough to be within reach, I grab her waist and place her on my lap so she straddles me, while digging my fingers into the lush flesh of her ass cheeks.

For several minutes, we just grind against one another, using my pre-cum as lubrication to assist with the friction.

"I'm going to destroy you and wreck that pussy of yours that you use as a weapon instead of a source of pleasure."

"Yes, please."

"You sure that is what you want? There won't be going back once you decide."

Penny nods. "I'm so horny that air is turning me on, as a gentle caress when all I want is something rough. And certain. And unapologetic. Can you be those things for me?"

Her words are airy and believable.

She wants this. I want this.

"Yes, Princess. I can."

"Then stop starving yourself."

I stand up with Penny wrapped around me like a bear cub on a tree and walk us to the bed.

"You did well, Princess," I praise, feeling her melt even more.

Placing her gently on the center of the bed, I trail my fingers along her legs, settling at her ankles and giving them some attention.

I rub and massage, enjoying the moans escaping from between her lips.

Penny likes being touched by me, and the realization sends a shock wave through me, because I very much love it as well.

My hands explore northward from her ankles up to her calves, and when they get to her inner thighs, I spread her wide. I want her open and vulnerable. If this is going to work short-term, then Penny needs to realize that I don't falter on my expectations. I like what I like and lack the desire to put a label on it.

I want her body to spell out the answers to my questions.

Does she like my tongue licking her folds?

Does she like to see herself in the mirror while I take her from behind?

Does she like to feel my cock pulsing in her mouth while she swallows my seed?

Does she like to go dizzy from her source of oxygen being obstructed?

I'm going to have so much fun bending her to my will. Deep down I know she wants to resist, but her need to please me will be stronger. I can sense it.

"Don't move, Penny."

"Okay…"

"You move? I stop."

I watch her throat as she swallows hard, her chest rising and falling as I kneel between her legs. Taking my time with her is the last thing on my mind, and yet I owe it to Penny to prepare her for my entry—despite the painful signals my cock is sending to me to hurry the hell up.

I want Penny with every part of my being and in every imaginable way. But I also want to make this a pleasant experience for her.

I want this to be her first time, erasing whatever horridness she's endured in the past.

Penny may be worried over compatibility, but I'm not. I've known it since her birthday party that she'd be the fire to my fuse.

For weeks we've been playing this seductive game where there's no real way to win, but also no way to not play.

My mind can't think about the endgame. I can only think about the now.

And right now, I will have Penelope Josephine Hoffman.

43

PENNY

No matter how many times I've played this scenario out in my head, nothing prepared me for the enigmatic Collins Stone. Never did I think the unyielding man would ever give in to the wishes of a girl like me.

Every touch of his hands running up my naked legs is intentional. He is slow and methodical. He says what he means and acts on what he says. Nothing Collins does is on accident or done without thoughtful consideration.

Every cast of his eyes warms me from head to toe, filling my insides with an energy that tingles through my limbs. He is seducing me with just his attention, and I'm melting under his approving gaze.

I didn't think Collins could soften his exterior shell long enough to let me into his life, but here I am fully submerged—and I plan to soak up every second he is willing to give me.

Except I'm so afraid to disobey him by moving and be the reason all of this stops.

To Collins, I'm probably a walking red flag, and I desperately don't want to wave that stop sign or make him second-guess his choices.

Because I want this.

I want him to erase my past bad experiences—or at the very least dull them enough to not be the focal point in my history.

I've been summoned to remain still and yet every inch of me wants to curl and mold myself around Collins's strong body, like a custom blanket. I want my own touch to be branded on his skin so he will remember this moment, just as much as I want to remember it.

But I remain motionless. I just lie here, waiting for him to bend just another inch forward. I wait here while his mouth hovers lower. I wait here while I pray he takes what I hope he still wants and never has a moment of regret.

Collins's kiss to my pussy is hard with the promise for more. His hands skate behind me to grip my backside, lifting me to his mouth and holding me there.

Then he pulls back, making me ache for more.

His lazy, nonchalant inspection of my pussy causes my posture to soften, coaxing me to melt my spine into the mattress.

I feel his greedy, rigid cock resting along my thigh. It's a steady reminder of just how much I affect him, and I relish in the knowledge that I can. And I will.

If I could bottle up this moment and set it on a shelf for a time in the future when I thirst for this level of closeness, I would. Because every touch and caress is a reminder that what we are doing, what we have voluntarily consented to, is just temporary.

We are temporary.

And the forbidden contract that I'll sign in a day's time will be the death sentence to our relationship. It will be the end after the time on the clock runs out.

While my heart yearns for forever, my mind knows that this fleeting version of Collins is way better than a diluted or nonexistent version of him.

I know my heart will ultimately be destroyed in the end, so it's best I savor this unfiltered taste.

Collins's fingers pull back the lips of my pussy, and he just looks at me.

He sees me in my state of vulnerability, as I consent to lie here immobile while he just stares at me.

With slow and methodical movements, Collins teases and tickles my flesh, dipping just a tip or two inside and pulling back out in a rush.

He's testing me, and I know I'm going to fail.

I know I won't be able to keep this up much longer before I wrap my legs around him and just thrust myself onto him like a depraved hussy.

Applying more pressure, Collins controls the pleasure rippling through me, sending jolts of heated electricity to every nerve ending in my body.

But I need *more*. And he knows it.

We are standing at the blurred edge of the cliff, not sure where the threshold is that will send us both plummeting over.

Yet we both know this slow dance isn't going to cut it.

Collins smiles. He fucking smiles, while I suffer in silence trying not to end this before it even gets started by disobeying him. Because I believe him when he says he'll stop if I move—even if it hurts him in the process.

He's a point prover, and I don't want to be his example.

"I've got you, Penny," he says softly, encouraging me with his light massaging. "You're such a good girl. Keep following my directives, and you'll be rewarded."

I watch as his lips curve upward, and I can't resist shivering. I don't even hide what his praise does to me. It must be written all over my face and etched into every goose bump. I want to be his good girl. But deep down, I think I'm craving the consequences of being bad.

"Bend your knees. Keep your heels flat and pushed back. I want to see all of your glorious body—every square inch. Present to me what is mine."

I remain silent and get a stern look from Collins. "What?" I whisper, unable to contain my confusion.

"Following orders and remaining still doesn't imply I want you to stay quiet, Penny. If I wanted you to be silent, I'd gag you. It's as simple as that."

Okay, then. "Understood."

"You are the most beautiful sight for my undeserving eyes. Forgive me while I take my time with you." His eyes smolder with heat. "Your body is meant to be worshipped. Every fucking inch of it."

I continue to melt under his attentive gaze, taking his words at face value. His eyes can't hide his true affections toward me, and I revel in knowing that my body can evoke this type of reaction from him.

"Take what I freely give to you, Collins. All of me."

"I can't wait to ruin you for every other man."

"Yes…"

"You are so fucking perfect that by the time I'm through, your body will only respond to my touch."

"Hmmm…"

Without more time to think, Collins leans even farther on his knees and blows right onto my wide-opened pussy. I hold myself still, only pressing my weight farther into the comforter that is covering the mattress. Every muscle in my body tenses, making me wonder if he could get me to orgasm—something I've only ever experienced by my own handiwork and even that is up for debate.

Then I feel it.

His lips…

His breath…

His fingers pulling my pussy lips wider.

Ever so slowly, his tongue outlines the curvature of my most private region, hitting every valley and hill along its path. Heat blossoms through me like a winter's wine, warming me and causing me to leak out all over the surface of his bed, without any conscious way of preventing it.

My entire pelvic region sparks from Collins's expert touch, igniting into a blaze that I don't think I can keep contained.

It's like a fuse is lit and the potential for a massive explosion is on the brink.

"That's it, my sweet girl," he says breathily on my most sensitive skin, eliciting a moan from deep within my throat. "You taste like strawberries and cream."

Hours ago, I was just an assignment. Now, I feel like we've evolved into more—so much more. A zing runs through me over the possibility of what the near future might bring, and if it feels like anything that mimics right now, then I'll be a happy girl.

"Hmm," I moan, as Collins adds more pressure to his movements.

He licks from my entrance up to my clit and then back down again—over and over, tonguing my pussy. I can't help but imagine what his actual cock will feel like when it's inside.

I feel myself gushing all over the bed, unable to stop the force spiraling through me, as Collins rushes to lap up all that I'm offering to him.

With a heart that continues to pound, my breathing picks up in uneven pants.

Collins is handling my body better than I've ever done on my own, and it already feels like he has insider's knowledge.

Placing a kiss on my clit, he raises his head to look at me, depriving me of his physical touch. "Relax and enjoy."

I grind my teeth at his wicked smile and stiffen my jaw, deflating into the mattress from the pause button being hit. Is he joking? There's nothing even remotely relaxing about any of this—especially when I'm forbidden to move. Surely he can see how hard it is not to shove my legs together under his inspecting gaze.

I can't hide from him. Even when I squeeze my eyes shut, I can still feel his predatory stare on me.

I'm going to be devoured. That's if he ever gets around to touching me again.

My body tenses as a finger presses against my entrance and then gently pushes inside. Collins fingered me in the viewing booth at Limit-X just last night, but now seems different—more stimulating.

Maybe it's how exposed I am…

Maybe it's how I've surrendered my body over to him…

When he hooks his finger, I moan out his name, and the man has the nerve to chuckle at me.

Dammit.

Collins knows exactly the effect he has on my body. It's not as if I'm hiding my true feelings either. From my panting breaths to the way my body is buzzing with excitement, how could he not know the extent he has me literally wrapped around his finger?

"More," I beg, urging him to speed up from his slow, intentional assault.

Making a tsk-tsk sound to shush me, Collins leans his head forward, capturing my entire clit into his mouth and sucking—hard.

Too hard, I think. Right?

I can't possibly—

"Ow!" I whimper. But then hovering on the sidelines is that unmistakable zing of pleasure. "Oh, fuck!" My words come out muffled. I'm on some brink I don't think I've ever been at before. Every time in the past I've touched myself has never felt like this.

Not like this.

Never even close to this.

It's too good. Yet too stimulating.

Every nerve ending is teetering between it being too much and not enough.

It's too much pain, yet not enough pressure.

If I could just guide him…

And then I do the unthinkable…

I move—not just a little. A lot.

Shit.

Maybe Collins won't notice.

Except he does.

All of the attention I've been enjoying halts, causing my entire world to stop spinning on its axis for the second time over the last twenty-four hours. Pushing up to my elbows, I watch as Collins stands up, then starts to walk away.

Oh, hell no.

While the sight of his muscular backside is something enjoyable to see, it's the last thing I need in my line of vision right now.

I don't need him giving up on me.

Not now. Not before this even really starts…

I won't be able to survive this ledge he placed me on, unless he jumps off too.

It's together or never. And I want together—dammit.

Rolling off the side of the bed, I chase after him, jumping on his back as he tries to get away.

"Hell, Penny," he grunts, stumbling forward but steadying himself as to not drop me. He grabs my legs and spins me around to his front like a floppy rag doll. My ass bumps into his cock, causing it to twitch. "What has gotten into you?"

"Not you!" I yell in fury, clinging to him like a deranged bear cub. We are glued together and yet missing the mark entirely. If I just lift and lower, we would fit as a human puzzle.

"You moved," he says simply.

"You made it impossible to stay still."

How is Collins not affected like I am? How is he able to keep his composure when I feel like some horned-up teenager? It's his dedication to discipline that makes me undisciplined. In comparison to his manners, I'll always mess up.

I don't stand a chance, and that revelation is sobering.

"You broke a rule—the only rule."

I pout my lips. "You wanted me to fail."

Smirking, his eyes darken, while his fingers extend over my naked ass cheeks. "It will be mighty fun for me punishing you."

I allow my body to go limp and slide down from my perch, rubbing my pussy against every hard inch of his cock on my descent.

Good. *Enjoy that attention while it lasts*.

I prop my hands on my hips. Collins is the first man I've been around where my first instinct isn't to conceal myself. He makes me confident—and a bit defiant.

"Then tie me the fuck up, but don't you dare end things the way you just did. This isn't a teachable moment, so quit trying to teach me a lesson I refuse to retain."

Collins's eyes twinkle with mirth. Why is he enjoying himself in my time of despair? He can be so annoying!

"Get back on the bed, Princess."

I do as I'm told. It feels foreign at first—yet indescribably relaxing. Maybe this whole following directions thing is what I need after all. It's like a revised game of *Collins Says*.

"Happy now?" I bite back. This new sense of confidence might get me into trouble, but the journey getting there will be all the fun.

"On all fours, ass in the air."

"Oh damn," I mumble. After a little hesitation, I slowly rotate my body, getting into position.

I feel his hand smooth out over my cheeks, humming to the rhythm of his movement. "Have you ever been spanked before, my naughty girl?"

"Only in my fantasies," I quip, looking back over my shoulder to catch his expression.

It's a semi lie, mostly because I've never considered it an option until I saw him with Daphne. I've been jealous of her ever since I caught them in the scene, silently wondering all this time what it would feel like to get marked by Collins Stone's hand print.

"You deserve more than I'm willing to deliver at this moment, but I can't wait to make you pay for all of your brattiness. You're going to be so fun to tame. But don't worry, I also like you wild."

Collins runs his hand up to my lower back, circling it and then sliding it back down to the tops of my upper thighs. I hang my head toward the comforter, bracing myself for whatever he plans to do.

It's the anticipation that gets to me.

When his hand leaves my thighs, I suck in a deep breath through my lungs and then wait.

And wait.

My body relaxes and then the whoosh of air resonates in my ears as the loud hollowing sound echoes into the room.

CRACK.

I flinch and then gasp as the pain in my ass cheek radiates through me. When the burning subsides, I'm left with this tingling sensation in my core and an aftertaste of confusion.

Do I want Collins to spank me again?

It wasn't as scary as my mind made it out to be.

Before I can decide, another whirling sound fills the room as my other cheek gets the same treatment.

"Ouch," I hiss, earning back a chuckle. "You are enjoying this too much."

"So are you. And your body is going to prove it."

The mattress dips and then his mouth is on my pussy. He spreads my folds for better access, driving his tongue into my entrance while using his fingers to tease my sensitive, swollen flesh.

Damn.

I don't think I could get more exposed. He can literally see every vulnerable part of me. But before I get a chance to second-guess what I'm doing, he pushes in what feels like just one finger.

Twisting it, he penetrates me deep, making me want to grind my hips back to get more of him. More of his finger and more of his tongue.

I need *more*.

Pulling out, he pushes in with more pressure.

Fuck.

Why do I feel like I'm so tight?

I've read that pain and pleasure are similar feelings that are often presented together but never really understood how…

Until now.

Right now, in this moment, I understand why this act can be so alluring.

Then I feel a finger at my other hole.

No.

"I can't," I whisper, trying to wiggle and clench off access.

"No square inch of you is off-limits, Princess. And one day soon I will claim you here"—he presses his finger right over my virgin hole—"and when your cries of pain morph into moans of passion, you will know I own you. Fully. And without reservation. But that takes a lot more prep work than I'm patient for right now. So for now, your virtue is safe."

I let out a sigh of relief, hanging my head. I'm definitely not ready for that right now and am glad he realizes it as well.

His mouth opens so wide I fear he will swallow my entire pussy.

I'm going to die a good death and will think my life was fulfilled because of his mouth.

Once he releases me, Collins moves back to give me the space I definitely don't need. I want him to—

CRACK.

"Dammit, you didn't even warn me," I scold.

CRACK.

And then I feel it—my pussy leaking. It's not from the pleasure he previously gave but from the zing of pain he just delivered.

It's as if my mind is playing tricks on me.

How can…

I feel the trail of liquid down my thigh, and when I hang my head onto the mattress and look between my slightly spread legs, I can see the glistening. I can also see Collins's expression of…

Adoration?

Pride?

Gratitude?

"You are exquisite, my sweet girl. So responsive and yet so curious. I'm going to have so much fun getting you to submit to my will."

Pulling my head up, I look over my shoulder. "Who says I'll submit?"

Running a hand up my leg, Collins gathers the product of my arousal onto his fingers. Leaning over me, he places two of them into my mouth, beckoning me to lick them clean. "You already are," he says smoothly, as I comply.

I moan around his fingers as he probes and pushes them into the back of my throat, testing my gag reflex I assume.

"But lucky for you, your sass just helps me think creatively about how to provide balance and the framework to assist you in fully discovering yourself."

Helping me to turn over and get settled on my back, Collins hovers over my body with his. He leans down to kiss my lips. This time it's much more urgent. Pushing back my hair with his fingers, he massages my cheeks with his thumbs.

"Are you sure you want to continue?"

I nod and give him my full attention. "I don't need any more safety checks, Collins. I'm sure."

His eyes spark. "Good. Because you're about to get all of me. And once we get acclimated, I won't be gentle."

"I appreciate your warning, but I'll be fine. I don't need coddled. I need devoured." I want primal. Feral. I want for someone to be so obsessed with me that their only serenity is being buried deep inside me.

Sliding a hand to my pussy, Collins cups it and growls, "No one touches this during our time together. Do you understand me, Penny?"

"Got it."

"Not even you without permission."

"Okay…" Surely he doesn't *really* mean that. I can ask for clarification later.

"I don't fucking share what's mine, and I don't plan to go long between reclaiming it. You've made me needy and on edge for weeks, so learn to accept the consequences like a good little girl. There might be days we don't leave this bed. So if you want to back out now, you better say so. And do it quick before I implode."

"Quit acting like we don't desire the same things," I bark out, driving my hips upward to show my wanton need. "I can handle you, Collins."

His eyes study me.

I'm not sure what he's looking for, but I hope he finds it soon.

"If you need me to pause or stop at any time, you will tell me. Understood?"

I nod.

"I need your verbal consent, Princess."

"Yes. I will tell you."

Reaching between us, Collins slips a finger inside me, pumps a few times, and then pulls out. He does this four more times. When I think he's going to just continue on with his frustrating torment of stop-and-go, he keeps one finger inside and then presses down with another hard on my clit, causing my body to shudder.

"Ahhh…"

It's as if he pulled the trigger on me.

My body erupts from the simple move. Giving me no time to enjoy the wave I'm riding on, he grabs a condom from the top of his nightstand, rips it open with ease, and then rolls it down his length. Then lining himself up, he presses the head of his cock into my entrance. Rocking his hips, he presses forward and then pulls back. A little forward…then back again. Each time he seems to go a bit deeper, stretching me to the point where I think I can't possibly take more. Forward…then back again.

But seeing that Collins is very much still hovering above me and the space between us isn't even closed, I am having my doubts that this will even work from a functionality standpoint.

"You're not going to fit," I whisper.

What if he doesn't fit?

What if all this prep work is one big misunderstanding and he changes his mind?

What if I'm too much work and not worth the effort?

"Get out of your head, Penelope."

"I'm scared."

Collins moves his mouth to my ear, gently nibbling at my lobe. "I know, Princess. But you have to trust me. Getting you broken in is the best part of the journey. I will fit. But first, I need you to stop with the self-doubt monologue probably running on repeat in your head. You have one job to do—lie here and take what I'm going to give to you. Let me worry over everything else."

"Okay," I say with hushed breath.

Pushing himself back up off me, he captures my eyes with his. "And Penny?"

"Hmm?"

"I'm not worried."

I look at him confused. "Why not?"

"Because your body was made for me."

Before I have a chance to react or to think, Collins slides his mouth to the hollow of my neck and kisses my sensitive flesh.

A hand grips my breast and squeezes.

I'm writhing underneath his attention, and slowly I feel the walls of my pussy loosen.

"That's my girl."

His sweet words are thick and needy, as warm as honey.

He applies more pressure.

A whimper escapes my lips. "It hurts…"

"Relax your core and let me inside your warmth."

"I'm trying."

"You're doing great, Princess. Let me make you feel good."

Throwing my head back on the pillow, I let out a labored breath. My face wrinkles and unwrinkles with the pinching pain I'm enduring.

Collins pushes some of my hair off my forehead, tucking it gently behind my ear, as he bends to kiss my eyes and then my nose. I can't possibly be looking my best right now, and yet the reflection of adoration reflected back in his eyes allows me the ability to relax into the mattress and absorb everything that is Collins Stone.

How can the same man treat me like a pampered princess and an insatiable slut all in one night?

I'd be lying if I said I didn't enjoy the contrast. It definitely keeps things interesting.

As I adjust to accommodate him, I trail my hands up and down his arms that are holding him up, as to not crush me.

"Am I doing okay?" My words come out raw, as my throat can't seem to find hydration.

His eyes soften, as he slides a hand between us to rub at my swollen clit. "You are taking me so well. I'm almost all" —he rocks his hips and pushes a little bit more forward— "the way in."

Then I feel it. The sudden fullness…

The burn of being stretched to my max overwhelms me, and the warmth of being this close to the man I thought I could never have is almost too much—too intense.

I'm immobile. I don't even think I could move if I was dared.

Collins studies my face, pausing all movements. "You'll tell me if it becomes too much?"

I bite my bottom lip and then suck it entirely between my top teeth while nodding, before quickly realizing that that will not suffice. "Yes."

"I'll know, but you *will* still tell me." It's an order—not a question.

"Yes," I echo, reaffirming.

Placing his forehead against mine, he sighs. "Good. I could stay buried in you forever, just like this, and be content."

Leaning down, he captures my mouth, tasting and

exploring, and allowing me time to get used to this new feeling of what it means to be in Collins's bed.

His nose nuzzles my hair, breathing in my scent, as one hand slides behind me to grip my backside, while the other tangles in my hair.

He begins to move again, pulling out moans from deep in my lungs with each simple movement.

My locks wrap around his fingers and he tugs to get my attention. "I can't wait to feel your pussy melt around my cock as it shudders from another orgasm." He grinds his hips into mine. "You're so fucking tight, and I'm going to find the greatest pleasure in stretching you out for my liking."

Lowering his hand, Collins grips my breast, kneading it while his mouth devours its twin. My lips part to exhale, as he alternates sides.

Sweat drips down my cheeks as I surrender my body over to a man who clearly knows how to command it.

"Collins?"

He slams into me a little harder, making me gasp out in pleasure while he pulls back out. "Yes, my dirty girl?"

"I'm close…"

It is shocking to even think I could have more pleasure to endure, when this slow burn rhythm has me in a weird state of need.

Collins places a kiss on my forehead, thrusting back into me. And then without warning, we roll, causing me to take ownership of our movements—from the top.

Helping me to sit up, he grips my hips to adjust my placement with his cock still buried deep within me.

"Use me, Penny. Make yourself cream all over my cock. Make that pussy weep for me."

"I don't think…" I don't like the pressure of performing, and most definitely not from this angle.

His fingers dig into the sides of my abdomen, lifting me up a few inches to force me to withdraw from the comfort I have when he is fully inside. Then he presses me down so my ass hits against his upper thighs.

"There's no reason to be shy now. Take from me what you desperately need."

Using the strength from my thighs, I rise all the way up until the tip of his cock is resting right outside my entrance. I circle my hips. My head drops back and my eyes close.

"I think I can get off just like this," I say breathily, enjoying the sensations.

Collins's fingers dig into my ass cheeks, while he thrusts his hips upward at an angle, never allowing more than an inch inside of me. "I very much agree."

Grinding my core onto him, I twist until I get the exact friction I'm looking for, and then I rub and slide until I feel those telltale signs that I'm about to go over the edge.

And I do—epically.

My mouth screams his name, as my body slumps forward. It's as if our hearts collide, drawing us closer to one another in a way I have never experienced before and probably never will again. It is that profound.

Within seconds, I'm on my back and Collins is reclaiming his control. He pumps inside a few more times while I detonate around him.

Then he pulls out, rips off the condom, and tosses it haphazardly to the floor.

Kneeling on the bed, Collins curls his fingers around his rigid cock as much as they will allow and pulls along the shaft in a rhythmic motion.

"Spread your legs, Penny. And accept my mark on you. Because next time, I'm shooting deep within you."

With bated breath, I wait until the first shot of his cum erupts from the tip and hits directly onto the lips of my pussy, coating me with the liquid heat.

An animalistic growl comes from deep within Collins's throat, making shivers run up my spine, as his eyes darken to nearly black.

But his pulsating cock doesn't stop. Splatters speckle my tits and my belly, marking me of his taking.

It is primal.

It is territorial.

And it is so freaking hot that I know this memory will be burned into my mind forever as a reminder of exactly who I belong to. And despite our arrangement being temporary, I have no doubt just how possessive and overprotective Collins will be during our contractual limits—a contract that has yet to be signed.

"Are you okay?" he asks, cutting through my own mental monologue.

"That…that…" I can't keep my brain under control. "Never happened to me before."

There's something so intriguing about this enigmatic man holding his rigid cock in his palm and painting my body with his seed.

"Well, thank fuck," Collins growls, looking at my body—his canvas. "I've never seen a prettier sight than the one lying before me right now, drenched in me."

“I feel like Jell-O.” And probably look like it too.

Collins kneels between my thighs, his semi-hard cock in his hand, and looks at me with utter satisfaction evident in his lazy smile. “You are the sexiest thing I’ve ever seen.” His spoken words echo my silent reciprocated ones. “I love this sight of you bathed in my cum like a good little girl who is accepting her fate and her purpose. I’m never going to want you to leave this bed.”

My pussy pulses with every dirty word he speaks. He makes me feel like a freaking goddess. Never in a million years did I think Collins Stone would cave to me, and soon I’ll be signing a document that will basically end us before we even begin.

Will I be able to walk away from this intoxicating man when the time is up?

And if I can, will I forever be a fraction of the woman I believe myself to be right now?

Collins lies down beside my spent body, pulling me to him.

His hand drifts over my breasts and then my stomach, rubbing in his cum as he goes, until he settles his palm against the warmth between my legs. Pressing deliberate circles into my flesh, he massages and makes the sparks come alive inside me at my core.

“Are you sore?”

“Yeah, a little,” I downplay.

Leaning over, he kisses my lips. “You are hurting more than a little, Penelope.”

My eyes catch his. How does he know?

But he does. So I just nod, as there’s no sense in denying it anymore.

Taking his fingers, Collins trails them along my outer lips, teasing me and causing tingles to resonate throughout my entire body. Picking up the pace, I feel my insides tightening, silently begging for…

Pressure?

"Roll over to your side, that's it. Good. Now grind yourself against my palm. You control it."

And I do.

And within just a couple of minutes, the slow and deliberate caressing causes another orgasm to be pulled from me without any real effort.

I am screwed.

Without a doubt—screwed.

My mind starts to wander, drifting in and out of being present and floating away.

"The next time we do this, there will be a formal contract binding us together," he says casually, as I keep drifting. "And no artificial barrier between my body and yours."

"As long as you make me feel like I do right now, I'll be…" My words slip off the edge of my tongue, entering a world where everything is still safe and right.

"Good night *for real*, my sweet girl."

And when the fog clears just a little…

I swear I hear…

"I don't think I'll ever be able to let you go."

So I whisper back, "I doubt I will either."

"I am prepared for everything in this life. Except for you, Princess."